timid

LARK COVE SERIES

USA TODAY BESTSELLING AUTHOR
DEVNEY PERRY

Editing & Proofreading:
Elizabeth Nover, Razor Sharp Editing
www.razorsharpediting.com
Ellie McLove, My Brother's Editor
www.mybrotherseditor.net
Julie Deaton, Deaton Author Services
www.facebook.com/jdproofs
Kaitlyn Moodie
www.facebook.com/KaitlynMoodieEditing

Cover:
Sarah Hansen © Okay Creations
www.okaycreations.com

Formatting:
Champagne Book Design
www.champagnebookdesign.com

dedication

To Mom and Dad.
My champions.

prologue

"**D**AD, IS IT OKAY IF I GET TWO—"

The Snickers bar in my hand slipped out of my grasp and dropped to the floor. My jaw was down there too, thanks to one glimpse at the man walking through the gas station door.

He was, without contest, the most beautiful man in the world. *No, the universe.* He'd stepped straight out of my *Seventeen* magazine and into the Lark Cove Gas 'N' Go.

His golden-blond hair was buzzed short to his scalp, a cut seen regularly in the hallways of my high school because most boys in Lark Cove had their moms whip out the bathroom clippers once a month. Except nothing about this man's haircut was boyish. On him, it was rugged. A little dangerous even. This guy couldn't be bothered to style his hair. He had more important things to do, like bench-press cars or battle zombies or rescue kittens from treetops.

Hidden in the candy aisle, I peered around a display of Doritos as he grabbed a bottle of water from the cooler by the register. He set it on the counter and dug out a wallet from his back jeans pocket.

"Just the water?" the clerk asked.

The man nodded. "And the gas on pump two."

A shiver ran down my spine at his low, rumbling voice. He made the words *gas* and *pump* sound hot.

The clerk punched in some numbers on the till. "Anything else?"

The man leaned back from the counter, eyeing the row of candy bars placed below for impulse buys, then grabbed a Snickers.

We liked the same candy. That *had* to mean something. Like . . . fate.

He handed the bar to the clerk before casually leaning an elbow on the counter. His shoulders pivoted my way, enough so I could get a better look at his face but not enough he could see me spying. With a smile, he nodded to the lottery ticket machine. "I'll take a Powerball too. Maybe it's my lucky day."

My knees wobbled at that smile. *Wowzah.* His soft lips stretched over straight, white teeth. His sky-blue eyes brightened. The smile softened his square jaw just enough that he became a whole different kind of dangerous. It was the kind that made me want to do stupid, embarrassing things just to get a fraction of his attention. It was a smile that vaporized the two-year crush I'd had on Brendon Jacoby, my lab partner in biology.

I couldn't like a boy now that I'd seen this *man.*

Who was he? He had to be a tourist passing through town. I'd lived in Lark Cove my entire life and never seen this guy before, which meant I'd probably never see him again.

My stomach dropped. Doing the only thing I could think of, I closed my eyes and said a prayer that we'd get a freak July snowstorm and the man would be trapped here for at least a week, preferably without a place to stay other than my house.

"Hey there, Jackson." My eyes popped open as Dad walked up to the register with his hand extended. "Nice to see you again."

"You too." A frenzy of excitement shot through my veins as the two shook hands. "It's Nate, right?"

"That's right." Dad smiled. "My wife, Betty, and I were down at the bar last week."

"For your anniversary." Jackson snapped his fingers as he put it together.

"Right again. Are you getting all settled into town?"

"I am. I didn't have much to move so it made unpacking easy."

Jackson said something else to Dad, but my heart was beating so hard I couldn't focus on their conversation.

Jackson. His name was Jackson. And he lived in Lark Cove.

"Willa."

Jackson and Willa. Willa and Jackson. Our names went together like peanut butter and jelly.

"Willa."

Maybe people in town would merge us into a nickname. *Will-son. Jack-illa.* Both were terrible, but I'd think of something better tonight.

"Earth to Willa!"

I flinched, my eyes whipping up. "Huh?"

Dad shook his head and laughed. "Lost in outer space again?"

"Yeah." Heat crept up my cheeks as I bent to pick up my fallen Snickers. With it in hand, I came out from behind the aisle.

"Jackson, meet my daughter." Before Dad could finish his introduction, the clerk stole his attention, asking if he wanted his weekly scratch ticket too.

"Hey." Jackson waved. "I'm Jackson."

"I'm Willa," I mumbled. Articulating words was impossible standing in front of him.

"Nice to meet you, Willow."

"It's, um . . . Willa."

But Jackson had already turned away. The clerk had his attention again, joking with both Jackson and Dad that if either won the lottery, he wanted a kickback.

With his purchases in hand, Jackson said good-bye to Dad and went right for the door and pushed outside.

"Ready to go?" Dad asked.

I nodded and handed him my Snickers.

As the clerk rang up my candy bar, Dad's ticket, a bag of M&M's and two cans of Coke, I peered outside, hoping to get one last glimpse of Jackson. But with the front windows stacked full of beer boxes and a rotating rack of maps blocking the only other free space, I couldn't see anything past our car parked right outside the door.

I drummed my fingers on the counter, willing the clerk to make change faster. Finally, he handed Dad a dollar and some coins, and I bolted for the door, stepping into the bright, summer sunshine just in time to see Jackson slide into an old Chevy truck.

"Did you forget something, honey?" Dad appeared at my side, handing me my Snickers and Coke.

"Whoopsie. Sorry, Dad."

He just laughed. "It's okay."

I took my things, then slowly walked toward our car, keeping one eye on Jackson's truck as it pulled onto the highway. When it disappeared behind a patch of trees, I sighed and resumed normal speed, opening the passenger door and sliding inside.

Luckily for me, Dad didn't comment on my strange behavior. He just popped the top on his Coke, took a sip and backed us out of the parking lot to go home.

"Um, Dad? Who was that?"

He pulled onto the highway, going the opposite direction

of where Jackson had turned. "Who was who?"

"That guy you introduced me to in the gas station. I haven't seen him around before." I added that last part hoping I sounded more curious than desperate for information.

"That's Jackson Page. He just moved to town to work with Hazel down at the bar. I think he's from New York or New Jersey. I can't remember."

"That's good." *More like freaking fantastic.*

Dad gave me a sideways glance. "Is it?"

Uh-oh. Maybe I hadn't hidden my crush as well as I'd hoped. "Totally!" It came out too loud as I scrambled for a recovery. "It's, um, good that Hazel has some help. Don't you think she's kind of old to be working at the bar all by herself?"

Dad frowned as he turned down the street toward our house. "Old? Hazel isn't all that much older than me and your mom. But I guess teenagers think anyone past thirty is old."

I giggled. "Ancient. You're practically fossils."

"Ouch." He clutched his heart, pretending to be hurt as he pulled into our driveway.

"Just kidding."

Dad smiled. "Try to save part of your candy bar until after dinner."

"Deal." I hopped out of the car, escaping inside while Dad went to check on Mom's progress in her vegetable garden.

I yanked my diary out from underneath my mattress and got comfortable on my bed. Then I tore into my Snickers bar, chewing as I opened to a blank page. My pen flew across the paper, leaving a trail of purple ink as I recounted every second at the gas station. When I was done, I closed the book and clutched it to my chest, smiling at the last line I'd written.

One day, I am going to marry Jackson Page.

I just had to get him to notice me first.

one

WILLA

Nine years later . . .

"T HERE'S ONE," I WHISPERED, POINTING TOWARD THE shooting star that streaked across the midnight sky. Even though I was alone, pointing them out had become a habit. My dad had been my stargazing partner for as long as I could remember. As a kid, he'd taught me about the constellations and galaxies. We'd have contests to see who could spot the most shooting stars.

These days, he preferred to sleep at night unless there was a special stellar occasion, like a comet or a lunar eclipse. So my nights counting falling stars were done alone. I'd come out to the playground behind my house, sit in the same swing with my eyes to the sky, then report to Dad the next morning how many I'd counted.

Sending some wood chips flying, I kicked off the ground and got my swing moving. My hands gripped the chains as I pumped my legs for some speed. When I had my momentum built, I let my head fall back. The tips of my long, blond hair nearly touched the ground as I smiled at the Milky Way.

Today had been a good day. No, an *incredible* day.

Months ago, I'd petitioned a charitable foundation in New

York to buy the Flathead Summer Camp, the children's camp where I worked as the director. It was owned by a local church, but after years of barely covering the overhead and maintenance costs, they'd decided it was time to let it go. The church had wanted to sell it to someone who'd continue it as a camp, but with no buyers, the camp would have to be closed down permanently and the land sold off for private development.

But kids needed that camp. They needed a place to escape for a week every summer without toys or iPads or video games. So I'd written a proposal and sent it to various charitable organizations around the country, then wished on a hundred shooting stars for a miracle.

I still couldn't believe my wish had come true. Earlier today, the Kendrick Foundation from New York City had agreed to buy my camp. And as a bonus, they were keeping me on as director.

Tonight, I wasn't wishing on falling stars. I was simply grateful.

My swing slowed to a stop. I pulled myself upright and took in the quiet night. Behind me was Lark Cove School. Its cream cinderblock walls glowed with reflected moonlight. The school and the long playground took up the whole block, except for five houses—three straight ahead and two to the left, one of which was mine.

My parents had never needed to build an outdoor play area. Instead, growing up, I'd just cross the invisible boundary that separated our lawn from the playground's and use the same swing set and jungle gym that I played on during recess.

All of the houses were dark tonight, the only light coming from across the street where a few porch lights were on. I was admiring a hanging basket of flowers when a dark figure strode onto the sidewalk.

I gasped, nearly falling off my swing as he stepped off the

cement and onto the grass.

My fingers slipped into the right pocket of my navy sun-dress, palming the small canister of pepper spray Dad had bought me for nights when I came out here alone. He'd also given me the whistle I was wearing around my neck.

I contemplated jumping off my swing and hurrying home, but stopped short.

I knew that stride. No, that *swagger*.

It belonged to the man who'd made my heart race and cheeks flush since I was seventeen.

Jackson.

Was he coming over here? I looked over my shoulder, expecting someone behind me, but there wasn't.

Forgetting the pepper spray, I used both hands to smooth down my hair. It had a natural wave that looked great for the first eight hours of the day, but somewhere between hours nine and ten, it grew exponentially in volume and frizz. With it sort of tamed, I swallowed the nerves in my throat just as Jackson stepped off the grass and into the wood chips surrounding the swings.

"Hey, Willa."

Oh. My. Goodness. He'd called me by the right name. Finally! After years of correcting him each time he called me Willow, hearing my name in his deep voice gave me wings.

Heat broke across my cheeks and I managed a breathy "Hi."

"Is this swing taken?"

I shook my head.

He grinned, then somehow fit his large frame into the small black rubber seat. His broad shoulders extended past the chains by at least five inches on each side, his jean-covered legs too long for the short seat.

"Nice night."

I nodded. "Yeah."

It came out quieter than I had intended, probably because I'd stopped breathing. So I ducked my chin into a shoulder and pulled in a long breath through my nostrils, hoping he couldn't hear me shaking.

The chains on his swing creaked as he dug a heel into the wood chips and propelled himself backward. "It's probably not safe for you to be out here at night."

"I have this whistle." I held it up so he could see it. "And some pepper spray in my pocket."

"Is that what you were reaching for when you spotted me?"

"Sorry." Mortification crept up my face, flaming my already hot cheeks. The last thing I wanted was for Jackson Page to think I was scared of him. Well, I was scared. More like terrified. But only because I'd crushed on him for basically my entire teenage and adult life.

"I'm just teasing you." He chuckled. "I'm glad you have the spray. Though I'd feel even better if you were behind a locked door at night, not sitting alone in a playground."

I gripped the chains on my swing tighter so I couldn't jump up and start dancing around. He was concerned about me. *Me.* Willa Doon, the girl who'd been trying to get his attention for nearly a decade.

Jackson pushed off the ground again, letting the silence of the night surround us.

Too shy to say anything, I resumed my swinging too. The color in my face drained away in the cool rush of air. Every time Jackson swung forward and I swung back, I'd catch a whiff of his spicy scent, cloves mixed with forest moss.

A combination that shouldn't have smelled so good, but boy did it ever.

"Crazy day."

"What?" I asked as it clicked what he was talking about. "Oh! You mean with Thea. Yeah. That was crazy."

Two executives from the Kendrick Foundation had flown to Montana today to check out my camp. I'd taken them on a tour and that's when they'd agreed to buy the place and keep me on as director. To celebrate, I'd taken them down to the bar for a drink.

The Lark Cove Bar was where Jackson had worked for years alongside his childhood friend, Thea. I'd gotten to know Thea and her five-year-old daughter, Charlie, over the years. They were awesome, but I'd never had the courage to ask about Charlie's father.

It turns out, I hadn't needed to ask. I'd had a front-row seat as Thea had dropped the bomb of a lifetime on one of the executives I'd brought to the bar.

Logan Kendrick, the chairman of the foundation and now my boss, had met Thea years ago in the city. I hadn't gotten the dirty details, but I'd deduced from the show that they'd hooked up without sharing important info, like last names or phone numbers. She'd gotten pregnant and come to Montana as a single mom. He'd come out today to buy a camp and gotten a daughter as a bonus.

It was the biggest drama we'd had in Lark Cove in ages.

"How is Thea doing?" I asked.

"I dunno." He went back to his swinging.

I pushed off the ground, swinging back and forth too, stealing glances at Jackson as our swings crossed at the bottom.

That was the story of my life, watching Jackson Page. It sounded like the title for a made-for-TV movie.

I'd been watching him for years, ever since the first day I'd seen him.

As a teenager, I'd search for him or his truck everywhere.

Occasionally, I'd see him at the gas station filling up. Or some-times I'd spot him at the town grocery store or eating at Bob's Diner. There weren't a lot of places to go in Lark Cove, and since he didn't go to our church and had no reason to come to my school, I'd been forced to settle for chaste glimpses every month or so.

My diaries had the exact dates and times.

I'd seen Jackson even less after high school. I'd moved two hours away to attend college in Missoula, and my infrequent trips home had meant six or more months between sightings. By the time I'd come back home, I'd been certain I would be return-ing to news that he'd gotten serious about a woman.

No sirree. He was still the same playboy he'd been for years.

Despite all the floozies and bimbos, I'd never stopped crush-ing on Jackson and I'd never stopped watching for him. It was just easier to do now that I was old enough to go into the bar.

Tonight was different though. Tonight, it was just the two of us. Not once in nine years had we shared a space alone. And because he wasn't putting on a show for his customers or flirting with every woman in Flathead County—well, except me—I saw something in his eyes I hadn't seen before.

Loneliness.

Deep, dark, empty loneliness.

I wanted to jump off my swing and hug it out of him.

Had Jackson always been lonely? Had I been so mesmerized by his handsome face that I'd missed this all along?

Outside of Thea and Hazel at the bar, I'd never seen him around town with a buddy. He'd never had a passenger in his truck or a partner in his fishing boat. The few times I'd seen him at the diner, he'd been eating alone.

Year after year of watching, it was sufficient to say that I'd become an expert on all things Jackson Page.

So how had I missed this loneliness he wore for all the stars to see?

I let my feet dangle and my swing slowed. Jackson gave his a few more pumps but then stopped too. As the two of us rocked back and forth, I took a deep breath and mustered the courage to speak.

"Are you okay, Jackson?"

His shoulders sagged, digging into the chains. He looked over with a sad smile. "I'm having a rough night."

"Want to talk about it? I'm a good listener."

He looked out over the grass. "It's crazy, don't you think? That after all these years, this guy shows up and all of a sudden Charlie has a dad?"

I didn't know if Logan's appearance would spell *miracle* or *disaster* for Thea and Charlie. But I did know that Jackson loved that little girl like his own. "For what it's worth, I spent some time with Logan today. He seems genuinely nice."

Jackson shrugged. "We'll see. Thea never said anything bad about him, but I don't trust the guy. I just . . . don't want things to change."

I didn't have anything wise to say or advice to offer. So I shuffled my feet, scooting my swing a bit closer to his before reaching over to give him a reassuring touch.

The moment my hand settled on his forearm, an electric shock zapped my fingers. What was that? I almost pulled back to examine my palm but stopped, not wanting to let him go. I'd never touched Jackson before, not even to shake his hand.

His face whipped to mine, his eyes widening. Focusing.

My breath caught at the intensity of his gaze, but I still didn't remove my hand. Instead, I wobbled a smile and stroked his skin with my thumb.

His eyes softened. "Thanks for listening."

"Anytime." With my cue to let go, I picked up my feet and swung back to my groove.

He pushed off the ground, resuming an easy swing. "What are you doing out here?"

"Just counting shooting stars." My eyes tipped up to the sky just in time to see another. "There." My finger shot in the air. "Did you see it?"

"Yeah."

"Aren't they pretty?"

"Beautiful." But he wasn't staring at the sky. He was looking at me.

I blushed and dropped my arm as my heartbeat raced. Had Jackson just called me beautiful? Because it seemed like it. I didn't have a lot of experience with men. None really. But that definitely sounded like flirting. And *gosh,* I liked it.

"Sure are a lot of stars. You don't see stars like this in the city."

I nodded. "I love it out here. I come out as much as I can in the summer to enjoy them. I live right over there." I pointed past him to the back of my parents' house. "Above the garage." Yes, it was borderline loser to live twenty feet from my parents, but it was free and there wasn't a huge rental market in Lark Cove.

Jackson's boots skidded on the wood chips as he stopped his swing and stood. With his hand extended, he nodded to my place. "Come on. I'll walk you home."

I practically flew out of my seat. The minute my fingers slid against his palm, I got another one of those zaps. My breathing came in erratic pants rather than smooth ins and outs as he led me toward my house. With every step, I wished home wasn't so close and my mom's garden miles away, not just yards.

I tried not to wiggle my fingers, keeping them still in his grip so he wouldn't let me go. But I was so excited to be holding

Jackson's hand, it was nearly impossible. Every atom in my body was buzzing. Never before had electrons whirled around protons and neutrons so fast.

Much too soon, we reached the base of the staircase that ran up the backside of the garage. I'd expected him to let go of my hand, but he didn't. He towered over my five-five with an odd stare.

Maybe it was the light, or lack thereof, but his eyes seemed duller than usual, the blue clouded by a slight haze, and they looked tired.

I would stand here forever holding Jackson's hand, but as exhaustion rolled off his wide shoulders, I reluctantly slipped my hand free. "I, um . . . thanks. Maybe we could—"

One moment I was trying to find the words to ask him out to dinner. The next, he was kissing me.

Jackson Page was kissing me.

On the lips.

His thick hands came to my cheeks. His calloused fingers slipped into the roots of my hair. And his tongue ran over my bottom lip.

My eyes went wide. Was this happening? His eyelids were closed. His nose was brushing mine. Our mouths were touching.

Jackson Page was kissing me. *On. The. Lips!*

I couldn't *not* smile. When I did, he took advantage of the part in my lips and his tongue slid inside, tickling the inside of my cheek.

I gasped and turned to mush. Gripping his forearms so I wouldn't fall, I relaxed completely into his kiss, letting my eyelids fall. His taste was incredible. It was minty with a hint of citrus. There was something else on his tongue too, but I wasn't sure what.

Hesitantly, I stroked my tongue against his. I had no idea if I was doing this right, but when Jackson moaned into my mouth, I did it again.

From there, whatever he did, I copied. When he crested his tongue over my top lip, I did the same to his bottom. When he nipped at the corner of my mouth, I gave him one right back. And when he sucked my bottom lip between his teeth, I waited until his was free, then did the same.

It was hot and wet and magic.

The scruff on his jaw made the skin around my lips the exact right amount of raw. An ache unlike anything I'd felt before curled in my belly. A throb pulsed between my legs. Without thinking, I shuffled my hips closer, brushing against the hardness in his jeans.

He hissed, sending a blast of air between us that cooled the wet skin above my lip. Then after one last lick, he pulled away.

"Sorry," he whispered, not letting go of my face. "I didn't mean—"

"Don't," I breathed. "Don't be sorry."

Because I'd never be sorry for that kiss.

My first kiss.

Something I'd avoided for years because I'd been waiting for *this* kiss with Jackson.

"I'd better go." His hands dropped from my face and he planted a soft kiss on my forehead. Then he backed away three steps before turning around. Even then, he glanced over his shoulder a couple of times as he walked through my parents' yard.

I waved and hurried up my stairs. The minute I closed the door behind me, I went to the window beside the door since it overlooked the playground. Crouched on my floor, hidden behind a curtain, I watched as Jackson passed the swings and the silver slide. It didn't take him long to step back onto the sidewalk and turn toward his house.

When he disappeared behind the corner of the school, I sank to the floor and let a happy grin stretch my cheeks.

After years of watching and waiting and hoping, Jackson had finally noticed me.

Me, the shy girl who'd loved him from a distance. Tonight, he'd made one of my dreams come true.

Sleep didn't come easy after my kiss with Jackson. I replayed it over and over and over, touching my swollen lips until eventually I crashed around four a.m. When my alarm went off at six, I jumped out of bed with a perky smile, like I'd slept for a day.

The smile stayed all day long. Every time I got weary, I'd think of Jackson's kiss and get hit with a fresh burst of energy.

By six o'clock, I was eager to get away from the camp. Not because I hadn't had a great day with the kids and my staff, but because I wanted so badly to see Jackson again. So instead of going home, like I normally did on Tuesday evenings, I steered my Ford Escape toward the bar.

The parking lot was full, but I squeezed into a tight space in the last row. I did a quick check in my visor mirror, pulling my hair into a topknot and smearing on some lip gloss. Then I popped a piece of cinnamon gum. I doubted Jackson would kiss me while working, but he might and I wanted to be prepared.

I walked into the bar with a confidence I hadn't felt in years, maybe ever. I strolled right up to the bar, sliding into a rickety old stool next to Wayne and Ronny, two locals who came down to the bar most nights. Normally, I picked a table in the middle of the room or a booth in the corner, somewhere I wasn't conspicuous.

But not tonight.

Tonight, I was going to be front and center.

"Hi, guys."

"Hey, Willa." Wayne patted my shoulder. "How are you today?"

"I'm great. How are you?"

"Can't complain."

I loved that Wayne always had a smile. I'd known him my entire life and couldn't remember a time when he wasn't in a good mood. Even during his divorce. He was in his late fifties, like my dad, and worked at the school doing maintenance. He'd always walk the halls whistling a cheery tune.

"Um, is Jackson here tonight?" I asked, my eyes scanning the bar.

Wayne didn't answer because at that moment, Jackson came out of the back carrying a pizza pan. He delivered it to one of the tables, then came back around the bar.

The minute he made eye contact, my heart jumped into my throat. "Hey," I breathed as the smile on my face got impossibly wider.

Jackson grinned. "Hey, Willow. What can I get for you?"

My smile faltered. *Willow?* I stared at him, hoping he'd start laughing at his not-so-funny joke, but he just stood there, waiting to take my drink order.

"It's Willa. With an *a*," I snapped. "Will-a."

He winced. "Sorry. I suck at names. Did you want a drink?"

I suck at names. That's how he was going to play this? He was going to pretend that last night hadn't happened? Was kissing me really so bad that he'd resort to childish games?

"I'll get your drink, Willa," Wayne offered. "How about a Bud Light?"

I nodded, unable to speak.

"Coming up." Jackson whipped a pint glass from beneath the bar and took it to the tap.

"It's still weird to me that you're old enough to drink." Wayne chuckled. "I remember you coming into the school every summer when you were just a little thing, helping your daddy get his classroom all ready for the school year."

I faked a smile for Wayne as Jackson set down my beer.

He turned and grabbed a bottle of aspirin from behind the cash register, opening the cap and popping a couple of pills into his mouth.

"Not feeling good?" Ronny asked.

Jackson shook his head. "I haven't had a bitch of a hangover like this in years. The damn thing has lasted all day. Remind me never to do tequila shots, then smoke a joint with the tourists again. I'm a fucking dumbass."

Ronny and Wayne both laughed.

I did not.

Tequila and weed. That was the taste I couldn't pinpoint last night. That was the reason for the haze in his eyes. He'd been drunk and high during my first kiss.

"Did you stay out late?" Ronny asked Jackson.

He shrugged. "Not really. I closed up around midnight after the tourists left the bar. Walked home and passed out."

I stared at his profile, waiting for his eyes to at least flicker my way. He was forgetting a stop on his stroll home. Was that intentional? Did he not want Wayne and Ronny to know he'd even talked to me? Or had he forgotten me completely in his inebriated state?

"You just went home and fell asleep?" I asked.

He glanced over. "Pretty much. Had some crazy dreams though."

I narrowed my gaze, assessing his expression. He wasn't

lying. He wasn't pretending. He wasn't omitting pieces of his story.

He really had forgotten.

He'd forgotten the best night of my life. The best first kiss in the history of first kisses.

He'd forgotten me.

The pain nearly knocked me off my stool. Jackson continued to chat with Wayne and Ronny while I stared unblinking at my beer glass. The bubbles collected on the rim, then burst.

Like my heart.

Enough, Willa. Enough.

My friends had told me for years to move on, to forget my schoolgirl crush on Jackson and go after a man who actually knew I existed.

But I'd nurtured and coddled the fantasy for nine years.

I'd finally had enough. This was the kick in the rear I'd needed to let him go. In a way, I was glad this had all happened.

Yep, glad. Super glad.

G-L-A-D, glad.

He was just a silly dream.

And it was time to chase a new one.

two

JACKSON

A S I WALKED PAST THE SCHOOL, I GLANCED ACROSS THE playground to the dark row of houses on the opposite side. My eyes immediately landed on the staircase behind one of the garages, and a wave of déjà vu hit hard.

Why were those stairs so familiar? I'd never been to that house before.

I shrugged the feeling away. They were probably familiar just because I'd walked down this street three hundred times on my way to work at the bar. I lived two blocks up in the same neighborhood—though my place wasn't nearly as nice as the homes on this road.

I kept walking but couldn't help a second glance at the staircase.

It had been over two weeks since the night I'd had five too many tequila shots and smoked a joint with a couple of tourists who'd stopped at the bar. And in those two weeks, I couldn't get this dream out of my head.

There was a girl. A beautiful girl.

And that staircase.

Fucking weed. There was a reason I rarely smoked.

Something about the mixture of marijuana and tequila did strange things to my mind. I didn't get the typical munchies or surfer-dude vibes. Things got hazy, nothing stayed in focus, and my memory took a hit.

Never again, Jackson. Never. Again.

I blamed this on Logan fucking Kendrick. The only reason I'd gotten drunk and smoked that joint was because he'd shown up in Lark Cove.

Why couldn't he have just stayed a stranger? Logan would be in Charlie's life, our lives, for good. Not that I didn't want Charlie to have a father—I wanted whatever was best for her— but change sucked and Logan was bringing a truckload of it to my simple life.

So the night he'd shown up in town, I hadn't handled it well. I'd poured a shot to take the edge off, followed by two more. When those tourists had come in, the bottle hadn't lasted long. And when one of the guys had passed me a joint, I hadn't thought twice before taking a hit.

The rest was a blur.

I remembered fuzzy pieces from that night. I remembered locking up the bar and taking a piss outside the back door by the Dumpster. I remembered walking past the playground. And I remembered the dream I had that night.

It was about a girl floating through the air with long, wavy hair the color of spun gold. Then there were flashes of those stairs.

After one last look over my shoulder at the staircase, I turned the corner of the block and headed down First Street toward the highway.

Toward my sanctuary, the Lark Cove Bar.

I'd moved to Lark Cove about nine years ago from New York City. The moment I'd driven through the small, lakeside town, a calm had settled over my soul. Moving here had been the best decision I'd ever made.

There were no blaring horns from taxis and angry drivers. We didn't have bums sleeping on our street corners. There were no smelly subway tunnels or towering skyscrapers. The only things on the horizon here were mountaintops.

It had only taken a week for me to adjust to the still nights, no traffic to lull me to sleep.

Lark Cove suited me. There were a couple of churches and a motel. A single school for all grades. The town only had one diner, but I didn't need a slew of restaurants to choose from. Most meals I ate at home or at the bar. If I had the extra cash, I drove the thirty minutes up to Kalispell for something different.

Though I preferred to leave Lark Cove only when absolutely necessary. With a small grocery store and a gas station, I could keep my fridge stocked with the essentials and fishing supplies.

I didn't need stores or shopping malls when I had the lake. When I was on my fishing boat, floating on the open water with a cup of worms in the cooler and my rod in a pole holder, I didn't need much else.

Just the lake and my bar.

Lark Cove was one of many small towns located along the highway that ran around Flathead Lake. The bar's neon sign lured a lot of tourists off the highway as they passed through. Though, we served a loyal local crowd too.

Other than the diner, we were the only establishment in Lark Cove that served food. Thea had come up with the idea to do brick-oven pizzas a while back and they'd been a huge hit. Add to that our cold beer and stiff drinks, and the bar was rarely empty these days.

Especially during the busy summer season.

We'd become a popular hangout spot for all of the nonlocals pretending to be local. This was a beautiful slice of Montana and it attracted rich people from across the country like flies.

They'd come in and buy up a chunk of land along the lake, then build a massive vacation home. Those houses sat empty except for a week or two each summer. Some people would stay into the fall, but as soon as the snow flew, they'd be gone.

Most of the local townsfolk didn't like the influx of out-of-staters each summer, but I didn't mind.

Paying customers were all the same in my book.

And there were usually a couple of hot women who'd come to town every summer looking for some no-strings-attached sex. They were more than willing to fuck the rugged Montanan for a few weeks before going back home, never to admit they'd slummed it with a bartender on their summer vacation.

That worked for me too. I got sex without having to worry about some girl becoming a stage-four clinger.

I didn't need drama in my life. I didn't *want* drama in my life. So I kept my inner circle small.

I had Hazel, the woman who was more of a mother than the real one had ever been. I had Thea, who was practically my sister. And Charlie, my niece, whether we were related by blood or not.

It was a short list by design, and if Logan took Thea and Charlie away from me, I'd never forgive the rich bastard.

I made it to the bar and opened the back door, walking down the short hall past Thea's office and the kitchen.

"Hey," I said, getting Thea's attention as I stepped up to the bar.

She looked up from the journal she'd been drawing in. "Hi. What are you doing here?"

I shrugged. "I was bored at home. Thought I'd come in and keep you company."

It was Thea's night to work, but I'd been too restless to stay at home. The unanswered questions were spinning in my head.

Would she move back to New York with Logan or would she stay in Montana? What would happen with Charlie? Before I knew it, I was off the couch, out the door and on my way to the bar.

"Want a beer?" Thea set down her pencil and sketch pad, then picked up a pint glass.

"Nah. I'll just have a Coke."

She gave me a sideways glance, probably because I rarely turned down beer on Saturday nights. "Are you feeling okay?"

"I'm good. Just don't feel like drinking."

I'd been drinking a lot lately and needed to slow it down. The last thing I wanted to do was become a drunk. Besides, the last couple of times I'd gotten drunk, I'd fucked up royally. First by smoking that joint two weeks ago. Then by drinking too many beers before Charlie's sixth birthday party and acting like an idiot.

"Been busy?" I asked after she set down my soda.

"Not bad. There was a good dinner rush tonight. Those guys in the corner booth have been here for a few hours. Wayne and Ronny were in earlier, but they both called it a night and left."

That was about normal for midnight on a Saturday. We were usually busy all afternoon and evening, but the crowd would thin to just a few diehards wanting to stick it out until we shut down at two.

"Where's Daddy Dearest tonight?" I muttered.

"Hey." She frowned. "Don't be like that."

I winced. "Sorry."

No matter how many times I told myself to give Logan a chance for Charlie's sake, I couldn't get past the fact that because of him, everything here was changing. Because of him, I could lose two of the three members of my family.

"It's okay," Thea said. "And he's at my house with Charlie."

I nodded and took a drink of my soda, swallowing a grumble.

"Are you sure you're okay with covering the bar all next week?"

"Like I told you yesterday when you asked me that same question ten times, yes. I can handle the bar all week."

"I know you can handle it. I just feel bad dumping it all on you short notice."

She'd come down last night and asked me to cover for her. Logan wanted to take her and Charlie to New York for a week. I'd told her she was moving too fast but promised to manage the bar.

And even though she knew I was more than capable, she would fret. Thea ran most of the business side of things at the bar. She'd taken them on after Hazel had decided to retire.

Thea kept the books, ordered from the distributors and made the schedule. At times, she treated me more like an employee than a partner. She'd forgotten that I'd spent years at this bar before she even moved to town.

"It's fine, Thea," I reassured her again. "Consider it my penance for the whole kissing thing."

Her face soured. "Don't ever do that again. That was disgusting."

"Disgusting? My kisses aren't disgusting."

"Don't pout." She scolded with a smile. "I'm sure all the women who throw themselves at you think you're a great kisser. But since I'm the closest thing you have to a sister, I can say it was disgusting."

"Yeah." I grimaced. "It was kind of gross."

Another bad decision made while drunk.

Our kiss had lasted all of two seconds before she'd pushed me away. I'd done it to see what Logan would do if he thought maybe he had some competition with Thea. *No more pre-partying for children's birthday parties.*

"Why don't you sit down?" She nodded to a stool. "I'm going to go check on that table and then we can talk."

As she left to check on the customers, I took my Coke and a tray of peanuts around the other side of the bar. When Thea was done refilling drinks, she pulled up a seat next to me and stole a couple of my peanuts, cracking the shells and then dropping them on the floor.

I loved that about this place. We weren't some fancy bar in the city where people were required to use coasters. We were all about the neon signs on the walls, peanut shells on the floor and classic country music on the jukebox. I didn't even care that I had to spend twenty minutes sweeping up shells after every shift.

"Do you want to tell me what's been bothering you?" Thea asked.

I grinned as I crunched a peanut. For as long as I'd known her, she never let me stew.

"Nothing." I scratched the scruff on my cheek. "I don't know. These last few years have been the best, you know? No drama like we had as kids. We've got a good gig here at the bar. Finally don't feel like I'm scraping pennies together. I guess I'm just pissed that things are changing. This guy . . . he's a game changer."

"Is that really so awful? Logan's not a bad guy, and Charlie adores him. She deserves a father, Jackson."

"I know." I sighed. "It's just . . ."

I trailed off, not wanting to admit that I was jealous. How did you tell your best friend that you didn't want her kid to have a dad because for the longest time, *you'd* been the guy playing that role?

I'd always suspected that Thea might meet a guy one day.

Hell, she deserved to be happy. I could compete with a stepdad. But I didn't stand a chance with a real dad, especially when he had millions of dollars and could give Charlie her every desire.

"I'm sorry." Thea shook her head, understanding settling on her face. I didn't have to tell her I was jealous. She'd already figured it out. "I didn't think of how you'd be feeling about all this. But you'll always be her uncle Jackson. She loves you so much."

I hung my head. "But I can't spoil her like he can. I don't have that kind of money."

"It's not a competition, and it's not about the things you buy her. She needs love from you both."

Did she? If Charlie had her dad, would she really need Uncle Jackson? She'd have her dad to play with her and he'd be the one to build her forts. He'd be the guy helping to sneak animals into their house when Thea wasn't looking. Logan would be the one to take her fishing or hiking around the lake.

That was, if they even stayed in Montana. I had a bad feeling that this "vacation" they were taking to New York would become permanent.

"She'll forget me if you don't come back."

"What?" Thea's eyes went wide. "We're coming back. This is just a vacation."

"You might decide to stay."

She shook her head. "No, I won't. I've already told Logan I won't be moving back to New York. This is just a vacation."

"Hope so." I stood from my stool and went behind the bar for a refill. "While you're there, go get a Giovanni's meatball sub for me. Damn, I miss those things."

Giovanni's had been our spot. Thea and I had each lived close to the restaurant as kids, and whenever we had the money, the two of us would share one of their famous foot-long sandwiches. Even after both of us moved out of Brooklyn for jobs in

Manhattan, we'd still go back for a meatball sub.

Usually we ate there when one of us was in a bad spot.

She'd taken me to Giovanni's after her boyfriend had cheated on her with her best friend. I'd bought our sub before breaking the news that I'd be moving to Montana.

For years, Giovanni's had been our safe place.

A sad, faraway look crossed her face. "I doubt we'll be spending much time in Brooklyn."

"Probably not." Logan was no doubt an Upper East Sider. "I wouldn't go back either."

Not to New York. I wouldn't go back to a place where there were more bad memories than good.

I took the soda gun and filled my glass, then grabbed Thea's sketch pad to flip through the pages. "You've almost got this one full."

"When I get back, you'd better have a new one waiting for me."

I chuckled. "Done."

Thea had been a perpetual whiner during the first few months after she'd moved to Montana. She'd complained constantly about how boring and slow it was at the bar. So I'd bought her a sketch pad, then told her to quit bitching and draw. Ever since, whenever she ran out of room in one pad, I bought her another.

"Who were you drawing tonight?" I asked, reaching the end of the book.

"You'll see."

I turned to the last page and nearly fell over.

That hair. It was the girl from my dream.

Even though the drawing was a black and white, it was obviously her hair was light and long and wavy. She was in profile, her high cheekbones resting perfectly over a shy smile. Somehow,

Thea had reached into my mind and yanked out my dream girl.

"She's hot." Hot wasn't the right word, but I didn't want to get all gooey in front of Thea. Beautiful. Stunning. Ethereal. Those big words would just lead to questions I didn't want to answer, so instead, I went with *hot*.

I looked up from the book and scanned the bar. I knew she wasn't here, but I wished she'd be back. "I'm sorry I missed her. Who is this?"

Thea's jaw dropped. "Seriously?"

"Seriously. Who is this?" I glanced at Thea, then back down again, wanting to keep my eyes on the page. "Was she just passing through or do you think she'll be back?"

Please, let her be here for the summer. Let this woman be real.

"Do I think she'll be back?" Thea's voice rose as she stood from her stool and rounded the bar, only to snatch the sketch pad away. "Give me that."

She looked at it for a moment, then shoved it in my face. "That is *Willa*, you dipshit."

"No fucking way." I yanked the pad from her hands. *Willa?* The timid blond girl? She was the science teacher's daughter and a kid. There was no way Willa was this gorgeous woman. "She doesn't look like this."

"Yes fucking way she does."

I bent closer to the paper, studying it before looking back at Thea. "She does?"

"Oh my god." Thea tossed up her hands and walked away to check on her customers. It gave me a chance to study the page.

This couldn't be Willow. *Willa.* I was shit at remembering names. When I'd first met her, I'd tried to memorize it just like she'd told it to me. Willow. Except I'd memorized it wrong. She'd corrected me a few times, but Willow had stuck.

Willa. With an a. Willa.

I repeated it ten times.

"Do you see it yet? Or am I really that bad of an artist?"

"Huh?" I jerked up, forcing my eyes away from the drawing as Thea came back. "I, uh, gotta go."

In a daze, I hugged Thea good-bye and walked out—taking her sketch pad with me. I was going to get to the bottom of this and find out why I'd been dreaming of Willa for two weeks.

Starting with a phone call.

My feet headed down the route home as I dug my phone from my pocket and dialed the number.

"You'd better be in jail if you're waking me up at this hour," Hazel answered.

"Not in jail." Not that she'd come bail me out anyway. She'd leave my ass in a cell until I'd learned my lesson. "Sorry to wake you."

"Are you okay?"

Am I? "Uh, sure."

"Then why are you calling me after midnight?"

I sighed. "This is going to sound strange."

In the background, blankets rustled and a bed creaked as Hazel shifted around. "Jackson, are you drunk?"

"No. I swear." I wasn't drunk, but I was really damn confused. "Do you know where Willa lives?"

"Willa Doon?"

"Yeah, Willa Doon. You work with her at the camp, don't you?"

Hazel had retired from bartending but got bored after a week, so she volunteered at the Flathead Summer Camp. I was pretty sure that Willa worked there too.

"Yes, I work with her. She's the director. Why do you need to know where she lives?"

Fuck. I should have gotten Willa's address from Thea. She

might have asked fewer questions. Though between her and Hazel, it was a crapshoot, since they both lived for giving me shit.

"I—I just . . ." How was I going to say this without sounding like I was drunk? There wasn't a good way, so I just blurted it all out. "I had a dream about her a couple of weeks ago and I can't get it out of my head. I want to talk to her."

Hazel stayed silent. All I heard was the sound of my own boots hitting the sidewalk.

"Hazel?"

"You had a dream and now you want to talk to her. At this hour?"

"Oh, right." It was dark. The curse of being a bartender. My day didn't start until lunch and went well into the night. I often forgot that most people didn't sleep until noon and go to bed after three. "Never mind."

"Wait, Jackson." Hazel stopped me before I hung up. "I don't have her address off the top of my head, but she lives at her parents' place. Above the garage."

My feet skidded to a stop. How had I known she was going to say that?

"It's that nice brown house by the school," Hazel told me. "The one with the big cottonwood tree in the front yard and the strawberry patch off to one side. Do you know which one I'm talking about?"

"Yeah." It was the house with the staircase on the backside of the garage. "Thanks. Sorry to wake you up."

Hazel laughed, her hoarse chuckle loud in my ear. "I love you, Jackson Page. I'm glad you've finally clued in."

Clued in? Before I could ask what she meant, she hung up.

I nearly called her back for an explanation, but I doubted she'd answer now that she knew I wasn't in trouble. So I stuffed my phone back into my jeans and kept walking. It didn't take me long to reach the playground, but before I stepped off the sidewalk and onto the grass, I paused.

Should I wait? Maybe it would be better to return tomorrow at a decent hour. *Yeah, after another night of that damn dream.*

I abandoned the cement for the lawn. There was no way I was waiting.

My long strides took me past the soccer goalposts and jungle gym. I slowed as I came toward the swing sets, studying them more closely as that déjà vu feeling crept back in. But I sloughed it off and kept walking, right up to the staircase.

When I reached the base, I stopped short of the first step. Okay, this was beyond weird. Had I been here before? This spot felt so familiar.

It had to be a part of my dream. This staircase was just something I'd fabricated, because there was no way I'd climbed these steps before. I took the first step, then the second and by the third, the weird feeling disappeared. I'd never been up here before, of that I was certain.

I would have remembered all these flowerpots.

Along the wall of the garage, planters filled with flowers overflowed onto every step. It was hard to tell the exact color of the petals in the dark, but the greenery had crept so far onto each stair that my size-twelve boots could barely fit without squashing leaves.

I was forced to climb the staircase right against the railing as I made my way to the landing at the top. The exterior light was on, illuminating the door, but inside it was completely dark.

Because it's one in the morning, dumbass.

I looked down the steps, debating whether or not I should knock. What was I even going to say? *Hey, Willa. Remember me? Turns out, I've been dreaming about you. Crazy, huh?*

She'd call the cops before I had the chance to finish.

Still, my doubts didn't stop me from rapping my knuckles twice on the tan door. I regretted it instantly.

I was going to scare Willa to death.

I turned, hoping she hadn't heard me knock. If I was lucky, I could make my escape and she'd never know I was here. But right as my foot landed on the first step down, a light flipped on inside.

Shit. I manned up and came back to the landing, shoving my hands in my pockets to keep from fidgeting. As I waited for the door to open, I said a quick prayer that I'd gotten the right house and I wasn't about to be greeted by an angry man with a shotgun.

A long, narrow window next to the door was covered with a sheer curtain. A dainty hand yanked it to the side and Willa's face appeared behind the glass. Her eyes flared as she looked me up and down.

"Hey." I slipped a hand from my pocket and gave her a corny wave.

Her face disappeared from the window and she freed the deadbolt. My heart was thumping in triple time as she turned the door's knob.

"Jackson?" She opened the door an inch.

"Yeah, it's me. Sorry, it's late."

The door opened wider and she stepped under the frame. Her hair was piled in a huge, blond nest on top of her head. She was wearing yellow pajama pants with white stars on the cotton and a thin, white V-neck tee.

"What are you doing here?" Her arms crossed underneath her breasts, thrusting them higher. In the cool night air, her nipples hardened.

My cock jerked behind my zipper and I used every bit of my

willpower to keep it from growing hard.

"I, uh . . . this is going to sound crazy." My motto for the night. "I've been having these dreams. About . . . you. I was wondering if maybe you'd want to, um . . ." I should have thought this through. What exactly did I want from Willa?

A date, I guess.

"Um, what?" she asked, waiting for an answer.

"Would you want to maybe go out sometime?"

Her mouth fell open, ever so slightly, and I stared at her bottom lip. It was so full and pink. Her lips were the perfect shade for her complexion. They matched the sexy blush of her cheeks.

"You want to go out with me?"

I nodded, the corners of my mouth turning up as I waited for the inevitable yes.

But my grin fell when she took one big step backward.

And slammed the door in my face.

three

WILLA

"**D**ID THAT JUST HAPPEN?" I ASKED THE DOOR.

Now he decides to show up?

Now he asks me on a date?

Now?

Unbelievable.

"Why?" I whispered to myself.

Why was he here now? Had he remembered our night under the stars? Was he drunk again?

I reached for the door, wanting answers, but before I touched the knob, I snatched my fingers away.

Don't open the door, Willa. Don't do it.

I'd spent the last two weeks kicking myself in the rear for my ridiculous crush on Jackson Page. I'd berated myself constantly for being so incredibly naïve. And I'd done everything in my power to block him out.

But the problem was, I'd spent too many years dreaming about him. Nine, to be exact. Thinking about Jackson, looking for him in town, had become ingrained into my routine.

Today, I'd finally made progress. I'd signed up for an online dating profile. I'd driven by the bar and hadn't let myself look for his truck. I'd even boxed up all of my old diaries, the ones filled with Jackson's name, and taken them to my parents' basement for storage.

I was moving on from Jackson Page.

Or so I'd thought, until he showed up at my door.

Why was he here? Why now? The curiosity was killing me. I reached for the knob again, jerking my hand back again just before my fingertips could brush the metal.

Gah! Why?

I had to know. Because maybe if I got some answers, I could stop being mad at Jackson for forgetting me. I could stop being mad at myself for letting this crush of mine go on for . . . far too long. This time I let my hand touch the knob.

I would get my answers, then it would be enough.

A rush of unfamiliar confidence surged as I twisted the knob open and yanked back the door. In my haste, I nearly hit myself in the nose.

Jackson was on the first step down, but when he heard me, he came back up to the landing. A hopeful, infuriatingly beautiful grin spread over his face.

"Why are you here?" I stepped right into his space, holding my chin high and narrowing my gaze.

He blinked and the grin disappeared. "Uh . . . to ask you out."

"That's it? There's nothing else you want to maybe discuss?" I strung the words out, giving him plenty of opportunity to fess up if he did remember our kiss.

"Uh, yeah." He gave me a sideways look. "That's it."

"You're sure?" I studied his face, searching for a flicker of recognition, but came away with nothing.

"Pretty sure." He cocked his head to the side. "Is everything okay?"

"Super," I muttered, leaning in closer. His eyes were clear, and there was no alcohol on his breath.

He really was here just to ask me out.

And it made me angry.

I was angry that he'd forgotten about the kiss.

I was angry at the part of me that wanted to say yes and do a victory dance.

I was angry that my feelings for him were so impossibly hard to let go.

"No." My entire body was vibrating with nerves and adrenaline. "I, um . . . no."

He leaned back, stunned. "No?"

"No. I don't want to go out with you. Not now. After . . ." I waved my hands in a big circle. "After everything."

His forehead wrinkled. "Everything?"

"Everything." With a short nod, I spun around, retreating back inside and kicking the door closed with my foot. My chest was heaving and the blood was rushing in my ears, but I still heard the soft knuckle tap on the window behind me.

"No," I groaned. Hadn't I made myself clear? Couldn't we just be done with this?

Couldn't *I* just be done with *him*?

Curiosity, that wretch, made me turn around and open the door again.

Jackson had this sheepish look on his face and—*blargh*—it was adorable. He lifted a hand and rubbed the back of his neck, looking at me from under his lashes.

"What am I missing here, Willa?"

I crossed my arms over my chest. "A lot."

"Care to explain?"

Explain? To explain meant giving Jackson too much insight into my past.

I'd been born and raised in Lark Cove, Montana. It was small and charming. Sheltered. My mom was a valued member of the community. My dad was a beloved teacher at the school.

Students loved his energy and feared his authority alike. Boys in high school had found it safer to stay in the friend zone, and since I'd had a massive crush on Jackson anyway, I hadn't minded one bit. I'd gone to prom with my cousin because all of the other boys in my class had already been paired up.

When I left town for college, I will admit my crush on Jackson faded—though only slightly. There were plenty of cute boys in the dorms and a few stole my attention. But then the unthinkable happened to my best friend Leighton at a party where we'd both been drinking. After that, well . . . things changed.

Boys became inconsequential. Partying was out of the question. We learned that the college experience so many bragged about wasn't all that it was cracked up to be.

The two of us moved off-campus and threw ourselves into our studies. I also got a part-time job at a preschool to ease the financial burden on my parents. So the years when most young women were experiencing their firsts, I was busy studying, working and supporting my best friend as she learned to stand tall again.

I didn't regret my college years. After what happened to Leighton, I made the conscious choice to only date men I knew and trusted. I went on a total of four dates in college, and though each of the guys had been a gentleman, none of them had been worthy of a first.

None of them made my pulse race. None of them made my breath hitch. None of them were Jackson.

It came as no surprise that after moving home, the crush I'd had on Jackson roared back to life. I fell back into the habits of my youth, daydreaming about him and no one else—not that there was a plethora of single men my age in Lark Cove. I let myself get caught up in the fantasy that he'd get all my firsts.

I knew it was rare for someone my age to be so inexperienced. Maybe my crush on Jackson had been an excuse. Maybe I'd convinced myself it was safer to love him from afar than risk an actual relationship with anyone else.

Or maybe it was real.

It felt real.

But at the moment, my feelings weren't to be trusted. And I certainly couldn't explain them, especially to Jackson.

"Willa?" Jackson prompted. When I didn't answer, he looked at his feet.

I stayed still, expecting him to leave, but he just stood there. Was he waiting me out? Did he think I'd cave and spill my guts?

He'd soon learn that I was an expert at staying quiet. I'd learned long ago that people always felt the need to fill silences with conversation. If you didn't speak up, eventually they would.

So I didn't utter a word.

Jackson began shifting his weight from one foot to the other, while I didn't move a muscle. I was a statue—on the outside.

On the inside, I was a twisted mess of anger and frustration and shame.

How many years had I waited? How many months had I wasted? All I'd ever wanted was for Jackson to take notice, or at least call me by the correct first name.

I'd just wanted one chance to see if there might be something real between us. I wasn't delusional. The chance of us falling in love, getting married and having babies was slim. Who knew if we'd work as a couple? But I would have settled for friendship.

Now even friendship was impossible.

A breeze blew across the back of the garage and goose bumps broke out on my forearms. Still, I didn't budge. The smart thing to do was to turn around and go inside. But my feet were glued to the wood underneath.

I opened my mouth to bid him good night, but nothing came out. So I clamped it shut with a click that echoed between us.

That made Jackson's face split in a wide smile, like he'd won the battle of silence.

I narrowed my eyes. As of two weeks ago, that smile had lost all of its power.

Well, not all. But a lot.

He crossed his arms over his chest, mirroring my stance with a dare behind those blue eyes. Then he ran his gaze up and down my body.

I loathed the shivers it left in its wake. It was intimidating, having his bulky, brutish frame tower over me. But still, I said nothing. Instead, I let my eyes wander, giving him the same languid perusal as he'd given me.

Jackson always wore jeans that were faded in just the right places to highlight the apex of his thick thighs. They molded over the best ass in Montana. He had on his standard black boots with the scuffed, square toes. The man must buy white T-shirts in bulk because they were always the same. They fit perfectly over washboard abs and chiseled biceps.

Most days, he covered the T-shirt with an open plaid shirt. My favorites were the blue and green ones. They had shiny pearl snaps instead of buttons. In the summer, the plaid was cotton. In the winter, flannel. Though, regardless of the season, he always had his sleeves rolled up, revealing his tanned forearms.

Today, Jackson was in a light blue plaid and it matched the color of his eyes. Normally, the plaid was left hanging open, but tonight he'd tucked his shirt into his narrow waistband.

He was breathtaking. He was more handsome now than the first day I'd seen him.

And here I was, in my jammies with bedhead.

The breeze picked up again and I was suddenly very aware of my nipples. I didn't need to look down to know they were on high beams underneath my cotton, V-neck tee, which had been washed thin.

Jackson shifted his weight again, then uncrossed his arms and sighed. "You're not going to tell me what I'm missing here, are you?"

I blinked once for no.

"Fine." His scowl was endearing. "Then I'll let you get back to sleep."

Without a word, I whipped around and scurried back inside. I used my foot to kick the door closed behind me so I wouldn't have to see him again. Then my shoulders collapsed, rolling in on themselves as I let myself breathe again.

Jackson's boots thudded down the steps, and when I was sure he'd made it to the bottom, I went to my bed and flopped down on the mattress.

"I will not go to the window. I will not go to the window."

I went to the window.

And I watched from behind the sheer curtain as Jackson crossed my backyard, stopping once to gaze up to my garage apartment before striding through the playground on his way home.

"You missed your chance," I whispered. "I have to let you go."

After Jackson left, I went back to bed only to toss and turn all night while I waited for my alarm to go off. Then I dragged myself into the shower and got ready for work. Caffeine, Snickers and chaos fueled my Sunday at work. After a hectic day of saying good-bye to one group of campers and welcoming the next, I should have slept like a log on Sunday night.

But thoughts of Jackson plagued my mind once again, keeping me up most of a second night. So by Monday morning, I was practically a walking zombie.

Like all Mondays, the day started off with a counselor meeting at the camp, so for an hour, I was able to avoid all thoughts of Jackson. After the counselors and I talked through our activities for the current day and the next, I chugged a huge cup of coffee. Then I spent some time in the office making sure all of the intake forms for this week's campers were ticked and tied. It took me twice as long as normal because I kept thinking back to Jackson on my doorstep.

Finally, I finished in the office and scarfed down a Snickers bar before joining a group of kids in the main lodge to make dream catchers to hang above their bunk beds. The kids always gave me energy, so I fed off them for the rest of the morning.

They were the reason I woke up with a smile most mornings. The kids were the reason I didn't care that my job would never make me rich. I lived for my week-by-week summers until the season ended.

It had become a bit of a challenge for myself over the years to see how much fun I could pack into a kid's single week at summer camp. It was my mission to make them fall in love with this little slice of Montana, with its tall trees and shimmering lakes, so that when they reflected on their childhood, the memories they made here were ones they'd never forget.

I hadn't been here long enough yet, but one day, I hoped to greet parents who'd been to my camp and were sending their kids here to make the same kind of lasting memories.

So while Jackson's late-night visit had upset me, I buried

those feelings and let the kids' smiles and laughter over craft hour give me a boost.

By ten thirty, I was starving and made my way to the kitchen. "Hi, Hazel," I said with a smile.

"Morning." She smiled back as she sipped her coffee. "So did Jackson ever track you down?"

My smile dropped. "He found me."

Since she was practically a member of Jackson's family, it shouldn't surprise me that she knew he'd come over.

"I hope you don't mind, but I told him where you lived."

"Ah." I went to the coffee pot and poured a refill in my mug.

Lark Cove was a small town, and after living here for a while, you learned where everyone else lived. I'd assumed that was how Jackson had known where to find me. A teensy part of me had hoped that maybe he'd actually remembered our night on the swings.

But no. He'd had to ask Hazel.

"What happened?" she asked.

"Nothing." Other than he asked me out on a date, something that two weeks ago would have sent me into joyful hysterics but now had me twisted in knots.

"Nothing?"

"Nothing." I nodded and went to the list she'd taped to one of the industrial refrigerators. "Is this the grocery list?"

"Yep. We're running low on a few basics so it's a bit longer than normal."

"No problem. We're under budget for the summer so we can get you all restocked."

Hazel had started volunteering at the camp a few years ago. She'd traded her nights at the bar for days at my camp. She came in for four to five hours every weekday and prepped meals for the campers.

The time she spent here meant my counselors could stay focused on the kids rather than scrambling to make meals in between activities. And it meant that I wasn't locked in the kitchen either. We all pitched in to make sure the kids were fed and happy, but without Hazel, things would be exponentially more stressful.

The fact that she'd insisted on not being paid had been nothing short of miraculous. Her volunteer status was one of the reasons I'd been able to scrimp and save on the church's meager budget and keep the place open until the Kendrick Foundation had stepped in as new owners.

That, and I hadn't taken a raise in over two years.

All Hazel had asked for when she'd started volunteering was that she could dictate the menu and that we let her bring Charlie along. I'd agreed immediately. So while Thea worked at the bar, Charlie came to camp with Hazel. The girl had become an honorary full-time camper these last couple of years. Along with her gran, she made my camp a better place.

"Are you going to stare at that list all day or tell me what happened with Jackson?"

"Stare at the list," I said, not looking her way.

"Fine," she muttered. "I'll just ask him. Hey, Jackson."

"Hi," a deep voice rumbled.

My head whipped to the kitchen door just as Jackson strolled inside.

He hadn't shaved this morning and the scruff on his jaw made the corners seem even sharper. His chin had a flat spot in the center. It wasn't a dimple, not really even a dent, just a feature that made his face even manlier.

His appeal was annoying.

"Hey." He smiled at me, then looked to Hazel. "Just thought I'd come in and say hello. Thought maybe I could take you for an early lunch at the diner before I need to open the bar. With Thea and Charlie gone to New York, I thought you might want company."

"Please," I mumbled, rolling my eyes.

Thea and Charlie had been gone a whole day, and Hazel was fine without them. Jackson wasn't here for lunch. He hadn't been to the camp in years, not since Hazel had first started volunteering.

He was here to pester me again.

"Lunch, huh?" Hazel wasn't buying it either.

"That's right." He grinned. "Willa, you can come too if you'd like."

"I'm not hungry." I took the grocery list and rounded the large stainless-steel table in the middle of the kitchen, going right for the side door that led to my office. "I'll get these supplies today, Hazel."

"Thanks," she said as I walked out.

I held my breath until I was safely in my office, then I plopped down behind my computer. My stomach rumbled. I needed another Snickers, but they were in the kitchen's candy stash.

Dropping my head into my hand, I stared unblinking at my desk. Why? Why was he here again? Why couldn't he just leave me alone to move on with a crush-free life?

"Knock, knock." Hazel walked into the office.

I peered around her, expecting to see Jackson on her heels, but she was alone.

"He left. I told him I was too busy for lunch and using me as an excuse to see you was lame."

I giggled. "Definitely lame."

She sat in the chair across from my desk, staring at me without a word. The silence went on long enough it was getting strange, but then she winked. "Make him work for it."

My eyebrows came together. "Work for it?"

"For you. Make him work to win you over."

"Oh, no." I waved my hands in the air, swatting that idea away. "I'm done with that. It's too late."

"Uh-oh." She frowned. "What did he do?"

Hazel knew I'd always had a crush on Jackson. Everyone knew, except for the man himself.

While I'd managed to hide my feelings from Jackson, I hadn't been so inconspicuous with the rest of Lark Cove. Apparently, my longing looks and sheepish waves were quite obvious. I did my best to hide those, but my traitorous cheeks always flushed when Jackson was near.

Hiding them wasn't as easy, especially in a town where everyone seemed to be watching and wondering, *Will today be the day Willa makes her approach?* The answer was always no. I'd never been brave enough to risk that kind of rejection.

Not that it mattered anymore.

"He didn't do anything," I lied. "I'm just ready to move on. He's not the man I thought he was, and I'm at the point in my life where it's time to get serious about finding the right guy."

Hazel's frown deepened. "Is this about him kissing Thea? Because there was nothing to that. He was just trying to piss off Logan."

"No." I shook my head. "It's not about that kiss."

Though, I wish I hadn't had to witness it firsthand.

Thea had invited me to Charlie's sixth birthday, and it took a lot of nerve for me to even attend the party since it wasn't long after Jackson had kissed me and forgotten. But I worked up the nerve to see him again because I didn't want to miss Charlie's special day.

I arrived at Thea's lakeside cottage—the one she and Charlie shared with Hazel—just in time to catch Jackson kiss Thea.

There was nothing quite like the pain of watching your long-time crush kiss another woman.

Especially a woman like Thea. She was gorgeous, with shiny, dark hair and seductive brown eyes. She was brave and confident and sexy. In other words, my polar opposite.

I ran away from the party, too upset to stay. A few days later, I'd all but convinced myself that Jackson was in love with Thea, so I mustered all my courage and stopped by the bar to ask for certain. Thea swore up and down there was nothing between her and Jackson but a sibling-type love. I believed her and decided it would be best to forget the whole thing.

Just like it would be best to forget all things Jackson.

Still, the mental image of his lips on hers made me nauseous. The idea of him and any other woman made my stomach churn.

Maybe that was the reason for his appearance last night. Had he run out of tourists to bang? Was I just next on his conquest list?

"I don't know what's going through your head, but steam is going to come shooting out of your ears at any moment."

I focused on Hazel. "Sorry. I'm . . . mad."

"At Jackson?"

"Yes." No. Not really. I was mostly mad at myself. I was mad for giving him my focus for so many years.

"Good," Hazel declared. "Be mad. Take it out on him. I'm sure that whatever he did, he deserves it. Just like he deserves a thump on the back of the head every now and again."

"He deserves it," I muttered.

"Just don't be mad forever. I'm not sure what has finally caused that boy's eyes to open, but I'm glad for it. The best thing that could happen to him is you."

I opened my mouth to respond, but I had no idea what to say, so I just nodded.

Hazel gave me a small smile and stood, going back to the kitchen without another word.

I stared at the empty doorway, replaying her words.

Make him work for it.

Maybe Hazel was on to something. Jackson had a lot of work to do if he was going to prove his sincerity. My guess was that he'd be bored with his pursuit within the week and move on to someone easier.

And after that happened, I'd truly be free to move on.

Maybe the quickest way to let him go was to watch him walk away.

Make him work for it?

I could do that.

four

JACKSON

"YOU KEEP STARING AT THAT DOOR LIKE YOU'RE EXPECTING someone." Wayne chuckled from his stool at the bar.

"Nah." I tore my eyes from the door and opened the dishwasher, letting the steam bellow out. As it did, my gaze drifted back to the door.

Wayne laughed again and took a sip of his beer. "Who are you waiting for?"

"No one."

That was bullshit. I was hoping Willa would come in, though I wasn't sure why. She'd blown me off today when I'd stopped by the camp under the guise of inviting Hazel to lunch.

I'd caught her off guard when I'd shown up at her door two nights ago. She'd made it clear that I'd done something to irritate her. I just had no idea what.

That's why I'd gone to the camp today. I'd assumed that in broad daylight and dressed in something other than pajamas, she'd explain the problem. But hell, she wouldn't even talk to me. She'd barely looked at me before whipping that hair around and rushing out of the kitchen.

When I'd asked her last night if I was missing something, she'd said yes. But what?

The only women I irritated on a regular basis were Hazel and Thea. Both of them were lousy at keeping their mouths shut, so whenever I pissed them off, I knew about it five seconds later. Willa's silence was bothering me, almost as much as being turned down for a date.

I never got turned down.

Though, I don't think I'd ever really asked a woman out before. I didn't date. I hooked up. And the women I hooked up with didn't get asked to dinner, unless they were eating here at the bar. They got asked to bed, then sent on their way after we were done.

But with Willa, I wanted more than an easy fuck. It wasn't every day I met a woman who had no qualms about slamming a door in my face. I had to admit, it was kind of a turn-on. I wanted to spend some time together and get to know her. Maybe that would shake the damn dream out of my head.

Though, dreaming about her and all that hair wasn't really a hardship.

Because, fuck me, that hair was incredible.

It's what had caught my eye in Thea's drawing. I wanted to spend intimate hours with that hair. I wanted it wrapped around my hands and threaded through my fingers. I wanted to feel the silky ends tickle my bare skin. Just thinking about her hair made my dick twitch.

I needed more of that hair and the woman who grew it. If she wouldn't agree to a date, I'd have to learn more about her in other ways.

"Hey, Wayne. You know Willa, don't you?" I asked.

He choked on his beer. "Willa Doon?"

I handed him a stack of napkins to clean the beer slobber on his chin.

He dried his face and gave me a sideways glance. "Yeah, I

know Willa."

"What's she like?"

"She's great. Her dad is the science teacher so I've known her since she was little. She used to come into the school with him during the summers. They'd practice his new experiments before school started."

"Nate's a good guy." He was one of the first people I'd met when I'd moved to Lark Cove. He didn't come down to the bar often, so I didn't see him much, but he always waved and asked me how I was doing whenever we bumped into each other around town.

I felt like an idiot for never noticing his daughter. How old was she? Nate wasn't all that old. And his wife, Betty, looked like she was in her forties, not old enough to have a grown daughter.

"How old is Willa?"

Wayne shrugged. "I don't know. I see so many kids at the school they all kind of blur together." He thought about it for a minute. "If I remember right, she graduated the same year I got divorced. And that was eight years ago, so . . . twenty-six."

Twenty-six. No wonder I hadn't noticed her years ago. She was too young.

I was thirty-one. She'd been a teenage girl when I'd moved to Lark Cove. I didn't have a lot of limitations when it came to the women I took to bed—women were beautiful creatures, no matter their shape or size—but they were all *women.*

Except Willa wasn't a teenage girl anymore. She'd grown into a stunning woman. A woman I should have noticed long before last night.

How had I missed her?

She came into the bar every now and then. I'd served her and her friends drinks. When she came in with her parents for pizza, she sat quietly and listened while Nate and I shot the breeze.

Oh, fuck. How many times had I called her Willow? I was such a prick.

"She does good work at that camp," Wayne said. "Her parents have been bragging for weeks about her saving it."

I nodded. "I'm glad it all worked out. I've heard nothing but good things about that camp, and it would be a shame to see it close."

Logan may have bought the camp, but I liked the idea of giving Willa all of the credit instead. My eyes went back to the door, hoping it would push open and she'd walk inside. But it stayed closed.

"Uh, I don't know if you know this or not, Jackson," Wayne said carefully. "I think Willa might have a little crush on you."

"No shit?" Then why had she turned me down for a date? Twice?

He shrugged. "Just a guess."

So not only had I not noticed her, but I'd also missed the fact that she was interested in me. How was that even possible? Wayne had to be wrong. Willa had never once batted her eyelashes my way, given me a seductive smile or flashed me a cleavage shot. I was good at picking up on subtle hints from women.

Wasn't I?

So how had I missed Willa's?

"Are we talking about the same Willa? Long, blond hair. Delicate face. Big blue eyes. That Willa?"

Wayne nodded. "The one and only."

"Well, if she liked me before, she's over it now," I told him as he drank his beer. "I asked her out twice in the last twenty-four hours and got shot down both times."

He sputtered his beer again. "You're kidding."

"I think I pissed her off."

Wayne started laughing. It began as a slow chuckle that

grew and grew until the other patrons in the bar all stopped talking to watch him belly laugh.

"Remind me to start charging you double for beers," I muttered after he pulled himself together.

"I don't know what you did," he wheezed, "but it had to have been bad. Willa is the sweetest girl in Flathead County. How'd you manage to make her angry?"

I shrugged. "I don't know."

He scoffed.

"Really!" I held up my hands. "I don't know. I know I've slipped a few times and called her Willow. But in my defense, I've always sucked at remembering names."

The only way I remembered a new name was to do what Hazel had taught me in high school. I said a name ten times in my head or I came up with a pneumonic device. But neither trick had helped me get Willa's right.

"You do suck at names," Wayne mumbled. "You thought my last name was Brown for the longest time."

Brown, like the color of his chocolate hair. "I—wait, your last name isn't Brown?"

"Christ, Jackson." He rolled his eyes. "It's Black."

"Sorry. Damn it," I huffed. "At least I'm great with faces."

Bullshit with me for twenty minutes and I'd remember you for years. Tell me your name once and ask me to repeat it weeks later, not happening. Working at the bar suited me perfectly. I recognized repeat customers by their faces and got away with calling them by a generic nickname.

Hey, man.

Good to see you again, sweetheart.

Welcome back, buddy.

No names required and I was still the cool bartender who remembered his patrons.

How was it that I hadn't really noticed Willa's face?

"You really don't know what you did to make Willa mad?" Wayne asked.

"No idea," I muttered and grabbed a glass. "I need a beer."

I filled it up, then shut off the tap. I examined the white foam around the rim, but before I brought the glass to my lips, I stepped over to the sink and dumped it out. Just two days ago, I'd made the decision not to drink as often and I sure as hell could go more than one day without a beer.

"So what are you going to do about her?"

Good question. I blew out a long breath. What was I going to do?

I could just leave her be. I'd asked her out and she'd rejected my offer. It was done. Things would probably be simpler if I just moved on.

There was a woman in the corner booth who'd been eyeing me all night. I bet she wouldn't turn me down if I asked her to come home with me later. But the problem was, I didn't have the slightest bit of interest.

When I'd delivered their latest round of drinks, the woman had eye-fucked me. Normally that look would be enough to stir some interest, but my dick was fast asleep. At the moment, it only came alive at the thought of Willa. Just remembering how she looked earlier today in the camp's kitchen, with her hair loose down her back, gave me a semi in three seconds flat. Saturday night, after she'd slammed the door in my face—twice—I'd walked home with a raging hard-on.

Something about her just did it for me.

So was I going to let Willa be? Would I take her rejection and move on?

Hell no.

I grinned at Wayne. "I'll think of something."

Maybe I'd swing by the camp again tomorrow. Maybe I'd leave a note with some flowers by her door. I was in the middle of brainstorming other ideas when the front door swung open and Willa walked inside.

I did a double take to make sure I wasn't dreaming.

The sunshine streamed in behind her, making her hair look like waves of gold. She had a heart-shaped face, her high cheekbones flushed and rosy. Her blue eyes were mesmerizing, the color of the lake on a sunny day.

How had I missed this? How had I missed *her*?

Willa looked around the room, searching. When she found me, she froze, still standing in the doorway.

I smiled and lifted a hand to wave, but before I could say hello, she was spinning back around and running out the door.

"Wayne," I called as I jogged down the length of the bar. "You're in charge."

He laughed and threw up his hands. "Free drinks for everyone!"

The bar erupted in laughter, but I didn't stop moving. I ran past the tables in the middle of the room, nearly slipping on a pile of peanut shells, and yanked open the door.

"Willa! Wait!"

She was halfway to her car already. At my call, she glanced over her shoulder but didn't stop. If anything, she seemed to be walking faster.

Just not fast enough.

My boots thudded hard on the gravel parking lot as I sprinted to catch up. I reached her side right as she beeped the locks on her SUV.

"Hey," I panted, standing by her door. "Why did you leave?"

"I, um . . ." She fiddled with the keys in her hand. "I changed my mind."

"Changed your mind about what?"

She closed her eyes, drawing in a long breath. Then she squared her shoulders, lifted her chin and looked me right in the eyes. "What do you want, Jackson? Why are you asking me out?"

Her questions caught me off guard. No woman had ever asked me why before. They'd all just said yes.

"I, uh . . . don't know."

"You don't know." She huffed and yanked open the door to her car, tossing in her purse before climbing inside, muttering, "Stupid idea. Stupid. Stupid."

"Wait." I grabbed the door before she could swing it closed. "What was a stupid idea? Coming here?"

"Yes," she snapped. "I should have stuck with my original plan."

"What plan?"

"To stay away from you." She tried to shut her door, but I held it tight. "Let go, Jackson."

"No. Just . . . just one second, okay? Clearly, I did something to piss you off. But I'm not sure what I did. So at some point, you're going to have to spell it out for me."

She frowned, tugging the door handle harder.

Still, I didn't let go. "You want to know why I'm asking you out? I guess . . . because I want to get to know you. I don't know, something about this," I waved my free hand between us, "feels different. Special."

Her mouth parted and her eyes widened, but she didn't say anything. Though she did stop jerking on the door handle.

"Come inside," I pleaded. "For just a little bit. Come sit in there and hang out. I'm sure Wayne's passing out free drinks at the moment so you can at least take advantage of one of those."

Her lips turned up, just a bit.

"Please?" I was begging now. I never begged.

Willa made me stand there, sweating from the summer sun and her intense stare, until finally she gave me the smallest of nods.

I did my best to hide my smug smile as she grabbed her purse and slid out of the car. As soon as she was clear of the door, I closed it behind her and walked with her back into the bar.

I opened the bar door for her, and sure enough, Wayne was making himself comfortable behind the bar. Though it didn't look like he was giving away drinks.

Thea and I never gave drinks away for free. It was a policy Hazel had drilled into us when we'd both started here, just as it had been drilled into her head long, long ago.

Hazel's parents had been the original owners of the Lark Cove Bar. When they'd passed on, she'd inherited it, as well as her childhood home. I'd worked alongside Hazel at the bar for years, until Thea moved to Lark Cove. With both of us running the place, Hazel had decided to retire, though her rules remained.

No free drinks.

It might be against the rules, but Wayne had just earned a free refill.

And Willa could drink for free any night of the week.

"Hey, Willa." Wayne smiled and winked at her as we approached the bar.

She smiled back. "Hi, Wayne."

I slid a stool out for her, and after she sat, I went behind the bar. "Thanks," I told Wayne, clapping him on the shoulder. "Next one's on me."

"Rain check. I've hit my two-beer limit for the night and it's time to go home."

With a quick wave to Willa and a couple others in the bar, he walked out the front door, leaving me and Willa alone across from each other.

"What would you like?"

"Just a water, please." She tucked a strand of hair behind her ear. Her fingers toyed with the edges of a cocktail napkin.

"Are you hungry?" I asked, filling up a glass of ice water and adding a lemon wedge. "I could make you a pizza."

She shook her head. "I ate at camp with the kids already."

"Want some peanuts?" I slid over a paper boat full without waiting for an answer.

"Thanks," she said but didn't crack one. She also didn't say a word.

My heart began pounding and my palms were sweating. Had talking to a woman always been this hard? It occurred to me that I didn't actually know how to get to know a member of the opposite sex, except in the carnal sense.

I decided to go with the only safe topic that came to mind. "So, uh, how are your parents?"

"Good."

"Your dad's a teacher, right?"

She nodded. "Science."

"And your mom? What does she do again?"

"She's an accountant. She helps out Bob with some of the bookkeeping at the diner and then does tax returns for a bunch of people every year. She likes it because it gives her the summers free to spend with my dad and to do her gardening."

"Is she the one who did all the flowers then? Up your stairs?"

"Yep." After another short answer, Willa examined her water glass.

I took a moment to glance around the room, trying to think of another topic to discuss. She wasn't giving me much to go on and I had a sudden case of stage fright. The only other conversation starter that popped into my head was the weather, and I refused to talk about the fucking weather.

"How are things at the camp?" I asked.

"Good." She sipped her water. "Busy. We just brought in a new bunch of kids yesterday so the first couple days are crazy as they all get settled."

"I bet. Do you ever have kids who get homesick, go home early?"

"Sometimes, but they rarely leave. It usually only takes a day for them to get comfortable and make some friends. Then they usually don't want to go home."

"I never went to camp as a kid."

"That's too bad. They're a lot of fun."

"I bet." I would have killed to escape my foster home for a week. There was no way I would have gotten homesick.

Behind Willa at one of the tables, a customer gave me a nod for their check. "Be right back."

I hustled to the till and printed out their bill, then delivered it and cleared some glasses. After I rang them up and wiped down their table, I went back to my spot across from Willa.

She was studying her water glass, and while I'd been gone, she'd pulled her hair back into a long ponytail so it was off her face. She was wearing a pair of jeans and a black, sleeveless blouse that showed off her slender arms. The collar of the blouse was high, but it had a deep cut. Her shirt was blousy and loose, and with the way she was leaned forward with her elbows on the bar, it hinted at her black lace bra underneath.

She didn't have large breasts, but that didn't stop me from trying to sneak a peek. I bet she'd blush something fierce if she knew I was attempting to look down her shirt.

"Hey." My eyes snapped away from Willa's chest to the woman standing by her side. It was the same one who'd been flirting with me all night.

She had her arms pressed tight to her ribs, forcing her breasts together. Out of habit, my gaze dropped to her chest. It was like a car accident on the side of the road. Those tits got a glance whether you wanted to see the carnage or not.

Unlike Willa's, this woman's top could barely contain her breasts. The material pulled as low as possible to show off her cleavage. This chick couldn't pull off subtle, unlike Willa, who was sexy without even trying.

"What can I get for you?" I asked.

"My friends are ready to go, so I just wanted to leave this for you." She set three twenties on the bar. On the top one was a name—Cee Cee—and a phone number written in red sharpie.

"Thanks." I took the bills back to the register and made change. "Here." I handed her a five and some coins.

"Keep it," she purred. "And call me."

I gave her a polite smile. "Thanks."

She turned, flipping her brown hair over a shoulder, then strutted back to her friends. She looked ridiculous, her ass swaying and her heels teetering with every step. If she wasn't careful, she was going to trip on a peanut shell and break an ankle.

It took forever for her and her friends to gather up their shit and leave, and when they were finally out the door, I turned my attention back to Willa.

It was just the two of us now, but I didn't know how long the privacy would last. My dinner rush was over and Mondays were normally our slowest night. But with my luck, someone would be here soon for a nightcap, ruining my chances of talking to Willa alone.

"Before someone else comes in, I wanted to ask you again. Would you like to go out for dinner sometime? Maybe hit the diner or even drive up to Kalispell."

Kalispell was the biggest and closest town to Lark Cove,

about thirty miles away on the north side of the lake. I hadn't been to many of the restaurants up there, but I did know they were fancier than the diner or my bar. And Willa deserved fancy.

"Listen, Jackson." She hitched her purse over her shoulder and stood from her stool. "I appreciate the offer, but I don't think it's a good idea."

"What?"

"I'm not what you're looking for, and I'm definitely not your type."

Not my type? She was exactly my type. "Willa—"

She cut me off. "It would probably be best if you just forgot about me. Again."

With that, she turned and hurried through the door, leaving me and my mouth hanging open behind the bar.

Again.

What the fuck did that mean?

five

WILLA

"ANY JACKSON SIGHTINGS LATELY, WILLA?" LEIGHTON asked.

It was the night after I'd foolishly gone to the bar and sat with Jackson. I was out at the diner with three friends from high school.

I shook my head. "I'm, um, kind of done with that whole thing."

Three shocked faces stared my way.

Giving up on Jackson was kind of a huge deal. Leighton, June and Hannah had known about my epic crush from day one. Though, Leighton was the only one who'd ever supported my feelings for Jackson. June and Hannah never spared their comments on how *ridiculous* it was.

At least one good thing would come from giving up on Jackson. I wouldn't have to deal with their snide commentary anymore when we met every other week for cheeseburgers.

Leighton set down her burger. "What do you mean, you're done with that whole thing?"

I shrugged. "I'm just . . . done."

June and Hannah shared a look.

"Well, I think it's great." June smiled. "And about damn time."

"Me too. Here, here!" Hannah raised up her Diet Coke for a toast.

June hoisted her glass of water right to the middle of the booth, both of them waiting for me and Leighton to join in.

A bruised heart wasn't something I felt like toasting, but I picked up my Coke anyway, reluctantly lifting it in the air. Leighton didn't touch her Dr. Pepper. She was too busy studying my profile.

I gave her *come on, let's just get this over with* eyes, and she finally joined in.

"Cheers!" June chimed. "Here's to Willa finally giving up on the hot bartender."

The hot bartender. They'd always called Jackson the hot bartender.

Their quips about Jackson made no sense. If I declared right now that I wanted to jump in bed with him and use his sculpted body for sex, they'd be all for it. All they saw when they looked at him was a tight ass and muscular arms.

Heaven forbid I actually like the man enough to want a relationship. That was just me being *naïve.* It didn't matter to them that he was funny and charming. They didn't care that he was so good with Charlie it made my heart skip.

He was just the hot bartender.

Maybe it was ridiculous to have feelings for someone I'd never spoken to on the phone or texted even once. I might be ridiculous for letting a high-school crush last beyond college. And it was ridiculous to think I stood a chance with a man who'd called me by the wrong name for years.

Ridiculous.

The last thing I wanted was to admit that they'd been right all this time.

"What happened?" Leighton asked.

"Nothing," I lied.

She didn't buy it, but she didn't push any further.

Leighton knew I'd tell her everything later. We shared no secrets.

I was the only person who knew what had happened to her our freshman year. Well, other than the scum who'd assaulted her. Two weeks into college, we'd gone to a party off campus. The two of us had had too much to drink and both had blacked out. Someone had raped her while I'd been passed out alone in a bathroom stall, draped over a toilet.

She refused to tell anyone but me about that night.

Or the miscarriage she'd had four weeks later.

We'd made a pact back then to be there for one another. So I would tell her about Jackson kissing me, then forgetting. I'd kept that story to myself this long simply because it was just too embarrassing to relive. But after tonight, Leighton would hear it all, from the swing set to his visit at the camp yesterday. And I'd tell her all about how he'd blatantly checked out a woman's breasts and butt last night right in front of me.

He'd asked me to stay at the bar and get to know him. Well, one could say I'd learned a lot.

I wanted to get Leighton's opinion on the matter, but not tonight and certainly not in front of June and Hannah. I wasn't quite ready to confess yet.

It was still too raw.

Leighton and I were closer to each other than either of us had ever been to June or Hannah. We'd all grown up together, but now June and Hannah lived and worked in Kalispell. While Leighton and I had always shared a special friendship, the same could be said of June and Hannah.

Still, the four of us tried to meet every other week or so for dinner. Sometimes, Leighton and I would go up to Kalispell.

Other weeks, June and Hannah would drive down here.

"Guess who I saw as I was driving through town?" Hannah asked. "Brendon Jacoby."

Goodness gracious. Here it comes. I picked up my burger and took an enormous bite so I wouldn't be able to talk. June and Hannah had been trying to set me up with Brendon ever since he'd moved back to Lark Cove last year. They'd never forgotten the crush I'd had on him my junior year. I guess now that Jackson wasn't in the picture anymore, they'd be even more ruthless in their matchmaking attempts.

"He's just as cute as ever."

I just kept chewing.

"My mom told me he broke up with that woman he was dating in Kalispell." Hannah wagged her eyebrows. "You should stop by his house. Say hi. Ask him to take you out for dinner."

June giggled. "Or to take your virginity."

I nearly choked on my bite as my face flushed bright red. Why was being a virgin funny? I finished chewing, wanting to say something back, but decided another bite was a better idea. When I got flustered or embarrassed, I never said the right thing.

The right retort would come eventually. I'd be sitting at home, stewing, and think of exactly what to say and how to say it. My comebacks were witty and hilarious. They were crafted with the perfect amount of sarcasm and bite.

They just came too late.

"Not funny, June," Leighton snapped.

"I'm just joking." She snickered. "Sort of."

Why were we still friends with June? I didn't remember her being such a mean girl in high school. Maybe I'd just missed it. But ever since we'd started this biweekly dinner after college, she'd brought along this attitude that more often than not rubbed me the wrong way.

One of these days, someone was going to put her in her place.

I just hoped I'd be there to watch.

"Whatever happened with that guy you liked from your office, Hannah?" Leighton asked.

I nudged her knee with mine, silently thanking her for changing the subject.

Hannah grinned and launched into a whole sordid tale about her seducing him last Friday night and screwing him in her office after everyone had left for the weekend. She didn't spare any details about her sex life. She never had. And every time she said the word *cock* or *fuck*, she looked right at me.

Leighton thought she did it to shock or embarrass me. Maybe she was right. Our senior year, Hannah had given us all the dirty details about her relationship with two football players and her stories had definitely shocked me back then.

They didn't anymore. I'd read erotic romance novels. I'd stumbled onto a rather educational account on Tumblr once. Heck, in college, I'd had to assist in teaching sex education during my one semester of student teaching.

The only reason I was blushing tonight was because Hannah was talking way too loudly as she described her lover's technique, and three tables down sat our former math teacher Mr. Rockman.

Couldn't we save these stories for margarita night?

Hannah went on and on and I focused on my cheeseburger, ignoring her constant looks from across the booth.

One day I'd find the right guy and he'd be my first. I wasn't in a rush to jump in bed with someone just because I was curious or felt the need to check *lose my virginity* off a list. I wanted it to be special. And for the longest time, I'd been holding out hope that my first time would be with Jackson.

A hollow feeling settled in my chest when I realized that dream was gone.

I was twenty-six years old. I had kissed one man, after which he'd forgotten. I'd never had a boyfriend or sex. I'd never been in love.

All because I'd been waiting for Jackson Page.

I didn't want to be twenty-seven and still single. I didn't want to be ridiculous anymore. I'd made the decision weeks ago to give up on him, but it hadn't really hit me until now. If I didn't move on—if I didn't let the illusion of him go—I'd be alone.

I shoved a huge bite of my cheeseburger into my mouth so I wouldn't cry.

Damn you, Jackson.

Damn you.

"Are we going to the bar for a drink tonight?" June asked after we'd all finished eating.

"I can't," I said, digging in my purse for a twenty. "I have to go back to camp and teach my constellations class."

Even if I didn't have to teach, I certainly wouldn't be going to the bar again.

We all dropped some cash on the table and slid out of the booth. I gave my friends each a hug good-bye and promised to call Leighton tomorrow. Then I went back to the camp and met a group of excited kids in the main lodge.

I gave them each a constellation map and flashlight, then led them on a short hike to a clearing in the trees next to the lake.

As the kids tried to find Ursa Major and Cassiopeia, I picked the brightest star in Sagittarius.

And I wished to forget Jackson Page.

There was a rustling outside my door.

No one was knocking, but there was a distinct rustling sound.

And muttering.

I barely made out the words *damn* and *shit*.

I sat up in bed, clutching the covers to my chest as I strained to listen. My parents were fast asleep so it couldn't be them. Plus, they didn't curse.

The list of my regular visitors was short—Leighton, June and Hannah. And since I was certain that they were all asleep in their own beds, there was only one person who would come to see me in the middle of the night.

Jackson.

I whipped off the covers and tiptoed across the cool maple floors toward the door. The curtain over the window was pulled back just enough on one side to peek through a crack.

And sure enough, there he was.

Jackson Page in all his glory.

He was fixing one of my mom's flowerpots he must have knocked over. Once he'd pushed it up against the wall and swept away the spilled soil, he stood and pulled a note from his pocket. He came right to the door and I shied back. With barely a sliver to see him through, I watched as he tried to shove a piece of paper into the slit between the deadbolt and the doorframe.

Why was he here?

I should have just let him leave his note and go, but I was curious. How long had I hoped for his attention? Too many hours to count. Now I had it and I wanted to know why.

Curiosity had turned me into a glutton for punishment.

Quickly, I righted my pajamas so the seams weren't crooked. My camisole was black, not as see-through as he'd seen the other night. My hot-pink pajama pants had little black bows on the cotton and were cuter than the yellow ones I'd been wearing during his last visit.

Just as I tugged my camisole up higher on my breasts, Jackson managed to get his note wedged by the lock and turned to leave.

I stepped over to the knob, undid the deadbolt and opened the door.

Jackson spun back around, his eyes taking in my bare feet and pajamas. "Hey. Sorry to wake you."

I crossed my arms over my chest, chilled from the night air. It was August but nights in Montana were still cool. Not to mention that being around Jackson gave me goose bumps.

"What are you doing here?"

He bent and picked up the note that had fallen when I'd opened the door. He held it out. "I swear I'm not stalking you. But I didn't think this could wait."

I took it from his hand and started to unfold it, but he stopped me. "Don't read it. Not while I'm here."

"Okay." I folded it back up, shoved it in my pants pocket and recrossed my arms.

I didn't say anything else, but I didn't go inside either. I just stood there as we stared at one another.

He'd chased me into the parking lot last night and told me that something between us felt special. Then he'd checked out that woman right in front of me. I'd had to sit witness as he'd drooled over her cleavage and raked his eyes over her ass as she'd strutted to the door.

Had he gone home with her after I'd left? Did he even realize how much he'd hurt me? He treated me like second place. I was just a consolation prize. A nobody.

I was right there—sitting right there in front of him—and

he picked someone else. Again. The pain I'd felt at the diner came back in full force.

I really needed that wish I'd made earlier tonight to come true.

"Good night." I gripped the door to close it, but before it moved an inch, he said the one word guaranteed to stop me and make me weak in the knees.

"Willa."

My name, said in his deep rumble, had never sounded so good.

"What?" I whispered.

"Dinner. Tomorrow at the bar."

Was that a question or an order? I shook my head, closing the door another inch. "Good night, Jackson. Just . . . good night."

"Wait." With one stride, he stepped close. Too close. My breath hitched as the heat waves from his chest radiated my way. My goose bumps grew their own goose bumps and it had nothing to do with the temperature.

"Why are you doing this?"

"Because I can't get you out of my head." Jackson lifted a hand and brushed his knuckles down my arm, all the way from my shoulder to my elbow.

A shiver took a slow roll down my spine. "M-me?"

"Yeah. You." He ran his hand back up to my shoulder, sending a tingle of electric sparks to my fingers.

The sensation made me sway on my bare feet.

Was I dreaming? This had to be a dream. Or was it a prank? My heart dropped to my stomach as I realized this could be some twisted joke. Like the time in ninth grade when Oliver Banks had asked me to the homecoming dance only because his friends had dared him to ask Mr. Doon's daughter. He'd danced with me once, then admitted he had a crush on Hannah and left to dance with her instead.

Maybe someone had put Jackson up to this just to get a laugh. Was he making fun of me because of my crush?

"Is this a joke?" I whispered.

"What?" He gaped at me. "Why would you think this is a joke?"

"Forget it." His astonishment made me feel slightly better. "I have a long day tomorrow so . . ." I shuffled back a few inches.

"Wait." He reached out and cupped my elbow. "Why the hell would you think this was a joke?"

"Just because," I said, fighting back tears.

I was exhausted and my wits were threadbare, so when I opened my mouth, the words in my head came out in a rush. "I've known you for years, Jackson, and you've hardly spoken to me at all. Then out of the blue, you ki—"

I stopped before I blurted out that he'd kissed me before. There was no need to relive that level of humiliation. Since he'd forgotten about our night in the playground, I was going to forget it too.

"I, what?" He nudged my elbow to keep talking. "What?"

"You come here," I said, recovering. "You come to my work. You tell me that something about us feels special, but then you check out another woman in the bar. Is that all you want? An easy score? Because I hate to break it to you, but I'm as far from easy as you can get."

"Whoa, whoa, whoa." He held up his hands. "I did not check that chick out last night."

"I was there. You looked right down her shirt and then at her butt as she left."

"That was not because I was interested in her. Trust me."

I frowned, sending him a silent *yeah, right.*

"It wasn't! You know what it's like when you drive by a dead deer on the side of the road? You don't want to look at the blood and guts, but you can't help it. That's how it was with that woman. And I only watched her leave because I was worried she'd twist her ankle with the way she was strutting around and then sue me."

"That's . . . gross." Although the roadkill analogy made sense.

"I'm not here as a joke, Willa. And I'm not here because I think you're an easy score." He paused, then chuckled. "I've put more work into trying to get you on a date than I have with any other woman in years."

My jaw dropped. Had he just said that? Right when I'd stopped wanting to slam the door in his face, he'd ruined everything with that last comment. My hands fisted at my sides, my spine straightening into a steel rod.

"Putting in some effort is funny to you? I know women normally just fall at your feet, but you'll have to excuse me for not stripping off my clothes and falling naked into your bed. Really, I'm so sorry to disappoint you."

For once, my sarcastic comeback came at the right moment. *Yes!* I mentally high-fived myself.

Jackson's smile dropped. "That's not what I meant. You took that the wrong way."

I didn't care to know what the right way was. "Good night, Jackson."

"Dinner. Just one dinner and I'll leave you alone." He took my elbow again, stopping me. "Look, we don't know each other all that well, but I'd like to change that. Start as friends. Go from there. Haven't you ever seen someone before and just felt this need to know them?"

Yes, I had.

Nine years ago in a gas station.

But timing had never been on my side. Back then—heck, three weeks ago—I would have agreed to dinner without question. Now, I wasn't sure if having Jackson in my life was a good idea.

I was inviting heartache to my front door.

Before I could reject him, he let me go and took a step back. "Think about it. I'll see you around."

Then he turned and jogged down my steps, crushing a few flowers with his boots as he went. Mom needed to get over and do some pruning. I was even having a hard time maneuvering the stairs amid all the greenery.

I stayed in the doorway, watching Jackson as he descended the stairs and crossed my yard. Like he'd done before, he glanced over his shoulder, giving me one last look before continuing onto the school's lawn.

When he was gone, I went inside and closed the door. Then I sat on the edge of my mattress and flipped on my bedside lamp. As my eyes adjusted to the light, I slipped the note he'd given me from my pocket.

Willa
I'm sorry for calling you Willow.
It won't happen again.
Jackson

I snorted a laugh. I didn't know what I'd expected to find in his note, but that wasn't it.

Setting the note down, I crawled into bed and snuggled in deep. I was beat and had another busy day ahead. I hoped I'd be able to fall asleep quickly and forget about the last ten minutes.

But, just like the last time Jackson had graced my doorstep, sleep didn't come easily. My thoughts were consumed with Jackson's handwriting.

And how much I liked seeing my name written in his sloppy scrawl.

six

JACKSON

THE WINDOWS ON MY TRUCK WERE ROLLED DOWN AS I DROVE through town the next morning, and the fresh air smelled like pine trees and dew. Not much could top this smell, except maybe Willa's hair. I'd only gotten a hint of it last night, but it was enough to leave me wanting more.

A lot more.

It was cool this early in the day, but by ten o'clock, the summer sunshine would burn off the chill and it would be a hot one. If I didn't have to work later, it would be the perfect day to take the boat out on the lake or go for a hike in the mountains.

I might not have been born in Montana, but this mountain air called to my blood.

Too bad my mother hadn't dumped me somewhere like this instead of New York City. I might have had a happy childhood. But I guess things worked out for the best. I'd met Thea and Hazel in the city, which had ultimately led to my move here.

And Lark Cove was where I was staying.

The only reason I'd set foot back in New York was if Thea and Charlie decided to stay there with Logan. They'd only been gone a few days, but damn I missed them. I missed talking about stuff at the bar with Thea. I missed hanging with Charlie in her fort behind their house.

For the first time in years, I felt the loneliness that had been so present during my childhood. *Damn, I hope they come back.* I wasn't sure what I'd do without seeing them on a regular basis.

Though I had to admit, chasing Willa this week had been one hell of a distraction.

There wasn't a cloud to be seen as I rolled down the highway, just the wide-open sky that was a shade lighter than Willa's eyes.

I stopped by the gas station to top off my gas tank and get a cup of coffee. Considering I walked most places in the summer, I rarely had to get gas this time of year unless I was taking out my boat.

But I took extra care with my truck, never letting it get below a quarter full. I also made sure the silver exterior was washed and waxed regularly. I changed the oil at exactly three thousand miles and detailed the interior every two months.

It was the nicest vehicle I'd ever owned. Actually, it was the nicest vehicle I'd ever been inside. When I'd finally had enough money to pay for a new rig outright, I'd driven my old Chevy up to Kalispell and come home with a big smile and a brand-new truck paid for in full.

After my truck, I saved up for my fishing boat—also brand-new and also paid for in full.

The only debt I had to my name was the mortgage on my house. It wasn't new, but it was affordable and I'd been making extra payments to ensure that before I turned fifty, I'd be free and clear.

I'd never wanted anything more than a life that was mine and mine alone.

I didn't want to depend on someone else's hand-me-downs just so I had clothes to wear. I didn't want to be at the mercy of the bus or train schedule in order to get to work. I didn't want anyone to tell me where I had to live or the chores I had to do.

My biggest goal was to be debt-free, and I was damn close to making that happen.

I wasn't a powerless kid anymore, stuck in a city alone. My life was mine, and it was a damn fine one at that.

I finished up at the gas station and sipped my scalding-hot coffee as I drove down the road toward Willa's camp. It was a gamble, showing up again this morning, but I was hoping now that she'd read my apology note, she'd finally cut me some slack.

It hadn't been easy to swallow my pride and write that note. But Willa was worth the hit to my ego and she'd deserved that apology for a long time coming.

I turned left off the highway and onto the winding gravel road that led to the camp. It was nestled underneath a grove of tall evergreens, right on the shoreline of the lake.

Properties like this had been slowly bought and developed in Lark Cove over the last twenty years. I had no idea how much the camp's land was worth, but I was guessing it was more money than I'd see in my lifetime.

I'd kill for a spot on the lake. I'd cherish a place where I could wake up and drink my coffee overlooking the water. I'd love a house with a dock for my boat so it could be ready and waiting at all times. But a home like that wasn't in my future. Instead, they were reserved for rich guys like Logan Kendrick.

At least he'd saved Willa's camp.

The gravel parking lot next to the camp was mostly empty, and just like I'd done the other day, I pulled my silver, half-ton Chevy next to Hazel's Subaru Outback. I got out and took a look inside, seeing Charlie's booster seat in the back. It was covered with snack crumbs, which meant it was time for me to take it for an afternoon since I kept Hazel's rig just as clean as my own.

With my coffee in hand, I followed the footpath down from

the parking lot to the campground.

The main lodge was closest to the parking lot and the first building visitors came upon. It was a huge log structure that blended in with the tree trunks. The main part of the building was a dining hall filled with wooden tables and folding chairs. At the back was the kitchen, bathrooms and Willa's office.

I'd gotten a tour of this whole place a few summers ago, courtesy of Charlie. I'd come out here to say hello to Hazel after she'd started volunteering and Charlie had dragged me all over the place, showing me each of the bunks and the inner workings of the lodge.

Had Willa been there that day of my tour? If she had been, I hadn't noticed. I'd been a blind asshole. All this time she'd been right there. If not for Thea's drawing, I may have never opened my eyes.

They were open now.

I found myself searching for her constantly. If I was working, I kept one eye on the door, waiting and hoping she'd come into the bar. And if she didn't, I'd hurry to close down the bar and hustle the few blocks to her street, wishing her light would still be on.

It had been just days since I'd gone to her house that first night, not even a week, and I'd become completely infatuated.

I liked how gracefully she moved, more like floating than walking. I liked the way her blue eyes were so pure and honest. I liked her shy smile and how she'd tuck her hair behind an ear when she blushed. It made me want to put my hand on her cheek with each flush just to feel its heat.

I liked her.

Willa kept asking me why I was into her, and though I'd done my best to explain it, I still didn't quite understand it myself.

She was just . . . special.

I wanted to connect with her on more than just a physical level. Maybe I'd get that chance today.

I scanned the rest of the buildings as I walked down the side of the lodge. Six small log cabins were scattered beneath the trees. Inside were kids' bunks, some for boys and some for girls. I imagined they got a little chilly at night since there wasn't much to keep out the cold, but I bet none of the kids cared when they were bundled up tight in a sleeping bag.

A couple of boys came running out of the shower and bathroom building situated between two of the bunkhouses. They came hurrying past me on their way to a large firepit built in the middle of a clearing. Past it, lake water sparkled in the sun. A couple boats were out today. As soon as Thea was back from her vacation, I was taking a couple days off work and my boat would be out there too.

My eyes tracked the kids as they hurried to take their seats on the log benches surrounding the firepit. There wasn't a fire—I assumed the counselors saved those for nighttime. I bet they let the kids roast marshmallows all week. I bet those kids had a blast from sunrise to sunset.

Would they let a thirty-one-year-old bartender come to camp? I'd missed all this kind of stuff as a kid.

From the entrance to the lodge, a whole other group of kids ran outside. Eleven or twelve, they looked old enough to spend a week away from their parents, but not old enough to get summer jobs.

I hit the double doors to the lodge and was about to step inside when a swish of blond hair caught my eye. From behind one of the small cabins, Willa walked toward the firepit with a group of girls.

They were giggling about something. One of the girls tugged on Willa's arm, pulling her down to whisper something in her ear. Whatever she said, Willa stood straight and began laughing with a wide and heart-stopping smile.

My hand came to my chest, rubbing at the sternum. She was so damn beautiful it felt like my chest was going to cave in.

I'd known Willa for years. I'd seen her face. Yet still, I'd missed her.

How had I missed her?

"You weren't paying attention."

My head whipped around as Hazel stepped through the lodge's doors and to my side.

"I didn't mean to say that out loud," I said.

Hazel laughed, her voice rough and hoarse from a thousand too many cigarettes. "You're back."

I shrugged. "I was up early. Thought I'd come over and say hello."

Willa reached the pit and stood in the middle with all the kids situated around her. She was in jeans again, like she had been the other night at the bar. They molded to her firm ass and trim legs, accentuating every curve. The cuffs were rolled up at her ankles, just above her sandals. And she was wearing a red Flathead Summer Camp tee.

Hazel was right. I hadn't been paying attention. I just hoped that it wasn't too late because I saw Willa now and wouldn't be looking away.

"How are you doing?" I asked Hazel as we stood and watched Willa with the kids.

"Good. It's quiet at home. Too quiet. I was thinking of coming down to the bar tonight to bother you."

I smiled and threw an arm around her shoulders. "That'd be great."

She leaned into my side, her arm going behind my back. Her frame was bonier now than I remembered as a kid. She'd gotten frailer these past few years. I'd been happy when she'd decided to stop working at the bar, but I wished she'd slow down even more.

There was no telling her that. Hazel Rhodes did what Hazel Rhodes wanted. Period.

"Have you heard from Thea and Charlie?" I asked.

She nodded. "They called me this morning."

"Are they having fun?"

"I don't think so."

I grinned. "Good."

Selfish as it was, I didn't want Thea and Charlie to be having a blast in New York. I wanted them to come home, though I was sure Logan would try and convince them to stay. He'd be a fool not to try, and Logan was no idiot.

"Don't worry." Hazel squeezed my hip. "They'll come home."

"I hope so."

I couldn't imagine them not being here and living with Hazel. As she got older, I worried about her alone in that cottage. But if Thea did stay in New York, I'd make sure Hazel was cared for.

"Are you here to check on me? Or to talk to Willa?" Hazel asked, cutting right to the chase.

I chuckled. "Both?"

She laughed too. "I'm glad you're finally seeing what's been in front of you all these years."

"Me too."

Maybe it wasn't that I hadn't been paying attention. Maybe it was the lonely ache in my chest I hadn't felt for years making me realize I wanted something more.

"But Jackson?"

I looked down. "Yeah?"

"Don't you break that girl's heart. If you think there's even a chance you'll hurt her, you walk away."

Did she really have no faith in me?

"I'm not going to break her heart," I snapped. "But I appreciate you thinking so highly of me that I'd go into this without thinking it through."

"Watch your attitude." She gave me the scowl she'd invented just for me. "I'm just making sure you know what you're doing."

"I do." I sighed. "I know she's something special."

"Then I'll say no more."

My eyes went back to the firepit, where Willa was reading from a clipboard. She had the kids' undivided attention as she spoke. They smiled up at her from their benches with complete adoration.

"She's good with them," I told Hazel.

"One of the best. She should have been a teacher like her dad. She's got the patience and a way of explaining things to kids that just clicks."

"I wish I would have had a teacher like that."

I couldn't remember a single one of my teachers' names because none of them had been memorable. The person who'd coached me through algebra and geography and made sure I graduated was Hazel.

"But I had you." I hugged Hazel tighter. "You made sure I didn't flunk. And that I knew exactly where Lark Cove, Montana, was on a map."

She laughed. "Brainwashing. I had to make sure either you or Thea came out here to keep me company. I lucked out and got you both."

"We're the lucky ones." I planted a kiss on the top of her hair.

The stress of those last few years mixing drinks and managing a small-town bar had turned her once-brown hair to a silvery white. Though she blamed the color on me instead of the long nights. I also got credit for the deep worry lines on her tanned and leathery skin. The puckering around her mouth was thanks to Virginia Slims.

Despite it all, she was still a beautiful woman. To me, she always would be, inside and out.

"Don't waste your sweet on me," Hazel said. "Save it for Willa." She swung an arm toward the firepit, then used her hand on my back to shove me forward.

I shot her a grin and walked toward the pit.

The kids were all huddled in groups of three, each team inspecting a sheet of paper as Willa watched on.

"Ready. Set. Go!" Willa called and the kids went dashing in all different directions.

Willa smiled, then steered one group of kids in the opposite direction. When she turned to watch them leave, she spotted me coming her way. Her face flushed, her cheeks not quite as red as her shirt. She tugged at her hem with one hand and held her clipboard against her chest with the other.

She was undoubtedly shy, but Willa had a fire inside her too. She'd given me a glimpse of her spirit these past few nights and damn if it wasn't sexy as hell.

I waved as I approached. "Hey."

"Hi." Her eyes raked down my green shirt to my jeans. Then she blushed deeper, her gaze darting to her clipboard.

Oh, yeah. She just checked me out.

Maybe my note had actually worked.

I stopped in front of her and leaned in close, dragging in a long breath of her hair. She smelled so delicious, like coconut and vanilla. Her head lifted up and I dropped my eyes to her clipboard, pretending she hadn't just busted me for sniffing her hair.

"Is that a scavenger hunt?" I pointed to the checklist on her clipboard.

She nodded. "Yeah. Good old-fashioned camp fun."

"Hmm. Let me see." I took the clipboard from her arm. "Pine cone. Green leaf. Wildflower. Feather." I read the rest of the list without narrating, then handed it back. "Cool. What do the winners get?"

"Um, bragging rights around the campfire? We do a new list every day to give the kids options if they don't want to do the nature hike or go fishing."

"So that wasn't all the kids?" I asked.

She shook her head. "No, just under half. Everyone else is out with the counselors exploring."

"Ah." I nodded. "I'd probably be out with them too if I were a kid. Though as an adult, I'd stay behind if that's where you were."

"Oh." She tucked a lock of hair behind her ear. "What, um . . ." Her fingers fiddled with the clip on the board. "What's up?"

"You read my note?"

She nodded. "I did."

"Good." That meant we could move on from the whole me-calling-her-by-the-wrong-name thing and get to the days where she wasn't slamming doors in my face. "Come to the bar and have dinner with me tonight."

"Was that an invitation or a command?"

I shrugged. "Does it matter?"

She frowned and I knew immediately that wasn't the right thing to say. Without a word, she marched toward the building between the bunkhouses marked SHOWERS.

"Hey, wait!" I ran after her, but she was walking fast. "What about dinner?"

She didn't answer. She just kept on marching all the way to the women's side, disappearing inside without hesitation.

Well, fuck.

I guess my note hadn't worked after all.

I debated going inside the showers but didn't want to terrify a young girl if Willa wasn't alone. So with a grumble and a kick at the dirt, I went back toward the parking lot.

I didn't miss Hazel watching from a window in the lodge, laughing her ass off. At least I was entertaining her.

She'd be in for another show soon, because I'd be back again tomorrow.

seven

WILLA

I MIGHT HAVE WATCHED JACKSON PAGE FOR YEARS, BUT THERE WAS a lot I didn't know about him. For one, the man was stubborn.

He was so darn stubborn it was driving me insane.

He'd been to the camp every day this week. Every. Single. Day.

After I'd escaped to the showers on Wednesday, I'd thought Jackson would give me some space and back off. But he hadn't, not even a little. If anything, my rejection seemed to encourage his behavior.

He visited the camp every morning to sit in the kitchen and drink coffee with Hazel. I made sure I was always out and about with the kids—hiding, basically. But I could only avoid my office and the kitchen area for so long. The best part of my job was hanging with the campers, but I also enjoyed the office work. I loved the behind-the-scenes tasks, the ones that made this camp *mine*. And though avoiding Jackson was a priority, there were bills to pay, phone calls to return and emails from parents to answer.

Jackson loomed outside my office whenever I was there. He didn't say much. He didn't invite me to dinner again or ask me to stop by the bar. He was just . . . there. As he talked to Hazel, he stood in the kitchen right where he could see through my office door. Every time I glanced up from my computer, he was watching me. He'd flash me a quick smile and go back to his conversation with Hazel.

Those smiles would fluster me so completely that I couldn't concentrate on anything. I overpaid our water bill by thirteen cents and most of the emails I sent were riddled with typos.

And it wasn't just his camp visits either.

Jackson continued leaving me notes in my door. Every. Single. Day. Each evening when I returned home from work, I found a note waiting.

The only reprieve I'd gotten from his presence was at night. His two-in-the-morning visits had stopped, but if he thought he was sparing me sleep, he was mistaken. My mind was too busy to sleep, pondering his notes.

He didn't press for a date in his notes or apologize again. Instead, they were just sweet and thoughtful and even funny—especially the first one.

Willa
I saw this today and it made me laugh. Thought you might like
it too.
Jackson

That message had been scribbled on a yellow Post-it and stuck to a clipping from last Sunday's *Daily Inter Lake* newspaper.

Craftsman Boat For Sale. Like New. $9,000.
Girlfriend Pregnant. Wife Pissed. Need Cash for Lawyer.

It wasn't a big thing but had made me laugh.

The next note wasn't as funny, but the smile it gave me was bigger.

Willa
In case your sweet tooth is like mine.
Jackson

He'd stuck that note on a Snickers bar. It had melted in its wrapper by the time I'd gotten home, but I'd stuck it in the freezer to harden it up. Even misshapen, it had hit the spot.

Today's note—left early in the day—had been simple. No gift or funny gimmick. Just a note.

Willa
I hope you had a good week.
Jackson

And it had been a good week.

I never considered a group of campers bad, but there were always weeks that stood out from others. This week's group of kids was amazing. They were all fun and energetic. Not a single one of them thought they were too cool for certain activities. We had full participation from every kid in every event.

It would be the week I'd remember from this year. They would be the group whose picture I'd frame for my office wall.

Jackson's notes had been the icing on the cake.

I'd collected a total of four notes from the week, and I'd had more face time with Jackson than ever before. He was weakening my resolve to forget about him. The crush I'd had for so long was being rekindled, this time burning even brighter.

Two more notes and I doubted I'd be able to say no to a dinner invitation.

I had a sneaking suspicion that he knew I was about to give in too. He was probably just waiting me out to see if I'd finally cave—more like when.

Jackson's charm was irresistible. It was like being surrounded by puppies. You couldn't not pet them.

The only reason I was still holding strong was because of my fears. I was scared. No, *terrified.*

Jackson had kissed me and forgotten. He'd overlooked me for years. I could get past those problems and let it all go. Deep down, I'd already forgiven him for forgetting about our night on the swings.

What petrified me was the realization that Jackson had the power to decimate my life. I was halfway in love with him already. If he made me fall the rest of the way, then tossed me aside, I'd be destroyed.

He'd leave me utterly and completely broken.

So here I was, standing at a crossroad. On one side was self-preservation. Jackson Page was on the other.

My phone rang on the kitchen counter and I rushed over to grab it. Seeing Leighton's picture on the screen, I answered with a smile. "Hey!"

"So? Did you get another note?"

I smiled. "Yes."

After our dinner with June and Hannah earlier in the week, I'd called and told her all about Jackson. She was on Jackson's side of my crossroad, waving me over.

"I'll be there in a sec." She hung up before I could respond.

I laughed and went to unlock the door since it wouldn't take her long to get here.

Leighton lived on the other side of town, the "lake side" whereas I lived on the "town side." The highway was the divider, separating the larger homes on the shoreline from the majority of businesses and locals' homes on the other.

She hadn't always lived on the lakeside. When we were kids, her family had lived a couple of blocks away. But her dad was in construction and had made a lot of money over the last twenty years building extravagant lake homes. He'd worked hard, and as a twenty-fifth wedding anniversary present to Leighton's mom, he'd invested in some lakefront property of his own and built them a beautiful home.

He'd also built a boathouse for Leighton, so like me, she lived on her parents' property but in her own space.

Ten minutes later, after she'd walked across the highway and up a few blocks to my house, Leighton was sitting next to me on the edge of my bed with Jackson's note in her hand.

"He loves you."

I rolled my eyes. "He doesn't love me. He just wants . . . well, I don't know exactly what he wants."

"It's not sex," she declared, earning another eye roll. "Okay, it's not *only* sex. If he wanted his normal *slam, bam, thank you, ma'am* kind of night, he wouldn't be leaving you notes and coming to see you at work."

My lips pursed and I swallowed the bitter taste on my tongue. I didn't want to think about Jackson doing any kind of slamming or bamming.

"What are you going to do?"

I shrugged. "I don't know. What would you do?"

"I think you should tell him about the kiss in the playground."

"No sirree." I shot off the bed. "As far as I'm concerned, that night never happened."

"Then I guess you'll have to go out with him. If that night never happened, then you have nothing to be mad about. Especially since he apologized for calling you Willow for so long."

I frowned, annoyed that she'd tricked me. "That's not what I meant."

"I know. But why not? I mean, you've liked this guy for an

eternity, so why not go out with him? Yes, he got drunk and high and kissed you, then forgot. Total asshole move. But it was one mistake. If you tell him about it, I bet he'll feel awful."

"I'm never telling him about it, Leighton."

She held up her hands. "Fine. What I'm saying is that he messed up and would probably own it. Just like this note."

She plucked the apology note from my nightstand. Was it pathetic that I kept them on my nightstand so I could sleep next to them? *Probably*.

"I don't want to tell him." I sighed. "It would be too humiliating."

"Then don't tell him. But if he really is interested, why wouldn't you go out with him?"

I went back to the bed and plopped down. "It hurt. So much. I've never felt anything like that before. And that was just after one kiss. What happens if we date for a while and then he dumps me? What if he breaks my heart?"

She set her hand over mine, her pink manicured nails such a contrast to mine, which were unpainted and cut short. "It's possible. But that's a risk no matter what. Don't you want to at least give Jackson a chance? I mean, if I had a guy who I've been crushing on for ages ask me out, I'd be too curious to resist."

I blew out a long breath. She was right, I could get hurt. But that was a risk everyone took when it came to love. "I'll think about it."

"Good." She put the notes back on the nightstand and scooted back into the pillows.

The couch over by the window was comfy and soft, but whenever Leighton was over, we always camped out on my bed, either to talk or gossip or watch TV. It was our spot.

"Mom and Dad are taking me out to dinner tonight. Want to come?" I asked.

She shook her head. "I can't. I, um . . . have a date."

"What?" I yelled, nearly jumping to the ceiling. "With who? When?" Leighton hadn't dated since high school, not since she'd been assaulted in college, and this was a huge step for her.

Leighton smiled and looked to her lap. "Brendon Jacoby."

"No way." My mouth fell open. "How did that happen?"

She picked at one of her nails. "I ran into him at the grocery store last night. He was buying salsa, and I was buying tortilla chips. We met by the nacho cheese and got to talking. He's having me over for tacos tonight."

"Yes!" I clapped. "I'm so excited!"

I might not have liked Brendon for myself, but he was a nice guy and perfect for Leighton. He was cute, in a clean-cut, wholesome kind of way. He didn't have the larger-than-life, drool-over-me presence that Jackson did, but when Brendon walked into a room, most women glanced his way.

"Me too." Leighton worried her bottom lip and she was about to ruin her nails if she kept picking.

"I'm proud of you. Are you okay?"

"I'm really nervous," she whispered. "I really like him."

"Don't worry," I said gently. "Just be yourself and he'll love you."

"Thanks," Leighton said with a sad smile. "What should I wear? Most of my stuff screams conservative English teacher. Not single lady who wouldn't mind a french kiss for the first time in ages."

I giggled. "Let's go back to your place and we'll find something."

She slid off the bed and stared longingly at a dress I'd laid out over the couch to air-dry. "Our friendship would be so much more convenient if we were the same size."

"Right?" Even as kids, the two of us had never been able to

share clothes.

Leighton had gotten her build from her dad, who'd always reminded me of a real-life Paul Bunyan. She was a knockout with her rich, chocolate hair and feminine curves. She was five nine with legs that went on for days and a bust that not even two of my bras sewed together would support.

"I want something like that navy sundress." She pointed to the dress I'd been wearing the night Jackson had kissed me on the swing set.

For the first time in our friendship, I was glad we couldn't share clothes like a lot of other girls did. That dress would be for me, along with the memories that came with it. No matter how much time passed, it would always remind me of that night with Jackson, even if the memory had turned sour.

"We'll find something." I slid into some flip-flops, then we traipsed through town and across the highway to her boathouse and got her ready for her date.

After picking out some skinny jeans and a simple green blouse, I left Leighton's place and walked home in no particular hurry, enjoying the warm sunshine of the early evening.

Saturdays were *me days,* because during the summer, it was my only day off in the week. Even then, I usually stopped by the camp for an hour or two, just to check in with the counselors. But today, I'd stayed away and let my capable staff run the show.

Tomorrow would be hectic, starting early with a sendoff for the current campers and ending late with a welcome party for the new group of kids. So I was enjoying the day to myself and catching up on some much-needed rest and laundry.

As I strolled down the sidewalk toward my house, my thoughts drifted to Jackson. Would there be another note waiting when I got home? My feet sped up, then I slowed as I remembered the time. He was already at work.

Thea was still in New York and Jackson had to open the bar. That was probably why I'd gotten today's note so early.

Dang. It had only been a few days, but I'd gotten used to having them by my door when I got home in the evenings.

I walked the rest of the way home, finding my mom sitting on the bottom step of my staircase with her garden gloves and a pair of scissors.

Her blond hair was twisted in a bun and trapped in a visor. She always dressed nicely, even when gardening. Today she wore a pair of navy linen pants and a cream blouse. The only thing casual about Mom was the pair of tan gardening clogs she wore when working outside.

"Hey, sweetie," she greeted, trimming back a flower.

"Hi. Want some help?"

"Sure! I didn't realize these had grown so much these past two weeks. I've been so focused on getting the strawberry patch in the front yard under control."

"It's okay. I just step around them."

"I think we'd better trim them back." She picked up a yellow petunia that had been trampled, probably by one of Jackson's boots.

I laughed. "You're probably right."

I picked up the watering can that I used every day to water the flowers and went to the faucet to fill it up. I watered quickly, then found another pair of scissors to help Mom.

It didn't take us long to work our way up the stairs, trimming until we could actually see the stairs again. When we got to the top, Dad came out from around the garage.

He was wearing his standard khaki chinos, short-sleeved shirt and loafers. The only thing different about his summer attire and his school-year attire was the lack of a tie. He still styled his light blond hair like he was going to work. And he starched and ironed his slacks every morning.

"You girls ready for dinner?" he asked.

"Almost," I told him, tying up the garbage bag we'd filled.

Saturdays were also my night to eat dinner with my parents. We'd started the ritual after I'd moved into the garage three years ago, so instead of going on dates or meeting friends, I spent my Saturday nights with Mom and Dad.

With the work done, Mom and I descended the stairs, meeting Dad at the bottom.

Mom pulled off her garden gloves and tossed them on a step. "I'm ready."

"You're wearing your visor and clogs to dinner?"

She shrugged. "It's just pizza at the bar."

"The bar? I thought we were going up to Kalispell." I wasn't mentally prepared to go to the bar for dinner. Or adequately dressed.

I normally wore dresses in the summer, except for jeans a couple times a week on days I'd spend outside exploring with the kids at camp. I never went to work without taming my hair and applying some makeup.

But today I'd made no effort. My face was bare and my hair hadn't been washed—or combed for that matter. It was just pulled back in a messy braid. I was wearing raggedy, olive-green shorts with a black tank top that sometimes doubled as a pajama top. The straps of my yellow bra were showing.

"We don't want to be driving around if we're drinking," Dad said.

"I can be the designated driver."

He shook his head. "No way. We're celebrating tonight! We're so proud of all the work you put into finding someone to buy the camp. Now it's safe for, hopefully, another fifty years, we want to toast to a job well done with our daughter. Besides, we haven't been to the bar in ages. I'm craving pizza."

"Fine," I muttered. "Can I have ten minutes to change?"

"You look beautiful." Mom took my hand and tugged me behind her down the driveway. "Let's go. I'm starving."

"But—"

"Oh, Willa," Dad said, catching up. "You look beautiful."

And that was how I ended up at the bar on my Saturday night with Jackson coming my way.

eight

WILLA

"HEY THERE, NATE. HI, BETTY. LONG TIME NO SEE." Jackson shook both of my parents' hands, then came to stand behind me at the table we'd chosen in the middle of the bar.

I scooched my chair in toward the table, trying to put a little more space between Jackson and me, but he wasn't having it.

He put both hands on the back of my chair, then leaned in close. "Hi, Willa."

"Uh . . . hi." I shivered at the heat from his chest on my bare shoulders.

Why was he standing so close? My parents were *right* there. Our table was one of four tall, square ones in the center of the room and there was plenty of space between tables.

Plenty. P-L-E-N-T-Y.

But was Jackson using any of that plentiful space?

No sirree. He stayed pressed against the back of my chair, like there were only three inches of usable space behind him, not three feet.

My skin prickled he was so close. I tried to nudge my chair forward again, but it barely moved. Sweat beaded on my temples and I pulled in a shaking breath.

Jackson's woodsy, rich scent was everywhere. It overpowered the stale beer, pizza and peanuts, and I inhaled a deep breath, unable to resist.

Sexy Hot Forest. That's what they'd call his cologne.

"Willa, you look flushed."

"Huh?" My eyes whipped to Mom, but she'd already turned to Jackson.

"You'd better bring her some ice water, Jackson."

"Sure, Betty." The vibrations from his rumble hit my neck, making my cheeks burn even hotter.

My face had been red since we'd walked in the door.

The moment Jackson had seen me trailing into the bar behind my parents, a smug smile had spread across his face. He'd gotten this sexy glint in his eye as he'd watched us take our seats. Well, as he'd watched *me* take my seat. Then he'd unleashed the swagger, rounding the bar with long, confident strides that made my heart race.

If that hadn't gotten me flustered enough, Jackson had foregone his standard plaid shirt. Tonight, it was just faded jeans, boots and a black T-shirt that fit snugly across his chest and biceps.

There was a lot of muscle action happening behind me. I willed my shoulders to stay straight and not give in to the temptation to lean backward and sink into that heat Jackson was radiating. I squirmed in my chair as a coil tightened between my legs.

This sexual tension was going to kill me.

I pulled in a deep breath, blocking out Jackson's smell, and did my best to get ahold of my internal temperature.

"I'll bring you all waters," Jackson told Mom and Dad. "What else can I get for you tonight?"

As he spoke, he drummed his fingers on the back of my

chair, brushing his knuckles ever so slightly against my shoulder blades.

Tingles shot down my spine, forcing me to straighten even more. My ribs slammed against the table, making the condiment rack wiggle.

"Sorry," I muttered, grabbing the bar menu that was sandwiched between a bottle of ketchup and one of hot sauce.

As I studied the same list of pizza toppings I'd memorized years ago, I took another breath. But with my torso pressed against the table, I couldn't get enough air.

Jackson shifted even closer, his forearms resting on the back of my chair. It put those dangerous knuckles up against my tank top, trapping me in my place.

"We're celebrating tonight, Jackson." Dad pulled his glasses from his shirt pocket to examine the row of liquor bottles behind the bar. "So I guess I'll have a vodka martini, please. Extra dry, no olives."

"Oooh!" Mom wagged her eyebrows at Dad and purred, "Feeling frisky tonight, Mr. Doon?"

"Eww, Mom," I groaned. "Gross."

She giggled, then looked up at Jackson and winked. "I'll have the same."

"You got it." He chuckled and bent his head lower, his breath whispering over my ear. "What would you like?"

A shiver ran down my back and my shoulders shimmied. The movement caused me to rub against his knuckles. It was just a slight touch, but the heat from his fingers singed through the back of my tank.

I jerked forward, making the table bounce again and winced as it bit into my rib cage once more.

"Willa!" Mom frowned. "Stop doing that."

"Sorry. This chair is, um . . . uncomfortable."

Behind me, Jackson chuckled. "I've got somewhere else you could sit."

I ignored him and shoved the menu back in its place. "I'll just have a Bud Light."

"You got it," he said, then finally backed away from my chair.

As soon as he was clear, I slumped in my seat, savoring the ability to breathe again. Both of my parents were inspecting me.

Mom had a goofy grin on her face. Dad's glasses had slid down his nose and his eyes were alternating between me and Jackson.

I gave them both a small smile, tucked my hands underneath my thighs and looked around the room, pretending like that hadn't been the most uncomfortable, yet exhilarating drink order I'd ever placed in my life.

I loved the Lark Cove Bar, and not just because of its staff. The building itself was full of character and rustic charm.

The high ceilings had exposed iron beams, and the battered floors were littered with peanut shells. None of the stools or chairs matched. The walls were paneled with warm wood and filled with a variety of signs and pictures that Hazel's parents had collected over the years.

She'd added her own special touches when she'd moved back to Montana to run the bar. After she'd retired, Thea and Jackson had put up some things of their own as well. There wasn't much free space left these days and I'm sure there were those who'd call it cluttered. I liked to think of it as a collection.

They'd each left their mark.

The bar itself was long and ran in an L shape across both of the back walls. Tall cocktail tables were in the center of the room, and a few booths lined the front windows. The black vinyl benches had been patched with electrical tape in a few spots.

It wasn't fancy or trendy, but it was perfect for Lark Cove.

"Here you go." Jackson came back quickly, setting down our drinks on square napkins along with a paper boat of peanuts. "Do you guys want dinner?"

"Yes, please. We need pizza." Mom turned in her chair to place our regular order. The entire time, Dad watched Jackson with a careful eye.

Probably because as soon as Jackson's hands had delivered the drinks, they'd gone right back to my chair.

I looked over my shoulder, up at Jackson. He flashed me a wink before focusing back on Mom as she rattled off our order.

Jackson's stance was intimate and claiming. He was leaning down, just a bit, into my space. His long legs were planted wide behind my seat, so if I wanted to stand, he'd have to move first.

It was no wonder Dad was suspicious. He hadn't missed the wink or the significance of Jackson's stance.

As Mom finished ordering, a new wave of nerves fluttered in my belly. I wanted Jackson to leave my chair, but I knew as soon as he left, I was in for some questioning.

Mom's detailed order of our three pizzas, all of which had their own special combination of five or six toppings, ended too soon.

"I'll get those going. Be back." Jackson rubbed a knuckle down the back of my arm before walking off.

One simple touch and my face was flaming again. Tingles worked their way down my elbow and to my fingertips. When I lifted my beer to my lips, my hand was shaking and a few drops sloshed over the rim.

Meanwhile, Dad sat across from me in silence, studying my every move.

Don't bring it up. Please don't bring it up.

"I think he likes you, sweetie." Mom's face was so full of

hope it made me love her even more. She so desperately wanted me to date, but there just weren't many single men my age in Lark Cove.

"Maybe." I sipped my beer, hoping that would be the end of it. I should have known better.

"You should ask him out." She nudged my elbow with her own. "He's cute."

"He, um . . . already kind of asked me out. I haven't given him an answer yet."

"Why not?"

"Is he making you uncomfortable?" Dad's chest puffed up as he straightened in his chair. "Do I need to talk to him?"

I shook my head and bit back a smile. "No. I'm fine."

Though I'd love to be a witness to that confrontation. Dad and Mom were both on the smaller end of the human-size spectrum. Mom was an inch shorter than me. Dad was five nine. Jackson had at least fifty pounds of muscle and brawn on him, plus quite a few inches.

But that wouldn't scare Dad away one bit.

"Are you sure?" he asked. "Because you looked uncomfortable."

I shook my head. "Really, Dad. I'm fine. I, um, I'm just not sure what to do about Jackson yet."

"You're not sure?" Mom nearly spit out her sip of martini. "You've had a crush on him since you were seventeen. I think the obvious answer here is *yes*."

"I'll think about it. Now can we talk about something else?" Anything else. We'd made a pact on my fifteenth birthday never to talk about boys, periods or bras in front of Dad. Maybe I needed to remind her that it was still in place.

"Fine." Mom shrugged and took another drink. I thought for a minute the discussion was over, but it wasn't. "Though for the record, I think you two would have the most beautiful blond babies."

"Mom!" I glared at her, then peeked over my shoulder.

Thankfully, Jackson had gone to the kitchen and hadn't heard her. I turned back around and gave Dad a pleading stare. He grinned and changed the subject, distracting Mom with a question about my cousin's baby shower in Kalispell the next weekend.

My shy demeanor certainly didn't come from my mother's gene pool. Mom had grown up in Kalispell and my three aunts still lived there with their families. All four of them were as direct and outgoing as you could get. If not for their petite frames and innocent faces, some would have called them rude. But due to their stature, they got labeled "sassy" or "spitfire."

I loved my aunts dearly, but the annual family reunion was something I'd spend months dreading because my mom was the tamest of the lot. Those get-togethers were always packed full of questions about my love life, or lack thereof, and awkward attempts to set me up with my cousins' single friends.

"Let's do a toast." Dad raised his glass. "To Willa. We're so proud of you."

"Thanks." I smiled and clinked his glass, then Mom's. "I appreciate all of your help."

Mom and Dad had both proofread my proposal to the Kendrick Foundation more times than I could count.

We sat and chatted for a while as we waited for Jackson to bring out our pizzas. It didn't take long for him to deliver all three, carefully squeezing them onto the table between our drinks.

"You guys need anything else?" he asked. "Another martini, Betty?"

"Do you mind?" she asked Dad.

I always thought it was cute when she did that. My mom's alcohol tolerance was low and after two martinis, she'd be a ball of giggles. She always made sure Dad didn't care if she got tipsy, which he never did. But she always asked his permission, not because she had to, but because above all else, they were thoughtful of one another.

"Of course not." He patted her knee. "Go for it. I'll have another too."

"Willa?" Jackson asked, nodding to my beer.

I shook my head. "Just a water, please."

"You got it." He left us to our meal, smiling at me as he walked away.

Wowzah. I'd seen that smile a hundred times, but rarely had it been just for me. Even though he'd been aiming it at me all week long, I still wasn't used to it.

A part of me hoped I'd never get used to it. Having a smile steal your breath away was a feeling like none other.

"I'm happy for you," Mom whispered as she dug into her pizza.

I lifted a slice of my own and gave her a smile. I was still scared. What I'd told Leighton was still true. But there was excitement and happiness there too.

The conversation at our table stopped as the three of us did what we always did at meal time: inhale food. By the time we were done, Mom, Dad and I hadn't spoken more than one word. Our three pizzas were gone except for a few pieces of discarded crust.

Jackson chuckled, returning to the back of my chair. "I was going to bring you a box, but I see you don't need one."

Dad laughed too. "We were hungry."

"Can I get you anything else?"

"Just the check." Mom smiled up at Jackson, her nose a rosy

red from the martinis.

"Will do," he told her. "Willa, you feel like sticking around for a bit?"

"Oh, uh . . . no. I'd better go."

"Come on. One more beer," Jackson pleaded. "I had this idea to do something special for Charlie and I wanted to run it by you."

I hesitated long enough for Mom to make my decision for me.

"Stay, sweetie." Mom patted my hand. "Your dad and I have business to attend to at home."

I groaned. "Blargh."

She giggled and batted her eyelashes at Dad. Two martinis and she was tipsy, even with all that pizza.

Dad was actually looking a little buzzed himself, and when he made a kissy face at her, I decided I'd rather brave time with Jackson than deal with these two as they groped each other on the walk home.

"Okay." I nodded. "I'll stay for a bit."

Jackson smiled as victory danced in his sky-blue eyes. "Finally."

nine

JACKSON

"I'M IMPRESSED YOU GUYS ATE THREE PIZZAS," I TOLD WILLA as I loaded up their empty pans.

"We were hungry." She shrugged, taking her half-full beer glass over to the bar.

Her parents had just left, snuggling together as they'd walked out the door.

Willa pretended to be grossed out by their not-so-subtle innuendo, but as she watched them leave, her dreamy smile told a different story.

As she sat on a stool, I hustled the empty pizza pans to the kitchen sink, then came back to clear the martini glasses and wipe down the table. After I did a lap around the room, making sure the other customers didn't need anything else, I went back behind the bar and stood across from Willa.

What I really wanted to do was kick everyone out for the night. I'd finally gotten Willa to agree to spend some time with me, and I wanted to give her my undivided attention. But it was busy tonight and I didn't have another option.

"Want another beer?" I asked.

"No, thanks. I've got a busy day tomorrow and I need to be fresh. Two beers make me a little woogidy the next morning."

"Woogidy?" I grinned. "That's not a word."

"It's kind of a word," she muttered. Her face flushed and she looked down at the bar.

Damn, she was cute. Cute in a sexy, drop-me-on-my-ass kind of way. I smiled at her rosy cheeks and the way her shoulders crept up to her ears.

I liked that I had the ability to unsettle her a bit. It meant that somewhere in there, her crush on me wasn't completely gone.

"Woogidy." I leaned in closer. "I like it. I might have to use that one myself."

She lifted her chin and gave me a shy smile.

"How about a Coke?"

"Please." She nodded and I filled her a glass.

A table of three caught my attention, so I left her to bring them another round. I came back and checked in with Willa just as a table of two signaled for their check.

And that was how the evening went.

When I wasn't filling a drink or waiting on someone, I'd stand at my post across from Willa. We chatted about nothing major, and while I worked, she watched the ballgame I had on the corner television.

I assumed after an hour of her sipping Coke and me being too busy to really talk much that she'd slip away.

But she stayed.

She sat quietly, taking the moments I had to spare until the place finally cleared out five hours later.

"Sorry." I set down the last batch of dirty glasses I'd collected from the room. "I haven't been good company tonight. But I'm glad you stayed."

"It's okay." She slid over her empty glass. "And me too. It's kind of fun watching you in action."

"Yeah?"

She nodded. "You work fast. I'm not sure how you keep everything straight, always doing three things at once. It's impressive."

Now it was my turn to blush. I don't think I'd ever been complimented on my bartending skills before. Other than the women who'd come in and compliment me on my body, I didn't get a lot of praise, even from Hazel and Thea.

Those two loved me, but aside from the occasional hug, razzing me was how they expressed their affection.

Willa's simple compliment made me feel ten feet tall.

"I like watching you work too," I told her. "You've got a gift with those kids at the camp. You should have been a teacher."

"That's what I have my degree in."

"But you didn't get a job at the school?"

She shook her head. "There aren't a lot of openings here. I probably could have moved to Kalispell and gotten a job there, but I wanted to live in Lark Cove. And the camp director position was open, so I took it instead. I figured it was a job I could keep until something else opened up, but then I just never wanted to leave."

"Then it's good that it all worked out."

She smiled. "Exactly. Maybe when my dad retires, I'll take his spot as the science teacher."

It was good she had a long-term plan, unlike me. If the bar were to ever close down, I'd be without another skill to fall back on if I wanted to stay in Lark Cove.

"Did you go to college?" she asked.

"Nah. I was lucky to graduate high school."

"Well, if you ever wanted to go, I'm sure you'd do great."

I blinked, surprised for the second time in five minutes.

Willa had such confidence in her statement. It was way more than I deserved, especially from a woman who had every right to consider me a cocky ass. But she looked at me like I could do anything in the world.

It was unnerving. It was a rush.

"College isn't for me," I told her. "I don't need anything other than my bar."

"Have you ever wanted to do anything else?" Her voice was only full of curiosity, not an ounce of judgment. She wasn't asking because she thought I could do better. She just wanted to know.

"Not really. I've been bartending ever since I turned eighteen. Liked it then. Still like it now. Someone has to serve pizza and beer, right?"

She smiled. "True."

"I like my job," I told her honestly. "I like working with Thea. I like that by working here, I can help fund Hazel's retirement. And I don't see myself living anywhere other than Lark Cove, so this all works."

"I'm glad. There are a lot of people miserable in their daily lives, always wishing for something bigger and better. It's nice to be around someone who just wants to enjoy a simple life."

I nearly toppled over. Who was this woman? Was she for real?

Most women who sat across from me thought I could do better for myself. To them, I was just a good-looking bartender with no ambition.

I didn't let it bother me. Hell, I capitalized on it. My occupation was the perfect way to get no-strings-attached sex because the rich women coming through town would only ever see me as a fling.

I wasn't the guy you brought home to meet Daddy.

Except I already knew Willa's dad. Her mom had practically ordered her to stay here with me tonight.

They didn't think less of me because of my job and neither did Willa.

"Thanks," I managed to choke out. "Not many people think like that."

She nodded. "I know. But I do."

Her smile was so warm and inviting, I leaned in a bit. *God, I could kiss her.* Her lips were such a pretty color. They were completely natural, free of heavy lipstick or thick gloss. They were just soft and pink.

And familiar.

Something in the back of my mind told me that if I kissed her right now, I'd taste peppermint lip balm. I'd bet the bar on it.

Weird.

That creepy déjà vu feeling was back. The one I still had whenever I looked at her staircase.

"Hey." Willa waved a hand in front of my eyes. "Where'd you go?"

I blinked, standing straight and swiping up a bar rag. "Sorry. You have nice . . . lips."

"Oh, um, thank you." She blushed again, this time pulling at her long braid over her shoulder as she attempted to hide among all that hair.

Damn, but I wanted my fingers in her hair. I wanted to take that braid and unfasten all the loops until the golden waves hung loose. I knew it would be like touching silk, just like I *knew* what she tasted like.

Which was fucking crazy because until a week ago, I hadn't known much about Willa Doon. I wanted to kick my own ass for being such a blind fool.

"I need to get things wiped down and cleaned up," I told her, wiping the bar by her side. "I'm not going to stay open until two. We can call it a night. But would you stay? I don't want you walking home in the dark."

"Sure, but only if I can help clean up. My butt is sick of this stool."

Willa stood and smoothed down her green shorts, running her hands over the tight globes of her ass. It wasn't meant to be sexy, but damn, this woman hit all the right buttons. Her smooth skin, tanned for the summer, was begging to be licked. Her toned legs would feel incredible wrapped around my hips.

Underneath her tank, a yellow bra strap was peeking out. Did her panties match? Whether they did or not, yellow was my new favorite color.

Especially the yellow color of her hair.

The sight of her stretching out stiff muscles had my dick straining against my zipper. I was just glad she couldn't see it from her side of the bar. I didn't need to freak her out with a bulge behind my jeans.

I tossed her a rag, deciding to keep my lower half hidden until my cock settled back down. "Just wipe down the tables and then we'll stack up the chairs."

"Okay." She smiled and got to work.

Willa made cleaning the bar more fun than it had ever been. A lot of bars had swampers, people who would come in during the early morning hours to scrub the place down. But Thea and I had always done the cleaning ourselves to save money.

Every night, we'd deep clean some part of the place. Once a month, the two of us would meet early on a Sunday morning and scour away built-up grime. It was a way we could afford to give Hazel a bigger cut each month.

Tonight, besides all the regular cleaning, I had to wash the windows. It normally took me over an hour to clean each night, but with Willa's help, we left after thirty minutes, both of us smelling like bleach and ammonia.

I led her out the back, locking the back door behind us. After tossing the last bag of trash in the Dumpster, I escorted her around the side of the building.

"Thanks for the help."

"No problem. It was kind of fun to see what you do after the crowd leaves."

"Sorry to keep you up so late. Are you going to be too woogidy tomorrow morning?"

She giggled as I used her word. "I'll be fine."

"You're welcome to join me every night," I told her. "I'll make you all the pizza you can eat for the chance to have your company."

She just smiled as we turned down the street that would lead us both home. It wasn't a flat-out no, so I'd take it.

We walked half a block quietly. Since her house was on the way to mine, it wasn't out of my way to escort her home. I lived two blocks up from her place, and after leaving her notes all week, I knew it took four minutes to get from my front door to hers.

"So, what was that idea you had for Charlie?" she asked.

"What?"

"You asked me to stay at the bar to talk about an idea you had for Charlie. What was it?"

Shit. "The truth? There wasn't anything. I was just desperate to get you to stay and I used her name as bait."

"Sneaky. I'll have to remember that in the future." She looked up, her blue eyes sparkling under the dim moonlight. "Though I would have probably stayed anyway."

"Good to know." Progress. I was making progress. *Finally.*

I wasn't sure if it was the cheesy notes or the visits to camp that had done the trick—maybe both—but I was glad she was giving me an inch. Not that it had been a hardship to spend time around her.

In truth, I liked visiting Willa and her camp. Those kids were always so excited and full of life. Watching them gave me more energy than my morning ten cups of coffee. And I liked writing her those notes too. Somehow, scribbling on a square, yellow piece of paper had become a highlight of my day.

We walked the rest of the way to her street in silence and slowed at the corner. There was an overgrown shrub crowding the sidewalk, forcing my body right beside hers. The gentlemanly thing to do would have been to let her go first, but I didn't want to lose her at my side. So I stayed close and when we rounded the corner, my arm brushed against the bare skin of hers.

It was an electric touch, sparking a flame under my skin. It made my heart pound and her breath catch.

Willa tripped on a seam in the sidewalk, but before she could fall, I grabbed her hand, steadying her with my grip.

"You good?" I asked.

She nodded, righting her feet as her delicate fingers stayed locked in my grasp.

We stayed side by side, neither of us stepping forward or breaking apart, even after she regained her balance. We just stood there as the night went still. The crickets chirping, the stars sparkling, the leaves rustling—it all disappeared until there was nothing left but Willa's hand holding mine.

I hadn't held a woman's hand in . . . well, ever. Was that right? Had I really never held a woman's hand before?

I hadn't expected it to be so intimate, maybe even more so than a kiss.

It made me dizzy and steady all at the same time, like the feeling I got after being on a boat for too long. Even when I got back to land, I would still sway with the waves.

"Is this okay?" I asked, squeezing her fingers. I didn't want to let them go but I would if she was uncomfortable.

"Um, yeah. It's okay," she whispered.

A rush of excitement stirred and I unstuck my feet and led us around the corner. As we passed the first house, I realized how great this felt, not just touching Willa, but simply being with her. I was proud to be holding her hand. I wished it wasn't dark so her neighbors could see us together.

The smile on my face stretched wider as she relaxed her hand, flattening her palm into mine. She pressed into me like she wanted to memorize our touch.

We reached her parents' house much too soon. I wanted to loop around the block a few times, but Willa had a busy day ahead.

"I can make it from here." She slipped her hand from mine as we stood at the end of the driveway. "Thanks for walking me home."

"You're welcome, but you're not home yet." I grabbed her hand again, grinning as I tugged her behind me.

"You really think the boogeyman is going to snatch me from my own yard?"

I chuckled. "Better safe than sorry."

She laughed as we crept past her parents' dark house. "I guess it's probably faster for you to get home by cutting through the playground anyway than circling the whole block."

Normally a woman admitting she knew where I lived would freak me the hell out. But like everything else about Willa, she was the exception. "Since you know where I live, maybe one of these days you'll leave me a note."

"Maybe."

I grinned. "Maybe you can tell me why you had a crush on

me at one point but don't anymore."

"Oh, um . . . it's not like that. I mean, it is. Kind of." She was getting flustered. "I did like you."

"And now you don't?" I asked her as we stopped by the base of her stairs.

"No."

I flinched. Hard. I hadn't expected that answer. I thought we were making progress, but she just laid it out there, clear as day.

She used to like me.

Now she didn't.

My hands fisted by my sides and I silently cursed the dream I'd been having for weeks. That fucking dream had twisted shit up in my head. It had made me believe there was more with Willa than there really was.

"Well, I guess I'll see you around." I made a move to leave, but her hands shot out and grabbed my wrist.

"No, wait! That's not what I meant." Her voice echoed off the garage. She sighed, then lowered her voice. "No, I do. I do still like you."

I about fell over. The relief that ran from my head to my boots told me exactly how much trouble I was in with this woman.

In a flash, I stepped right into her space, erasing the inches between us. I broke free of the grasp she had on my wrist and cupped her face, holding it still as I crushed my mouth to hers.

I swallowed her gasp, keeping my eyes open. Hers stared right back, wide and bright and so blue.

I slowly molded my lips to hers, pressing in even deeper, until her eyes finally drifted shut. Then I let mine do the same to concentrate on kissing this amazing woman breathless.

My hands drifted off her cheeks and into her hair. *Silk.*

My tongue traced the seam between her lips, persuading them apart for a taste. *Peppermint.*

Just like I'd expected.

As my tongue dove deeper, Willa tensed for a split second. It was enough to make me pause and realize that I'd stolen this kiss. So I backed off a bit, letting my tongue retreat. She shocked me by following my tongue with her own, out of her mouth and into mine.

Her hands, which had been hanging loose at her sides, came to my waist. They traveled up slowly and her fingertips dug into my T-shirt as they crawled all the way to my shoulders. Then she wrapped her arms around my neck and pulled herself up so that her breasts were flush with my chest.

I groaned into her mouth, loving the feel of her against me and wishing we weren't separated by these damn clothes.

The kiss turned from hot to scorching in an instant. I wrapped her up tight, forgetting her hair as my hands traveled up and down her back. When she didn't push away, I went farther, molding my palms to the curves of her ass.

"Jackson," she moaned into my mouth. Her arms clutched me like I was going to run away.

But I wasn't going anywhere.

I poured everything I had into this kiss, not wanting her to forget it anytime soon. When I showed up at her camp tomorrow morning, I wanted her running toward me, not away.

So with her ass in my hands and her tits against my chest, I devoured her. I led the way and she followed, copying my every move like we'd kissed a million times. The strokes. The nips. The flutter of a tongue. It was magic.

It was . . . not the first time.

I broke away from Willa, panting for breath. She stood back and looked up at me with hooded eyes. Her lips were swollen and her hair mussed.

I'd seen it all before except it wasn't from my dream. A night I'd forgotten came rushing back, fast, sending me rocking backward on my heels.

I caught my breath and scowled down at Willa. "When were you going to tell me that we've kissed before?"

ten

WILLA

"WHEN WERE YOU GOING TO TELL ME THAT WE'VE kissed before?"

He remembered? *Oh. Shit.* I didn't cuss much, but this situation called for a curse word, even if it was mental.

"Um, never?"

His jaw clenched. "Never?"

"I don't know." I sighed. "Maybe someday." No, *never*.

Jackson shook his head, taking a few moments to put it all together. "That's why you were pissed and avoiding me. Not because I called you Willow."

"Right," I admitted.

The timing was ironic. On the walk home, I'd made the decision to let go of our playground kiss. Since Jackson was oblivious to that night, I wasn't going to hold it against him any longer. But just my luck, he remembered.

I'd been hoping to avoid this conversation for all eternity, but the look on Jackson's face told me there'd be no getting out of an explanation.

What I really wanted to do was run upstairs and bury my red face in a pillow. This discussion was going to bring on a whole new level of humiliation, worse than even the going-to-school-naked dream I'd had for two months straight my junior year.

"I can't believe you didn't fucking tell me we've kissed before." Jackson was fuming. "When was it? At a party? At the bar? I assume I was drunk. I never would have forgotten you otherwise."

That actually made me feel a teensy bit better.

I didn't get a chance to answer because he slammed a hand down on my banister. "Why the fuck didn't you tell me when I showed up here that first night?"

"You forgot," I hissed, looking over my shoulder to make sure we hadn't woken up my parents. My embarrassment fizzled away as my temper spiked.

Jackson didn't get to be mad. He didn't get to yell at me. *He* was the one who *forgot*!

I turned and stomped up two stairs, leaving him behind with a hair swish, but when my foot landed on the third, I spun back around and poked a finger toward his nose.

"Why didn't I tell you? Uh, why do you think?" I asked with an eye roll. "Do you think that's something I wanted to admit? That a guy who I've known for years, the one who calls me by the wrong name, randomly wanders into a park one night and kisses me? Then the next day, he doesn't remember who I am? Golly gee, I wonder why I didn't say anything."

I whipped back around and pounded up the remaining stairs. With the pruning Mom and I had done on the flowers earlier, I could actually stomp without leaving flower carcasses in my wake.

"Willa, wait." Jackson's footsteps sounded behind me, but I didn't stop. I kept going right to my always-unlocked door and straight inside, slamming it closed behind me.

"Grr!" My growl filled the dark room.

I kicked off my flip-flops, sending them flying across the loft in different directions. Then I whirled back to the door and jerked it open.

Jackson was standing in the middle of the landing with his arms crossed, just waiting.

"You hurt my feelings!" I shouted, startled by my own volume.

"What happened?" When I didn't answer, his eyes softened and his arms dropped to his sides. "Please, tell me. If you're mad, you can yell and cuss. Don't hold back, not from me. Tell me what happened."

"You hurt my feelings," I confessed again.

He nodded but didn't say a word as I stepped through the doorway. Something about being on my doorstep, my turf, made admitting the truth a bit easier. That, and I just *knew* that Jackson wouldn't run away, no matter what I said.

He was here to listen.

"I was watching the stars from the playground and you were walking home. You came over. We talked. Then you walked me here. *You* kissed *me* and the next day when I came into the bar to say hello, you called me Willow. You told Wayne and Ronny you didn't remember much from the night before because you were drunk and high. That's what happened. That's when you kissed me."

Jackson's shoulders fell, but he remained quiet, sensing I wasn't quite done yet.

"Do you have any idea how long I'd been waiting for you to notice me? How many times I'd walked into the bar and wished you'd finally just *see* me? Then you did and I was so happy. And then you forgot."

He nodded, still standing in silence as words came out of me I didn't even know I'd needed to say.

"You don't get to be mad at me for not telling you. Of

course, I didn't want to tell you about it. It's mortifying. The first person to ever kiss me forgot."

His stoic stance faltered and he staggered backward a couple of inches. "The first?"

"The first." I nodded, tears filling my eyes. I hadn't meant to let that slip, but it was out there now along with everything else. "I'm not bold. Or daring. But you . . . you were my risk. I put myself out there for you and it didn't work. So yeah, I didn't tell you about the kiss."

Jackson stepped closer, his eyes narrowed. "I'm sorry, Willa."

Why did his apology make me feel worse? Before, I'd only felt bad for myself. Now I felt bad for dumping all of this on him too.

I dropped my chin, drawing my arms around my ribs even tighter, like I was physically trying to dam up the tears. But the wounds were open now, my pain on full display, and the water in my eyes just welled deeper.

"Hey. Don't cry. I'm the asshole here. I'm sorry." His hands cupped my face like they had when he'd kissed me. A tear fell and he brushed it away with his thumb. "What can I do?"

I sniffled and stepped back, forcing him to let me go. With some space to collect myself, I pulled in a shaking breath and brushed away the welling tears. "I'd be okay if we never talked about this again."

"Can't do it." He shook his head. "Not until I know this isn't going to come between us."

Us. U-S.

Two simple letters that made up possibly my newest favorite word in the entire English language. One tiny word that made some of the hurt wash away.

He didn't want anything to come between *us*.

"It won't."

"Promise?"

I nodded. "Promise."

"Good." Jackson didn't let me keep my space. With one stride, I was in his arms again and he was stealing another kiss.

This one was different from the others. It was careful and tender. He peppered small kisses all over my mouth, not letting even a little bit go untouched. Then he slid his tongue into my mouth in a slow invasion, letting his taste seep in behind it. After a few gentle strokes, he backed away, planting one last wet kiss on my lips.

He ran his fingers over my ears, tucking away a few frizzy strands of hair. "You deserved a better first kiss."

"No." My hands slid around his waist. "It was actually quite perfect."

"I'm sorry."

"I know," I whispered.

He opened his mouth to say something else, but I didn't want to talk about it anymore. So I stood on my toes, hoping he'd get the gist and meet me halfway. I was too short to make it to his lips on my own.

Jackson didn't disappoint. He dropped whatever he was going to say and grinned before giving me the kiss I'd been after.

I kept my hands wrapped around his narrow waist, exploring up and down from that position. I pressed my soft curves against his hard ridges and used my fingertips to study every contour of his muscled back. He was so . . . hard. Everywhere.

From beneath his jeans, there was a definite bulge digging into my hip. Knowing that I was the one turning him on—me—skyrocketed my desire. I clung to him, pulling him closer to let him plunder my mouth until he finally broke away, panting.

"We'd better slow down."

I nodded, though it sounded like a bad idea. All these years,

I'd been waiting for a kiss, his kiss. The time to wait was over.

"Want to come inside?" I asked.

He looked over my shoulder to the door, then down the stairs. "I shouldn't, but yes."

Yes. The butterflies in my stomach fluttered as I let him go to step inside. But the moment I crossed the threshold, I froze. The butterflies dropped dead.

My laundry was piled up on my couch. Clean panties were folded and stacked on the coffee table. There were five bras air-drying in the kitchen.

I spun back around and shoved my hands into his pecs, stopping him from coming in any farther. "Can I, um . . . can you cover your eyes for a sec?"

"Huh?"

"Can you just cover your eyes?" I took one of his meaty paws and lifted it toward his face. "Just for a second."

He chuckled but kept his hand over his eyes.

"Don't move." I turned him away from my couch and kitchen, just in case he peeked. "And don't look."

"Are you hiding a dead body?"

"Of course not." I ran over to the couch and swiped all of my laundry into a single pile. All of the shirts and pants and panties I'd folded earlier—that I'd refold tomorrow—got tossed into a basket. Then I hustled to the kitchen, triple-checking that the bras I'd hand-washed this morning were no longer hanging on cupboard doors.

With it all cleared away, I shoved the laundry basket behind the small bar in the kitchen. "Okay. You can take your hand away now."

He did, turning around to face me. In my haste, I hadn't even turned on a light. He reached for the switches by the door and flicked them on. Then he nodded to himself as he assessed the room. "Cool place."

"Thanks." I came out of the kitchen, toying with the hem of my tank top. It was nerve-racking to have him in my space. No one but my parents and some girlfriends had ever been in here.

Jackson walked right down the center of the room toward my now-clean couch. The slanted ceilings were too short for him at the edges, and as he got closer to the exterior walls, he began to crouch, bending lower and lower until he collapsed into the sofa.

"This probably feels like a dollhouse for you."

He grinned and kept looking around. "Kind of. But I bet I'll only whack my head on the ceiling a couple of times before I get used to it."

A couple of times. I shouldn't have liked the thought of him hitting his head, but I did. Because that meant he was coming back.

I walked over to the couch, maneuvering around the coffee table and feeling more self-conscious than I'd been on the stairs. It was easier to be adventurous and brave in the night. Now that we were inside, I was worried Jackson would pick up on all the little things I'd been able to hide in the dark.

Jackson was sitting in the middle of the couch, leaving me exactly half a cushion of free space between him and the plethora of throw pillows by the armrest. The moment my butt hit the cream upholstery, he tossed an arm across the back of the couch.

He sat there so comfortably, claiming my couch. It was almost as if he'd been the one to haul it up the stairs and squeeze it through the door.

"Did your parents build this for you?" he asked, inspecting my bed at the other end of the open room.

"No, they had it built a while back for my grandma. My

dad's mom. She lived here for a year but then started to show signs of Alzheimer's. It broke my dad's heart to move her into a home in Kalispell."

"Sorry."

I shrugged. "It's okay. She's happy."

Grandma didn't remember any of us now, but that hadn't stopped us from visiting her often. A lot of my things were actually hers. I'd kept them here as a tribute to her beautiful taste.

The loft was divided in half by the front door. On the left was my bedroom area. On the right was my kitchen and living room.

The pitch of the roof was at the tallest by the door so you could walk in comfortably, but in other areas, the walls tapered at the edges to only about five feet.

My kitchen was my favorite part, even though it was small. But with bright-white cabinets and a large window over the sink, it felt bigger than it actually was. The butcher-block counters were Grandma's request. She'd loved to bake her own bread and had insisted on wooden counters rather than granite because she swore it made the bread taste better. I didn't know if it was true or not, but her dinner rolls were legendary.

On the other end of the room, situated outside the single bathroom, was my bed. It was covered in Grandma's favorite white quilt, one she'd bought from a church bazaar. It was simple and understated, much like Grandma herself. But it was stunning too, with intricate white flowers stitched on the soft white cotton.

The entire place was full of muted colors and warm woods. The floors were a chocolate brown that matched the wooden beams in the ceiling.

The only thing I didn't like about it was how warm it got in the summer. Without an air conditioner, it was miserable in the afternoon and evenings until the night air cooled my room down.

I should have opened the kitchen window, but now that I was settled into Jackson's side, I didn't want to get up.

Neither of us spoke as he finished his inspection of my place. When his eyes stopped roaming, he focused on the opposite wall and sat there, just breathing in and out.

Was this awkward? Or was this normal? I didn't know how to act after a midnight confession and three amazing kisses. I hadn't invited him inside for a specific reason, more just because I hadn't wanted to see him go.

So if he was waiting for me to make the next move, we were going to be here forever. I'd used up all my courage on the stairs.

"Willa . . ." Jackson trailed off and sighed.

My body strung tight at the warning in his tone. Was he about to give me a long apology about how he was sorry he'd kissed me? Maybe he needed someone with more experience, and now that he knew that woman wasn't me, was he going to bolt?

I braced, waiting for him to continue as he shifted in his seat to look at me.

"I know I've been coming on strong," he said. "But that was before I knew about everything else."

Definitely not going to like this. "Okay," I drawled.

"You shouldn't have to put up with that kind of shit from a man. I'm a mess. If you want me to stop so you can find someone better, just say the word. I'll walk away."

Better? I snorted a laugh.

There wasn't better than Jackson Page. In my book—literally in my diaries—he was as good as it got. I didn't know a lot about Jackson's history, but it was likely he'd come from rough beginnings.

None of that mattered to me. What did matter was that he seemed down on himself. It left an uneasy feeling in my stomach. Maybe he wasn't as confident as he liked people to believe.

"Don't walk away," I told him. "And you're not a mess."

He scoffed. "I kissed you when I was drunk and high, then forgot. That's the definition of a fucking mess. You deserve better than that."

"Better is up for interpretation." I settled into the couch, scooting closer to his side to tell him a story. "My mom dated this rich guy when she was younger. Obviously, that was before she met my dad. She grew up in Kalispell and he was her high school boyfriend. His family had a lot of money."

Jackson relaxed a bit, wrapping his arm around my shoulders as I continued.

"They dated for a couple of years in college, but Mom says neither of them were really into it at that point. They'd grown apart, so she broke up with him. A few weeks later, she met my dad. One look at him and she knew she'd made the right choice."

I'd been a preteen when Mom had told me about how she and Dad had met, but it was a tale I never forgot. Mom and Dad were a classic example of love at first sight.

They were the reason that, as a younger me, I'd never felt my crush on Jackson was ridiculous or silly or pathetic.

"So Mom came home on spring break not long after she met Dad and ran into her ex. I guess he wasn't so happy he'd been replaced in such a short amount of time. He claimed to be 'better' than Dad and asked her to get back together with him. You can guess how that conversation ended."

Jackson chuckled. "I sure can."

I smiled up into his beautiful blue eyes, glad I'd been able to make him laugh. "I think what's important is finding a person who makes *you* better. And someone you can trust with your heart. And, Jackson? I trust you with mine."

Even after our rocky start, I trusted him.

"Can I tell you a secret?" He leaned down and whispered, "I have a crush on you."

I smiled. "It's about time."

He laughed and dropped his forehead to mine as I laughed too. When we stopped, he blew out a long breath and muttered, "I'd better go."

"Okay." As much as I'd like to make out with him on the couch all night, I had a long day tomorrow. I stood first and he followed, standing too fast and hitting his head on the slanted ceiling.

"Ah, fuck." He rubbed the back of his head, ducking as he maneuvered to the center of the room.

I winced. "Sorry."

"Told you." He shrugged. "One more time and I'll remember not to stand up so fast."

"I'll stock up on ice packs."

He grinned and snagged my hand, dragging me into his chest. "Next time maybe we'll be horizontal on the couch and I won't have to worry about it."

Oh. My. Goodness. My core quivered and I was suddenly quite aware of my nipples. Horizontal couch time was definitely a go. I wasn't sure exactly what it meant, but I'd figure it out as we went along.

"Thea comes back Monday," Jackson said. "I'm hesitant to ask, given the other times you've shot me down, but since I've had a rough night, I'm hoping you'll take it easy on my ego. Dinner? How about Tuesday or Wednesday?"

I'd have to cancel my weekly dinner with the girls, but I didn't care. The only one I'd really miss seeing right now was Leighton, and even though it was after two in the morning, I was calling her the second Jackson left.

"I can do both nights."

He grinned. "Both it is."

"No, I meant either."

"Too late. You agreed. We'll go up to Kalispell on Tuesday and do something nice."

"I could cook," I offered.

"You can cook on Wednesday."

I smiled and nodded. "You got it."

With a quick brush of his lips on mine, he gave me a soft, sweet kiss, then walked to the door. "Lock up after me."

"I will." I nodded and closed the door behind him. When the deadbolt clicked, his boots thudded down the stairs.

I pressed my fingers to my lips as I watched through the window next to the door. He looked back over his shoulder twice this time as he crossed the yard. And somehow, he knew I was watching because he blew me a kiss.

Air kisses. Sweet kisses. Soft kisses. Hard kisses. Wet kisses. Tonight, I'd learned it all.

And I couldn't wait to see what he'd teach me next.

eleven

JACKSON

THE MORNING OF MY DATE WITH WILLA, I STOPPED BY THE BAR to check on Thea. It was nice to have some time off now that she was back from New York, but it was hard to enjoy when she looked so miserable.

As I came down the hallway from the back door, I found her in her office. Her shoulders were hunched over a list. Her eyes were rimmed with red as she sniffled. She'd heard me open the door and was trying to hide her tears.

"Hey," I said as I leaned on the office door.

"Hey. I didn't think you'd be in this morning." She swiped her cheek with the back of her hand, then went about shuffling a stack of papers. "Thanks for taking care of everything while I was gone. Looks like things went well. I'll get all of the cleaning supplies from your list before we open today. Anything else you need?"

"No, that should do for now." I stepped into the office and went right around to her side of the desk, perching myself on the edge. I held out a hand, waiting for her to place her palm in mine. The moment she did, the tears came back.

"Sorry." She swiped at them with her free hand, but they were falling too fast.

"Don't be sorry. Is there anything I can do?"

She shook her head, pulling herself together. That was one thing about Thea: if she did cry, it never lasted long. "We'll be fine. It's not like we didn't know this would happen. Logan lives in New York. We live here. It's for the best to end things now before it gets even harder."

After their trip to New York, Thea and Logan had decided to end the relationship they'd been testing ever since he'd found out about Charlie earlier in the summer. His job as a prominent lawyer and philanthropist for his family dictated he live in New York.

But with Thea's history there and her desire to raise Charlie in a place where she'd flourish, they needed to be here in Lark Cove.

So Logan and Thea had sacrificed their happiness together, knowing it was best for their daughter.

It had been a huge relief when Thea had called to say they were back. A part of me, a big part, had expected her to tell me they were staying in New York. I'd expected to be left behind.

But they came back, and while I was so damn happy, they were sad. After the relief subsided, the guilt settled in because my happiness was at the expense of their misery.

It wasn't right.

"It's no secret I wasn't happy that Logan showed up."

She scoffed. "Really? I hadn't picked up on that."

I grinned, glad she wasn't too upset to still tease me. "But I'll give the guy credit. He did the right thing by not forcing you to move to New York."

"I almost did," she whispered. "It was so tempting. But being there was . . . hard. Harder than I thought it would be. And it just wasn't the right place for Charlie."

"I missed you guys when you were gone," I told her. "Things weren't the same without you around."

That was an understatement, but I didn't want Thea to feel bad for leaving. She didn't need to know how lost I'd felt the day they'd left for New York, wondering if they'd come back. She didn't need to know how scared I was that I'd lose yet another family.

"We missed you too."

"I know I acted like an ass when Logan showed up. I was pissed things were changing because of him. But I should have been more supportive. I guess it took you guys leaving and the scare that you might not come back to realize I was just worried about myself. I felt like my family was slipping away and I didn't handle it well. I'm sorry."

She squeezed my hand. "It's okay."

Maybe it was them leaving that had opened my eyes to what I'd been missing in my life, but if Thea wanted to be with Logan, I wouldn't stand in the way. He wasn't the enemy I'd made him out to be.

"I'm glad you're home," I told her. "But if you do decide to move, know that I'll be here for you. I just want you and Charlie to be happy. Hell, I'd even come out and visit."

Thea pulled her hand from mine and stood from the chair. Then she threw her arms around my shoulders. "Thank you. But we're not going anywhere."

I hugged her back. "Good."

We stayed like that for a few moments until she patted my back and sat back down. "I'd better get back to work."

"Yeah. And I'd better get going. I'm heading over to the camp to hang with Charlie for a while."

I'd seen them briefly the day after they'd come home, but we hadn't really had much time together. I'd missed Charlie too and was just as worried about her as I was Thea, maybe more. Leaving Logan had been hard on her little heart. I hoped some time to just play and laugh and do the things she loved most would make her smile.

"She'll love that. She really missed you and Hazel while we were gone. I'm sure she'd like to spend some time with you."

"Call me if you need anything," I said as I walked out of the office.

"I will." She waved, then dove back into the paperwork stacked on her desk. I'd taken care of all the logistics for the bar while she'd been gone, but I'd left her the bills to pay and supplies to order. Thea loved mixing drinks, but she had this weird thing where she got off on paperwork.

Which was fine by me. I hated that shit.

From the bar, I went straight to the camp and into the main lodge. Willa was nowhere to be found. Actually, the entire place was quiet—the campers must be out on an adventure.

I lucked out and found Charlie in the first place I looked: the kitchen.

She was sitting on the table, eating a bowl of trail mix. The faded ball cap I'd given her was on her head. Her knees were dirty and she was swinging her legs back and forth. Her shoulders were turned down and her expression heavy.

It broke my heart to see her sad. Like Thea, she was missing Logan.

"Hey, Chuck."

Her head whipped up from her bowl, sending her long, brown hair flying to the side. "Uncle Jackson!"

The smile on her beautiful face made my world a brighter place. I rushed for her at the same time she set her bowl aside and hopped off the table, flying across the tiled floor into my arms.

I needed that hug just as much as she did.

I held her tight, hoping to chase some of her sadness away.

Over her tiny shoulder, I saw Hazel in the back corner of the kitchen. Willa snuck in from her office door at the back.

I winked at them both, then gave Charlie all of my attention. "Feel like hanging out in your fort for a while?"

"Yeah." She nodded and stepped out of my embrace. Then she went back for her bowl of snacks, tucking it under her arm and leading me out of the kitchen. "Let's go."

I waved to Willa and Hazel, then followed Charlie outside, where we spent the morning exploring the woods. As we collected cool rocks and sticks and brought them into the fort she'd made beneath two evergreens, Charlie told me about her trip to New York. She'd met Logan's family, *her* family, and explored the city.

I did my best to lift her dampened spirits. Because she never failed to brighten mine.

Parked in the gravel lot at the camp later that evening, I popped a piece of gum in my mouth as I waited for Willa to take her on our first date. I was rattling with nerves. My thumb was drumming on the steering wheel in a fast beat and I was sweating even though the AC was cranked.

She hadn't kissed anyone before me. Had she ever dated? I didn't want to wreck this for her like I'd ruined her first kiss. I didn't want to wreck any of her firsts, including her first time with a man if she chose that man to be me.

Maybe if I'd had more experience taking a woman to a nice restaurant, I wouldn't be so worked up. Maybe the pressure wouldn't feel so overwhelming. But since I didn't date often, or ever, this was likely to be the blind leading the blind.

I kept drumming as a group of kids came out of the lodge,

and right behind them was Willa. She waved good-bye to a counselor and then started up the trail to the parking lot.

My thumb stopped.

She'd changed since I'd been here earlier. Instead of the simple green dress and cream cardigan she'd been in this morning, she was wearing a—*what did women call them?*—little black dress.

My pulse spiked as I took her in. Her dress was elegant and sleeveless. It showed just enough skin to be sexy. The way it hugged her hips and molded to her perky breasts showed off subtle curves. The skirt rode down her toned legs nearly to her knees. It wasn't short, but with its tight fit, it would ride up her thighs as she climbed in my truck.

And if the dress weren't enough to get my blood pumping, her hair would have done the trick. She'd pinned the top back from her face but left long waves to cascade down her back.

I liked knowing that if I made her blush tonight, she wouldn't be able to hide it from me in her hair. I also liked knowing that when I kissed her tonight, the pink lipstick she was wearing would smudge.

She was almost to the truck so I made a quick adjustment to my dick and swallowed my gum. Then I took a deep breath and whispered, "Don't fuck this up."

For some reason, Willa had picked me. She wanted me for her first kiss and her first date. I didn't want to be a disappointment tonight.

That would come later.

One day, Willa would realize I wasn't anything special and I couldn't give her what she needed. I wasn't a marriage-and-babies kind of guy, but until then, I'd do my best to make this good for her.

Starting with a first date.

As she approached the truck, I leaned over the center

console for the door handle. *Shit.* I should have gotten out. But Willa didn't seem to care. She just smiled and waved. "Hi."

"You're beautiful."

She blushed and started to step up, but her dress was too tight.

"I can help." I unbuckled my seat belt, but she stopped me with a hand.

"I've got it." Smiling, she planted a hand on the door and the other in the seat, then hopped. Her hair bounced as she propelled herself into the seat, laughing as she landed. "Whoopsie." One of her heels had slipped off in the process. She giggled again as she toed it back on and shut the door.

And I watched it all with a slack jaw. Did she have any idea how sexy that was? She was graceful and adorably clumsy all at the same time.

When she looked my way, I came unstuck, leaning over the console to kiss her cheek. "You're beautiful."

It was worth repeating.

"Thanks." Her eyes ran up and down my torso. "You're not so bad yourself."

I grinned and leaned back in my seat, rebuckling and putting the truck in reverse. I wasn't dressed as fancy as she was, but I'd found a darker pair of jeans without frayed hems and a solid-gray button-up shirt. I'd even tucked it in.

"I like your truck," Willa said as we pulled onto the highway. "It's very clean. Unlike my car, which is a disaster zone."

"I'll clean it for you. I take care of Hazel's."

"Oh, you don't have to do that."

I reached over and lifted her hand from her lap. "I'd like to. Clean vehicles are kind of my thing."

"Then have at it. I hate cleaning my car." She flattened her hand into mine, pressing our palms together.

She didn't thread our fingers together. Instead, she let me hold her hand entirely. I could close mine all the way around hers, holding it tight, and if she wanted to slip free, I had to let her go first.

"How was the rest of your day?" she asked.

"Good. Productive. Cleaned the truck. Cleaned my boat. It was nice to get away from the bar for a change."

"I bet. Charlie was sure happy to see you this morning."

"I was happy to see her too. She'll be back in school soon. I won't get to see her as much."

Willa sighed. "Yeah. I always get lonely when school starts in September and the camp closes for the winter."

"You can come and keep me company. I get lonely at the bar too."

She looked over and nodded. "I'd like that."

Lark Cove quieted down substantially in the fall and winter. The bar got a rush of activity during hunting season and we'd see the occasional skier. But it was a different town when the weather turned cold.

"What do you do when there isn't camp?" I asked.

"Go crazy." She giggled. "It's usually busy for a couple of weeks after the last set of campers leave. We have to winterize the buildings and I make sure that all the bills are paid. But after that, I don't have a lot to do. I go in occasionally to check on things and do any office work, but it only takes five or six hours at most. I've been thinking about getting another job."

"Yeah? Like where?"

"I don't know." She shrugged. "I can't get a year-round job because I need my summers free, so that limits my options. I saw the gas station was looking for a part-time cashier."

"No." *Fuck no.* "You can't work at the gas station." The idea of her in a gas station, alone in the dead of night while working the graveyard shift, gave me anxiety pains.

"Huh?" Her face whipped to mine. "Why not?"

"It's not safe. You'd be a sitting duck for any random creep passing through town."

"Oh," she muttered. "Okay. No on the gas station."

I eyed her, waiting for more, but there was nothing. She just looked out the window, watching as we rolled down the highway.

"That's it?"

Her forehead furrowed. "That's it, what?"

"You're not going to bust my balls for telling you where not to work? Or call me a dick for ordering you around?" Thea or Hazel would have told me to fuck off if I'd told them they couldn't work somewhere.

But Willa just smiled. "I can't get mad at you for wanting me to be safe. If you had another reason, then maybe I would disagree. But being concerned for my well-being is, well . . . sweet."

Sweet? Well, shit. Was this woman for real?

Ever since Saturday night, something had shifted between us. She'd dropped her hand and wasn't keeping me at arm's length.

Instead, she'd just pulled me straight into her world.

On Sunday, the morning after she'd told me about our real first kiss, I'd gone to the camp with a double vanilla chai latte— her favorite, according to the owner of the coffee hut. Since I'd been the one to keep her up late, I figured she'd need an extra dose of sugar and caffeine.

What I hadn't realized was that she'd be thriving on organized chaos. The parking lot had been full of parents collecting their happy kids. Willa had been running around like crazy when I'd gotten there, and I'd half expected her to shoo me away.

But instead, she'd thanked me for her coffee with a kiss and ordered me to follow her and "talk as we walk."

So as she said good-bye to campers and coordinated the clean out of the bunkhouses in preparation for the next batch of kids, I'd been right there by her side. Whenever she took a sip of her coffee, she smiled up at me. Whenever she ran into a counselor, she introduced me without delay.

The smile on her face never faltered.

Maybe the campers would forget that smile, but I never would.

Sunday night, after she'd made sure the new group of kids were settled at the camp, she came to the bar for a late dinner. By then, the exhaustion had finally settled in, so I'd gotten her a Coke and made her a pizza. After she'd eaten, I'd sent her home early to get some sleep.

Yesterday had been more of the same. Coffee. Work. Pizza. And a kiss at the bar before I sent her on her way before dark.

And now I was finally getting my date. It was just her and me, off to do something together.

"How is Thea doing?" Willa asked.

"Okay. Sad, like Charlie. I think she's glad to be home, but they both miss Logan."

"I hope they can work it out. Do you think Thea would ever move to the city?"

I shrugged. "I doubt it. Neither of us have a ton of fond memories from that place." Though as hard as it would be to see them go, I'd rather have Thea happy in the city with Logan than brokenhearted in Montana.

Willa hummed but didn't push for more.

I could have left it at that, but for once, I felt the need to explain. I wanted to offer Willa something more than a blanket, closed-off statement. "Did you know that's where we met? Me and Thea and Hazel?"

She shook her head. "No. I guess I've never heard the story of how you all found one another."

Hardly anyone had. Thea and I didn't share a lot about the past with patrons at the bar, just like we didn't gossip about people around town. We were probably seen as a bit of a mystery, and honestly, we liked it that way.

But for Willa, I'd spill it all. I felt safe telling her anything in the world. I hadn't a clue why, but I was trusting my gut.

"Do you want to know?"

She smiled, pressing her palm deeper into mine. "Only if you want to share."

I took a deep breath, kept my eyes on the road, and started at the beginning.

"My mom was shit. Or is. I don't know. I haven't seen her in over twenty years. When I was nine, she packed up our stuff, shoved it in our car and drove us from Pennsylvania to New York. Then she dropped me off at my aunt's place and I never saw her again."

Willa's gasp was barely audible over the whirl of the truck tires against the pavement.

"My aunt kept me for about a week before she turned me over to the state. I don't know why because I never saw her again either. All she left me with was the backpack my mom had packed full of clothes and a few wrinkled papers."

One of which had been my birth certificate. I didn't realize it at the time, but I guess that was Mom's way of saying she wasn't ever coming back.

I'd wanted to go after her for years. A couple of times, I'd tried to run away from my foster homes and hitchhike back to the small Pennsylvania town where we'd lived. According to my birth certificate, it was where I'd been born. But every time I'd tried to run, I'd gotten caught by the authorities and hauled back into the system.

By the time I was old enough to make a successful runaway attempt, I hadn't bothered. I'd found Thea and Hazel by then, and I'd written off my mother.

"Then what?" Willa asked.

"Foster care. I bounced around a lot."

Families didn't want an older kid with abandonment and attitude issues, so I'd moved from home to home until my freshman year. "The longest I stayed in a home was during high school. And it wasn't because of the home. It was because of Thea and Hazel."

"Why's that?" she asked.

"How much of Thea's history do you know?"

She shrugged. "Not much. She's a private person."

I chuckled. That was the truth. We both were. But like I trusted Willa with my story, she could be trusted with Thea's. And since our stories were intertwined, I couldn't tell one without the other.

"Thea doesn't have parents either, but she didn't grow up in foster care. She lived in this orphanage."

"They still have those?" Willa asked.

"I doubt they do now, but at the time, yeah. It was one of the last in the city, from what I remember. I think after Thea graduated and moved out, it closed down. For a while during our senior year, she was the only kid that lived there."

"I bet that was lonely."

"Yeah, it was."

Though at the time, I'd always envied her. Thea didn't have to share a room or house with others. I'd been just as lonely as she had been, even with a foster home full of people and hardly any personal space.

I shifted a bit in my seat, never letting go of Willa's hand.

"Thea and I went to the same high school, but we didn't meet there. I actually met Hazel first. I was at the grocery store trying to shoplift a candy bar. She caught me before the clerk did."

"Uh-oh." Willa winced, proving she knew Hazel well. "I bet she was pissed."

I chuckled. "You could say that. She grabbed the Snickers and hauled my ass up to the checkout line. I thought for sure she was going to turn me in, but instead she just added it to her basket of groceries. After she bought it, she told me I could eat it but only after dinner."

To this day, I wasn't sure why I'd gone with her back to the orphanage. I'd been fifteen years old and had just topped six feet. I hadn't been quite as tall or brawny as I was now, but it wouldn't have taken much to escape Hazel.

I never even tried. I just followed her through our Brooklyn neighborhood without question.

"Hazel worked as a part-time cook at the orphanage, so she took me there. Then she sat me down at the kitchen table, told me to get started on my homework while she put the groceries away and whipped up dinner."

Hazel had also shoved a bag of frozen peas on the black eye my foster father had given me, but I didn't want to share that with Willa. She didn't need to know that he was a mean bastard who loved a good fistfight. He'd put up a makeshift boxing ring in the garage, then paired us foster boys off with one another, jumping in and taking over a fight when we weren't "taking it seriously."

I think he got his rocks off when he landed a good punch or two. And since it was boxing practice, something to teach us respect and discipline and give us a physical challenge—such bullshit—teachers and social workers overlooked the bruises.

When I finally learned to fight well enough to land him on

his ass, I let him win instead. I stroked the asshole's ego and put up with the lack of food and four kids per bedroom all because I couldn't risk getting thrown out of their house and sent away from Hazel and Thea.

"I was sitting at the table doing my homework when Thea came into the kitchen at the orphanage," I told Willa. "I recognized her from school, but we'd never talked before. She hugged Hazel, got out her own schoolwork and sat next to me until dinner. Then I split my Snickers with her. We've been friends ever since."

Willa gave me a small smile. "I'm glad you found them."

"Me too." I squeezed her hand.

They were my only family.

Hazel had been the person who made sure my homework was done. She'd been the one to feed me when I was hungry. If not for her and that orphanage, who knew where I'd be? *Jail, probably.*

Willa's face turned to the side window and she watched the lake through the trees as they streaked past. Her mood darkened, changing the atmosphere in the truck. The air got heavy, weighing down on my shoulders as my heart beat even louder.

I shouldn't have shared all that. What was wrong with me? My history was too serious for a first date.

Not ten minutes from town and I was fucking this up already.

Willa wiggled her fingers and I let go of her hand. It killed me that she needed some space.

I opened my mouth to apologize but stopped when Willa turned and flipped up the console. Then she unbuckled her seat belt and slid into the middle seat.

My arm automatically went behind her shoulders as she dove into my side. One of her arms wrapped around my waist and the other slipped behind my back.

Then she hugged me.

"I'm sorry," she whispered.

I dropped my cheek to the top of her hair. "It's okay. It all worked out."

Somehow, her arms got tighter.

"As much as I like this, I don't want you unbuckled."

"One more second." She squeezed me again, then slipped her arms free.

I figured she'd slide back to the passenger seat, but she didn't. She just let me go and dug out the lap belt that had fallen between the seats. She strapped it on and smiled before looking back down the road.

This bench seat? It was my new favorite feature of my truck. Thank god I hadn't gone for buckets.

The heavy air disappeared and I relaxed into my seat. The smell of Willa's coconut-and-vanilla hair infused the cab, smelling far better than the blue tree freshener I'd tucked under the backseat.

With every mile, I felt lighter. Years of baggage got smaller and smaller in my rearview mirror. Unloading my past to Willa had been freeing. And though my past had been hard, I couldn't regret it. That road had led me here, to Lark Cove and to her.

"Can I ask you something?" she asked.

"Sure." My hand went to her knee.

"Do you ever think about finding your mom?"

"No," I said immediately. "She's dead to me."

"Okay." Just like before, I waited. But she said nothing.

"That's it?"

She giggled again. "Yeah. That's it."

"You're not going to try and convince me otherwise? Both Thea and Hazel think it would be good to find out where she'd disappeared to all those years ago. They think it will give me closure."

"If she's dead to you, then she's dead to me. That's it."

I eyed her profile, amazed that she was on my page. My tires thudded against the rumble strip as we drifted toward the shoulder.

"Watch the road, Jackson," she said. "I'm starving, and crashing into a tree would put a dent in our dinner plans."

Grinning, I turned my eyes back to the highway. "Well, we can't have that, Willow."

She flinched, her gasp much louder this time. With her mouth hanging open, Willa turned and gaped at my profile.

I chuckled. "What? Too soon to joke about the name thing?"

Her mouth snapped closed and she pursed her lips. The corners didn't want to stay flat, even though she tried.

"Jerkface." She shoved her elbow into my ribs, then giggled.

With that, the seriousness of our conversation disappeared. Willa stayed tucked into my side as we drove down the road to dinner, talking about everything light and airy. By the time we'd both scarfed down two huge ribeyes and made it back to Lark Cove, I knew one thing: I'd never have a better date in my life.

And when the time came, it was going to be damn hard to walk away from this woman.

twelve

WILLA

B E BOLD.

That was my new motto.

Or at least it had been my motto for the last two minutes.

Jackson and I had arguably the best date of all time. He took me to a nice restaurant in Kalispell, a steakhouse I'd only been to once before with my parents. When I ordered the largest ribeye with sautéed mushrooms, a loaded baked potato and a side salad, Jackson didn't even blink. He just grinned at the waitress and ordered the same.

Then we laughed. We talked—maybe more than I'd ever talked during a meal. Jackson wanted to know all about growing up in Lark Cove and my experiences in college. I wanted to know about funny stories from the bar. Hardly a moment went by where one of us wasn't telling the other a story.

I may have watched Jackson from a distance for years, but tonight, I'd really gotten to know him. And everything I'd learned made me crave more.

"I had fun tonight," he said as he escorted me up my staircase.

"I had fun too." At the top step, I glanced over my shoulder. *Be bold.* "Would you like to come in?"

"Sure."

I smiled, excitement bubbling in my belly as I unlocked the door. "Shoot." I turned abruptly just inside the door. "My car is still at the camp."

Jackson put his hands on my shoulders and spun me back around, urging me inside. "I'll come get you in the morning and take you to work."

Or you can just sleep here.

If I was really being bold, I would have said that out loud, but I guess I needed more practice. Still, the thought of Jackson in my apartment again sent a rush of nervous energy to my insides.

Was tonight the night I'd go all the way?

The thought of losing my virginity didn't scare me—much. My fingers fumbled with the clasp on my pink clutch as we entered my loft. What would it feel like? Would it hurt? Would Jackson like it?

I glanced up at Jackson as I led him toward the couch. *I really want him to like it.*

More than anything else, I was nervous I wouldn't be good at sex for Jackson. It was guaranteed I'd be awkward, there was no escaping the first-time jitters. But I was more anxious about Jackson's reaction than I was for myself.

He'd take care of me. I just wanted to take care of him too.

My mouth was full of cotton; anxiety had parched me dry. So instead of going to the couch with Jackson, I turned for the kitchen. "Do you want something to drink?"

"I'm okay. Thanks." He crouched as he approached the wall, ducking so he wouldn't hit his head before sinking into the couch.

"I'm just going to . . ." I pointed to the kitchen, then followed my finger.

Hurrying to the cupboard with the glasses, I took one out, filled it from the tap and chugged it in three hard gulps. Then I set it in the sink and took a deep breath as I looked out the kitchen window.

Be bold.

I could do this.

I left the kitchen and took a seat next to Jackson. A silence settled over the room as my shoulder pressed into his arm, but neither of us moved. Neither of us said a word. Though we were both breathing harder than normal.

Should I touch him? Maybe stroke his leg or something?

My hands wouldn't move off my lap.

Be bold.

I could kiss him. I bet he'd really be surprised if I swung up and straddled his lap. Except in this dress, there'd be no swinging or straddling. And dress issues aside, I probably wouldn't have done it anyway.

"I can hear the gears turning, Willa. What's going on in your mind?"

"Nothing." I stared at my lap. "I, um . . ."

Be bold. For once in your life, be bold.

I took a deep breath, then blurted, "Do youwannastaythenight?"

"Say that again?"

My eyes squeezed shut. The courage I'd scraped together to say it once had nearly wiped out my reserves, but I summoned just a smidge more. "Do you want to stay the night?"

"Yes."

My eyes flew open as I looked up at him, astonished. "Really?"

"Yes, but I'm not going to."

"Oh." I wanted to crawl under the couch cushions and

hide. "Okay."

"We need to talk about a few things first." He angled his body on the sofa, turning my way. When I didn't move or look away from my lap, he put his hands on my shoulders, gently twisting them sideways.

I still didn't budge.

"Work with me here, babe."

No one had ever called me babe before, and I always thought men used it when they couldn't remember a woman's name.

"I don't know if I like being called babe."

Jackson laughed. "Then I'll think of something else. Now will you spin this way and look at me? Please?"

I sighed and turned, reluctantly lifting my eyes to meet his.

"You're the best kiss I've had in my life."

Me? I was a good kisser? "No way."

"Yes, way. And that tells me that everything else we do is going to be off the charts. But I messed up your first kiss. I'm not going to mess up the rest. If I stay tonight, I doubt I'll keep my hands to myself."

There was so much running through my mind it nearly exploded. So I began processing his speech one piece at a time, starting at the beginning.

I was a good kisser? I was a good kisser. No, *the best*. My inner diva was about the size of a gummy bear, but she was standing tall tonight, giving me a burst of confidence.

My fingertips left my lap to trail up his jean-covered thigh. "What if I don't want you to keep your hands to yourself?"

"Willa," he groaned, the sound part torture, part pleasure. Before my fingers could get too far, his hand slapped down on mine. "Stop."

I'd finally had the nerve to make a move and I'd been rejected. My gaze dropped, assessing the couch cushion again as a hiding spot.

"Hey." Jackson's hand came to my chin, tipping it back. "Can we just talk this through for a sec?"

I nodded. "All right."

"I'm not going to lie to you." He blew out a long breath. "I'm . . . nervous."

"Nervous?" Why would he be nervous? It's not like he hadn't had sex before. "Why?"

"I really don't want to fuck this up. You know? Your first," he gulped, "time. It should be special. Not me fucking you on the couch after dinner."

His confession, albeit crude, melted my heart. I loved that he cared to make sure I was comfortable. I loved that he was putting my feelings above his own needs.

I cupped his cheek with my palm. "Thank you."

"Can I ask you something?"

"Sure."

"Why'd you wait?"

I dropped my hand, then looked to my lap, unable to look him in the face as I spoke. "It wasn't like it was something I planned. My virginity has never been sacred to me. Sex just . . . never happened. I didn't date in high school. I went out a couple of times in college, but the guys, they just weren't right."

I didn't get into Leighton's story—that was hers alone to share. But it had definitely impacted my own choices when it came to sex and men.

"I was never so concerned with being a virgin that I felt the need to seek out someone to take it," I admitted. "I guess I just always assumed that when the time was right, the time was right."

"And is tonight that right time?"

Was it? Yes, I wanted to be with Jackson. But I could use

a few more dates and some time with Jackson to work out my nerves. Was I ready yet? Now? "No."

"Okay."

"You don't care?"

"Look at me," he ordered, gently forcing my gaze to his. "You drive the boat. How fast or slow we go is up to you. Okay, Captain?"

I smiled. "Okay. As long as you promise never to call me *Captain* again."

"I can do that."

I sighed. "Can we at least make out or something? I feel like I've been waiting my entire life to kiss you, and now that I can, it's all I want to do."

The words came out of my mouth so fast, my brain didn't have time to stop them. But once my ears heard it all, I definitely wanted to hide under the couch cushion.

I was begging for a kiss. Begging. *Golly gee, Willa. Be bold, not desperate.*

My hands came to my face, hiding my hot cheeks. "I can't believe I said that."

Jackson chuckled and tugged my hands away. Then his mouth slowly descended toward mine. "We're definitely doing something, cupcake."

I grimaced. "No on cupcake."

He chuckled. With his lips so close, the vibration skimmed my cheek. "Sugar?" He kissed the corner of my mouth.

My eyelids drifted closed as I whispered, "No."

"Sweetness?" Another kiss, this time to the other corner of my lips.

"No." I wasn't a donut.

Jackson's soft lips trailed up my cheek, leaving tingles as they went to my ear. "Darling?"

"Uh-uh."

He sucked my earlobe into his mouth and I went limp, falling forward into his chest. Who knew his tongue in my ear would be such a turn on?

"More." My hands went to his chest, pressing into the cotton of his gray button-down shirt.

His lips followed their trail backward toward my mouth. His smooth jaw was hot and hard against my cheek, and even without his normal stubble, it left a burn.

"Dear? Honey?"

"Dad calls Mom dear. He calls me honey."

Jackson growled, taking his lips away from my face and ducking down to attach them at my collarbone.

I sagged into the back of the couch, completely dazed that he found all these new spots to make me melt.

"Princess?" he murmured against my neck.

My head lulled to the side. "That's for little girls with pigtails."

"Boo?"

"Absolutely not," I breathed. "Keep going." My hands went to the back of his head, his short hair soft against my palms as I pulled him closer.

His tongue came out, licking as his lips peppered kisses across my neck. "Doll?"

"Uh-uh."

Another peppered kiss. "Cookie?"

I shook my head, inching my butt across the couch to get closer.

Straddle him. Now was the time for straddling.

My fingers left his chest and came to my skirt. I gathered the hem in my fists, dragging it up my thighs.

To my surprise, Jackson's hands came down to help. His

calloused fingers skimmed the sensitive skin of my legs, sending my heart into overdrive. The minute my knees were no longer constricted by the hem, I spread them apart.

In my haste, I pulled too hard and a small ripping noise came from the slit now bunched by my rear. That didn't stop me. This was my most expensive dress, but I'd have Mom mend it later.

My hands shoved at Jackson's brawny shoulders, sending him back into the couch, as I climbed onto his lap.

The second my core settled against the rough denim of his jeans, I let out a soft moan. His erection was sizeable beneath his zipper, beneath me, and it made my mouth go dry again. I was dizzy and hot and the tension coiling in my center was making me squirm.

It. Was. Incredible.

Riding Jackson's lap was unlike anything I'd ever felt before. A couple of times, I'd experimented with things down below. After some girlfriends in college had tried to explain what an orgasm felt like, I'd gotten curious and touched myself in the shower.

But my fingers hadn't built me up like this. Having Jackson's mouth on my neck, his hardness rubbing against my lace panties, was so erotic I was trembling.

"Fuck, Willa," he said into my neck before pulling back. His hands came to my face, pushing away the locks of hair that had escaped the clip in the back. "You're perfect."

I smiled, then leaned in and kissed him softly.

It didn't stay sweet for long. Jackson's fingers dug into my hair, angling my head the way he wanted so his tongue could explore every corner of my mouth.

The throbbing between my legs escalated and I ground my center into him, stretching my dress even further. The sound of splitting seams echoed in my room.

Jackson's hands left my hair, wandering down my shoulders to my breasts. He cupped them both and rolled his thumbs over my nipples, peaking them even through my clothes.

This seemed way beyond a simple make-out session, but I was definitely not complaining. A rush of nervous excitement sent my hopes soaring into the stars as one of his hands drifted lower, disappearing beneath my skirt.

"Do you want me to stop?" he panted against my lips. "Just say the word."

"No." I wrapped my arms behind his neck. "Touch me."

The minute his fingers touched the soaking wet center of my panties, my sex clenched. My shoulders shivered and my eyes rolled into the back of my head.

Jackson's fingers were a thousand times better than my own.

"More?" he whispered.

I nodded and one of his fingers slipped beneath the lace of my panties. It stroked through my folds twice before finding my clit.

"Jackson," I gasped as he circled my bud. My hips slid deeper into his hand, needing more pressure.

The hand he had on my breast dropped to my skirt. His fingertips tickled my thighs as he slid it up toward my panties. With a rough tug, he yanked them to the side, making room for both of his hands.

I was so primed, he didn't meet any resistance as he slipped a finger inside, curling it to stroke my inner walls. With his other hand, he swapped out a finger for the pad of his thumb to work my clit.

He was drowning me in ecstasy.

"Fuck, you're tight," he whispered against my neck as his finger plunged in and out. His lips came to the soft spot beneath my ear, kissing it just as he added another finger. The stretch of them both was unbelievable.

If his fingers felt this way, having him inside me would be otherworldly. Judging by the bulge on his lap, he was big. Would he even fit?

That particular worry fell away as Jackson picked up the pace of his thumb. There wasn't much space between us, but somehow, his strong arms and unbelievably capable hands fit right where they needed to be.

As the tension built higher, I let my hips rock back and forth as I held on to his shoulders for balance.

"That's it, babe. Fuck my fingers." His hoarse whisper made my core clench. "You like my dirty mouth, don't you? Just wait until I use it instead of my fingers to make you come."

"Yes," I moaned, long and loud.

Jackson's mouth latched onto my neck, sucking hard like he was trying to draw out my taste. The friction of his fingers and his hot, wet lips sent me spiraling higher until I was strung so tight, all I could do was snap.

My body shook as I came, my core squeezing Jackson's fingers in hard pulses. My body jerked out of my control and white spots burst behind my eyelids. Pulse after pulse, the shocks ran through every muscle until I was limp and draped over Jackson's chest.

When the aftershocks of my orgasm subsided, Jackson gently removed his fingers from my panties, righting them back into place. As the fabric settled over my sensitive clit, a ripple of shivers ran down my spine.

"You're beautiful when you come," Jackson whispered into my hair.

His comment would have embarrassed me on most days, but now, it just made me smile. I didn't have the energy for embarrassment. "Thanks."

With his hands on my hips, he shifted me down his thighs and off his erection with a groan.

My eyes shot open. "What about you? Should I . . ." I swallowed. "Do you want a hand job?"

Hand job? Turns out, I had plenty of energy left to be embarrassed, and I was never saying *hand job* again.

"No, that was just for you." Jackson smiled as the heat crept up my cheeks. "Come here."

He shifted on the couch, tossing up both of his legs so he was lying down. As he moved, he shifted my legs to one side, positioning me so I was tucked down his entire length.

I was trapped between his strong body and the back of the couch, lying on his chest.

Not a bad place to be stuck.

The skirt of my dress was still bunched up my thighs, so I wiggled it down. My gaze tracked down his body, his long legs hanging well over the other armrest.

"I need a bigger couch."

"Nah. This one works just fine."

I giggled, snuggling deeper into his side.

"Your hair is so soft." With the arm underneath me, he toyed with a strand.

"So is yours." I'd thought it would be spiky, but it felt more like velvet. "I like that you keep it short."

"Me too. I hated it when Hazel first made me buzz it off, but then I got used to it. It's actually a bit curly when it grows out."

"Really?" I kind of wanted to see him with curls. "Why did Hazel make you cut it?"

"Lice," he grumbled. "My whole foster home got it one year. I used the shampoo and shit to kill them, but Hazel didn't want to take any chances that I'd pass them on to Thea. So she made me buzz it all off. After that, I never grew it back. It's easier this way."

Lice. Just the word made my scalp itch, but I resisted the urge. "That sounds awful."

"It was. There was this little girl who lived with us at the time. She had this long, brown hair. It had the same kind of waves as yours. No matter how many times they shampooed her, they'd still find eggs so they made her chop it all off. I've never seen a person cry so hard."

As a woman who loved her hair, my heart hurt for that little girl. "Poor thing."

"I didn't really get it at first. I thought it was just a girl thing to get so worked up over a haircut. But later she told me that her mother was getting out of jail soon and she was worried that without her hair, her mom wouldn't recognize her to take her home."

And now my heart broke for the little girl. "Did her mom come back for her?"

"Yeah. She got released a few months later and took the girl home. I always wondered if her mom stayed out of trouble."

I dropped my cheek back onto his chest. "I hope she did. For the girl's sake."

"Me too, babe."

Babe. He'd called me babe earlier, right before I'd come. Maybe it wasn't so bad.

Maybe it was actually kind of perfect.

"That one. Babe. I think I like it now."

"Thank god." He laughed. "I was running out of options."

thirteen

WILLA

"SO HOW'S IT GOING WITH JACKSON?" MOM ASKED before taking a bite of her salad.

"Good." *Wonderful.*

It had been two weeks since Jackson and I had had our first date and I was simply floating. Things between us were just so . . . easy. We fit seamlessly into each other's lives like there'd been an empty space all along, just waiting for the other person to fill.

Jackson would come to the camp every morning with my favorite coffee. We'd chat in the kitchen with Hazel or take a stroll together outside until I had to get back to work. Then he'd go do his thing during the day while I worked.

After I left the camp, I'd go and sit with him at the bar. I'd become a regular, just like Wayne and Ronny. I'd stay until closing, then help him close down before driving him home.

On the nights Thea was at the bar and he was free, he'd come over to my place and let me cook him dinner. Afterward, we'd spend hours making out on the couch and fooling around.

He never let it go too far, but things were definitely progressing. He'd touched every inch of my skin, testing which spots drove me wild. And I was learning exactly what it felt like to touch a man.

I blushed just thinking about the sound of his deep, throaty groan as he'd come in my hand last night. It was the most intense moment we'd shared. My hand on him. His fingers in me.

"Oh, Willa." Mom laughed. "I can practically see your thoughts. Just be safe as you play with his naked body."

"Mom." I choked on my bite of lettuce. "Seriously? Can we not talk about that, um . . . stuff at dinner?" *Or in front of Dad?*

He was sitting across from me, shaking his head. The expression on his face was pure torture, like Mom had just shoved bamboo shards up his fingernails.

"Come on, Betty," he grumbled.

"Sorry." Mom held up her hands, then looked to me. "I'm just happy for you, honey. From the sounds of it, you're having the time of your life."

I opened my mouth to say thanks, but the look on Dad's face stopped me. He was about as green as the cucumber he was halving.

"What?" I asked him, then looked at Mom.

"What?" Her eyes widened. "Nothing!"

"You said, 'From the sounds of it, you're having the time of your life,' and then Dad practically gagged. What do you mean, *the sounds of it?*"

She grimaced and the fork in my hand dropped to my plate, sending lettuce flying.

They could hear Jackson and me at night? *Nooooo.*

I stared at Mom, hoping she'd say it wasn't true, but she just shook her head. "We leave our windows open at night. You do too. Sound carries across the backyard."

My dinner was dangerously close to coming back up.

Up until two weeks ago, I hadn't even known I had the ability to make some of the noises Jackson could conjure as he toyed with my body. The shy girl was a screamer. Who knew?

But those sounds were definitely not ones I wanted drifting into my parents' bedroom at night.

I buried my face in my hands, wanting to crawl under the table and die.

I'd never been this embarrassed before. Never. Not when Jackson had forgotten about our first kiss. Not the time my junior year that I'd leaned in too close to a Bunsen burner in chemistry and accidentally singed off part of an eyebrow. Not even the time in seventh grade when I'd sneezed during the silent prayer time at church and accidentally farted loud enough for three pews to hear.

This was worse.

So. Much. Worse.

"Sorry," I said into my hands.

"You don't need to apologize." Mom took one of my wrists, tugging my hand away from my face. "Now that it's getting cooler, we'll close our windows at night."

I nodded. "Me too."

"So how did the last week of camp go?" Mom asked, thankfully changing the subject.

"It was great," I told them. "It's always hard to say good-bye to the staff."

"They'll be back." Dad gave me a reassuring smile, doing his best to move on from the awkward moments.

"I hope so."

My camp was structured differently from a lot of others around the state. Other summer programs had limited staff on hand, typically just a director and maintenance manager. The kids were chaperoned by volunteer parents at whichever organization was sponsoring the camp.

But at mine, we employed a full-time counseling staff. They were all college kids who wanted to spend their summers in

Lark Cove. They were content to live in a bunkhouse with their sleeping bags and limited space for personal belongings, right alongside the kids. It wasn't glamorous, but they did it for the experience.

I paid them as well as possible because of how much they were giving up. They didn't get many days off to hang out with friends. They didn't get a lot of free time to spend on the lake. Other than the staff lounge in the main lodge, they didn't even have their own private space.

But their energy never waned.

Somehow, every year I managed to find a group of counselors who could match my enthusiasm beat for beat. It wasn't uncommon for counselors to return for a second year, some even three. And when they knew they weren't going to come back because they were graduating or had other job offers, they helped me recruit a replacement.

More often than not, the outgoing counselor put the incoming recruit through a more rigorous examination than I ever could.

I'd miss the counselors who'd be moving on after this season.

"Did you hear back from the coffee hut?" Mom asked.

"Yeah." I frowned. "They don't have any positions open, but they said they'd keep me in mind if something changes this winter."

And since I didn't know of any other place looking for part-time help, I was facing another boring winter.

It wasn't all that surprising. There wasn't much employee turnover in any Lark Cove business. People wanted to work close to home, so they held on to their jobs with a death grip.

"All ready for school to start, Dad?"

He nodded. "Ready as ever. I've spent the last couple of

weeks rearranging my classroom. Now that you're not so busy at camp, you'll have to come by and check it out."

"I'll be there."

I loved going back to the school, not just because it brought back memories from my own time as a student, but also because it brought back memories of when I'd gone in as Dad's special assistant.

Every summer, he rearranged his classroom. He'd test out the new experiments he wanted to try with his classes. He'd redecorate his bulletin boards. And I'd be his helper.

I missed those days.

As Mom, Dad and I chatted more about Dad's plans for the first day of school, my appetite returned and I finished my plate. "Thanks, Mom. That was delicious."

"Yes, it was." Dad stood from the table. "Thanks for dinner, dear." He kissed her on the forehead, collected both their plates and took them into the kitchen.

Mom smiled as she watched him walk away. "Your dad and I were going to rent a movie tonight. Will you stay and watch it with us?"

I checked the clock on the wall. I'd promised Jackson I'd come down to the bar to keep him company and it was about time to leave.

"Please?" Mom placed her hand over mine. "Your dad feels like he's losing his baby girl. It would mean a lot if you stayed."

"Okay." The bar would be there tomorrow. "Just let me text Jackson."

She smiled and cleared my plate as I took out my phone to tell Jackson I'd be down after the movie.

His reply was fast. *Sounds good, babe. Don't walk if it's dark.*

I smiled at the screen. He was always so concerned with my safety. Nothing bad ever happened in Lark Cove so it was sort of unnecessary, but I didn't argue.

Jackson's past explained a lot about him. He didn't trust easily. Other than Hazel and Thea, his instinct was to keep people at arm's length. Even me, to some degree. He was slowly letting me in, but it would take time.

My theory was that Jackson expected people to abandon him.

People had disappeared from his life, one after another. As far as I knew, he didn't know his father. His mother was . . . well, I didn't have nice words to say about her. The same was true for his aunt.

And I wasn't sure how many foster siblings he'd watched come in the door and go right back out.

Jackson didn't have a constant. He didn't have a person dedicated to always being by his side, someone who would choose him first. He didn't have a champion.

Until now.

Since my confession about our actual first kiss, I'd let go of all my fears and doubts. I was holding nothing back when it came to our relationship. Because maybe if I let him in completely, he'd do the same with me.

Maybe he'd trust me with his heart.

"Willa?" Mom called from the kitchen. "Do you want popcorn?"

"Sure." I wasn't really hungry but undoubtedly I'd eat a bowl or two. Popcorn was a requirement for movies in this house.

I tucked my phone into the pocket of my hoodie and stood from the table, taking the remaining silverware to the kitchen. The evenings were cooling down quickly now that it was almost September. I'd worn jeans tonight for dinner but had pulled on a pink, hooded pullover since I knew I'd be walking down to the bar. My days of wearing sundresses and sandals would soon come to an end for the six-plus long months of winter.

Jackson would be trading out the T-shirts he wore under his plaid shirts for long-sleeved thermals soon. I'd always loved watching his transition to warmer clothes and this year would be even better than most.

Instead of drooling over his broad chest under those thermals and wondering what his biceps looked like underneath his thick flannels, I'd already know.

Jackson hadn't been fully naked in front of me yet, but things were progressing. I was becoming addicted to his hands and mouth on my body. Since that first time he'd made me orgasm, I'd been in a constant state of desperation, needing him just a little bit more and more.

As I walked into the kitchen with the dirty utensils, Mom smirked. "Thinking about him again?"

"Yeah." I smiled.

"I remember those days." She looked longingly down the hall where Dad had disappeared into the living room to get the movie started. "Oh heck, I still have days like that."

"I'm glad."

Their marriage was the one I wanted.

Mom and Dad hadn't been able to have more kids because of Mom's blood pressure during her pregnancy with me. She'd been willing to try, but Dad had refused. He hadn't been willing to gamble with her life, because they were a pair. Two pieces to a whole. They didn't just love each other, they were best friends.

I wanted that kind of devotion.

"I'm happy for you, sweetie."

"Thanks, Mom." I finished helping her with the dishes as she made the popcorn, then we joined Dad in the living room for a repeat viewing of his favorite Marvel movie.

By the time the Avengers were battling alien invaders, the

popcorn bowl was empty except for some kernels, and I was stretched out on the chaise lounge, nearly asleep.

Between the chaos of the summer camp and the long nights with Jackson, I was worn out. So close to dreamland, I barely felt my phone vibrate in my pocket. I shook myself awake on the third ring, scrambling to answer it before it stopped.

"Hello?"

"Where are you?" Jackson asked in a panic.

"At home. What's wrong?"

"Have you seen Thea?"

I sat up, a chill creeping up my neck. "No. Why?"

"Fuck," he spat. In the background, beer bottles crashed as he threw them in the garbage. "We need to find her."

"What's going on? Is she okay? Is it Charlie?"

"Charlie's fine. Thea went for a walk and we can't get ahold of her. I guess there's some shit going on with somebody emailing her threats. I don't fucking know. But Hazel called worried and Thea's not answering her phone. Now the cops are out looking for her."

"What?" I gasped, slapping a hand over my pounding heart.

"Let's go, guys. You gotta get out of here." Jackson's voice was muffled as he stifled the protests. He must be kicking people out of the bar.

I waited for him to come back on the line, sliding on my flip-flops that I'd kicked off earlier.

"I'll call you later, babe. I'm trying to get this place closed so I can go help find Thea." The fear in his voice terrified me. He'd never sounded scared before.

"I'll come help."

"No," he snapped as more beer bottles crashed. "Stay home."

"Jac—"

The phone went dead. When I pulled it away from my ear, Dad had paused the movie and both he and Mom were looking at me with worried eyes.

"I need to go." I shot off the couch. "Something is happening with Thea, and Jackson is really worried. Someone has been threatening her and the cops are searching for her. I couldn't really understand, but I should be there for him."

"Okay, honey." Dad stood too, following me down the hall and to the front door. "Let me walk you to the bar."

I nodded, glad for his company. As he slid on his loafers, I stepped outside and looked up and down our street for any sign of Thea.

"Lock this, Betty," Dad told Mom.

"I will." She waited for him to join me on the sidewalk, then shut the door.

The walk to the bar was more of a sprint with Dad hot on my heels. I went right inside, passing two guys on their way out, with just enough time to see Jackson grabbing his keys from next to the cash register.

"Hey."

He whipped around with an angry scowl. "What the fuck, Willa? I told you to stay home. You shouldn't be out walking around by yourself."

I pointed over my shoulder just as Dad came inside.

"Nate." Jackson's anger deflated. "Thanks for walking her down."

"You bet." Dad placed his hand on my shoulder. "I'm going to get back to your mom. Let me know if we can do anything."

"Okay. Thanks, Dad."

He kissed my cheek, then nodded good-bye to Jackson.

I unglued my feet from the door and hurried behind the bar, sliding my arms around Jackson's waist.

He wrapped me up tight. "Sorry for snapping. I'm just worried."

"It's okay. What can I do?"

"Lock the front door." He let me go and handed me his keys. "I need to put some food in the fridge, then we can go."

As he disappeared into the kitchen, I locked up the front and swiped a few dirty glasses from a booth in the corner. When I got back to the kitchen, Jackson was practically throwing things in the refrigerator.

I helped him clear off the big prep table in the center of the room, then followed him as he marched out the back door. He took one of my hands and with the other called Hazel.

"Fuck. She's not answering."

"Let's just go to her house."

He nodded, his hand gripping mine even tighter as we changed direction to cross the highway.

Hazel and Thea's cottage was nestled right against Flathead Lake. Most of the locals lived on my side of the highway, except for a few remaining homes like Hazel's that had been there for sixty-plus years.

She could probably make millions if she sold her lot to a rich out-of-stater who wanted the lakefront property, but money wasn't all that important to Hazel. I think she liked to wake up each morning to the sound of waves hitting their shoreline and have a beautiful view as she worked in her vegetable garden.

I'd make the same decision if I were in her shoes.

It didn't take us long to reach Hazel's cottage. Jackson normally held back his strides when we walked together, but tonight, I was practically jogging so he didn't have to slow down.

The moment we turned down Hazel and Thea's street, I spotted three sheriff's cars parked in front of the cottage. Two deputies were standing in the center of the lawn while Hazel stood off to the side.

Jackson let go of my hand and ran right to her. The minute she saw him, she opened her arms and waited for him to rush into her embrace. I wasn't sure who was holding who.

When I caught up, Jackson let Hazel go with one arm so he could tuck me into his free side.

"Any word?" Jackson asked.

Hazel nodded and looked over her shoulder. "She's right there."

The three of us awkwardly spun around to see Logan holding a shaken and pale Thea around the corner of the house. They were talking to Sheriff Magee.

Jackson's entire body relaxed, his arm around my shoulders getting heavy as he sighed. "Thank fuck. She's okay?"

Hazel nodded. "Someone came after her. I don't know who or why."

"When did Logan get here?" I asked.

"Earlier tonight. He was the one who found her."

Found her where? Who had threatened her? I held back my questions, hoping someone would offer us an explanation soon. Maybe Jackson already knew what was going on and he'd tell me later.

Sheriff Magee said something to Logan, then gave Thea a pat on the shoulder. The three of them ended their conversation and walked our way. The sheriff rounded up his deputies and they all loaded into their cruisers while Thea and Logan came toward us.

Logan was wearing suit pants and a starched white shirt, probably having come from a business meeting. But his suit jacket was missing, along with his usual collected presence. His dark hair had been raked back one too many times and the dark strands were askew. His face was nearly as pale as Thea's.

She looked more frazzled than I'd ever seen her, her eyes wide and dazed. Her hands clung to Logan's waist as she walked, but she forced a small smile as she looked at me and then Jackson.

"You okay?" Jackson asked, letting go of Hazel and me. He took one step forward and captured Thea in a hug.

"Not really." She hugged Jackson for a few moments, then patted his back and he let her go. She went straight into Hazel's arms. "We have to go down to the station and talk to them about everything. The sheriff asked us to keep names and specifics quiet until they get things under control. But the bottom line is I'm okay."

"Okay." Hazel nodded. "You go. I'll be here with Charlie."

"Thanks." Thea rested her head on Hazel's shoulder, then held out a hand for me. I took it immediately.

Jackson held out his hand to shake Logan's. "Glad you made it back."

"Me too." Logan looked at Thea. "Just in time."

"Thanks." Jackson's voice cracked as he looked at Thea too. "Thanks for getting to her."

Logan nodded. "I've got them covered."

"Yeah, you do." Jackson let go of Logan's hand and clapped him on the shoulder. "Sorry it took me so long to figure that out."

At Jackson's apology, Thea's hand squeezed mine and we shared a look.

It was no secret that Jackson and Logan hadn't been fast friends. From the moment he'd come to Lark Cove, Logan had been trying to win Thea, and Jackson had stood in the way, acting as the protector for the only family he'd ever known.

But over the last week, something had changed. Jackson had stopped grumbling and griping about Logan. I think he'd realized that the best thing for Thea and Charlie was Logan. And above all else, Jackson just wanted them to be happy.

"We better get down to the station," Logan said. Thea nodded and reluctantly let go of my hand. Hazel reluctantly let go of Thea.

"Call me as soon as you can," Jackson told Thea. "I want details."

"I will." She nodded, then looked at Hazel. "We'll be home in a bit."

"Take your time." Hazel waved as Thea and Logan walked to her car. As they drove away, Hazel blew out a long breath. "I'd better check to make sure Charlie slept through the chaos."

"Do you want me to stay?" Jackson asked.

She shook her head. "No. You take Willa home and get some rest. We'll get all the details tomorrow."

Jackson nodded and walked her to the door. Before Hazel disappeared inside, they hugged again. She whispered something into his ear, then patted his cheek and vanished inside.

"Let's get you home, babe." Jackson took my hand and led me home, this time walking at our normal pace.

We made our way through town in silence and I texted Dad to let him know Thea was fine. Or she would be—Logan would see to that.

As we walked up the driveway toward my garage, Mom poked her head out of the living room window. She gave me a short wave, then shut off the lights.

At my staircase, Jackson went up first to open the door. His fists were clenched as he stepped inside, as if he were expecting someone to be in there.

"Lock up from now on," he ordered, flipping on the lights.

"Okay." I nodded. Whatever had happened tonight had freaked him out, and I bet as we all learned the details, it would freak me out too. If Jackson hadn't insisted on me locking my door, I was sure Dad would have anyway.

I closed the door and flipped the lock. The second I turned back to the room, Jackson pulled me into his arms to breathe in my hair.

"Do you want to talk about it?" I asked, wrapping my arms around his waist.

He shook his head. "She's okay. That's all that matters. We'll get the rest figured out tomorrow."

"Would you like something to drink? I have a couple of beers left over from dinner the other night."

"No, I should go. I'm all keyed up."

"You can stay." I ran my hands up and down his back.

He groaned into my hair as my hands disappeared into the back pockets of his jeans. When I dug my fingertips into those incredible, rounded muscles, he hissed and stepped back, forcing my hands away.

Jackson ran a hand over his stubble. "I don't have it in me to stop tonight, Willa."

I stepped closer. The adrenaline from the evening had me on edge and I needed to be close to Jackson. "What if I don't want you to stop?"

"No." He stepped back again, his head getting closer to the ceiling. "We should plan a special night in a hotel. I'll get candles and flowers or whatever else you want. I just . . . I don't want you to be disappointed."

"That's impossible."

He shook his head. "You've built me up in your head into something great. I'm not."

Why couldn't he see what I saw? He was a wonderful man with flaws. I wasn't blind. He wasn't perfect.

But he was perfect for me.

I stepped right into his space, taking his face in my hands

and tipping it down so I had his full attention. "I haven't built you up into anything, Jackson. I just see you for the greatness you already are. I don't need candles or flowers or a fancy hotel room."

"You deserve special."

"Yes, I do," I declared. "And no matter where it happens, it will be. This is already going to be one of the most special experiences of my life, simply because it's with *you*."

fourteen

JACKSON

UCK. HOW WAS I SUPPOSED TO RESIST HER?

Never had a woman stared at me the way Willa did. She looked at me like I was a king. The adoration in her eyes had nothing to do with my face or body. She saw straight to my center, and it was the sexiest thing I'd ever seen.

"You're sure?"

A playful smile tugged at the corner of her lips. "I'm sure."

Planning a special night at a hotel was ancient history now. Thea's ordeal tonight had scared me enough to abandon those plans. Why hold off the good moments when bad ones were around every corner?

And if Willa wanted me here, in her own bed, then tonight was good enough for me.

I crushed my lips down on hers, swallowing her yelp of surprise. She must have been expecting me to put up more of a fight.

But what she couldn't know was that I'd been fighting this for weeks. I didn't have the strength to wait any longer. There was only so much a guy could take and she'd worn my resolve thinner than my threadbare T-shirt—the one she was tugging out of my jeans as my tongue devoured her mouth.

I groaned as she pressed in closer, her stomach pressing

against my throbbing dick.

Her hands slipped between us, going right for the button on my jeans. The shyness she'd had with me on our first date had disappeared over the last couple of weeks. She'd grown bolder, more comfortable with my hands on her body.

When she came, she made the hottest damn noises I'd ever heard. She didn't hold back her moans or stifle her cries. Hell, two nights ago when I'd gone down on her, I'd thought for sure she'd wake up the whole neighborhood.

It had taken every bit of willpower not to sink into her tight, wet heat. Tonight, I wouldn't have to pull back. I wouldn't have to walk home with an aching cock just to get myself off in the shower as I imagined how Willa's pussy felt around me.

Tonight, I'd make this good for the both of us.

She worked the button free on my jeans and went for the zipper, but before she could pull it down, I reached between us and captured her hands, breaking off our kiss.

"What?" she panted. Her eyes were hooded as she looked up at me, confused. "I thought—"

"In a minute." I dropped my forehead to hers. "I don't want to rush through it."

"Oh, okay." She nodded, her cheeks flushed and her lips a shade darker than their normal pink. She worried the bottom one between her teeth.

Willa may have grown bolder when it came to our physical activities, but perhaps she was getting too deep in unfamiliar waters. I wanted her in control of how fast we took things, and there was no doubt she wanted all of me tonight. But there was also no doubt she was ready for me to take the helm.

"I, um . . ." She trailed off as she walked over to the end table next to her bed. Just the sight of her next to her mattress made me weak.

Don't fuck this up. Do not fuck this up.

I had one shot to make this experience special for her.

I wasn't going to fuck it up.

She turned to face me with a shy smile on her mouth. From the nightstand, she lifted out a box of condoms. "I bought these."

Damn it. I should have told her I'd already taken care of the condoms. Buying them couldn't have been easy for her. I crossed over into her bedroom and took the box from her hands, tossing it onto the bed behind her.

"I want to talk to you about something."

Her forehead creased. "What?"

"I want this to feel good for you." I ran my knuckles over her cheek. "Don't feel pressured to say yes, but I got tested a couple of weeks ago. I'm clean. And I've never not used a condom. So if you're okay with it, then I don't want anything between us."

She nodded fast. "I'm on the pill."

"I know." I grinned. "I kind of snooped in your bathroom one night."

I'd known this would eventually happen and I hadn't wanted to put her at any risk. So I'd driven up to Kalispell and gotten myself tested right after our first date. I'd also picked up my own box of condoms in case she wasn't willing to take that chance.

"This is your decision. If you want the added protection, I'm fine with that."

She dropped her eyes, taking a moment to think it over, then she shook her head and looked back up. "No, I trust you."

I wasn't sure why.

I'd messed up for years, not giving her the attention she deserved. Then I'd blown her first kiss. She had to know that before this was over, I'd fuck up at least a dozen more times. But still, she trusted me and it meant the world.

I trusted her too. I'd never gone without a condom, no

matter how many times women had begged me to go bare. I'd provided the protection. Always.

Except for now.

Willa was special. She was the exception to all my rules, because with her, there was no need to guard myself against manipulation or deception.

She was the type of woman who did things the right way. In the right order. Date. Engagement. Fancy wedding. Her dad would walk her down the aisle and her mom would cry as they shared their father-daughter dance. After she was married, her husband would buy her a puppy. Then they'd have kids.

Since that guy—whoever he was—would be getting those moments, I was taking this one.

"Jackson?" Willa's sweet voice snapped me out of my head. "Are you okay?"

I smiled, shaking off the uneasy feeling in my gut. "Never better."

Dipping low, I gave her a soft kiss on the corner of her mouth, trailing my lips along her cheek to her ear. Her entire body trembled whenever I kissed her ear, so I captured an earlobe between my teeth, tugging at it before letting it go to drag my tongue up the curved shell.

"Gosh," she breathed.

My arms banded around her back, pulling her flush against my body as I returned to her mouth. I went at her with full force, using every trick I had to leave her breathless.

Our chests were heaving against one another's when I finally unglued myself from her mouth. When had simple kissing gotten so damn good? Her tongue twisting with mine was enough to get me so worked up I could blow at any second. "God, Willa."

"Don't change your mind," she pleaded, assuming I'd

stopped for a different reason.

I grinned. "I won't."

Loosening my arms, I slid my hands down her sides and picked her up, laying her down on the bed. Then I swatted the box of condoms away.

She sat up and gripped the hem of her hoodie, but I stopped her. "Let me. Just close your eyes."

"Okay." Her hands shook as she dropped her shirt and lay back on the bed.

"It's all right to be nervous," I told her as I slid off her flip-flops.

"I'm not." She lifted her head, locking her gaze with mine. "I'm not nervous. Not with you."

She had so much faith in me—more than I deserved.

Do not fuck this up.

"Close your eyes."

She nodded, lying back down on the white quilt with her blond hair spread out to the sides. When her eyes drifted closed, I ran my hands slowly up her legs. The tremors in her body increased as I skated up her thighs toward the waistband of her jeans.

While my fingers undid the button, I swung up on the bed, straddling her knees as I loomed over her. She smiled when my weight hit the bed but kept her eyes closed like I'd ordered.

"God, you're beautiful."

She smiled wider, proving my point.

I undid her jeans and peeled them off her lean legs. Then I tossed them on the floor and feasted my eyes on her red lace panties.

Her sexy-as-fuck lingerie had shocked the hell out of me at first. I'd expected to find prim and proper white, cotton briefs under Willa's sundresses. But my woman was always in lace or silk. Sometimes she wore bikinis and other times a thong. No matter what color her panties were, her bras always matched.

Undressing her was like opening a present.

I didn't know if the underwear was for me, but I didn't care. If she did it to make herself feel pretty, I'd gladly be the guy who got to enjoy it too.

"Are you wet for me, babe?" I ran a finger over the gusset of her panties, making her squirm. "You're wet."

But she'd need to be wetter for me to fit. I went for the hem of her hoodie, pulling it up her ribs, making sure my knuckles raked across her creamy skin as I pulled it up. I grinned when I got a glimpse of her red bra. It had lace cups, like her panties, and her hard nipples were pink and puckered underneath. I lowered my mouth, sucking one into my mouth, lace and all.

"Jackson," Willa moaned, her hands coming to my head.

Those sounds she made drove me wild. We'd been getting pretty hot and heavy these last couple of weeks and I'd worked hard to get to know her body.

Our foreplay wasn't just about putting in my due diligence to get the prize. It was about worshiping her body so she could trust me with it. It was about discovering her tells so I'd know when I hit the right spots.

I abandoned one nipple, moving toward the next, dropping kisses along her sternum as I did. After giving her other nipple some attention, I trailed my mouth down, kissing at the soft swells of her breasts. I kissed at the sensitive skin over her ribs because it made her breath catch. Then I kissed down the softness of her stomach, lingering on her belly button for just a moment because I loved how it made her hum.

Willa's hips pivoted back and forth, searching as I slowly went lower. I kissed down her mound, then like I'd done with her nipples, I sucked her clit into my mouth through her panties.

"Oh my god," she cried, nearly bucking off the bed.

I smiled, rubbing her bud with the tip of my nose. She didn't usually say *god*. She said *gosh* or *goodness*. I'd laughed my ass off when she'd let a *golly gee* slip once.

She said *god* when I had my mouth on her.

Wanting to see her bare, I leaned back and tugged at her panties, pulling them down her hips. As soon as I got them to her knees, she kicked them off and sent them shooting to the floor.

"Be patient." I chuckled.

She shook her head. "You're killing me here."

"Well, we can't have that." With a firm grip on her knees, I pressed her thighs apart, then dove in. My tongue found her hot and sweet center. I worked up and down her slit, lapping her up, though I avoided her clit to make it last. She was so responsive, especially when I gave her a hard suck. But tonight when she came, it was going to be around me.

Damn, I was glad she'd pushed for this. I needed to sink inside her soon and shred the remaining barrier between us.

As she moaned my name again, I realized she'd been right. We didn't need anything other than us to make this special.

Taking her to a fancy hotel could have made her uncomfortable. It was better here, in her own bed and her own space. She could be as loud as she wanted. She could cry if it hurt.

Hating the idea of her in pain, I did my best to at least make this part feel good. I feasted on her, savoring her taste on my tongue until she was writhing and breathless. Then I leaned back to take her all in.

Her hoodie was bunched above her breasts. Her knees were splayed open. And her eyes, full of lust and devotion, were aimed at me.

Only me.

I was the only man who'd ever seen that look on her face.

"Sweatshirt and bra off, babe."

She nodded, scrambling to sit up. While she yanked it over her head and unclasped her bra, I whipped off both my plaid shirt and the T-shirt underneath.

"Pull back the covers," I ordered. "Get in bed." I didn't want to risk getting blood on her grandma's quilt.

Willa nodded again, obeying my commands without question.

As she scooted under the bedding, I stepped onto the floor and ripped down my jeans while simultaneously toeing off my boots. When I turned, Willa's eyes were wide and aimed right at my bobbing cock.

"Touch me," I whispered, stepping up to the bed. Then I took one of her hands and brought it to my dick.

She looked up at me as her palm fitted around my shaft. Her hands were so dainty but damn if she didn't have a fierce grip. As her fingers closed around me, I fitted my hand on top of hers, just like I'd done when I'd taught her how to jack me off.

We stroked in unison, our eyes locked as our hands moved. A flush of color spread across her bare chest, rising up her neck as her grip tightened.

"Fuck, your hand feels good." I closed my eyes and dropped my hand, letting her work me for a minute. When her thumb touched the drop at the tip, my eyes opened just in time to see her lick her lips.

Shit, I was going to come if she kept at it. I grabbed her wrist, pulling it away from my cock. Then I planted a knee in the bed and urged her onto her back. I settled into the space between her legs, careful not to crush her with my weight.

"You okay?"

She nodded.

"Tell me, Willa. Tell me you're okay."

"I'm okay." Her hands came to my cheeks. "Promise."

I leaned down and gave her a soft kiss. "Say the word and we'll stop."

"I don't want to stop." She angled up her hips, brushing her damp curls against my dick.

"I'll go slow." I reached between us, gripping my cock at the base. I used the tip to toy with her clit over and over as I latched my mouth onto hers and kissed her deep.

Her legs began to tremble and her tongue twisted in a frantic rhythm against mine, so I gave her clit one last flick and then positioned at her entrance.

The change made her freeze and her eyes pop open. I broke my mouth from hers and held her gaze as my hips inched me forward.

"Okay?"

She nodded.

The tip slid right through her wet folds, her heat beckoning me further. I balled my fist in the bedding, using every scrap of willpower to take it slow. Inch by inch, out then in, I worked myself deeper until I was seated to the root.

She winced as I planted myself deep and I cringed. "Fuck, I'm sorry."

"It's okay." She shook her head. "It's not that bad. Just give me a sec."

"Take your time." I hovered above her, careful not to shift until she was ready. When she opened her eyes and gave me a small smile, I smiled back. "You're amazing, babe."

Her shoulders relaxed. "You're not so bad yourself, Jackson Page."

"You ready for the good stuff?"

She giggled. "Show me what you've got."

I pressed the base of my cock into her clit, earning a soft

purr before pulling out slowly. My strokes began slow and measured, as I wanted to make sure she wasn't in pain. But when her legs wrapped around my hips, urging me on faster, I lost control.

Thrust after thrust, I pistoned into her until her moans filled the room. When I reached between us for her clit, it barely took two flicks and she was coming apart, squeezing me so damn tight, I nearly blacked out.

"Fuck, Willa!" I roared to the ceiling as her inner walls clenched, milking my own release. I kept my hips moving, my finger on her clit, until the stars cleared from my eyes and I collapsed after the most intense orgasm of my life.

Willa let out a contented sigh as she came down from her high. Her arms wrapped around my back and her legs around my ass.

"I think you killed me, woman," I murmured into her hair, making her giggle. I took one last drag of her sweet scent and lifted up to see her face. "Are you okay? Are you hurt? That got a little rougher than I'd planned."

"I'm perfect. *You* were perfect."

This woman. She always knew exactly what I needed to hear. "I don't know what I did to deserve this but thank you. I'm honored you wanted it to be me."

Willa swallowed and looked to the ceiling, blinking furiously as she tried to keep the tears away.

"Come on." I kissed the tip of her nose, then pulled out of her slowly, knowing she'd be sore. "Let's take a shower."

I stood first, then scooped her up in my arms to carry her into the bathroom. When the water was hot, I helped her under the spray.

It was a tight space for two people, but we made it work. As she stood close, I took my time washing her hair and body, savoring the steam filled with the smell of her coconut-and-vanilla shampoo. When we were both clean, dry and exhausted, I carried her back to bed and tucked us in.

"Good night," Willa whispered, snuggling her back into my chest.

"Night, babe." I closed my eyes and relaxed into her down pillows.

My arms pulled her even closer as peace settled over her dark bedroom. Being here, being Willa's big spoon, was exactly the right place. Things just felt *right*.

"Jackson?"

"Hmm?"

Her hand slipped under mine. "Thank you."

"For what? Sex?" I chuckled. "You don't ever have to thank me for sex."

"No." She laughed. "Not for sex. For making a dream come true."

She'd done it again. She said things that made my heart beat too hard. She said things that made me unable to speak.

So I kissed her hair and held her close as she dozed off.

I was glad I'd been able to give her this dream. Some other man—a man who believed in love—would get her others.

But at least I'd gotten this one.

fifteen

WILLA

"**M**ORNING, BABE." JACKSON WRAPPED HIS ARMS around me as I stood at the stove. "What are we trying for breakfast today?"

I smiled up at him. "French toast."

"Sounds good. Want more coffee?"

"Sure."

He kissed my neck before letting me go and grabbing my mug. He went to the other side of my kitchen to refill it, delivering it with another kiss, then he got out his own coffee cup from the cupboard. After he filled it, he leaned against the counter to watch me cook.

He was wearing nothing more than a pair of navy boxers, his muscles on full display. His eyes were still heavy with sleep as he sipped his coffee. The longer strands of his hair on top were disheveled.

It was my favorite time with Jackson.

Had I known how handsome he was in the morning, I would have worked harder to get his attention all those years ago.

Not even the view of the lake in the spring with the flowers in bloom after a long winter, with the grass neon green and the mountains royal blue in the distance, was as beautiful as the sight of Jackson Page standing in my kitchen drinking coffee.

It had been over a month since the first night we'd had sex, and Jackson hadn't slept at his own house once. He'd settled into my tiny loft apartment so quickly it was hard to remember what it had been like here without him.

"Want to get out the syrup and butter?" I asked. "These are about done."

"You bet." He took his coffee into the living room along with our supplies and put it all down next to the plates I'd already set out.

I didn't know how he could sleep through the noise I made in the kitchen each morning, but I figured it was because he was simply dog-tired. He'd gotten here late last night after closing down the bar.

I'd opted for a night at home instead of keeping him company, and I'd been surprised that he'd had to stay until closing for an early-October Thursday. When I'd called down to the bar to check on him around midnight, he'd told me there'd been a group of bow hunters who'd come in looking to unwind after a long, unsuccessful week of hiking in the mountains. I'd been dead to the world when he'd climbed into bed sometime around three.

Luckily, neither of us had anywhere to be this morning so we'd slept in and were having a late breakfast.

I took the final pieces of french toast out of the pan and shut off the stove. Then I gathered it all up and took it into the living room, setting our food on the coffee table, which doubled as my dining room. I settled into the couch next to Jackson and served him up five pieces.

I'd made ten because I knew he'd be hungry. That, and because I still hadn't figured out exactly the right egg-to-bread ratio for two people.

"Well?" I asked after he'd slathered his toast in butter and syrup and shoved a huge bite in his mouth. "What do you think?"

He grinned, his mouth full as he spoke. "Love it."

"Good." I smiled, cutting up my own bite.

I'd been on a mission to teach Jackson about breakfast over the last month. One morning, not long after he'd started sleeping with me, I'd asked him about his favorite breakfast foods. He'd just shrugged, saying that breakfast had never been a big deal and he mostly ate cold cereal.

I didn't do cold cereal. And breakfast *was* a big deal.

Everyone deserved to wake up to the smell of bacon and warm syrup.

So I'd taken it upon myself to make breakfast a special meal for him. I didn't make us feasts every day, mostly just eggs and some kind of meat—his muscles required protein. But once a week, I'd make something new. So far, his favorite was my biscuits and sausage gravy. He'd loved my crepes too.

There would be no more granola bars, Pop-Tarts or Frosted Flakes if I had anything to say about it.

"Are you working today?" he asked.

"Yeah. I need to go in for a little while and pay some bills. And I want to make sure everything on my checklist is done for winter."

We'd had a few cold nights this past week where the temperature had dropped to nearly freezing. The last thing I needed at camp was a broken water pipe, so I was going to triple-check that we were prepped for snow.

"You don't have to be at the bar until four, right? Want to come with me?"

He shook his head, swallowing a bite. "I can't, babe. Sorry. Thea wants me to come down to talk about a few things."

"What things? Is she okay?"

"She's good. I'm sure she just wants to go over some

numbers. She likes to bore me to death with the bar's finances at least once a month."

I giggled. "Don't ever let my mother know how much you hate accounting, okay? It would crush her."

Jackson laughed too, forking another bite. "Nah. Betty loves me no matter what."

He wasn't wrong. Mom was overjoyed that he and I were dating. Dad was too. They were both trying to let us have our space, but I'd definitely noticed a change in their routine.

Our weekly dinners, the ones that had *always* been on Saturday nights, were now more fluid. If Jackson was working on Saturday, they rescheduled to a night when he was free, even when I'd offer to just come over alone. And those two had eaten more meals at the bar over the last month than they had in the past year combined. One or both had a constant "hankering" for pizza these days.

I actually thought it was kind of endearing how much they loved spending time with Jackson. I loved spending all my time with him too.

"After I get done at the camp, I'm going to do some cleaning and laundry. But then I'll come down and keep you company for dinner."

"Sounds good," he said. "I'll be there whenever you come down."

Thea was scheduled to work all morning and afternoon, but Jackson had been spending extra time at the bar this month, even if she was on shift. Logan had been spending a lot of his time there too. After what had happened last month, neither of them wanted to leave her alone for long stretches of time.

The night Thea had been attacked had left its mark.

Jackson and I learned all about what had happened the night we'd frantically walked to the cottage in search of Thea.

The next day, he and I had gone down to Hazel's cottage and gotten the scoop.

Thea had been receiving harassing emails from Ronny, one of the bar's regulars. Things had escalated and he'd come after her that night. Luckily, nothing bad happened because Logan got to her in time, and the man who'd been harassing her was now facing time in prison for criminal stalking.

The threat was gone, but Thea was under a near-constant watch. I think Jackson and Logan had worked out some kind of secret system where one, if not both, was at the bar with her. Which meant even if it was Jackson's night off, he was more often than not still at the bar, taking on more and more.

Now that the camp was closed, it didn't bother me. I spent my nights there with him, eating dinner, visiting and helping him shut down before we came back here to bed. But I was worried that he was getting burned out.

He needed some time for himself too.

"Will you take me fishing?"

"Fishing?" He swallowed the last bite of his breakfast. "You want to go fishing?"

"Yeah. I want to see your boat. And pretty soon the lake will freeze. What if we went next week?"

He looked down at me with an odd expression in his eyes. I'd seen it many times over the last month, usually when I said something he wasn't expecting, and it always tied my stomach in a knot.

His gaze held a strange mix of wonder and pain. It had taken me a while to read the look, but I'd finally put my finger on it.

He stared at me like he was trying to memorize my face. Like he was already preparing for me to walk away.

I gave him a soft smile, trying to ease some of his fears. In time, he'd see I wasn't going anywhere. We just needed more breakfasts together and more nights spent in each other's arms. We needed more mornings where he'd wake me up with a kiss before sliding inside me.

Maybe we needed five or fifty fishing trips, just the two of us, but eventually he'd see.

I wasn't letting him go.

"So? What do you think?"

He blinked out of his stare, then ran his hand down my back. "Yeah. I'd love to take you fishing."

"Goodie." I smiled, then stood to clear our plates. "Do you want me to go over to your place and get your laundry? I'd be happy to toss it in with mine."

"You don't have to do that." He followed me into the kitchen with the syrup and butter.

Jackson hadn't let me into his place much. He had a nice house, though it was a little outdated. It was definitely a bachelor pad without much for decoration.

I'd actually only been there twice, both times in and out quickly, stopping only so he could change clothes. Every time I'd asked him if he wanted to stay the night there or hang out and watch a movie on his much bigger TV, he'd find a reason to keep me away.

I was trying not to make a big deal out of it since we'd only been together a short time. But the whole situation was bothering me.

I'd let him into my home completely, even giving him his own key. All I'd seen of his home was the entryway, living room and kitchen. I wasn't sure if he was ashamed of his house. Or maybe it was a mess and he didn't want me to see—though I doubted it because he kept the truck immaculate.

Whatever the reason, I was determined to break through.

"I don't mind," I told him. "Once I'm done at the camp, I

have nothing else to do all day. I can certainly tackle my boy-friend's laundry."

"Don't worry about it, Willa. I'll do some this weekend."

I sighed. "Okay."

He didn't trust me to wash his jeans yet, but he would.

Things would get easier.

We needed more time, just the two of us.

After breakfast, Jackson and I both left my apartment. I went to the camp while he went to the bar.

I finished my work in an hour, then returned home to do laundry and clean, which didn't take me long. With Dad teaching, I stopped by my parents' house in hopes that Mom would be up for an afternoon visit, but she was busy working on book-keeping for Bob's Diner. So I went down to the bar much earlier than I'd planned.

It was empty except for Thea standing behind the bar, dust-ing the shelves and bottles along the mirrored wall.

"Hey, Willa!" Thea smiled as the door closed behind me. She looked beautiful today, with her dark eyes and thick hair. She looked beautiful all the time, but lately, she'd had an extra sparkle in her eyes.

She and Logan had gotten married a couple of weeks ago in a small celebration in the backyard of their sprawling lake house, and she'd had that sparkle ever since.

"Hi! How's it going?"

"Good. You?"

I slumped into a stool at the bar. "Good. But I'm going kind of stir-crazy. This time of year is always tough. I miss the camp and it takes me some time to adjust to the slower pace."

"Yeah." She set down her duster and came to stand across from me. "It's hard when Charlie starts school. It's so . . . quiet."

I nodded. "Exactly."

"Jackson said you were thinking about getting a part-time job this winter."

"I was, but I haven't found anything yet."

"I think the gas station was looking for an evening clerk."

"No." Jackson's voice came from the back hallway before he emerged. "She's not working at the gas station."

Thea rolled her eyes and spun around. "Why not? Wait. Let me guess." She held up her hand before he could speak. "It's not safe."

Jackson grinned at the sarcasm in her tone, walking right past her. "You know? Willa never argues with me about stuff like this. She just knows I'm looking out for her. So why do you have to bust my balls every time I say something that's just for your own good?"

Thea winked at me. "It's fun. Busting your balls is one of my hobbies."

I giggled as she and Jackson went into one of their stare-downs. Seeing them together reaffirmed what Thea had always told me: they were siblings of the heart.

All the moments when I'd been jealous of Thea had been silly. The way Jackson looked at her was nothing like the way he looked at me. There was no attraction between them, only affection.

It made me wish I had a brother or sister of my own.

Jackson broke the staring contest first, shaking his head as he came closer. He leaned across the bar to softly kiss my lips. "Hey, babe."

"Hi," I whispered. Just one little kiss and I was nearly breathless. "So did you guys have a good meeting today? I see she didn't bore you to death with the accounting."

Thea scoffed. "Is that what you told her? That my monthly update is boring? Rude. I spend a lot of time putting that together so you know what's happening."

"Traitor." Jackson tried to hide a smile as he glared at me. "And yes, it was good. The best review of those damn spreadsheets I've ever had."

"I'm taking them home to Logan," Thea declared. "At least he'll appreciate them."

"I'm sure he will," Jackson agreed, getting a glass out to fill it with Coke. He set it down right in front of me with a napkin.

"Thanks." I loved that he didn't ask me anymore what I wanted to drink. He knew I'd stick to Coke until dinner and then have a beer. Sometimes two. Then I'd switch to water until it was time to go home.

"We do have some news, though." Jackson looked to Thea, getting a nod of approval to share. "Thea's going to step back a bit. Not work as many nights. She's cutting back on weekends too."

My heart sank. This was exactly the opposite of what I'd hoped for today. Jackson needed some time for himself, not more long nights at the bar.

"So we're going to hire another bartender."

"What? Really?" I perked up. "That's great!"

Thea smiled. "I think so too. It's been a long time coming." She turned to Jackson. "And we've earned a break."

"Damn right."

I wanted to ask if they could afford to take on a staff member, but I held my tongue. I trusted that Thea—and Jackson, for all his complaining—knew the business well enough to make the decision.

They wouldn't do this if it would put their financial futures in jeopardy. Or Hazel's. She was still technically the owner of the bar and they paid her a portion of the profits each month.

I guess none of that really mattered anymore. Logan would take care of Thea and Hazel no matter the financial situation at the bar. The man had more money than I'd ever see in my lifetime. Thea and Charlie, if they'd ever gone without before, would never be without again.

Logan Kendrick would make their dreams come true.

Even if that meant letting Thea work her dream job managing this bar and living a simple life here in Lark Cove.

Much like Jackson, Thea didn't need or want fancy. She just needed her family, their love and a happy home.

Maybe if Jackson wasn't here all the time, he'd get to settle into a home too.

"Any leads on an employee?" I asked.

"No, but we're not in a hurry," Thea said. "We'd rather keep things as they are and wait for the right person."

"That's smart. I'll keep my ears open for anyone looking for a job." Well, other than myself.

Thea smiled and changed topics. "You're friends with Leighton, right?"

"Yeah." I nodded. "We've been best friends since we were kids. Why?"

"I ran into her at school yesterday when I was dropping off Charlie. She invited me to one of those kitchen party things she's hosting next weekend. I've never been to one, but Logan thinks I need more 'me time.' I was thinking of going but was hoping you'd be there too."

"Yes, I'll be there and my mom will too. You should definitely come. There won't be a lot of us, but it will be fun. I'm making my famous wheat chili."

"That sounds delicious." Thea leaned her elbows on the bar

top. "I was thinking about expanding our bar menu this winter. Wheat chili could be a huge hit with the tourists. Is it hard?"

Before I could answer, Jackson cut in. "While you two swap recipes, I'm going to go change out the keg of Bud Light."

He leaned over the bar again, giving me another kiss before disappearing into the back.

I got a healthy dose of his backside as he walked away. I'd long admired his behind, but now that I knew exactly what it felt like beneath my hands, how firm his ass was when he was on top of me, it made admiring it so much better.

Thea was grinning when I looked back to her. "You two are so cute."

I smiled, blushing a little before launching into my recipe for the chili. I was just explaining how I prepped the wheat berries when the front door opened.

Thea looked over my shoulder with a smile to greet her customer. "Hi, there."

I turned to see a woman walking across the room. She looked to be about as old as my mom, likely in her late fifties, judging by the fine lines on her face and the gray sprinkled through her dark blond hair.

She was wearing skintight jeans with black cowboy boots, the stitching on the toe a bright red. Her black leather jacket was covering an old Rolling Stones tee, one that looked as if she'd gotten it from an actual concert.

"What can I get you?" Thea asked as the woman came to stand at the bar.

"I'm actually lookin' for someone. Heard he worked here."

There was only one man who worked here. The hairs on the back of my neck prickled as Thea's face changed. Gone were her easy smile and sparkling eyes. A fierce, protective look settled in their place.

"And who's that?" she asked.

The woman didn't get a chance to answer as Jackson stepped out from the back. His entire body went rigid except for one arm that lifted and pointed right toward the door as he bellowed, "Get the fuck out of my bar!"

sixteen

JACKSON

HOW MANY YEARS WAS IT GOING TO TAKE TO ERASE THIS woman's face from my memory? Even after decades, I still recognized her.

My mother didn't look much different now than she had the day she'd left me standing in the middle of my aunt's living room. Her hair was a lighter blond and shorter now. I didn't remember her being so thin. But her voice was the same. It sounded exactly like it had the day she'd left me with my aunt, telling me I'd be happy there.

Lying bitch.

Why the fuck was she here? After all these years, why had she come now? She must have had some kind of sixth sense to know I was actually happy, so she'd come to ruin it.

But I wasn't going to let her. I wasn't a kid anymore and she didn't have any power over me or my life.

"I'm not going to say it again," I barked. "Get the fuck out."

She didn't move. "You look good, Son. Grew up to look a lot like your granddaddy. But you got my eyes."

The room, which was already silent, went wired as Willa and Thea realized this woman was my mother.

"I spent a lot of time tracking you down." She smiled. "How are you?"

Did she expect me to be grateful? She sounded like she was doing me the favor here. I crossed my arms over my chest. "You wasted your time coming here. Get out."

"I need to talk to you about somethin'."

"No," I snapped. The hold I had on my temper was about to break. "I've got nothing to say to you."

Her sugar-sweet smile fell away. "Jackson—"

"You heard him." Thea cut her off with an angry snarl. She looked like she was seconds from leaping across the bar to throat punch my mom. "Get out."

Thea knew all about my mother, and so did Hazel. It was a good thing she wasn't here today because she would have already kicked Mom's ass through the door.

"Leave." Thea rounded the bar. "Now."

Mom glared at Thea but didn't move.

Willa slid out of her seat, standing with her arms crossed over her chest. Her shoulders were stiff. I was betting the look on her face held anything but her normal cheery smile.

Mom turned away from Thea and scowled at Willa, then looked her up and down. She was about four inches taller than Willa and trying to intimidate her. But Willa just stood straighter, not backing off an inch.

My shy Willa, ready to throw down against my shitty mother. If I hadn't started falling for her already, that would have tipped me over.

Mom puffed her chest out, inching closer to Willa. The movement unfroze my feet. I did not want Mom infecting Willa's space.

"Fine. You don't want to leave? I'll toss your ass out myself." With long, angry strides, I walked out from behind the bar and went right up to Mom, gripping one of her arms and hauling her toward the door.

"Let me go," she spat, trying to shake her arm loose.

"Out." I opened the door with my free hand and shoved her through it. Then I pulled it closed, fighting the hydraulic, and gripped the knob tight.

"Jackson!" she shrieked from the other side of the steel. "I need to talk to you!"

She pounded her fists against it a couple of times, trying to open the door again, but I kept a firm hold on the knob. It didn't take long for Mom to get the hint and stop her banging and shouting.

Thea crossed the room to stand by one of the windows in the front. I didn't move as she watched the parking lot, waiting.

"There," Thea said a few moments later, leaving the window. "She's gone."

She grumbled something else and pulled her phone from her pocket. With it pressed to her ear, she marched through the bar toward the back, probably to call Logan or Hazel. Or both.

I closed my eyes and took a breath, sagging into the door. My heart was racing and I felt like someone had just punched me in the gut.

Why was Mom here? Why now? What could she possibly want? Maybe I should have talked to her.

As my head spun, a pair of delicate arms wrapped around my waist from behind.

Willa's cheek pressed against my back. "Want to talk about it? Or pretend it never happened?"

"Pretend it never happened."

"Okay."

Okay. That was it. She wouldn't push. She'd just ride shotgun and let me navigate this.

I just wish I had a fucking clue which direction to go.

"Hazel is coming down here," Thea announced as she

returned, pissed off and snarling. "If that bitch comes back, I swear to god I'm going to beat her ass."

"I'll help," Willa told her.

I chuckled. Only she could make me smile after having just thrown my mother out of my bar.

I loosened her hands from my stomach and turned, bending to give her a soft kiss. "I'm going to get back to work. Shake this off. Are you going to hang with me tonight?"

"I'm not going anywhere."

And she didn't.

Willa sat stoically on a barstool all afternoon and evening, keeping a watchful eye on the door the entire time. Right beside her was Hazel, who'd come down minutes after Thea's phone call.

"You should go home," I told Hazel. It was one in the morning and she was yawning every other minute.

She yawned again. "I think I will. I'm too old to stay until closing anymore."

"Thanks for coming down." I leaned across the bar and kissed her cheek.

"You sure you're okay?"

"I told you, I'm fine. It was just a shock."

That wasn't entirely true, but I refused to talk about my mother's surprise visit.

Thea had given Hazel all the details earlier, then the two of them had sat and ranted about it for a couple of hours. They'd pestered me for a while, wanting to talk about my feelings, but I'd told them I was fine.

I think Willa must have said something to the pair at one point while I'd been in the kitchen because when I'd come back out, the topic had been dropped completely.

Thea had left the bar shortly before dinner to go home

and eat with Logan and Charlie. Hazel and Willa had stayed to eat here with me and bullshit with the random tourist who'd plopped down in the seat next to them.

"Will you call me immediately if she shows up?" Hazel asked, standing from her seat.

If? More like when.

I had no doubt Mom would be back, but I wasn't going to play her games. "If she shows up again, I'll keep kicking her ass out the door until she gets the hint."

Hazel frowned, dismissing me and turning to my girlfriend. "Willa, will you please call me immediately if that woman shows up again? I have some things I'd like to say to her."

Willa just bit her lip, trying not to smile.

"I see how it is. You're on his side now." Hazel gave me a pointed look as she slung her purse over her shoulder. "Don't forget I have spies everywhere, and I'm going to have my five minutes with that woman."

"It would just be a waste of your time."

Mom's face hadn't held an ounce of remorse. She could have earned five minutes with me, but she hadn't said the magic word. *Sorry.*

"I've got nothing but time these days, Jackson. And I don't want to talk to her because I think she'll hear a word I say. Telling her off is for me." Hazel gave me a sad smile. "And you."

"Fine." I sighed and gave her a nod. "I'll call."

Hazel had earned the right to a confrontation with Mom years ago when she'd stepped in to take Mom's place.

"Stop by and see me tomorrow." Hazel gave Willa a hug. "You too."

"We will," Willa said. "Have a good night."

"Do you want another beer, babe?" I asked as Hazel walked out the door.

Willa shook her head. "Just water."

"I'll take another beer." The tourist who'd been sitting on Hazel's side held up his empty glass. Then he moved into the seat Hazel had just left to sit next to Willa. The guy had already had four beers, but he didn't seem too drunk, so I poured him a fresh glass.

"Be back," I told Willa, winking at her before leaving to check on the other customers.

The Friday-night crowd had mostly cleared out, but there were still a few people lingering over by the pool table and jukebox.

The pool table was a newer addition to the bar. Hazel and her parents had kept one for years before I'd moved to Lark Cove, but it had been so beaten up that she'd decided to put it in storage. Thea and I had dug it out about a year ago and gotten it refurbished.

Our customers loved it, but the only downside was that it kept people in the bar later at night. The group playing tonight still had a whole stack of quarters lined up and it didn't look like they'd be leaving anytime soon.

All I really wanted was to go back to Willa's place and spend the rest of the night forgetting all about this day while I was buried deep inside of her.

Because she had the power to make it all better.

I stuttered my step as I walked, crushing a peanut shell. Willa had power over me. Even in a positive light, it was still power. The realization scared the hell out of me.

I'd been relying on myself for so long I wasn't good at leaning on anyone else. I didn't want to be at anyone else's mercy, even if it was just to give me comfort.

I glanced over my shoulder and took a long look at Willa's back.

Maybe I was getting too close. I'd started this whole thing with Willa because I'd just wanted to get to know her. I'd wanted to date her for a while until we got bored with one another.

But I wasn't bored, not in the slightest. The more I was around her, the more I wanted her.

Maybe I'd gone too far already. I didn't want to get married. I didn't want kids. I was good with Charlie because I had fun uncle written all over me, but being a husband and father was a whole other story.

I didn't have that kind of love in me to give.

When Willa and I got to that point in our relationship, when we talked about the future, she'd see pretty damn quick we didn't have one.

Maybe I should let her go now, before that point?

Not yet.

We were still having fun. I'd delay a serious conversation for just a little while longer. Then I'd let her go.

I shook off the feeling and finished checking on my customers. Behind me, Willa was still sitting at the bar.

I'd miss catching glimpses of her long blond hair as I worked. I'd miss having her at the bar every night, talking to me about nothing. I'd miss having her in my arms at night, chasing away the loneliness that I'd lived with for so long.

But it was right to let her go. *Eventually.* She deserved a guy who could love her like she deserved.

Willa must have felt my eyes on her because she looked over her shoulder and smiled. Then she turned back around to the guy at her side.

The guy smiled at her and scooted his stool a little too close to my girlfriend.

I scowled at his back, hoping he felt my glare, but he just kept on talking to Willa.

She nodded as he spoke. She didn't move farther away. She let him bump her shoulder with his.

A jealous haze coated my vision as they laughed over something he said.

Why was she laughing with him? She was supposed to be here for me tonight, not to flirt with some random tourist. Had they been like that all night?

I'd been too busy to pay them much attention. And Hazel had been between them for most of the night. Had they just been biding their time until she'd left them alone?

My jaw clenched tight as I cleared off a table. With two empty beer bottles in my hand, I went back around the bar and threw them, hard, into the trash can. They shattered instantly.

Willa jumped, startled by the noise. She looked at me, worried, but the guy next to her said something else and stole her attention. She laughed with him again. She gave him her smile.

Fuck this day.

Things had gone downhill since french toast, starting with my meeting with Thea.

I knew eventually she'd suggest we bring in some extra help. But this had been our place for years. Just her, me and Hazel. Bringing in someone new was a change I didn't want to make, even though I would.

I'd already been irritated by the time Mom walked through the door. Now Willa was laughing with this guy.

When we parted ways, she'd probably end up with his type. He wore nice jeans and a starched shirt with sleeves worn down to the wrists. His hair was styled and he probably paid someone to trim it every two weeks. He had an Audi keychain and a gold money clip.

I'd never owned or would ever own a fucking money clip.

Fuck this day, I was done.

"Last call!" I shouted.

The crew around the pool table all grumbled, so did Willa's newest fan, but I ignored them all. The angry glares I sent around the room were enough to have people downing their drinks, dropping a few bucks for a tip and heading out into the dark night. The tourist at Willa's side was the last to slither out, but eventually he left after a longing glance at Willa.

Asshole.

"Did you drive down or walk?" I asked Willa once the place was empty.

"I drove."

"Good." I nodded. "Grab your stuff. I'll walk you out."

"What?" she asked. "Don't you want some help cleaning?"

I shook my head. "No. I need some space tonight. You go home. I'll catch you later. Tomorrow or something."

I ushered her to the door, like I'd done with my mother. Except my touch was gentle and light on her elbow rather than the firm grip I'd had on Mom.

Damn it. Had I hurt Mom? What if I'd left a mark? I'd never lost my temper with a woman like that before, and shitty mother or not, I wasn't that guy.

"Jackson." Willa pulled her elbow free and stopped at my side. "What are you talking about? You'll call me tomorrow or something? What is that supposed to mean?"

"Just like it sounds," I snapped. "I'll call you tomorrow. Or sometime. I don't know. I'll see you around."

She frowned, stepping closer to touch my arm. "Don't do this. Don't push me away because of what happened today. If you want to talk about things, I'll listen. If you don't, then we don't have to. But shoving me out the door and saying you're going to call me 'tomorrow or something' isn't the answer. Let me help you."

"Then what is the answer, Willa? Huh? Because you didn't seem to be helping me much when you were flirting with that guy earlier."

"Flirting?" She stepped back, her forehead furrowed. "What are you talking about? I wasn't flirting with that guy."

"Sure looked like it to me."

"He told me a joke and I laughed. I might not be as experienced as you, but even I know that's not flirting."

"Whatever." I walked to the door and pushed it open.

Willa stared at me for a moment, frozen to her spot. She couldn't believe I was kicking her out either.

"Jackson," she whispered, pain crossing her beautiful face.

"Night, Willa."

She stared at me, tears sheening her eyes, until finally she dropped her gaze to the floor and hurried outside to the dark, deserted parking lot.

I stood in the doorway watching as she jogged to her car, making sure she got inside safely and onto the highway to go home.

"Fuck," I hissed. My hands fisted at my sides. "Fuck!" My shout disappeared into the night.

I'd made Willa cry all because I didn't know how to deal with the emotions swirling in my head.

I went right back inside for my keys, bringing them back to lock up, then went straight to the liquor bottles. I didn't care that there was a dirty tumbler on the center table or bottles next to the pool table. Fuck the pint glass that douchebag had been drinking from while he'd sat by Willa.

Fuck it all.

Fuck the feelings, all of them. I'd burn them away.

I popped the pour spout off a bottle of tequila and put it right to my lips to chug.

The tequila became an eraser.

I didn't want to remember Mom's face or her voice. I didn't want to remember how alone I'd felt when she'd abandoned me.

I didn't want to remember Willa's eyes full of tears.

I didn't want to remember any of it, so I gulped down some more booze, shot after shot.

Walking home wasn't an option. I'd pass Willa's staircase and there was no way I'd be able to resist going to her soft bed. I wouldn't be able to resist pulling her into my arms and falling asleep with my nose buried in her hair.

So I didn't walk home.

I got drunk and passed out on the pool table knowing that I'd just fucked up the best thing that had ever happened to me.

seventeen

WILLA

"WHAT DO YOU THINK?" I ASKED DAD.

Dad sighed. "I think you just need to be patient. I don't agree with how he reacted, but I do understand."

After Jackson had kicked me out of the bar last night, I'd come home only to toss and turn for hours. I hadn't slept as I'd replayed things over and over. None of it made sense, so I'd come to Mom and Dad's first thing this morning for some coffee and advice.

"I didn't do anything wrong." I didn't care what Jackson had said, I had *not* been flirting with that guy at the bar. I didn't even know how to flirt.

"No, you didn't." Dad patted my knee. "But Jackson's guarded, honey. Seeing his mother couldn't have been easy on him, and I can see why he'd lash out. Give him a chance to realize he messed up."

It didn't surprise me that Dad's advice was to cut Jackson some slack. Dad was the most understanding person on the planet.

We were sitting at the dining room table, staring out the big sliding glass door that went out to the back patio. Mom was in the kitchen doing the breakfast dishes. She'd escaped after we ate, leaving me and Dad alone to talk.

She'd always done that. She let Dad tackle the tough conversations because the outcome was always better. I loved Mom, but her forward approach usually just made me cry. I loved that she knew it too. When it was something really important, she'd always weigh in. She made sure Dad knew her position and opinion.

But she left the delivery up to him. She recognized that Dad and I were kindred spirits.

"Thanks, Dad."

"Anytime." He sipped his coffee, looking across our yard to the playground beyond.

Had Jackson walked home last night? Had he even cared at all when he'd passed this way? Had he hesitated, wanting to come apologize? Or was this the end?

My eyes filled with tears just thinking about it.

I was so angry at him. How could he accuse me of flirting with another man? Didn't he see how much I cared? Didn't he see that I only had eyes for him and had for years?

I wanted to scream at the top of my lungs. I wanted to pound my fists on the table because it was so unfair.

But I didn't. I silently took another sip of my coffee and stared blankly at the yard.

Jackson may have treated me badly last night, but it hadn't changed my feelings toward him. If he knocked on my door right now, I'd forgive him instantly. Unless he did something truly nasty or spiteful, I'd always be there for him.

But I wasn't going to chase him.

If he still wanted me, it was his move to make. I deserved an apology.

Sniffling, I wiped my eyes dry and focused on the playground. It was cold this morning and the grass was covered in white crystals. I was studying the frozen blades just as a man came down the sidewalk on the far side of the playground.

A man wearing a green plaid shirt, faded jeans and black boots, the same thing he'd been wearing last night.

I sat up straighter, leaning forward as I watched Jackson walk.

Dad spotted him too because his posture matched my own.

Jackson was walking past the playground with his eyes aimed at the sidewalk. His hands were stuffed into his jeans pockets. His shoulders and neck were bunched.

It was as if he was trying not to look over at my house. He looked like he was forcing one foot in front of the other while his face pointed stoically to the cement.

Temptation must have gotten to him because about half-way down the sidewalk, he glanced over once. After two steps, he glanced over again.

My heart was pounding as I watched his indecision. Step. Glance. Another step. Another glance.

Would he stop? Would he go home and call me "tomorrow or something?"

Stop, Jackson. Just stop.

The tears came back as he kept walking. He wasn't going to stop.

He'd almost reached the corner of the school, where he'd disappear from sight, when he slowed, his stride about half its normal distance. He took two more shuffled steps before his feet halted on the sidewalk. His chest heaved with a long sigh before he turned on a heel and stepped onto the grass.

I let out a little cry, the relief causing a tear to fall.

At my side, Dad put his hand on my shoulder and gave it a squeeze. Then without a word, he stood and left the dining room.

Jackson made the trek across the playground quickly. The closer he got, the faster he seemed to walk, and by the time he crossed into our backyard, he was jogging.

Before he reached the stairs to my apartment, I opened the sliding glass door and stepped outside. I closed it behind me, crossing my arms over my chest to tuck my hands in. The wood on the deck was freezing against my bare feet and the cold air gave me goose bumps, even under my bulky sweater and thick jeans.

"I'm over here," I called.

Jackson's face whirled from the garage to me and his feet immediately changed direction. He didn't slow down as he ran over to the porch and bounded up the steps, coming right into my space.

His chest crashed into mine and his arms closed around me tight to keep me from falling.

The moment I was in his embrace, the tears came back.

Jackson didn't speak as I cried into his shirt; he just held me, resting his cheek against my hair. I felt his apology in his strong arms and racing heart. I felt it as each one of his breaths got easier and the tension left his back.

It was the best *sorry* I'd ever had, even better than the one he'd written me on a Post-it.

I burrowed into his shirt, wrapping my arms around his waist. My hands, still cold, slipped beneath the loose hem of his plaid shirt and into the back pockets of his jeans.

We stood there, holding each other, for a long while until behind me the door slid open and Dad's voice broke through the silence.

"Come on inside, you two. It's cold. Jackson, would you like coffee?"

"That would be great," Jackson said over my head.

"Thanks, Nate."

I kept my arms tight around Jackson even as Dad moved back inside the house. But the door was still open, letting the cold into the house, so I reluctantly let him go.

"I'm sorry." Jackson's hands came to my shoulders, holding me captive. "I'm so sorry. I fucked up and acted like a dick."

"Yes, you did." I sighed. "But I get it. You had a lot on your mind."

"I'm still sorry." Jackson let me go and looked me up and down. When his gaze landed on my bare feet, he frowned. "Shit. You're probably freezing. Come on."

I wasn't cold, not in Jackson's arms, but I didn't argue as he grabbed one of my hands to drag me inside. Just as he was closing the door behind us, Mom and Dad came back to the dining room, each with two coffee cups.

Dad handed one over to Jackson as Mom gave me mine, then Dad motioned to the table. "Sit down. We need to have a discussion."

Jackson gave me a sideways look, hesitantly pulling out a chair. His eyes were bloodshot. He smelled like the bar and a bottle of tequila. As he sat, he rubbed the back of his neck, trying to work out a kink.

The only explanation for him being in the same clothes and walking home this morning was that he'd slept at the bar.

I might not be mad at him anymore, but I didn't feel bad for him either. He could have slept in my warm, soft bed but he'd chosen not to. If his solution was to get drunk instead of talking through his problems, then he deserved this hangover.

Though I'd still massage his neck later.

"So we might as well not beat around the bush," Mom said. "Willa told us about what happened with your mother yesterday."

Jackson shot me a look. "Did she?"

Whoopsie. I probably should have gotten permission before spilling his life story to my parents. I'd only told them because I'd needed them to understand the entire story before asking their advice. Still, it wasn't my story to share.

Before I could apologize to Jackson, Dad spoke up. "We don't keep secrets in this family."

"No offense, Nate," Jackson shot back, "but we're not family."

Dad's face hardened. "Do you have feelings for my daughter?"

"Yes," Jackson replied immediately.

"Then you're a part of this family, and when one of us is having a hard time, we talk it through."

Jackson slumped, knowing that Dad was talking about me. His shoulders hunched forward as the guilt from last night weighed them down.

"I think you need to confront your mother," Mom declared. "Get it out and over with. Find out why she's here, then you can dictate what will happen next. Right now, she has the power because she surprised you. You need to take it back."

Mom's direct approach might not always work when giving me advice, but it seemed right up Jackson's alley. She was a younger version of Hazel and she was going to go all mama bear for him.

After Hazel had her five minutes with Jackson's mother, my mom would be next in line.

"I don't know if I should see her or not," Jackson confessed. "Nothing good can come from her being here."

"Maybe. Maybe not." Dad shrugged. "But I wouldn't see her because she has something to say. I'd see her because *you* do. This could be your chance to get some closure. You deserve that much."

"Maybe," Jackson mumbled. "I'll think on it."

"Do you think she left town?" I asked.

He shook his head. "Thea texted me this morning and said she saw her car at the motel."

"She probably wants something," Mom muttered. "Any idea what it could be?"

"Money?" Jackson guessed. "Maybe she thinks I have some."

"Is there any chance she wants to make amends?" Dad asked.

Jackson stared at his coffee mug. It took him a few moments, but he murmured, "No."

My heart broke for him, but he was right. If that woman had wanted to apologize for dumping her son in the middle of New York City to fend for himself, that would have been the first thing out of her mouth yesterday.

"I hate her," I whispered.

The entire table's eyes were on me, probably because I hadn't ever said those words in my life about another person. Mom and Dad had taught me not to hate. Dislike, sure, but not hate.

I did though. I hated Jackson's mother and I didn't even know her name.

"What's her name?" I asked Jackson.

"Melissa."

"Melissa," I repeated. "I hate her."

I hated her for all that she'd done to break Jackson's spirit. I hated her for abandoning him. I hated that because of her, he didn't trust anyone. It was her fault that he'd closed off his heart.

Jackson's hand came to my knee. "Maybe your mom is right. Maybe I should confront her. Find out what she wants. Then we can all let her go. For good."

The concern in his eyes wasn't for himself, but for me, because he didn't want his burden to bring me down.

"Okay. It's settled." Mom stood from her chair. "Jackson, have you had breakfast? You look like you need some greasy food. I'll make you an omelet."

"Thanks, Betty."

Dad stood too, grabbing Jackson's coffee mug. "I'll get you a refill."

As they disappeared into the kitchen, Jackson spun in his chair. He took my face in his hands and gently kissed my forehead. "Thank you."

"For what?"

"For not staying mad at me even though I deserve it. For getting so worked up over my mother that you'd throw down right beside Hazel."

"I've never thrown down before, but I think I could win."

He chuckled. "I'd put my money on you."

We both knew that was total crap. I'd never gotten violent before in my life. But I wouldn't turn down the chance to punch Jackson's mother in the face—or at least nod along as Hazel said some not-so-nice things.

"I'm sorry for spilling everything to my parents without asking," I told him.

"I get it. You were upset and needed to talk. I'm just not used to sharing."

"I know."

"But I'm glad you did." He pressed his forehead to mine. "Feels kind of good to have the Doon family in my corner. And I think your mom is right. I need to do this on my terms. I don't want to keep waiting for her to show back up again."

"Do you, um . . . want me to go with you?" I wanted to be there for him, but I also understood if this was something he had to do alone.

"Would you?"

I nodded. "I'm there."

"Thanks, babe." He kissed my forehead again. "Maybe we can go down this afternoon. I need a nap first. I feel like shit."

"I could use a nap too. I didn't sleep much last night."

"That's my fault. Sorry."

I patted his leg. "It's done. After breakfast, we'll crash for a while, then wake up and start the day fresh."

"Sounds like a plan. Though I need to work in a shower somewhere in there."

I winked. "I'm sure we could arrange that."

A spark of heat hit his eyes. "I want to kiss you so fucking bad right now."

"Then do."

"Not until I find a toothbrush," he grumbled.

I giggled. "Did you know I've only been drunk once?"

"No shit?" he asked.

"My friends always told me that when you wake up with a hangover, you feel like a cat took a crap in your mouth. I didn't understand that until I had too many drinks at a party my freshman year and blacked out."

"Blacked out?" His mouth turned down. "I don't like the idea of you drinking so much you blacked out."

"Me neither."

Because the night I had gotten drunk had been the night Leighton had been assaulted. Maybe I could have prevented it if I hadn't guzzled jungle juice for an hour. Maybe it would have been me instead. The two of us had gone over that night time and time again without answers. Finally, we'd agreed to leave it in the past and neither of us had had the desire to drink heavily again.

"It was my one and only party," I told Jackson. "I haven't been drunk since."

"I think you're on to something. I feel like death," he moaned.

I cupped his stubbled cheek. "I'll make you feel better."

"You already did." With a quick grab, he yanked me out of my chair and into his lap. Then he buried his face in my neck as his arms held me tight.

I closed my eyes and rested my head on his shoulder as he breathed into my hair. I don't know how long we sat like that, but I'd almost fallen asleep in his arms when I heard my parents.

"Just let them be," Dad whispered.

"What about his breakfast?" Mom whispered back.

"Willa will take care of him."

And I would.

eighteen

JACKSON

It hadn't been hard to track down my mother. Like Thea had written in her text, Mom's green sedan was in the lot of the motel.

The car was a hell of a lot nicer than the one I remembered from my childhood. But I guess when you got rid of your kid, your expenses dropped and you could afford a newer vehicle.

I didn't want to explain to the motel owners why I needed Melissa Page's room number, so with Willa at my side, I parked my truck in the lot and walked up to the door directly in front of her car. The motel was fairly empty this time of year and even if I knocked on a few wrong doors, it was worth the hassle so people in town wouldn't know who Mom was.

With a deep breath and a glance over my shoulder at Willa, I pounded on the door. Behind it, someone shuffled and mumbled before it swung open.

"Jackson." Mom looked me up and down before doing the same with Willa. "Finally decided to talk to me?"

I took a step back and crossed my arms over my chest. From the corner of my eye, I saw Willa do the same. Her protective streak was a mile wide right now and I fucking loved it. It felt almost as good as it had when her parents had called me family this morning.

I wouldn't ever be an official member of the Doon family, but like I'd done with my foster families, I'd get to claim them for a time. That was good enough for me. They were a hell of a lot better than the woman standing in front of me.

"What's it going to take to get you to leave and stay away for good?"

"Just assume I want somethin'?" She frowned. "What if I was here to stay?"

"You wouldn't be welcome."

Her face turned down, like she was hurt that I didn't give her a hug, a kiss and a *Hey, Mom, I missed ya!*

As she stood there, looking like the victim, my temper roared. Feelings I'd kept buried deep for years were boiling to the surface. I clamped my arms across my chest, keeping my arms and fists pinned. I didn't trust myself with this much anger rolling through my bloodstream. The only thing keeping me composed was Willa and my desire to get some answers.

"Seems like a waste of time to track me down," I told her. "You could have found me a long time ago. Instead, you dumped me with a damn stranger and never looked back."

"Oh, please." She waved me off. "My sister, your own aunt, is hardly a stranger. Don't act like I abandoned you. You were with your family while I had to take care of a few things."

I scoffed. "Yeah. I was with family. For. A. Week. Then this *family* dumped me too. When you drove off to take care of these things of yours, did you at least look back once or twice in your rearview? I can't remember. I do remember your sister—my own aunt—didn't look back. Not once. Aunt Marie didn't even get out of the car when she dropped me off at social services. Nope. Just pulled up to the curb and told me not to forget my backpack."

I waited, hoping for a flash of surprise or remorse to cross

Mom's face, but it never came. "I didn't know she would do that."

"No," I said through gritted teeth. "You were long gone by then. So back to my original question. What the fuck is it going to take for you to leave Lark Cove and my life for good?"

Because then I could block it all out.

I'd forget about that scared little boy who stood outside the social services building all day until finally, a social worker came outside to ask if he was lost.

I hadn't been lost, just left behind.

Lost came later as I moved from foster house to foster house, never once finding a home. All because this woman had *things* to take care of.

"Forget it," I clipped. She wasn't sorry. She didn't care. There would be no answer for me today.

As of now, she was dead to me.

"Let's go, Willa." I turned to leave but stopped at the sound of a new voice.

"Mom?"

I froze as Willa gasped. There was no question which motel room that voice had come from or who it was addressing.

I turned around slowly, facing my mother just as a boy emerged from the motel room. But he wasn't just a boy. He was her kid.

What the actual fuck? *She had another kid?* She'd left me to fend for myself at nine years old, then she'd had another son.

The boy stood by Mom's side, staring right at me before he whispered, "Is that him?"

Mom threw her arm around his shoulders. "Yep. This is your big brother, Jackson."

"Hey." The kid smiled like he'd been waiting his entire life to meet me.

I stared at him with a slack jaw. Was this why she'd come here? To introduce me to my younger brother?

I had no idea how old he was, maybe eleven or twelve, like some of the kids at Willa's camp. What I did know was that his jeans were four inches too long and his sweatshirt would have fit me better than it did him. Why was he wearing such baggy clothes? Couldn't Mom afford ones in his size?

He didn't look a thing like her—or me for that matter. The only similarity I had with her was light hair and the color of our blue eyes. He didn't even have that. His skin was darker, like his dad had been African-American. His eyes were a rich brown and his curly black hair was cropped short.

My half-brother.

The kid stepped forward, away from Mom, and held out a hand. "I'm Ryder."

Ryder? This just kept getting better.

"Ryder?" I huffed, ignoring the kid and glaring at Mom. "Are you fucking joking? You named him Ryder? Did you forget that you already used that for my middle name?"

The kid flinched, but I kept my glare on Mom.

She shrugged it off, staring at me with complete indifference.

I hated her. Jesus, fuck, but I hated her. The tension on the sidewalk was stifling, making the cool fall air heavy and hot.

The kid shifted his weight back and forth as his extended hand dropped slowly along with his eyes. But before he could shrink away, Willa stepped up and caught his hand, returning the handshake that had been meant for me.

"Um . . . hi, Ryder. I'm Willa."

He gave her a shaky smile as they shook but then looked right back to me with big, brown, hopeful eyes.

I recognized that hope—I'd had that same look once.

After Mom and my aunt dumped me, I'd longed for someone

to welcome me with open arms. I'd needed someone to accept me. But the people in the first foster home hardly paid me any attention. They only kept me for a month. The next home was the same, though they kept me for two months. The third let me stay a week.

And each time I packed up my backpack, hope faded.

I wouldn't be the guy to take that from this kid, so I held out my hand. "Hey, Ryder. I'm Jackson. Nice to meet you."

"You too." He shook my hand with a bright smile, then let it go. "Mom told me about you."

About what? She didn't even know me. I looked over his head to see Mom looking bored.

"Is this why you came?" I asked her. "For a family reunion?"

"Ryder, give me a minute with Jackson." Mom stepped farther out onto the sidewalk, nodding for Ryder to go back into the room. "And shut the door."

"Okay," he mumbled. He gave me another smile before going inside and closing the door.

"How old is he?" I asked Mom before she could talk.

"Twelve."

"Twelve," I repeated, shaking my head. After I'd spent my entire childhood needing a mother, she'd found it in herself to become one to someone else.

"So is he why you came to find me?"

She nodded. "Need you to take him for a while."

The disgust tasted worse in my mouth than my hangover breath. My mother was disgusting. Simply disgusting.

She'd tracked me down after all these years to pawn off another one of her kids.

"You want me to take him?" I asked. "Are you serious?"

"You're his only family and he's a good kid. He won't give you any trouble."

A memory came rushing back of the day she'd left me at Aunt Marie's. Mom had said those exact same words about me.

"So you came to pawn him off on me. Does he know?" Was that why he'd looked at me like I was his salvation?

Mom shook her head. "Thought it would be best to tell him together."

"Of course, you did," Willa said dryly. "You always put the needs of your children first."

"This ain't your business," Mom snapped at her.

"Why?" I asked before Willa could respond. "I want a reason why you're leaving him here."

"That ain't your business either. But you either take him or he's on his own."

What choice did I have? She'd backed me into a corner, piling all of this on my conscience so that if Ryder went into the system, I'd feel guilty.

"You're a fucking bitch." The words were cathartic.

Mom rolled her eyes. "Now you sound like your granddaddy."

"Too bad I didn't get to meet him. I think we would have had a lot in common."

"You gonna take Ryder or not?" She was getting flustered, the color in her cheeks rising.

"How did you even find me?"

She shrugged. "Wasn't that hard. Hired a guy to track you down online with your social security number."

Because she'd needed a place for my brother. I bet she had a backpack all loaded up for Ryder, just like she'd done with me.

"Get the kid. Get his shit. And get the fuck out of Montana."

She grinned, knowing she'd won. Without a word, Mom

went back inside the motel room, closing the door at her back.

"Oh, Jackson." Willa came to my side. "I cannot believe this is happening."

My arm went around her shoulders, holding on to her. "Me neither."

I'd come down to the motel for closure and hadn't gotten any. Instead, I'd gotten a twelve-year-old kid brother who would be living with me indefinitely.

"I don't know what else to do," I whispered. "If I don't take him, then—"

"You have to take him." Willa's entire frame shook with fury. "You need to get him away from her. She's toxic."

"What am I going to do?"

I didn't know anything about raising a kid. I worked at a bar. Who was going to watch him when I was working until three in the morning? Who was going to help him with his math homework? Who was going to make sure he was eating the right shit from the food pyramid?

For fuck's sake, I'd slept on a pool table last night. I wasn't equipped to be responsible for another person. It was one of the reasons I didn't want kids of my own. I wasn't that guy.

"We'll figure it out," Willa reassured me.

"Yeah," I muttered. I didn't have a choice. I wouldn't let a kid, let alone my brother, go through the same childhood hell I'd gone through.

The motel door opened again and I let Willa go.

Ryder's face had paled and his eyes were wide as he walked out the door with a backpack slung over one shoulder.

Mom was right behind him, rolling out a cheap black suitcase.

Ryder's eyes were full of despair as he stood on the sidewalk. The poor kid. There was no doubt that Mom had just dropped the bomb on him.

"Sounds like you'll be staying with me for a while." I clapped him on the shoulder. "That cool with you?"

He shrugged and looked at his tennis shoes. He had big feet and was probably going to be tall after he grew into them.

"Willa? Would you help Ryder get his things loaded into the truck?"

"Sure." She practically yanked the suitcase handle out of my mother's hand. Then with a parting glare, she walked to the truck.

Ryder waited a beat, then followed her. He didn't even turn to say good-bye to Mom. He didn't give her a word or a look. And he didn't seem surprised, just . . . disappointed.

How many times had she left him before? I remembered my years with her being full of babysitters and neighbors. Maybe our time with her wasn't all that much different. I bet she'd promised him a fun trip to meet his brother, just like she'd promised me a fun trip to meet my aunt.

Mom didn't say anything as Ryder walked away, certainly not a promise to return. Instead of watching her kid leave, her eyes were glued to my truck and a greedy smirk spread across her mouth.

She was going to ask me for money. Guaranteed.

"Get out of town." I shuffled closer, growling down at her. "Now."

"I need money."

This bitch was so predictable.

I hated the idea of giving her a damn cent, but if it got her out of Lark Cove and away from me and Ryder, I didn't care.

I ripped my wallet out of my back pocket and pulled out the stack of cash I'd shoved in there. It was ten days' worth of tips—about five hundred bucks. I'd planned on running it up to the bank in Kalispell this week.

Instead I shoved it into her chest. "I never want to see your face again."

She took the money and stuffed it in her jeans pocket. "I need more money if you don't want me coming back."

I stepped even closer, sending her back on her heels. "That's all you're ever going to get. You don't see me again. You don't see him again. You're dead to us. Got it? If I see your face again, you won't like what happens next. I got no love for you, lady. But I got a lot of rage."

The threat erased some of her arrogance. She stepped back farther, looking at me once more before turning into the motel room and slamming the door.

My shoulders collapsed as I breathed. I gave myself until the count of five, then went to the truck and climbed into the driver's seat. Willa was sitting shotgun, her face etched with worry.

I reached over the console and took her hand as I glanced in the back. Ryder was looking out his window, away from the motel and Mom's car.

"You got everything?" I asked him.

He shrugged. "I guess."

Was this really happening? Two hours ago, it was just Willa and me curled together in her bed. Two hours ago, I was just a bartender lucky to have a girlfriend who'd forgiven him after he'd acted like a dick.

Now I was some sort of pseudo-parent to a kid I'd met less than fifteen minutes ago.

"Are you hungry?" I asked Ryder.

He shrugged again.

"I'm hungry," Willa said.

"You're always hungry. Ryder, do you want to see Willa

stuff an entire pizza in her mouth? She can inhale one in about three minutes."

She smiled, going along with my attempt to lighten the mood. "More like ten."

Ryder didn't laugh or respond. He just hung his head, turning even further into the window. One of his hands slid up to wipe his nose.

I opened my mouth to say something else but closed it instead. There was nothing to say. So I looked ahead, glancing one last time at my mother's motel room door. Then I fired up the truck and reversed out of the lot.

Before I even hit the highway, Willa was texting on her phone. She was calling in reinforcements. Thea was already at the bar. Hazel would likely be there soon. So I focused on the road, driving us the few blocks down to the bar where I'd find help.

Where my real family would be waiting.

nineteen

WILLA

"Missed you," Jackson whispered as he wrapped me up in his arms. The stubble on his jaw tickled the skin on my neck as he kissed my bare shoulder.

"I missed you too."

It had been a week since Jackson had confronted his mother and discovered his little brother. And in that time, we hadn't spent a single night together. Instead, Jackson's focus had been exactly where it should have been.

On Ryder.

When we arrived at the bar after leaving Melissa Page behind—hopefully for good—Thea was waiting by the door to welcome us. Hazel came in two minutes later. And while I sat with Ryder and discussed pizza toppings, Jackson pulled them into the back and explained the situation.

From that moment on, life became a flurry of activity as we all tried to get Ryder settled into his life here. Hazel took it upon herself to get his room set up in Jackson's house. Thea was in charge of getting Ryder clothes that fit and decent shoes. I made sure Ryder was enrolled in school and had all the necessary supplies.

So while the three of us were taking care of logistics, Jackson was with Ryder. Around the clock. They toured town.

They ate meals together. They spent evenings on Jackson's living room couch watching movies.

And since I'd wanted them to have a chance to bond, I'd stepped back. I saw them both during the day as I came and went from his house, but at night, I stayed home alone.

We both knew it was the right call. Ryder had needed time in his new home without Jackson's girlfriend around. But now Ryder was comfortable in their house, and on Monday, he was starting school.

He was settled.

So last night, Jackson had insisted I start spending the night. For the first time in a week, we were waking up together. For the first time ever, it was in his bed, not mine.

"I like your bed," I told him.

"I like you in my bed."

I wanted to ask him why he'd never wanted me to stay here before, but I didn't want to touch on any subject that could make him uncomfortable, not on his special day.

"Happy Birthday," I whispered.

He kissed my hair. "Thanks, babe."

I loved that I was the first person to tell him. I'd told him at midnight, after we'd had sex and were cuddled in each other's arms. We'd gone at it hard last night, both of us needing something hot and wild to ease our stresses. It had been a challenge to keep quiet, but Jackson had swallowed most of my cries with his mouth.

He'd done the same this morning.

"How about breakfast?"

"You and your breakfasts." He chuckled and his arms hugged me tighter. His smile tickled my shoulder. "I wouldn't say no to your french toast."

"Perfect." I'd brought over a huge haul of groceries yesterday and had an extra loaf of bread just in case that was his choice. "I hope Ryder likes french toast."

"I'm sure he will. That kid seems to eat just about anything. Makes me wonder how often he got regular meals."

I sighed. "I was thinking the exact same thing last night."

We'd gone out to dinner at Bob's Diner for Jackson's birthday and all ordered a double cheeseburger. Even I had trouble eating an entire one.

Ryder had inhaled two.

"I'll give it to the kid." Jackson sighed. "He's taking this in stride."

I nodded. "He sure is."

Ryder had been closed off at first. As we all buzzed around him, frantically setting him up in his new life, he'd stood by and watched with few words. But after a couple of days, he'd begun to relax.

As Hazel set up his room, he'd pitched in, moving furniture as she gave direction. He'd found a new friend in Charlie. Thea had taken them both shopping for school clothes and since Charlie preferred boy clothes to girl, they'd bought matching shirts.

And with me, he'd become my right-hand man.

When I went to the grocery store, he came along and pushed the cart. When I had to stop by the camp to ensure everything was okay, he came along too. Ryder had taken one look at my camp and fallen in love, begging me to sneak him into one of the camps next summer.

After just a week, he was laughing and joking with Jackson and me like he'd known us his entire life. The only time he'd clam up was when we asked about his past.

"He won't talk about your mom." I'd tried a couple of times to broach the subject, just to see how he was holding up.

But Ryder had just frowned and gone quiet. Much like his older brother, he seemed to bottle things up.

"Can you blame him?" Jackson asked.

"No, but I worry he's holding too much inside." It had been like pulling teeth just to find out what school he'd gone to so I could call and get his records transferred. "Maybe he'll talk to you."

"Maybe," Jackson muttered.

The sound of clanking pans came from the kitchen, interrupting our conversation. Though I had a feeling it had been over anyway.

When we'd first started dating, Jackson had been so forthcoming about his past. Honestly, it had surprised me that he'd shared so much with me about his childhood on our first date.

But ever since his mother had shown, he'd shut down.

It wasn't just that he was busy with Ryder either. There was something going on with him. The problem was, I didn't have any specific examples to confront him about. He was still sweet and sexy and my Jackson. But there was something heavy surrounding him.

When we were having a serious conversation, he'd end it with something short. *Maybe. I'll think about it. We'll see.* They all meant he was done talking, and I'd heard them more in the last week than ever before.

"Ryder must be hungry," Jackson said as the clanking in the kitchen continued. "It's been over five hours since he ate so he's probably on the verge of starvation."

I smiled. "Then I'd better get started on breakfast."

Jackson let me go and I slipped from his bed and into the en-suite bathroom.

As I brushed my teeth, I studied the room. It was outdated, much like the rest of Jackson's house. The laminate counters and vinyl floor were clean but had been well used. This home had been built in the seventies and was full of wood paneling in the bedrooms and living areas, making the entire place seem like a man cave.

Still, I loved being here in Jackson's space. This house had such potential to be a bright and happy home. The bathroom could be easily updated with lighter colors and newer finishes. The living areas just needed to be refreshed. And with new cabinets and countertops, the kitchen had the potential to be a dream.

I finished with my teeth and went back to the bedroom, passing Jackson as he went to the bathroom. As I pulled on some pajama pants, a bra and one of his sweatshirts, I made a mental list of improvements for his room.

It wouldn't take much to create the perfect bedroom. The paneling had to go and a bigger closet would be ideal. Visions of me and Jackson waking up here, morning after morning, filled my head. I pictured my clothes in his closet and my books on his nightstand.

I hoped I'd get the chance to update it one day.

When another sound echoed from the kitchen, I gave up my interior design dreaming and walked out of the bedroom and down the short hall to find Ryder studying the stove.

"Good morning," I greeted as I tied up my hair.

"Hey." He smiled. "How do you turn this thing on?"

"It's a gas stove so you have to light the burners."

"Oh." He searched the counter, probably looking for matches. "I was going to make some breakfast."

"How about I do the breakfast?" I went to the stove, taking over his position in front of a frying pan. "Do you want to be my assistant?"

He nodded and we got to work. An hour later, Ryder had

learned how to not only light the stove but also make french toast. And the three of us were devouring the biggest batch I'd made in my life.

"Don't eat that one." I plucked a mangled piece of french toast from the bottom of the pile before Ryder could grab it.

"Why?" Ryder asked, his mouth full of food.

"It's all woogidy. I'll eat it."

Ryder stopped chewing. "Woogidy?"

Jackson chuckled, taking another two pieces for his own plate. "Willa makes up words."

"Woogidy." Ryder grinned. "I like it."

I shot a *so there* look at Jackson. "Thanks."

"So what do you want to do today for your birthday?" Ryder asked his brother.

Jackson winked at me. "I had a request to go fishing before the lake freezes. Figured we could take the boat out today."

Ryder and I high-fived.

"Cold?" Jackson asked.

My teeth chattered. "I'm okay."

He frowned and stripped off his thick, canvas coat to drape over my shoulders. The body heat trapped in the flannel lining warmed me instantly.

"What about you?" I asked. "You'll freeze."

"I'm good." He kissed the top of my brown stocking cap.

We were in the middle of Flathead Lake on Jackson's boat. The sun was shining down on the water. The air was cool and crisp. But the slight breeze wafting over the water had seeped through my jeans, sweater and brown puffer vest. I'd been fine in town, but as Jackson had sped his boat across the water, I'd turned into an icicle.

"I should have worn my snow gear." And I would have except I'd wanted to look cute on Jackson's birthday and wear my new Wellington boots.

"Yeah." Jackson grinned. "Next time dress like Ryder."

I giggled and looked at Ryder sitting at the back of the boat. His fishing rod was gripped firmly in his gloved hands. He'd even brought along his backpack, full of whatever extra provisions he'd packed inside.

After breakfast, Jackson had told him to get ready and wear warm clothes. Ryder had immediately gone to change, emerging from his room in the snow pants, winter coat and Sorel boots that Thea had bought him earlier in the week. He looked ready for the ski hill, not fishing.

But at least he was warm.

"Do you think we'll catch anything?" I asked.

Jackson shrugged. "Maybe."

"I hope we do, but even if we don't, I'm glad I got to see your boat."

Jackson's fishing boat was the nicest one I'd ever seen, larger than any waterskiing boats docked next to it at the marina. The aluminum frame was shiny and I loved the sound of the waves slapping against the hull.

The bow was closed in with a railing and the roof above Jackson covered his driver's chair and my passenger seat. The two bucket seats in the back swiveled around completely. And the massive twin engines meant it hadn't taken us long to get to the middle of the lake.

"I hadn't planned on buying one this big, but when I saw it, I couldn't pass it up." Jackson looked adoringly around the boat.

"I'm glad you didn't." Fishing next summer would be a blast. "How's it going, Ryder?"

"Good." He nodded, staying focused on his fishing pole.

"Are you excited to start school next week?"

"I guess."

"You'll get to be in my best friend's English class. Her name is Leighton and she's a teacher there. My dad teaches there too, but you won't have him for a few years. He teaches high school science."

"If I'm still here by then," he muttered.

My eyes shot to Jackson. He was just as surprised by Ryder's statement as I was. Why wouldn't Ryder be here? Did he think Jackson would get rid of him?

"Why don't you set that pole in the holder?" Jackson asked.

Ryder shook his head. "I got it."

"Just for a minute." Jackson stood from his seat, striding to the back of the boat to help Ryder with the pole. Then he took the empty seat at the back. "Look kid, we gotta talk."

Ryder's entire body tensed. "Are you getting rid of me?"

"What? No." Jackson put a hand on Ryder's knee. "What did Mom tell you about me?"

"Not much. Just that I had an older brother but he didn't live with her."

"Because she dumped me. She took me to New York and left me with her sister. Except her sister didn't want me so I went into foster care. Long story short, I jumped from home to home until high school. It sucked but I got to meet Hazel and Thea, which eventually led me here."

"Mom left you too?"

Jackson nodded. "Yeah. She did."

"But she never came back?"

"No."

Ryder's head fell, his entire frame slumping in his seat. "She comes back for me."

My teeth gritted together. The cold from earlier was completely gone now that I was angry. Jackson had suspected she'd left him before, and he'd been right.

I hated Melissa Page. That woman was such a *bitch*.

"She's left you before?" Jackson asked.

Ryder nodded. "She does it a lot. She leaves me for a while, then comes back to get me. She promised me last time was it. That we were coming up here to see you and be a family. But it was just more of her bullshit."

The curse word from his mouth startled me.

Ryder cussed with ease, so I knew it wasn't the first time. I didn't like that it made him sound much older than twelve. He shouldn't have things to cuss about at that age, not yet.

Though for his mother, I'd say *bullshit* too.

"So she comes back?" Jackson asked.

"Yeah. She disappears but comes back eventually to take me with her."

"Not this time." Jackson shook his head. "She's not taking you again. You're here."

Ryder studied Jackson's face, like he didn't believe that could be true. "Really?"

"Really, kid. We'll make sure she can't take you again."

Tears welled in Ryder's brown eyes. He sniffled, trying to clear them up, but a week's worth of high emotions was too much. He broke down, slouching in his seat, and cried. Jackson's hand stayed on his knee the entire time.

Jackson looked at me, his face a mixture of fury at his mother and pain for his brother. I gave him a reassuring smile and hoped he knew he wasn't in this alone.

Melissa Page might not realize it yet, but she'd lost both of her sons. Now that they'd found each other, they wouldn't need her ever again.

It took a few minutes for Ryder to calm down, and when he did, he pulled in few shaking breaths before looking at Jackson. "I don't want to go with her again."

"You won't," Jackson declared. "I'll go talk to a lawyer on Monday. We'll figure out a way for me to become your legal guardian. But that means you need to tell us all about the past. I gotta know what happened with you and Mom. No surprises."

"Okay." Ryder nodded. "Like what do you want to know?"

"Well, to start, let's go over where you were living. Las Vegas, right?"

Ryder had given us enough information about his school that I'd been able to call and get the records transferred up to Lark Cove. But other than the school's name in Las Vegas, we didn't know much else. They would only transfer the records to the school so I hadn't gotten to see them.

"Yeah. We lived in Vegas for a while with Mom's boyfriend. Christopher." Ryder rolled his eyes. "He's an asshole."

"Why'd you guys leave Vegas?"

"Christopher dumped Mom. They got in a big fight one night, and the next morning, Mom loaded us up and drove us to Denver. That's when she got the idea to come looking for you."

Because she'd needed a place to leave her kid.

"Where did you live before Vegas?" I asked Ryder.

"All over. Kansas. Alabama. Iowa. I was born in West Virginia."

Which meant after Melissa had abandoned Jackson in New York, she likely hadn't gone back to Pennsylvania where he'd been born. She'd slowly made her way out West.

"What kind of jobs did she have?" Jackson asked.

Ryder shrugged. "None really. She always had a guy or something. A couple times we lived alone, but it never lasted."

"And who'd she leave you with when she'd disappear?" I

asked. "Was it other family? Or your dad?"

"No. I don't know my dad. She never told me his name. Mostly, she left me with her friends and neighbors. It was never for long. A couple weeks and then she'd be back. The longest was a month."

If that pattern continued, it meant she'd be back and back soon.

As harsh as it sounded in my head, I wished she'd do to Ryder what she'd done to Jackson—leave and never look back. It would be hard for Ryder, but I still felt like it would be better for him never to see that woman again.

"Did she say she was coming back?" Jackson asked.

Ryder shook his head. "Not this time."

Jackson and I shared a look, wishing for the exact same thing.

We both wanted Melissa Page to just become a bad memory.

The fishing pole in the holder whizzed and the line strung tight, ending our conversation. Jackson and Ryder both jumped into action, springing for the reel. I took out my phone and walked to the back of the boat, videoing the entire thing as the guys brought in a beautiful rainbow trout.

We took a picture, commemorating Ryder's first fish, then set it free.

After the excitement from the first fish, we didn't talk about Ryder's past again or their mother. We just enjoyed our afternoon and looked on as Ryder caught three other fish.

I'd made us peanut butter and jelly sandwiches for the boat, but by the time we made it back to Jackson's house and parked the boat in his garage, I was starving.

"I'm so hungry," Ryder and I said it at the same time, then shared a look and laughed.

"How about we all get cleaned up and go out to dinner in Kalispell?" Jackson suggested as we all came inside the house and piled coats onto his living room couch.

"Sounds great." I smiled.

"Cool! I'll get in the shower." Ryder disappeared down the hall to his room on the other side of the house from Jackson's bedroom.

"I know what I want for my birthday," Jackson said, stepping close.

"What's that?"

He bent and gave me a soft kiss, pressing his hips and the growing bulge behind his jeans forward. "Shower with me?"

I let out a soft moan. "Well, I might have gotten you a little something else, but a shower sounds nice too."

I'd gotten him a new pair of boots for his birthday. The soles of his others were coming loose so I'd splurged. These were the same style as the ones he already had, but new and the nicest brand on the market.

"Maybe we should get a little dirty before we clean up?" I whispered as he kissed my neck.

"I like the way you think, Willow."

"Willow? You jerkface!" I poked his side, trying not to laugh.

He grinned. "Still too soon to joke about that, huh?"

"Since it's your birthday I'll let it slide."

"Thanks." He kissed me again, this time letting his tongue linger a bit on my bottom lip. He pulled away, but instead of heat in his eyes and a playful grin, Jackson's face had a hint of worry.

"What's wrong?"

He sighed. "I just keep thinking that she'll be back."

"Me too. But if she does, then we'll deal."

He dropped his forehead to mine. "Thanks for everything. For helping get Ryder settled this week. For helping me."

"You don't have to thank me." I wrapped my arms around his waist, snuggling into his chest. "We're a team."

He hummed.

But he didn't say anything else.

twenty

WILLA

"SO WHAT'S NEW?" HANNAH ASKED ME AND LEIGHTON. She was sitting across from us in a booth at Bob's Diner. "You two have been so busy lately we've hardly seen you."

I sighed. "Sorry. Things have just been a little crazy."

It had been a month since the fishing expedition on Jackson's birthday. Ryder was getting into a rhythm at school. Jackson was adjusting to being a stand-in parent. And I was doing everything in my power to help them both, which meant dinner with my girlfriends had been skipped—a lot.

Actually, dinners with June and Hannah had been few and far between ever since I'd started dating Jackson. I'd canceled on dinner with them more times than accepted, mostly to spend time with him.

Truth be told, I didn't really feel like being here tonight either, but the guilt of being a bad friend had eaten away at me. When Hannah had called, I hadn't been able to say no.

Ryder was sleeping over at the cottage tonight with Hazel, and what I really wanted was to spend the evening with Jackson at the bar, then sleep at my apartment, since we hadn't been there in forever.

But I also missed the girls, especially Leighton.

"How are things going with Brendon?" June asked Leighton, waggling her eyebrows.

My best friend smiled that dreamy smile she'd been wearing for months. "Amazing."

"They're in love." I swooned, nudging her shoulder with my own.

"We so are." Leighton and Brendon were nearly inseparable these days, and she'd missed about as many girls' dinners as I had.

While I hadn't seen much of Hannah or June, Leighton and I always made time for each other. She knew all about me and Jackson. I knew all about her and Brendon. And I had a hunch that those two would be headed down the aisle before long.

I was overjoyed that she'd found a man who loved her un-conditionally. And that she'd found someone to confide in about her assault besides me.

"Aren't you jealous, Willa?" June teased. "She took your man."

"No." I laughed, toying with the paper wrapper I'd stripped from my straw. "I have a man, thank you very much."

"How are things going with Jackson?" Hannah asked.

"Wonderful."

"Obviously," June said, fanning her face. "I mean just look at that man. Those eyes. That ass. He's so damn hot. I bet he's good in bed too. God knows he's had a lot of practice. If there was a guy I wanted to fool around with before finding my husband, I'd pick Jackson too."

My entire body stilled. "We're not fooling around. We're together."

"Oh, Willa." She gave me a pitying smile. "Come on. Jackson's not that kind of guy."

"What kind of guy?"

"The kind you marry. He's the one you fuck senseless *before* you find the guy to settle down with and have kids."

"What? That's not . . . no. It's not like that."

Somehow in a matter of seconds, she'd cheapened my most special relationship. And she made him out to be some kind of insensitive man whore. Yes, Jackson had experience and I hated thinking about it. But none of that mattered now. It was in the past and his future was with me.

"Have you guys talked about getting married?" Hannah asked.

"Um, no."

Hannah and June shared a smug look.

"They don't need to talk about that yet," Leighton said, coming to my defense.

"Have you and Brendon talked about it?" June asked.

"Well, yeah. But Willa and Jackson are different."

We are? "Why?"

"Not in a bad way," Leighton said. "You're just at a different point in your relationship. Brendon and I are moving at warp speed, talking about getting married and having kids. We both want that. You and Jackson are still getting to know one another. You're not as serious yet."

Not as serious? Had she not been listening to me during all of our phone calls when I'd spilled my guts about every tidbit of my relationship?

"We are *just* as serious. I love Jackson." I hadn't told him yet, but he knew. Didn't he? And he loved me too. There's no way we could connect like we did and not be in love.

"You can love someone without marrying them," Hannah said.

"You can fuck someone without marrying them too," June snickered.

"Stop it. Stop saying f-fuck."

She rolled her eyes. "Sorry. I didn't realize we were back in high school."

"I don't care if you say fuck." *Gosh, it sounds stupid when I cuss.* "I just don't like you saying it when it comes to me and Jackson. We're not just having casual sex. We have something special."

"I'm just trying to be your friend," Hannah said. "Jackson doesn't seem like a guy who wants the whole marriage, babies, Sunday-brunch-with-your-parents thing. He's what, five years older than we are?"

"Six," I corrected now that he'd had his birthday.

"Whatever. Don't you think if he wanted to get married, he would have by now?"

The sting of angry—no, furious—tears pricked my eyes. Jackson hadn't gotten married because he hadn't found the right woman yet. *Me.*

I refused to believe anything else.

Why couldn't my friends just be supportive? Why did they always make me feel ridiculous and naïve?

I dug into my purse and yanked out some cash from my wallet. We'd ordered, but it hadn't arrived yet, so I threw it down in the middle of our empty table, then slid out of the booth with my purse and winter coat in hand.

"Willa," Leighton said. "Wait. We didn't mean to make you upset."

I turned around. "None of you know how my relationship works. None of you know Jackson. All you've ever made me feel was pathetic for having a crush on him."

"It is," June muttered.

Hannah shushed her and Leighton shot her a glare.

"You know what's pathetic?" I snapped at June, stepping

right up to the table. "You. You come here and try to embarrass me with all your talk of sex and *fucking*. You try to make me feel stupid for loving a man who deserves it. I don't give a crap what you think about Jackson or me. It's none of your damn business, so butt out."

All three faces at the table stared up at me like I'd gone bonkers. My outburst was so out of character it even surprised me a bit.

"He's the best thing that's ever happened to me," I told them. "He might not be ready to get married today, but you know what? Neither am I. And the bottom line is, it is none. Of. Your. Business."

With that, I spun back around and marched for the door. I wasted no time getting into my car and peeling out of the parking lot, driving straight to the bar.

I drove straight to the man who'd make it all better.

"Hey, babe." Jackson smiled as I walked through the door. But as I stomped across the room, my shoes crunching peanut shells, his smile dropped. "Uh-oh. What happened at dinner? Did they burn your cheeseburger?"

"No." I slumped into a stool. "I kind of yelled at my friends."

He chuckled. "They must have deserved it then. My girl doesn't get riled up much."

They had deserved it. Maybe. June had for sure. Except I felt bad for lumping Leighton into the mix, and Hannah had been genuinely trying to give me advice.

Jackson walked around the corner of the bar, taking the stool next to mine. He spun me to face him so my legs were between his.

"What happened?" he asked gently.

"Nothing." I waved it off. "I don't want to talk about it."

Discussing the diner situation would involve me asking

Jackson if he wanted to get married and I didn't want to freak him out.

"Are you sure?" he asked.

"Yeah. I'm just glad to be here now."

"Me too." He leaned forward, giving me a soft kiss.

"See?" I whispered. "All better."

He cupped my face in his hand and I leaned into his palm. We sat there, just staring at one another for a moment until the door opened and Leighton walked in with apology written all over her face.

"Hey, Leighton," he greeted.

"Hi, Jackson."

"I'll give you two a minute." He slid off his stool, kissing my forehead. "Are you hungry?"

I nodded. "Yeah. I didn't eat."

"Okay. I'll make you something. Be back."

Leighton took the seat Jackson had abandoned as he strode behind the bar and disappeared down the hall toward the kitchen.

"I'm sorry," we both said at the same time, then laughed.

"You were right," she said. "It's your relationship. Don't let any of us tell you what's right or wrong. Just follow your heart."

"He is my heart. He always has been."

Leighton smiled. "I know. And there's nothing pathetic about that."

"June thinks so."

She scoffed. "June is jealous and always has been, which makes her opinion invalid."

"Maybe," I muttered. "I still feel bad for snapping at her and Hannah."

"Don't feel bad. They deserved it, we all did. I'm glad you stood up for yourself."

It wasn't so much me I'd stood up for but my relationship

with Jackson. Where he was concerned, I had a lot more spirit than usual.

"I'm starving." Leighton's stomach growled. "Would you care if I invited Brendon down to share a pizza?"

I smiled. "Not at all."

Two hours later, my bad mood from the diner was gone and my stomach was full of my favorite pizza.

"I like the way he looks at you," I told Leighton after Brendon excused himself for the restroom.

She giggled. "I was just thinking the exact same thing about Jackson."

I looked down the bar, where Jackson was cashing out a customer's tab. He gave me a wink when he caught me watching.

"Can I ask you something?"

She nodded. "Of course."

"When did you tell Brendon you loved him?" The pair had said it a couple of times throughout the night. It had been lovey-dovey and so cute.

Leighton and I had been talking constantly about our boyfriends, but I hadn't asked her for specifics about when they'd exchanged the words. I just knew they said them and often.

"About a month ago. Why?"

I shrugged. "Just curious. Did he say it first?"

"Technically, no." She smiled. "We were at his place one Friday night about a month ago and we'd each had a few glasses of wine. He was all glassy-eyed and smiley. We started kissing, but then he stopped and asked, 'Do you love me?' I couldn't lie to him so . . . I said it. Then he said it back."

Leighton looked over her shoulder to make sure Brendon wasn't coming back, then she leaned in close. "He was so happy that he let me sit on his face for almost an hour."

My cheeks flushed as she giggled and took another drink of

her beer.

"I, um . . . we haven't done that before," I whispered.

"You're missing out."

I made a mental note to ask Jackson about it later. With him, all of our boundaries had been erased and I felt comfortable asking him about sex. June might judge him for his "experience," but I was reaping the benefits.

"Ready to go, sweetheart?" Brendon asked, appearing at Leighton's side. They really were a beautiful couple, each tall with dark hair. Their babies would be enormous.

She nodded, drinking the last swig of her beer. "All set."

They each pulled on their coats and hugged me good-bye before saying the same to Jackson. Then they left us to an empty bar, walking out the door hand in hand.

"Let's close up," Jackson said, leaning across the bar.

I stood on the railing, meeting him in the middle for a kiss. "My place?"

He nodded. "Yeah. I've missed you."

"I've missed you too."

It wasn't like the two of us didn't see each other every day, but with Ryder and all the other things happening, it hadn't just been us.

We closed down the bar in record time and Jackson followed me in his truck back to my house. I missed our summer strolls along the sidewalk, but with winter coming, we wouldn't be walking again until spring.

The minute we got inside my apartment, Jackson attacked my mouth, his lips ravenous for my own. Just like always, I met his ferocity beat for beat, stripping off my own clothes as he shrugged out of his.

"Jackson," I panted between kisses. "I want to try something."

His mouth moved down the column of my neck as he whipped off his flannel shirt. "What?"

I unzipped my jeans. "I want to sit on your face."

He stilled, leaning back with a grin. "Yeah?"

My cheeks felt hot. "Yeah."

"Fuck, yeah." His hands gripped my hips, picking me up off the floor. In two fast strides, he'd tossed me onto the bed.

I giggled at the wolfish grin on his face. "When did you decide you wanted to try this?" he asked as he yanked off my knee-high brown boots.

"Leighton." I tugged my sweater over my head and unclasped my bra.

"I knew I liked her." He chuckled. "Get your jeans off."

I did as I was told, wiggling them free from my hips so he could pull them to the floor.

"Up." He ordered me to my knees. "Panties off."

I obeyed, the excitement running through my blood making my fingers fumble on my thong. But as soon as I had it around my ankles, I kicked it to the floor.

Jackson still had his jeans on. They were unbuttoned, hanging from the delicious V that I loved to trace with my tongue. When I reached for the zipper, he grabbed my wrist and stopped me. "Leave them."

He climbed on the bed, lying right in the middle on his back. His gorgeous face looked up at me like I was his last meal.

"Get over here, babe."

"Okay," I breathed. "Where?"

He pointed to his mouth. "Right. Here."

A shiver ran over my shoulders as I straddled his waist. Then inch by inch, I scooted my knees forward. My center hovered over his washboard abs, then over the valley between his hard pecs. Finally, he helped me over his arms so my knees were planted right by his ears.

"Grab the headboard."

I nodded, placing my hands on the frame in front of me. "Like this?"

"Mm-hmm." He hummed right against my pussy. "Hold on tight." The feel of his hot breath on my clit made my inner walls quiver.

Jackson dragged his tongue along my slit in a slow, torturous motion.

"Oh. My. God." My head lulled to the side as he did it again.

"You taste so fucking good, Willa."

I moaned as his hands came from underneath my legs, gripping the curve of my ass. His fingertips dug in hard, sending a rush of heat to my core.

"Now ride my face."

I wasn't sure what he meant, but as his mouth latched onto my clit, alternating between sucking and lapping me up with his flat tongue, my body figured it out fast.

My knees and legs were shaking as I rocked against his mouth and his stubble tickled the insides of my thighs.

The cries that came from my chest were free and loud, filling my small apartment with pure ecstasy as Jackson added his own groans.

"I'm going to come," I gasped.

He responded with a hard suck on my clit, sending me over the edge. Pulse after pulse, I came over his mouth. He kept me from falling with his hands, and when I was a boneless mess, still quaking from the aftershocks, he carefully helped me off his face.

"Wowzah." I swiped the sweaty hair from my forehead as I took Jackson's place with my back on the bed.

"Liked that, huh?" He smirked as he worked off his jeans.

When his thick, hard cock bobbed free, I licked my lips.

"My turn?" I suggested, but he shook his head.

"I'm going to come inside you tonight and not in your mouth." With a tight fist, he stroked his swollen flesh up and down until a glistening drop formed at the tip. He kneeled on the bed, letting go of his cock so he could grab my knees and spread them wide.

"I missed you," he whispered, lining himself up with my entrance.

"I missed you too."

I held his eyes as he inched inside, stretching me as he buried himself deep. Then he bent, touching his forehead to mine, and let go of all restraint. He drove us up high, using hard and fast strokes until I was whimpering and ready to explode. His big hands came to my breasts, tugging on my nipples and the sensation sent me over the edge.

I cried out, practically screaming his name as he dropped his face into my hair and shot his hot release inside me.

Yes, Jackson had fucked me. It had been hard and rough and perfect. But it hadn't been the cheap sex June and Hannah bragged about. Jackson and I fucked and we loved.

We had both.

I was delirious as he fell to my side, pulling me over his chest to hold me while we regained our breath.

"I missed you." It was the third time he'd told me tonight.

"I'm right here."

"I know." He sighed. "We just haven't had this for a while. Just me and you."

I softly kissed his chest. "It will get easier."

"Yeah." He hugged me tight before letting me go to use the bathroom and clean up. When I came back out to the bedroom, he'd climbed beneath the covers. Normally, he always tugged the quilt down so it wouldn't get messy, but we'd been in such a hurry tonight, he'd forgotten.

I climbed into bed, snuggling my naked little spoon into his naked big spoon.

As I closed my eyes, a rush of pity for Hannah and June hit, not because I'd snapped at them, but because they didn't have this. They might get the sex, but they were missing this part. They were missing the love.

Jackson's breathing began to draw out, his body not far from sleep. So before he could conk out, I whispered his name.

"Hmm?"

I took a deep breath. "Do you love me?"

His arms around me jerked and his body stilled.

My eyes shot open, staring at the nightstand as I waited for a response.

It wasn't the one I wanted.

Jackson relaxed his arms and kissed my hair. "Get some sleep, babe."

twenty-one

WILLA

"WE HAVEN'T HAD LUNCH TOGETHER HERE IN A LONG time," Dad said.

"No, we haven't." I smiled.

The last time I remembered coming to the school to eat lunch in his classroom was when I'd gotten my job as director at the camp. I'd made us peanut butter and jelly sandwiches, then come down to surprise him with the good news.

Just like then, he was on his side of his tall desk, I was on the other. In the corner was the same periodic chart that had been there for decades. The cabinets at the back of the room were full of beakers and Bunsen burners. Above us was a replica of the solar system I'd helped him make a few summers ago.

"Remember in high school when you'd come here on Thursdays to eat with me?"

I nodded. "Best lunch day of the week."

I'd ditch my friends in the cafeteria to come and eat with Dad. Once, a kid in my gym class had made a snide comment about it, calling me a daddy's girl. I'd just shrugged and walked away because it was true. I was a daddy's girl. Spending forty-five minutes in his classroom had never been an embarrassment.

Most of those lunches, Dad and I would talk about my homework or my friends. If something was bothering me, his classroom was my escape.

Like today.

"Is there something wrong, honey?"

I swallowed a bite of my sandwich and chased it down with a swig of Coke. "No," I lied.

He frowned. "Willa."

"It's nothing." I was lying to myself too.

The last two weeks had been miserable. Ever since I'd asked Jackson if he loved me, things between us had been off-kilter.

We still saw each other every day, but he was distracted. He didn't laugh with me anymore and the rare smile he'd give was forced. Whenever I asked him if he was okay, he'd get irritated and tell me he just had a lot on his mind.

Maybe a braver woman would have pestered and pressed him until he admitted what was bothering him. Maybe she would have stood up to him, demanding he lose the grumpy attitude.

But I wasn't that woman. I let him be a grouch during the day because at night, he'd still sleep with me in his arms.

Jackson might not want to talk to me much, but he didn't seem to have any trouble taking me to bed.

Was it pathetic that I let him? Maybe a woman who didn't love him so much would have cut him off.

But I just couldn't. On the nights when Jackson wasn't working, I went to his house to make dinner for him and Ryder. We'd eat, then all watch TV on his worn leather couch.

The nights when Jackson worked, Ryder would stay with Hazel. He didn't invite me down to the bar to spend the evening with him. He was spending more and more time at the bar during the day too. Whenever I'd ask him to go to lunch or hang out, he'd be meeting with Thea or helping Hazel with this or that.

Still, he'd show up at my apartment in the midnight hours.

I never once pushed him away as he crawled into my bed.

"You can always talk to me," Dad said.

"I know. Thank you for that." But this was a conversation for Mom or maybe Leighton. I needed some female advice.

"Ryder seems to be adjusting to school just fine."

"I think he is too." I nodded. "He's a great kid. And it sounds like he's already made some friends."

Dad grinned. "From what I've seen, he's Mr. Popular."

"I'm not surprised at all."

Dad and Ryder had met a few weeks ago, but since Dad wasn't his teacher, they didn't see one another often. Though I was glad both he and Leighton were here to keep an eye on Ryder.

I wasn't just in love with Jackson. His little brother had me wrapped around his finger.

Ryder was sweet and funny. His handsome face was constantly smiling and there was a twinkle in his eye that reminded me of his brother's. It showed a lot these days, especially since Jackson had petitioned the district court to become his legal guardian. It was amazing how a set of papers waiting to be evaluated by a judge could erase a mountain of worries from a young boy's mind.

He was the only reason why things between Jackson and I weren't miserably uncomfortable. Ryder provided a buffer on the evenings we spent together. Jackson didn't have trouble giving him gentle smiles or laughing at stories about Ryder's new adventures at school.

It was just me who he was pulling away from.

And it was all my fault.

I'd been so worked up by my friends' comments that I'd pushed Jackson too soon. He wasn't ready to confess his feelings.

For all I knew, he'd never said those words to anyone before.

I refused to believe that he didn't love me. *He did.* This was just a big step for him and he needed time. The idea that he didn't love me, or never would, hurt so badly I couldn't breathe.

Was it pathetic to live in denial?

My perpetual boredom didn't help. With nothing to do all day, I thought about Jackson constantly. I needed a distraction.

"I'm bored," I told Dad. *And lonely.*

He laughed. "Well, if bored means you'll come eat lunch with me, I can't complain."

"I wish I could have found a job this winter. There are only about five hours of work a week to do at the camp and I'm going crazy. I was thinking of expanding my search to Kalispell."

It was only thirty miles away but driving up there every day in the winter had never been appealing. The highway that wound around the lake was often covered in ice this time of year, so a thirty-minute drive could easily take twice as long. When it got really bad, they'd close the road entirely.

But with nothing else to do but sit at home alone and fret, it might be worth risking the roads.

"What kind of job do you want?" Dad asked.

"My options are limited. I don't want to take a job where they'd be counting on me to work for longer than a few months. So it doesn't leave much. I was thinking maybe seasonal holiday work. I bet I could find something at the mall for Christmas."

Though I doubted I'd be all that good in a retail shop. I wasn't exactly the outgoing salesperson type. But a holiday job would get me through January. Then I'd only have a few months to wait until things picked back up at the camp.

"I don't know." I picked at the crust of my sandwich. "I'll start looking and see what's open."

Footsteps echoed down the empty hallway, and out of habit,

Dad and I both turned to stare at the door.

When Jackson passed by with an angry scowl on his face, I nearly fell out of my seat. What was he doing at school? Was there a problem with Ryder?

Before I flew out of my chair, Dad was off his, walking to the door to call Jackson into his classroom.

Jackson followed Dad into the room, looking tired and worried. The moment he saw me, a smile tugged at his lips, but then it fell.

That's what always happened. It was like he forgot for a second to be disappointed with my presence.

My goodness, it hurt.

"Hi." I waved, not getting up.

"Hey." He came over and bent to kiss me on the cheek.

He hadn't kissed me on the lips since the night I'd asked him if he loved me, not even when we were in bed together. He kissed me everywhere else—the forehead, my neck, on top of my hair—but not the lips.

Every kiss on the cheek made my heart sink. It put more distance between us. He was standing right by my side, but he might as well be orbiting around a different sun.

All because I'd asked him one silly question.

Do you love me?

No. No, he did not.

And pathetic, stupid, naïve me didn't care. I stayed with him anyway.

"So what brings you here?" Dad asked Jackson, though he was staring at me. The worry on his face made my heart ache even more.

Jackson rubbed his jaw and sighed. "Had a meeting with Ryder's teachers."

"Is everything okay?" I asked.

"No. He's behind the other kids. They said we need to start thinking about holding him back a grade."

"What?" I gasped. "But it's only November. The school year's not even halfway over yet. Why would they want to talk about that now?" My last question was aimed at Dad.

"How far behind is he?" Dad asked Jackson.

"Far enough that they don't think there's any way to catch up."

"Sorry," Dad said. "I didn't realize."

How would he? He wasn't Ryder's teacher; otherwise he would have given us a heads-up much sooner.

"Is there anything we can do?" I asked.

"No." Jackson sighed. "There's nothing I can do."

I said *we*. He said *I*.

"Tutoring," Dad suggested. "One-on-one help makes a big difference. It might get him caught up enough to at least be able to stay in the right grade. He probably won't get perfect grades, but at least he won't fall behind. And if you keep it up, maybe by the time he gets to high school, he'll be on the right track."

"I'm no tutor." Jackson shook his head. "I barely passed school myself."

"I could tutor him." My eyes met Dad's, a grin playing on his face. He was already five steps ahead of me.

Maybe I wouldn't need that job in Kalispell. I loved spending time with Ryder and it would give me something to do. It was perfect.

Except Jackson shut me down. "Nah. You're busy. I'll just see if Hazel or Thea could help."

My shoulders fell. He knew I wasn't busy and he knew I would love to help Ryder. But he wasn't even going to let me do that.

The writing was all over the chalkboard. Jackson was pulling away from me before he made the clean break. He didn't want me tutoring his brother because he had no plans to keep me around.

"Well, that's probably for the best anyway, Willa," Dad said. "You can't be tutoring Ryder if you're going to get a job in Kalispell."

"What?" Jackson's eyes snapped to mine. "You're getting a job in Kalispell?"

I shrugged. "Maybe."

"It's winter." He planted his hands on his hips. "As soon as the snow sticks, the roads will be shit. You're not driving up there every day."

This man confused me to death. He didn't want me around, but he didn't want me to drive to Kalispell for a job to keep me occupied.

"Then I guess you'll have time to tutor Ryder," Dad said, trying not to smile.

Jackson dropped his gaze to the piece of paper in his hands. It looked to be some sort of report card. After a heavy sigh, he nodded and handed it over. "Fine. Let me talk to Ryder after school and tell him what's up."

"Okay." I took the paper, seeing a list of Ryder's classes with his grades next to each. Every single one was an F.

"I gotta go." He turned around and took two steps but then stopped. He came back, gave me a quick kiss on the forehead, then waved to Dad. "Later, Nate."

"Bye, Jackson." Dad waved back.

Neither Dad nor I spoke as Jackson's boots echoed down the hallway.

"I'm losing him," I whispered. "He's just . . . drifting away."

Dad reached across the table to place his hand over mine. "Then pull him back."

My chin quivered. "I don't know how."

"Talk to him. Don't just let him drift away. If your relationship is going to end, you deserve to know why. Stand up for yourself, honey."

"You know I'm not good at that."

Dad patted my hand. "I think you're a lot better at confrontation than you think. You just choose your battles."

I didn't want to fight this battle, because I wouldn't win.

Jackson had all the weapons. He held my heart in the palm of his hand.

How was I supposed to fight? I couldn't demand that he fall in love with me. I couldn't make him feel those things.

When we ended, I'd be shattered. My life would be forever changed. I couldn't stay in Lark Cove without him, not with memories of us together around every corner. I'd end up leaving my beloved camp. My parents. My home.

Everything.

"Do you have dinner with the girls tonight?" Dad asked, always knowing when to change the subject.

Though that topic wasn't much better.

"No, not tonight. June and I are kind of fighting. And you know Hannah, she always takes June's side."

Dad nodded. "And Leighton always takes yours."

"Yeah."

I hadn't called June or Hannah since the night at the diner two weeks ago. I would eventually—we'd been friends too long to just throw it all away—but I wasn't quite ready yet. And I didn't know how I'd face them if they ended up being right about Jackson.

"What happened with you girls?" Dad asked.

I gave him a sad smile. "I stood up for myself."

And look where it had gotten me.

"So how did Ryder take it?" I asked Jackson later that night.

We were lying in his bed, him on his side, me on mine. It was another thing that had changed these last two weeks.

There was no more spooning.

"About as well as you'd think," Jackson muttered. "He doesn't want to get held back."

"He's smart. We'll get him caught up."

"We might not," he said. "The fact is, Mom was too busy dragging him all over the country to worry about keeping him in school. He might have to repeat this year. So don't promise him something that might not happen."

"Okay," I whispered, wounded by his sharp tone.

A chill settled into the bed as silence consumed the room. I'd never wanted to escape Jackson's bed before, but right now, I just wanted to go home and cry.

"I think I'm going to go." I sat up, ready to run away, but Jackson grabbed my shoulder, forcing it down and back into the mattress. It was the first time he'd touched me since I'd come over after dinner.

"Stay." He sighed. "I'm sorry. It's just . . . let's get some sleep."

It was only nine o'clock. Jackson was a night owl, so nine o'clock to him was like five o'clock to others. We'd never gone to bed this early, which showed me just how much he wanted to avoid any sort of conversation.

"Fine." I settled back into my pillow.

I didn't feel like staying, but I also didn't want to go home. It felt like once I left here, that would be the beginning of our end.

I burrowed under the covers, bringing them all the way up

to my ears. Then I turned my back on Jackson, curling into a little ball so I'd stay warm. Without his arms around me, I'd be cold tonight.

Then with tears prickling my eyes, I drifted off to sleep.

Hours later, in the dead of night, I woke up cold and alone.

"Jackson?" I sat up in bed, swinging the covers off my legs.

He wasn't in bed or in the bathroom, so I got up and pulled on a sweatshirt to go searching. His hushed voice came from the living room and it sounded like he was on the phone, but I hadn't heard it ring.

By the time I made it to the bedroom door, the front door opened and closed. I hurried down the hallway toward the living room but was too late. I walked to the front window just in time to see Jackson's truck pulling out of his driveway. It had started snowing and his headlights illuminated the flakes as he backed onto the road and drove away.

Was something wrong? Was it Thea or Hazel? Rushing back to the bedroom, I swiped my phone from the nightstand. My finger hovered over his name, ready to call, but I stopped.

If he'd wanted to share, he would have told me. He would have woken me up before he disappeared in the middle of the night.

His silence was just another rejection. It was another dagger to my heart.

I clutched my phone to my chest and crawled back in bed, hoping he'd call.

He didn't.

Three hours and seven minutes later, I heard his truck pull back into the drive. Then a few moments later, the front door opened and closed. He stomped his boots and thudded down the hallway.

I kept my eyes closed and stayed curled into my little ball, pretending to be asleep. My body was perfectly still as I listened to him strip off his clothes. The entire time I wished he'd say something and explain where he'd been.

He didn't.

He finished undressing, crawled into bed and passed out.

When he began snoring, I rolled over to study his face. As I leaned closer, a heartbreaking smell filled my nose.

My boyfriend had left me alone in his bed only to come back hours later smelling like tequila and women's perfume.

twenty-two

JACKSON

"RYDER, WHAT WOULD YOU LIKE TO DRINK?" BETTY ASKED as she opened the refrigerator in her kitchen. "I've got apple juice, milk, water, lemonade and SunnyD. That was Willa's favorite when she was your age. Oh, and Nate bought a case of Sprite because he is trying to give up Coke. Don't ask me how trading one soda for another will help him quit the former because his reasoning makes no sense."

"It makes perfect sense," Nate said, walking into the kitch-en. "I don't like Sprite."

"See?" Betty winked at my brother. "No sense."

Ryder laughed. "I'll try the SunnyD."

"You got it. Jackson, what would you like?"

"Water, please."

Betty nodded. "You guys make yourselves at home. I'll get your drinks and come find you."

"Can I help cook?" Ryder asked her. "Willa's been teaching me."

"A young chef. I like it." Betty smiled as she filled a glass with ice. "Yes, you can help. You can help Willa peel the sweet potatoes."

I glanced over at Willa at the sink. The moment we'd walked into the house, she'd gone right for the kitchen, practically ripping the potato peeler out of her mom's hand to take over.

She looked over her shoulder at me, then turned her eyes down. She'd barely made eye contact with me over the last week. And whenever she did look at me, the pain in her eyes nearly broke me apart.

It was Thanksgiving and we were spending it with her family. Two months ago, I would have looked forward to a day at Nate and Betty's place, eating a big meal. Maybe watching some football.

But now, I was coming out of my skin.

The last place I wanted to be was with Willa's family. I didn't want Ryder bonding with them. I didn't want Nate and Betty to think this would be a new tradition.

This would be the one and only holiday he or I spent with the Doons.

The time for my inevitable split with Willa was here.

I should have cut her free sooner, but I'd been a coward. A big dumb coward. I hadn't been able to walk away from her, because I wanted her too much. I needed her too much.

She kept me calm and collected. She'd been the one to keep me sane as I'd tried to fit Ryder into my life. Being the selfish asshole that I was, I'd clung to her because I needed her, and in the process, I'd let her get in too deep.

She was in love with me.

Somehow, I'd fooled her into thinking I was the kind of man she should love.

The night she'd asked me if I loved her, I should have ended it. I should have climbed out of her bed and walked away. But did I do the right thing? No, I'd just kept holding on, and in the process, I was hurting her. I told myself it would be just one more night. One more kiss on her hair. One more time to hold her in my arms.

One more time, then I'd let her go.

Except I still hadn't worked up the nerve to say good-bye. I'd held on too long and now I was here with her family, getting ready to eat a turkey dinner that I sure as fuck didn't deserve.

"So what do you normally do for Thanksgiving, Jackson?" Betty asked as she handed me my water.

"Thank you." I forced a smile. "Normally I spend it with Hazel and Thea at the cottage."

"Ahh. And where are they this year?"

"At Thea and Logan's new place."

They'd invited Ryder and me to come over, but Nate and Betty had already planned on having us here. Besides that, I couldn't be around Thea and Logan right now. They were too happy.

Thea had announced this week that she was pregnant. She and Logan were over the moon to be having a baby and Charlie was thrilled to be a big sister.

I was glad for them, but it was more change. I suspected Thea would eventually quit the bar—her husband was a billionaire so she didn't need to work. They'd have more kids and get on with their lives. I wouldn't be surprised if they moved to New York one day.

Sooner or later, everyone leaves.

I watched Willa as she worked on the potatoes. Her long, beautiful hair was streaming down her back. She'd spent time curling it this morning, something she didn't do that often, but I loved it when she did. She'd tamed the natural waves into these perfect swirls and the tips swished delicately at her waist.

I wanted to walk over, pull her into my arms and take a deep breath of that hair. I wanted to pull in the smell, just one more time. Instead, I shied toward the back wall of the kitchen, getting as far away from her as the room would allow.

Willa hadn't stayed a night at my house for the last week, not since I'd gotten that late-night phone call to come down to the bar. Not since I'd made one of the biggest fucking mistakes of my life.

I missed her in my bed. It wouldn't be the same without her.

Ryder said something to Willa as they peeled potatoes side by side and it made her smile.

That smile was sheer agony.

I was going to miss her so damn much, and I knew nothing would ever fill that void.

I'd never forget the musical sound of her laugh. I'd never forget those silly words she'd make up or the breakfasts she'd cooked me in her apartment.

I'd never forget the way it felt to have her in my arms as she drifted off to sleep.

"Well, I'd better go out and check my fryer," Nate said, popping the top on a can of Sprite. He took a sip and grimaced. "Jackson, feel like some fresh air?"

"Sure." Fresh air and some distance from Willa sounded like a great idea. I pushed off the wall and followed him to the back deck.

"Have you ever deep-fried a turkey?" Nate stepped through the sliding door and into the cold.

"I haven't. Thea always makes them in the oven."

"We normally do too, but I've been wanting to try this for years now. Betty made us do a test run a couple of weeks ago just to make sure I knew what I was doing. Dang, it's good. This will be the best bird you've ever had in your life."

"I believe it." I took a long breath of the cool air as he turned on his fryer.

I let my eyes wander over their backyard and across the school's playground.

I'd never be able to look at those swing sets again. I'd never be able to walk across a wide lawn and not think of climbing Willa's staircase.

I rubbed my face, knowing the hollow feeling in my gut wouldn't go away anytime soon. What was I going to do when she did find someone new? How was I going to stay in Lark Cove? I guess watching from a distance as she found the love she was supposed to have would be my punishment for hurting her.

And my reward.

Once Ryder graduated, maybe I'd leave Montana. I'd always come back to see Hazel, but for the first time, the idea of escaping Lark Cove didn't seem all that bad.

Do you love me?

I wished she hadn't asked. I wished I could have said yes. But I'd never told another person that I loved them before. Not Hazel or Thea or Charlie.

No one.

I didn't know shit about love and Willa deserved someone who did. She deserved to have her dreams come true.

I was no dream maker.

"How are you?" Nate asked, coming to stand at my side.

Fucking miserable. "Good. You?"

"Oh, just fine. How are things at the bar?"

"Good. Slow this time of year."

"I bet."

We stood there, surveying his yard. It had snowed an inch last night so the grass was mostly covered in white. It looked peaceful, the exact opposite of the torment plaguing my heart.

Nate had to know things between Willa and me were ending. Yet he hadn't turned us away. He'd welcomed me and my brother into his home to share a meal his wife was cooking.

Nate Doon was a good man, the best really. He'd be there

for Willa after I broke her heart, helping her put it back together.

He clapped a hand on my shoulder, then gave it a squeeze. I looked at him, but neither of us spoke. Nate just gave me a nod, dropped his hand and went back inside. A few moments after he disappeared inside, the sliding door opened again.

"Hey." Ryder appeared at my side. "What are you doing out here?"

"Nothing," I told him. "Just getting some air."

"Are you, uh . . ." He kicked some snow off the porch. "How are you doing?"

"I'm good," I lied. "What about you? You doing okay?"

"You ask me that a lot."

I chuckled. "Yep." At least once a day.

I had no clue how to act like a parent to this kid, so I'd told him early on that he had to tell me if something was wrong. Still, I checked on him constantly, just so he'd know I cared. I could count on two fingers the number of people who'd had asked me if I was doing okay when I was a kid.

"I'm good," he promised.

"You sure?"

He shrugged. "Do you think Willa can help me get caught up at school?"

"She'll try."

Ryder wanted so badly not to fall behind it was all he talked about. That, and if Willa could be his tutor. I hated to burst his bubble, but I didn't want his hopes to get too high. Willa would tutor Ryder, even after we broke up, but I wouldn't put her in that position.

"Listen, kid." I turned away from the yard to face him. "If Willa can't tutor you, then I will. So will Hazel and Thea. We'll do whatever we can to help."

His eyebrows furrowed. "Why wouldn't Willa be able to

help? Doesn't she want to?"

"No, she does. But she's got other stuff going on. It just . . . it just might not work out."

"Oh." He hung his head. "I get it. You guys are breaking up, aren't you? I saw Willa crying the other morning in the kitchen. I don't think she saw me, but I saw her. And then she hasn't been back."

Fuck. That must have been the morning after I'd gotten drunk at the bar. The same night I'd gotten a phone call I never should have answered.

"Is it because of me?" Ryder asked.

"No." I put my hand on his shoulder. "It has nothing to do with you."

It is all on me.

"I don't want you to worry about it, okay? Just have fun today. And eat a lot of turkey."

He smiled. "I can do that. I'm hungry."

"We just had breakfast an hour ago."

"Yeah, but I only ate two bowls of cereal because I didn't want to get too full before lunch. I normally have three."

I grinned. "I'm sure Betty won't let you starve."

The sliding door opened again and we turned to see Willa. She folded her arms over her chest as she stepped out into the cold air.

"Mom has a snack for you," she told Ryder.

He immediately bolted for the door, leaving Willa and me alone.

"Good timing," I said. "He just told me he was hungry."

"I think he's grown an inch since he moved here." She watched Ryder as he disappeared inside.

"I think you're right." Now that he was getting all the food he could eat, Ryder had sprouted. There was no question he would be tall like me. And if my hunch was right, he'd fill out and have the frame of a linebacker. He just needed groceries.

"Are you going to stay out here?" Willa dropped her eyes, looking anywhere but at me as she spoke. Meanwhile, I stared at her, soaking her in while I still could.

"For a while."

She pursed her lips, then went back to the door. But before she opened it, she paused and turned around. "Do you even want to be here?"

Tell her the truth. "Not really."

Pain flashed across her face as she stood there, staring at her feet. After a few seconds, she squared her shoulders, and when she looked up, her beautiful blue eyes were filled with angry tears.

"Are you ever going to tell me why? Or are you just waiting until I've finally had enough and end this for you?"

"That's not what I'm doing."

"Isn't it? Then why? I might be new to this, but I'm not stupid. You don't want to be together, so tell me why."

The pleading in her voice was killing me. "Let's talk about it later, okay?"

She shook her head. "Let's talk about it now."

"I don't want to wreck your Thanksgiving."

"Too late," she whispered. "Why? I want to know why."

My shoulders fell. The last thing I wanted was to do this today, or any day, but she deserved an explanation. At least today, she'd be here with her family. So I took a deep breath, met her gaze and dove headfirst into a conversation I'd been dreading for weeks.

"We want different things."

"Different things?" she repeated. "Like what?"

"Marriage. Kids."

"You don't want to get married."

I shook my head. "No, I don't."

"Ever? Or just to me?"

"Ever." The last thing I wanted was for her to think it was because of her. If there was a woman I'd marry, it would be Willa.

But I wasn't that guy. I saw the way she looked at her parents. She wanted what they had. Commitment. Love. Till death do us part. I wasn't the man to give her those things.

"So what if I told you I didn't want to get married either?" she asked.

"You don't want to get married?"

"Yes, I do. I want to get married. I want to have what my parents have." She looked over her shoulder at the house. "But I want to know if marriage was off the table, would you still be doing this?"

"Yes."

She gritted her teeth. "Why?"

"You're going to want kids."

"How do you know?" she fired back. "You've never asked me. How do you know I want kids?"

Because I knew her. Inside and out, I knew Willa.

And at this moment, she needed to play this little game. I'd go along with it and answer her hypotheticals if it made it easier to say good-bye.

"Well?" I asked. "Do you want kids?"

"Yes, I do."

"Then there you go. I don't."

She dropped her arms, fisting her hands at her sides. The last time I'd seen her this frustrated, she'd been on her doorstep in her pajamas. I'd never forget how beautiful she was the first night I came to her house.

"Why?" she asked.

"Why, what?"

"Why don't you want kids?"

"I just . . . don't. I don't want kids. I don't want to get married. You do. End of story. End of us."

She rocked back on her heels like I'd shoved her. "So that's it?"

I nodded. "That's it."

"Okay," she whispered, dropping her chin. A tear fell, landing in a scuff of snow by her boot.

My hand reached for her on instinct, but I forced it back and into my pocket. "I'll go. Do you want me to take Ryder?"

She shook her head, wrapping her arms around her stomach. "No. Let him stay."

I opened my mouth to tell her good-bye but the words wouldn't come. My feet wouldn't move off the edge of the deck, because the moment I stepped off, this would be over.

I took one last long look at Willa, the woman who'd given me the best summer of my life, and whispered, "I'm sorry."

She didn't respond. She didn't look at me.

She just let me go.

I stepped off the deck, nearly collapsing as a lead weight settled on my shoulders. My boots were so heavy I had to practically drag my feet across the yard and onto the school's property.

Every step I took, I got colder. I felt sicker.

This feeling was the reason I didn't get close to people. This was the reason it was better to live alone. It hurt too much to say good-bye. It was damn near crippling.

I walked faster, angry at myself and this entire situation. And I was angry at Willa for making me feel this way.

Why had she waited so long for me? Why had she made me crave her? Why couldn't she have gone to college and met her future husband? That way, I never would have known her. She would have always just been *Willow*.

This was just as much her fault as it was mine.

My strides got longer as I played the irrational blame game. I didn't play for long. I wanted to be mad at Willa, but I couldn't.

She was innocent, just a victim of my fucked-up life.

Maybe I wasn't so different from Melissa Page after all. I'd stolen a page from her playbook today, making sure that I was never the one in the rearview mirror again.

I'd almost reached the swing set when an angry word rang across the playground.

"No."

What? My feet stopped and I spun around.

Willa was right behind me, not five feet away. Had she been following me this whole time?

"Willa—"

"No," she cut me off again, closing the distance between us.

"No, what?"

"No, you don't get to leave."

I sighed. "Go home, Willa." *Please go home.* I didn't have it in me to say no if she asked me to stay.

She looked up at me with a defiance like nothing I'd ever seen before. She looked fierce and bold and beautiful.

And she told me, "No."

twenty-three

JACKSON

"WHY ARE YOU DOING THIS?"

She crossed her arms over her chest. "Because I want an explanation."

"And I just gave you one."

"It wasn't good enough."

Her chin rose as she spoke. She stood taller today since her knee-high boots gave her a few extra inches. I still towered over her, but her stance was almost intimidating. When had she gotten this backbone? She never challenged me on, well . . . anything.

"I don't know what else to say."

"Why don't you want to get married?"

I shrugged. "Because I don't. I never have."

"Why?"

"I don't know. I just don't."

"Is it because you don't believe in marriage? Or because you don't want to make a commitment?"

My hands fisted. "No."

"Then what?" Her voice was getting louder. She was as frustrated as I was. "Why don't you want to get married? You said it wasn't me, so why? Because the way I see it . . . you either don't want to get married to me and you're lying. Or you are just scared."

Should I lie? Should I tell her I didn't want to marry her?

It would be pointless. She'd see right through my bullshit, and I couldn't do that to her. Some sick part of me wanted Willa to love me—just a little—even after this was over.

"It's not you," I confessed.

"Then you're scared. Why?"

"Why does not wanting to get married mean I'm scared?"

She narrowed her eyes. "You're scared."

"I'm not scared, Willa."

"Then what?" She uncrossed her arms, throwing up her hands. "Why? I want to know why."

"I don't know why!" I shouted. "Okay? I don't know why. I just know that I don't want to get married. I don't want to feel trapped."

"So you feel like I trap you?"

I sighed. "No."

"But you just said that being married would mean you'd be trapped. Is that what you think about all marriages? Do you think Thea feels trapped by Logan? Or my dad feels trapped by my mom?"

"No."

"Then your reason is shit."

I jerked back and frowned. She rarely cussed and it always took me by surprise.

"I don't know what else to say, Willa. I don't want to get married. I don't want kids. I'm not going to be the guy who takes those things away from you."

"So you're doing all this to set me free?"

"Yes." I closed the space between us. "I'm not husband material. Or father material. Go. Be with someone who is."

She searched my eyes, trying to decide if I was telling the truth. Every passing second was killing me.

Walk away, babe. Just walk away.

"No," she whispered.

"Please." I closed my eyes. "Please. Go."

"Just tell me why."

"I don't know." It was the truth. "I don't know anything about being a husband or a father. I don't know how to love. What I do know is that people walk out more often than they stay. I don't want to be the guy who walks out on his family. You need someone you can depend on. That's not me. Eventually, I'll let you down. I'll fuck all of this up."

All of the confidence in her face vanished and her shoulders drooped. "So you're worried you're going to leave me and break my heart, yet here you are, leaving me and breaking my heart. That doesn't make any sense."

No, it really didn't. But it was the right thing to do. "I don't know how to love you."

With that, she dropped her chin. When her shoulders began to shake, the pain in my heart multiplied tenfold. I couldn't handle it when she cried. I couldn't breathe. All I wanted to do was pull her into my arms and promise it would be okay, but since I couldn't make that promise, I had to stand here and watch.

A sound escaped her mouth and she slapped a hand over her lips. Her hair had fallen in front of her face, shielding it from me.

"Please, just go insi—"

She threw her head back and laughed.

She's laughing?

She was, and loud. The entire playground echoed with it as she dropped her hand from her mouth. The pain on her face from thirty seconds ago was gone. Instead, she wore a wide smile full of triumphant joy.

It was beautiful but damn hard to look at. She was happy I was letting her go? Never in a million years would I have expected her to be relieved, and *fuck* did it hurt. But I guess it would make everything easier, wouldn't it?

She looked back at me, the smile still on her face, and she shook her head. "I was right."

"Right about what?"

"You're scared." She stopped laughing and swiped the tears from the corners of her eyes. "You love me and it scares you to death. Not because you're worried that you'll leave me. But because you're terrified I'll leave you, just like everyone else has always done."

"That's not—I'm doing this for you."

She rolled her eyes and guffawed.

Was I scared? Maybe I was. Maybe she was right. Maybe I was terrified that she'd crumble my heart into a thousand pieces. But the fact still remained.

"You deserve more than me."

She shook her head, closing the remaining space between us. She put her hands on my chest and locked her eyes with mine. "There is no more than you."

"Willa—"

"Do you love me?"

Her question sent ice through my veins. Pure. Petrifying. Ice. I wanted to lie and run away. I wanted to tell her no and be done with this. But with her blue eyes searching mine, only one word came to mind.

"Yes."

The corner of her mouth turned up. "I knew it."

"But," I dropped my forehead to hers, "that doesn't change anything. This can't work. It would be better for you to just walk away."

She shook her head. "I'm not much of a fighter and I rarely stand up for myself. But I'm standing up for you. I'll fight for you." Her hands slid up to my cheeks, pushing me back so she could look me in the eye. "I'm not letting you go. And I'll never leave you behind."

I closed my eyes, trying to work up the nerve to leave. But fuck, I wanted to keep her. Forever. Would she stay? Would Willa be that one person to stick?

Yes.

She was my courageous champion. My warrior. My lover. My friend.

My everything.

Willa *was* the one.

"I love you, Jackson Page," she whispered. "Don't run away from me. Please."

I leaned back and swallowed hard. I'd never told anyone that I loved them. She made it seem easy, but the words were stuck in my throat. "I, uh—"

"Don't." She pressed her fingers to my lips and smiled. "It's okay."

Relief rushed over my shoulders as I stared at her winning smile. It was the same one she'd had a few moments ago, but it wasn't smug, just happy and free and stunning. I was torn between staring at it for an hour and kissing the hell out of it.

I went with option two.

I slammed my mouth down on hers, swooping her up in my arms. My tongue dove into her open mouth, twisting and tangling with hers. When her legs wrapped around my hips, I gripped her ass, tugging her even closer.

With her arms wrapped around my shoulders, I kissed her until I was dizzy.

My chest was heaving as Willa leaned back to look at me, but I didn't set her down. I kept her in my arms so we could stare at each other nose to nose.

I ached to show her how I felt so I took one step, then another. With Willa in my arms, I marched us across the snow-covered grass toward her house. She didn't move or look away, not once. She just held on to my shoulders as I took her right to the place where we both wanted to be.

When I hit her yard, I turned toward her staircase. Only then did she glance over my shoulder to her parents' house. She gave someone a small smile as I hit the first step.

I wasn't sure who was outside, but I didn't turn to check. I just carried Willa up and into her apartment.

The moment the door closed behind us, she pressed her mouth onto mine again. She clawed at my back as her legs pulled her center even closer. When it was just the two of us, she shed all of her inhibitions.

Willa let it all go because she trusted me. She loved me like no other person ever had.

The realization hit me like a bullet, sending me back two steps. I broke away from her mouth, panting as I took in the flush reddening her cheeks and the lust darkening her eyes.

"My Willa," I whispered. "Only mine."

"Only yours." She nodded, then buried her head into my neck. She knew I loved it when she nipped at the line of my jaw.

I crossed the room, kneeling on her bed. She let me go and sank back, scooting right up to the pillows. Normally, I liked to strip her down, but we were both too frantic.

While she pulled her sweater up and over her head, I unbuttoned my jeans. Then I yanked at the snaps on my shirt, sending them all free with a fast stream of clicks. Once it was tossed to the floor, I made fast work of the rest. Jeans. T-shirt. Boots. It all went flying as Willa did the same.

Naked and aching for her skin on mine, I crawled on top of her, using my weight to press her deeper into the bed. Her arms wound around my neck, pulling my lips close. But I wouldn't kiss her. I backed away just enough so she could see my face.

"Do you love me?" I asked.

The light in her eyes danced as she smiled. "What do you think?"

I smiled back, lining myself up with her slick heat. I pressed in just a little, using all of my willpower not to thrust deep and hard. "Say it again."

"I love you." She arched up, begging for more.

"Do you love me?" I notched myself in another inch.

"Yes," she panted. "I love you."

"Again. Say it again." Maybe if I heard it enough, I'd learn to say it back.

"I love you, Jackson Page." She tugged me closer to whisper in my ear. "I love you. It's always been you."

I drove deep, all the way to the root. Willa cried out as I stilled with us joined. It was just her and me. Just us.

She wouldn't find another man to make her dreams come true.

I was her dream and she was mine.

"I love you, Willa." The words came easy. "Only you."

She lifted up to kiss me and I kissed her right back, wrapping myself tightly around her body. "Move," she pleaded against my lips.

I eased out, slowly, because I liked the way she trembled in my arms. Then I slid back in, slowly and deliberately, as her shuddered breaths feathered against my cheek.

I'd always scoffed when people said they'd *made love*. Wasn't that just a fancy way to say sex? I'd always thought it was a term that women liked to use because it sounded more intimate than fucking.

Damn, I was a fool.

As I moved inside of her, in and out with our eyes locked and our bodies entwined, I finally got a clue. I was making love to Willa.

If she wanted to get married, I'd put on a suit and stand at an altar and say *I do*. If she wanted babies, I'd make them with her.

Only her.

"Love you," I whispered again as I thrust in and out. She said it right back, holding me tight with her legs around my hips.

"Jackson," she moaned, her limbs shaking.

"Give it to me, babe. Give me everything." I reached between us, finding her clit. I pressed against it, circling twice, and that was all it took for her to detonate around me. She clenched me so tight with her pulsing inner walls that I lost all control.

I worked my hips faster, harder, taking away my hand and grinding into her clit with the base of my cock. The pressure built in my spine and my balls tightened. I wanted to hold back and give her another orgasm, but I couldn't keep my release at bay. With my neck arched back to the ceiling, I roared and came in hot spurts inside of her.

The room was spinning as I came back down and I collapsed on top of her. I grinned at myself as I breathed in her hair. Sex with Willa was awesome, the best I'd ever had. But making love to her just blew my fucking mind.

"Oh my goodness," she panted. "That was . . ."

I nodded into her hair. "Yeah. Holy fuck."

She giggled and I forced my muscles back to life, rolling us over so she was lying on my chest. Her legs were still straddling my thighs, my softening cock still inside her.

She made a move to get up, but I held her tight. "Not yet."

"Okay." She didn't fight me. She just collapsed and gave me all her weight until we both regained our breath.

"Thank you," I whispered.

"For what?"

"For being a fighter."

"I'm not." She kissed my chest. "But I'll always fight for you."

"Why me?" I asked.

"Because you're you."

I lifted up to see her face. "That's it?"

"That's it." She nodded with a smile. "What if I asked you the same? Why me?"

I grinned. "Because you're you."

"Exactly." She rolled off, slowly disconnecting us. Then she tugged my hand, pulling me up from the bed. "We'd better get back for Thanksgiving. I don't trust Ryder not to eat all the pre-dinner snacks and I'm hungry."

I chuckled, following her to the bathroom. We cleaned up, then came back to the bedroom and sorted through the mess of piled clothes.

As she finished pulling on her boots, she looked up at me. "Are my cheeks still red?"

"Yep." It would take at least ten minutes for the sign of her orgasm to go away.

She sighed. "My parents are going to know exactly what we were doing."

"Yeah." I pulled her into my arms. "Make-up sex."

She giggled. "We should fight more. Just not on holidays when we have to spend the day with my parents and your little brother."

"Good idea." Though I was sure that all three would be more than happy to see us together. The strife between us hadn't been missed by anyone.

"Come on. Let's go." I took her hand and led her back outside. As we walked down the staircase, I took a long look at the playground.

The battleground.

Until the day I died, I'd never forget how Willa had fought for me by that swing set.

"Can I ask you something?" Willa asked as we walked toward her parents' deck.

I glanced down at her. "As long as it isn't *why*. You hit your quota for that one already today."

"It's not why." She smiled. "I was just wondering where you went the other night."

"What other night?" I asked, even though I knew exactly what night she was talking about.

"Last week when you left in the middle of the night. Where did you go?"

"Oh, uh, just the bar. I was restless so I went down for a drink. I was being a dick to you, and all the shit with Ryder . . . I just needed to get my head right. So I went down and had a couple of drinks and made sure the new bartender was doing okay. Sorry. I didn't realize you'd even heard me."

"Hmmm." She frowned. "In the future, talking to me might be the better decision. Contrary to popular belief, tequila isn't exactly a problem solver."

"You're right." I kissed the top of her head. "I'll work on it. Sorry."

I would work on drowning my problems with booze, but sometimes, a man just needed a drink. And that night, I'd needed a big fucking drink. Luckily, our new bartender, Dakota, had been more than happy to pour them for his boss.

"Was that who called you?" she asked. "Dakota? I thought I heard you on the phone before you left."

I looked her right in the eye, hoping like hell this was the one lie I could pull off today. "It was no one. Just a wrong number."

twenty-four

WILLA

"HEY!" I SMILED AND STOOD FROM MY CHAIR AS JACKSON strode into my office at the camp. "This is a surprise."

He was supposed to be driving to Kalispell this morning in my car. We'd swapped vehicles because he wanted to clean mine on his trip to town. Apparently, he had a favorite car wash in Kalispell and he was going up there to shop for Ryder's Christmas presents. So while he was running errands, I'd come to the camp to get some work done before a meeting with Logan.

"What are you doing here?" I asked as he came around the desk.

He answered by taking my face in his hands and crushing his lips down on mine.

It took me a second to catch up, but as soon as I did, I closed my eyes and wrapped my arms around his waist, pulling myself closer. I gripped the back of his Carhartt coat, fisting the thick canvas.

His tongue invaded my mouth and his fingers threaded into my hair. When he broke away, the world was spinning and my lips were deliciously swollen.

"Gosh," I breathed. "What was that for? Not that I'm complaining."

He grinned and kissed me again, this time soft and sweet. "Thank you."

"You're welcome?" I had no idea what he was thanking me for, especially since I was the one getting the favor today. I hated cleaning my car.

"I got a call from Ryder's math teacher this morning," he told me. "He got a C on his test yesterday."

"Yes!" I clapped. "I knew he could do it."

"It's all because of you."

I shook my head. "No, he gets the credit. He's been working his butt off."

Ryder was such a bright kid. He just had some gaps in the fundamentals of his education. We'd been working together nonstop over the last two weeks. When he wasn't at school, he was with me.

We'd do his English papers in my apartment or his social studies assignments in Jackson's living room. We always seemed to find ourselves at my parents' dining room table when there were math and science problems to work out. I was Ryder's primary tutor, but Dad had dubbed himself the assistant.

"You get some credit too," Jackson said. "There's no way he would have passed that test if I had been helping him these last couple of weeks."

I shrugged. "It's been my pleasure." Tutoring Ryder was the best winter job I could have asked for.

Jackson kissed me again, then stepped back. He winked at me before turning and striding out of my office.

"That's it?" I asked his back. "You're leaving already?"

He glanced over his shoulder as he strode through the kitchen while I hurried to follow. "I've got a busy day. I need to get your car cleaned and then talk to Hazel. Ryder's having a last-minute sleepover because tonight, you're mine."

A shiver rolled over my shoulders as I followed him into the main room. "My parents asked us over for dinner, but I think I'd better decline."

"You'll be too busy fucking me to worry about dinner."

"Wowzah," I whispered, enjoying another shiver.

He wore a sexy grin as he walked down the center aisle in the quiet main room.

All of the tables were clean and the chairs were pushed in. In the summer, chairs were never in their rightful spot. There was always something on a table, either kids' art projects left out to be finished or snacks for campers to grab and take along on their next adventure. And there was always someone coming or going from the main room.

I longed for the clutter and the noise.

Everything outdoors was covered with snow. The firepit and all the log benches were buried. The trees had a glittery sparkle. And beyond them, the lake was a flat sheet of ice. I hoped the highway wouldn't be too icy on the way to Kalispell.

"Drive safe," I told Jackson as he stopped at the double doors.

"I'll call you when I get back and we can make plans." He kissed me one last time, then went outside. I waved good-bye and turned to go back to the office but stopped when I saw Logan and Jackson meet along the path up to the parking lot.

I watched from inside the main room as the two shook hands and laughed about something.

Logan and Jackson were getting along so well these days that I'd actually consider them friends. I loved that Jackson was expanding his group. It wasn't just Hazel, Thea and Charlie anymore. He had all of us. Me, Ryder, my parents and even Logan.

He was opening up. He was letting others love him. And I

think for the first time in his life, he wasn't worried that we'd all disappear.

If he didn't want to get married one day, I'd be okay with that. Like I'd told Leighton on the phone last week, I didn't need a white dress and fancy party. I just needed Jackson. If he didn't come around to the idea of marriage, I'd let go of that dream.

I had the one I'd really been after anyway.

The babies thing? That was a different story. I wasn't going to let go of that dream so easily. One day, I had complete faith that Jackson would get over his fears and realize any child would be lucky to have him as their dad.

Jackson and Logan said good-bye and I stepped away from the window to go back to the door. I opened it for Logan as he stomped the snow off his boots.

"Morning," I told him.

"Good morning." He stepped inside and looked around the room.

I put my hands in my jean pockets, then took them out. I tugged at the hem of my sweater, making sure it hadn't ridden up. Then I looked around the room, trying not to stare at Logan as he did his minor inspection.

No matter how much time we spent together, Logan Kendrick always made me nervous. He had this raw power that rolled off his body. That, and he was the most handsome man I'd ever seen besides Jackson.

Logan's dark hair was always styled and his face shaven. Even in his casual jeans and black winter coat, he was classy. The boots he wore were the same style as Jackson's, but they weren't worn or scuffed. Everything about Logan was polished.

And his air of confidence and command was completely intimidating.

"How are you today?" he asked.

"Good, thanks." I gave him a shaky smile. "And you? H-how are you?"

"I'm good."

"Oh, that's great." My voice was airy and quiet. "Would you like coffee? I made a pot. It's in the kitchen." *Obviously, Willa. Geez. Get a grip.*

"Sure." His gentle eyes were doing their best to put me at ease. "Lead the way."

I ducked my head and walked toward the kitchen. I took a few deep breaths, reminding myself that he was just Logan, my boyfriend's best friend's husband. It didn't matter that he had more money than anyone I'd ever met or that he was my boss.

By the time we made it to the kitchen, I'd relaxed some. Nerves still fluttered in my stomach, but I was able to speak normally and with slightly more confidence.

"How do you like your coffee?" I asked.

"Black is fine."

I nodded and took a cup out of the cupboard, then filled it from the industrial pot. It wasn't as good as the coffee Hazel made. Somehow hers always tasted better than mine, even though the process was the same. But it was hot and good enough for the day.

"How is Thea feeling?" I handed him his cup.

He smiled. "She's had a lot of morning sickness since Thanksgiving, but she handles it like a trooper."

"I bet Charlie's excited."

"She wants a baby brother so badly." He chuckled. "We've been trying to tell her that a sister would be okay too, but she's got her hopes up."

"And what about you? Do you have a preference?"

Logan shook his head. "Happy and healthy is all I want."

The dreamy smile on his face made my heart melt. He loved

his family so much it was hard not to swoon.

"Should we meet in your office?" he asked. "Or would you like to chat in the main room?"

"I've got some things in my office." I led the way into the office and took a seat behind my desk as Logan took the guest chair opposite me.

My office wasn't much. It was dark without a window and always cold. It was cramped, with just enough room for my desk and a couple of file cabinets. But I'd put up a ton of pictures of campers from over the years and it made the room cheery. How could you not smile when you were surrounded by happy kids?

"I've been hearing great things about the camp." Logan paused to take a sip of his coffee. "And you. Everyone at the foundation has been very impressed. I'm told it's been the most organized transition in Kendrick Foundation history, all because of you."

"Really? Thank you." I blushed, tucking a piece of hair behind my ear. "Everyone seems so nice at the foundation office. I've only gotten to talk to them on the phone, but you have a great team."

"I'm lucky. And now you're a part of that team so I'm even luckier."

"Thank you. Again. So what did you want to talk about today?" I'd been shocked when he'd called me to arrange this morning's meeting. I figured that CEOs of large charitable foundations didn't meet with tiny camp directors like me.

"Well, I'd like to discuss the plans you proposed for the improvements this spring."

"Oh." My heart sank. "Did I ask for too much?"

We were in dire need of some facility updates. I'd tried to limit my requests to the areas in the worst shape, but the camp had been short on funds for far too long.

"On the contrary," Logan said as I took a sip of coffee. "I'd like to see what we can do if I double the amount you requested."

I choked on my coffee, coughing and spurting it all over my desk. A couple of drops even managed to fly far enough across the desk to land on his hand.

"Oh my gosh. I'm so sorry," I gasped, still coughing as I scrambled for anything to clean up my mess. Where were the paper towels or napkins? Why didn't I keep an unlimited supply in here just in case? "Here. Use this." I handed him the scarf I'd worn to work today. "I'm so sorry."

"It's fine." He chuckled and wiped his hand on his jeans. "It was worth the coffee shower to see the look on your face. I've never seen anyone's eyes that big before."

My mouth fell open as I sank into my chair. No doubt my face was the same shade of magenta as the bra I'd put on this morning. "I'm—" I stopped at the look on Logan's face. "You're teasing me, aren't you?"

"Definitely."

Relief washed over me. "You really want to double the improvement budget?"

"I do. This camp has become something of a personal favorite of mine, so it gets special treatment."

"There's a lot we could do with that money. The bathrooms need a complete overhaul. The kitchen could use a new stove and refrigerator. It wasn't at the top of my priority list, but I'd love to have some of the windows replaced in the bunks."

"We'll do it all and then some." He took a pen from a cup holder and grabbed a pad of sticky notes from the desk. "All right. How about you start listing off all the things you want and then we'll estimate cost and rank them."

"Actually." I opened my desk drawer. "Here." I handed him a notebook where I kept my wish list plus bids for each improvement.

Now it was his turn for his eyes to get wide. "You're organized, aren't you?"

"Just a smidge." I smiled. "I started that list my first year here and I update it every year."

"Not much has been crossed off."

I shook my head. "No."

He clicked the pen and smiled. "Let's change that."

A swell of excitement ran through my body, making me bounce in my chair.

An hour later, the two of us had planned all of the improvements to do this year plus some for next. Despite having spent little time at the camp—something he would no doubt be changing this coming season—Logan even had some ideas for improvements of his own.

He wanted to have a larger beach area built so the kids could spend more time by the water. He wanted to have a permanent "fort" built, something where the kids could escape to play in the trees. It was something I was sure his daughter would wholeheartedly approve of since Charlie had already built a makeshift fort in the trees last summer.

It would be incredible.

"I just . . . thank you." I took the notebook from Logan and put it back in my desk. "This will make a huge difference and I know the kids will love it."

"My pleasure." Logan grinned and leaned back in his chair. "I have something else I want to talk to you about. How would you feel about working for me part-time in the winters?"

I blinked in surprise. "Work for you? Doing what?"

"Whatever comes up." He shrugged. "I'm trying to cut back on work now that the baby is coming. I don't want to miss out on anything. But with everyone on my staff still in New York and the uptick of work we've gotten at the foundation lately, I could use someone to help me keep it all straight."

"And you want me?" I pointed to my chest. "I've never been an assistant before."

"You're organized and smart. You won't have any trouble figuring it out."

My mouth was hanging open at his compliments. Working for Logan seemed like the perfect opportunity, but I wanted to run it by Jackson and my parents first. "Can I think about it?"

"Of course. There's no rush."

"Is there anything else you want to discuss today?"

He shook his head and stood from his chair to look at some of the photos on the wall.

I was just about to tell him a funny story about the picture in which me and some of the kids were wearing togas when a knock sounded at the office door.

Porter Hannagan, one of the sheriff's deputies, was standing at the door. He was in a uniform of jeans and a dark brown shirt with his badge and gun hooked to his belt.

"Hey, Porter." I stood and went over to greet him. "How are you?"

The two of us had gone to high school together. He was a year older than me and had left to go to the police academy after graduation. We didn't see each other much, but I always waved when I saw him in his patrol car along the highway.

"I'm good, Willa. I saw your car here on my way to the station."

"Is everything okay?" The worry lines on his forehead had my heart pounding. My thoughts immediately went to Jackson and my parents, hoping they were all right.

Before he could answer, Logan stepped up to my side, his hand extended to Porter. "Hello, Deputy Hannagan."

"Porter, please." Porter shook his hand. "Good to see you, Mr. Kendrick."

"It's Logan," he corrected. "So what brings you here?"

Porter's eyes shifted down to me. He had such kind eyes, but even though they were gentle, the look in them sent every worst-case scenario running through my head. Was it a car crash? Had Mom gotten hurt at home? Was there an emergency at the school?

He spoke before I could ask. "I'm breaking protocol by being here, but Jackson asked me to personally come down and tell you. He didn't want to tell you over the phone."

My arms began shaking and I wrapped them around my stomach. "What happened?"

He took a deep breath. "Sheriff Magee arrested Jackson about an hour ago."

"What?" My jaw dropped. "That's impossible. Jackson is in Kalispell, getting my car cleaned."

"No, he's not. Sheriff found him at the bar and brought him into the station. Like I said, he could have called you, but he asked me to come down."

"Why? Why was he arrested?"

Porter took another long breath. "He's the primary suspect in a murder."

My legs turned to jelly and I nearly fell over. I would have if not for Logan grabbing my elbow to steady me.

"This has to be a mistake," I said. "It's a mistake."

"Who is he accused of killing?" Logan asked.

Porter's eyes reluctantly came to mine. "His mother."

twenty-five

WILLA

"IT'S THREE," MOM SAID AFTER CHECKING HER WATCH. "RYDER will be getting out of school before long. One of us should be there when he gets home."

I nodded. "Would you mind going to Jackson's? I don't want to leave."

"Of course." She gathered up her purse and coat from a chair in the sheriff's station's waiting room. I'd called her on the drive down here from the camp because for situations like this, I still needed my mom. "Call me if you hear anything."

I nodded again and dug Jackson's truck keys from my puffer coat. His truck was in the parking lot next to Logan's SUV. My car was parked at the bar because he'd been brought to the sheriff's station in the back of a cop car like a criminal.

My mouth flooded with saliva and I swallowed it down. The nausea took a second to go away, but it would be back. Every time I thought of Jackson in a jail cell, I fought the urge to puke.

I was desperate for information but we'd been sitting here for hours and no one had told us a thing.

With tears in my eyes, I took Jackson's house key off the chain and handed it over to Mom. "It's for the side garage door."

"Okay. I'll take care of Ryder. You just stay strong." Mom

squeezed my shoulder, but before she could leave, I grabbed her wrist.

"Don't tell him anything."

She shook her head. "I won't."

Someone would have to explain to Ryder that his mother was dead and Jackson was being accused of her murder. That someone should be Jackson.

Or me, if he was going to be held in custody all night.

As Mom walked out the door, I pulled my coat further up my neck, burrowing inside. It was freezing in the little lobby where we were sitting, or maybe it was just me. Everyone else had taken their coats off and seemed fine with the room's temperature.

But I couldn't stay warm, even with the coffee cup that people kept refilling for me. The thought of Jackson being accused of murder chilled me to the bone. The thought of having to tell Ryder this was happening made me shake. I wanted to go back to this morning when Jackson and I had been snuggled warm in his bed.

The front door to the station opened—Hazel coming back inside from her smoke break.

"Anything?"

I shook my head as Thea did the same from the chair across from me.

Thea's hands kept patting her stomach. You couldn't tell she was pregnant—it was too soon for her to be showing—but that gesture gave it away. It was her nervous tell, whereas mine was my bouncing feet on the floor.

Thea and Hazel had walked into the sheriff's station just seconds after I'd come in with Logan. Hazel had led the charge to the front desk, marching up to the deputy stationed there and demanding to see Jackson.

The deputy had politely but firmly told us it wasn't possible. Jackson had to be "processed" and "questioned" before they could determine whether or not he could be released.

Hazel protested and she put up a good fight, but the deputy didn't budge. So we'd all sat down in the lobby while Jackson was somewhere in the building. The nausea rolled again when I thought about him getting fingerprinted and having his mug shot taken.

He was not a criminal.

Hazel dropped her pack of cigarettes and lighter into her purse. "I'm going to go ask again."

She stomped up to the desk and put her hands on her hips. Her back was blocking the view of the deputy's face so I couldn't make out what he told her. I didn't need to. The way her shoulders sank and her arms fell to her sides said it all.

Hazel nodded to the deputy, then came back to her seat next to Thea.

"This is ridiculous," she muttered. "Do you know him?" she asked Thea, nodding backward at the deputy.

"No, he's new. I think he lives up in Kalispell and commutes down here. He hasn't been into the bar yet."

Hazel frowned. "I used to know all of the deputies. I had them all on speed dial in case there was a problem at the bar."

"I've got Sheriff Magee's and Porter's numbers both memorized." Thea hung her head. "But I haven't called either of them in ages. If there's a problem, I call Jackson first."

She looked up and met my eyes. We were both thinking the same thing.

What will I do without him?

Our stare was broken up when Logan walked over, tucking his phone into his jeans. He'd been on and off various calls since we'd walked into the station.

"They got ahold of her." He sat on Thea's other side and took her hand. "She's getting off the ski hill and will be here as soon as possible."

Logan's first string of phone calls had been to attorneys up in Kalispell. There wasn't a plethora of lawyers in rural Montana, especially those with experience in murder investigations. But after numerous calls, Logan had found one who had excellent references and adequate experience—or so he'd deemed.

The problem was that the lawyer Logan wanted for Jackson, a Rita Sperry, had taken the day off to go skiing. Her office had called her a thousand times, mostly after each one of Logan's thousand calls to see if she'd checked in yet.

Finally, after we'd sat here all day feeling lost and hopeless, help was on the way.

I just hoped Jackson hadn't said too much already without an attorney present.

"I think we'd better make a plan just in case he doesn't get out," Thea told Logan.

He shook his head. "We'll get him out."

"How do you know?" Thea rubbed her belly in fast circles. "This lawyer might not be able to do anything today. This is a criminal charge, Logan. He could go to prison. He could—"

"Hey." Logan placed his hand over hers. "We'll get him out today, then we'll figure out the next step."

Tears welled in Thea's eyes. "But what if he did it?"

I winced so hard my chair squeaked. How could she have let that thought even cross her mind?

"He didn't," I declared. "He did not do this."

I looked over at Hazel for some support, but her gaze was down in her lap.

"He *did not* do this," I repeated.

Hazel looked up and gave me a sad smile. "I don't want to

think that either. But—"

"No," I snapped. "No. He didn't. He *wouldn't.*"

Thea checked over her shoulder to make sure the deputy at the desk wasn't listening. When she saw he was on the phone, she turned back and leaned in close. "He hated her. He had every right, but he hated her."

"Enough to murder her?" I hissed. "That's not Jackson and you know it. Yes, he hated her. But do you really think he would hurt her?"

She sighed. "No, I don't."

I turned my eyes on Hazel. "Do you?"

Hazel shook her head. "No."

"Logan?"

He shook his head too.

"Okay then." I leaned back in my seat and crossed my arms. "He needs us behind him, one hundred percent."

The lobby went silent again except for the dull murmur coming from the deputy on the phone. I unbuttoned my coat as my frustration with Hazel and Thea warmed my insides.

How could they think he was guilty? How dare they? Shame on them for doubting him. Even if it was just for a moment, it still made me angry.

I wished Mom were still here. She wouldn't have contemplated the worst. Or would she? Had she already considered that he could be guilty too? Was I being naïve to not at least consider all of the alternatives here?

Sheriff Magee was good at his job. He wouldn't have arrested Jackson if there weren't a reason. Which meant Jackson was a suspect because there had to be some sort of evidence against him.

But what? It had been two months since his mother had come to Lark Cove. He hadn't seen her since the day she'd abandoned Ryder.

Right?

Had he seen Melissa again and hidden it from me? We'd been in such a good place these past couple of weeks. The two of us had become closer than ever and we talked about everything. We confided in one another. We trusted each other.

At least, I thought we did. So if he had been in contact with Melissa, why hadn't he told me about it?

"This doesn't make any sense," I muttered.

"What was that?" Logan asked.

"This doesn't make any sense," I repeated, louder. "She left Lark Cove months ago." I looked at Thea and Hazel. "Did he say anything about her coming back?"

Hazel shook her head. "Not to me."

"Me either," Thea said. "As far as I know, he hasn't seen her since she left town after dropping off Ryder."

Unless he was being framed, that meant he'd hid something from all of us.

He'd lied to me. A lie of omission, but a lie nonetheless.

The questions began to roll through my mind, an endless string with nothing but a question mark to separate them. When had this happened? How had she died? When had Jackson found the time to see her?

I'd been with him almost constantly these past few days. The only time we'd been apart was when he'd been at the bar working and I'd been at his house tutoring Ryder. So when? When could he have possibly seen his mother again?

There was no way he could have killed her. The entire thing made no sense. I couldn't picture Jackson hurting someone, no matter who they were. He rarely lost his temper. When he was upset, he didn't lash out. He shut down.

Except that wasn't exactly true.

The night he'd thought I was flirting with that guy at the bar, he'd lashed out. He'd shattered those beer bottles so hard in the trash can I'd nearly startled off my stool. And he'd been so angry that night, saying such hurtful things. I hadn't seen him like that before or since.

Maybe his mother had come back while he'd been drunk. He'd blacked out the night he'd kissed me this summer. Maybe he'd been drunk when his mother had come back to town and he hadn't told me because he didn't remember.

But when? When had he been drunk? The only night that came to mind was weeks ago when he'd left in the middle of the night and come home smelling like booze.

I closed my eyes as my stomach churned.

Oh, no. Jackson, what did you do?

That phone call, the one he'd told me was a wrong number, had to have been from his mother. It was the only explanation.

I ticked the days off on my fingers, counting backward. That call had come before Thanksgiving, in the middle of November. It had been almost three weeks ago.

Three weeks and it was all starting to make more sense.

He'd been acting distant. He'd been short and snappish. He'd tried to break us apart. Was it all because his mother had come back to Lark Cove?

None of it made any sense. Jackson wasn't a murderer. He was sweet and loving and kind. He wouldn't do this to me and he especially wouldn't do this to Ryder. Something wasn't adding up.

If I could just talk to Jackson, we'd figure this out.

I stood from my seat and went to the front desk, giving the deputy a slight wave as I approached.

"I'm sorry, ma'am," he said. "I don't have an update for you."

"That's okay." I looked beyond him. The counter that separated us ran the length of the small lobby, effectively creating a barrier to the rest of the building. You couldn't get into the station unless he unlocked the door to my side.

I stared at the door longingly, wanting to go through it and search for Jackson. My attention snapped back to the deputy just as Porter and Sheriff Magee came from the doorway at his back.

My eyes went to Porter's first, hoping to see something promising in his face. But he didn't spare me a glance as he handed a file folder to the front desk deputy.

"Hi, Willa." Sheriff Magee extended his hand over the counter.

I gave him a small smile. "Hi, Sheriff Magee."

It had been a while since I'd seen the sheriff. I'd run into him at the grocery store a year back in the beer and wine section. He had teased me about not being old enough to buy alcohol. He hadn't been able to believe I was the same little girl who'd he'd once helped up after a bike crash in front of his house.

I'd grown up. Sheriff Magee had changed a lot too since then.

His black hair, which was normally pulled back into a ponytail and covered with a Stetson, had grayed substantially. The lines on his tanned face were deep. Even his stout frame seemed to have lost some of its bulky mass.

But he still had the same warm smile I remembered, an older version of Dakota's, his nephew and the bar's new bartender.

They had the same eyes, nearly black, with high cheekbones and a strong chin.

"Can I see Jackson?" I asked him.

He sighed. "I'm sorry. Not yet. We need to ask you a few questions."

My heart sank. "Okay."

"Sheriff." Logan appeared at my side, holding his hand out.

"Logan. Thea." He nodded to them both. "Hi, Hazel."

"Xavier," she grumbled.

No one ever called the sheriff anything other than Magee. He went by either Magee or Sheriff Magee. Not even my father used Xavier and he'd known Sheriff Magee for decades. Why did it not surprise me that Hazel, of all people, called him by his first name?

"Where's my boy?" she asked him.

"We're asking him some questions."

"Are you about done? We've been here all damn day."

He frowned. "I need to talk with Willa. And I might have some questions for you too."

"Fine." She narrowed her eyes, sending him a glare that would have made me cry.

"Can I do that?" he asked. "Or did you want me to stand here so you can glare at me a little while longer?"

She dismissed him with a flick of her wrist. "Get on with it."

I looked back and forth between them, wondering what the deal was with these two. Everyone liked Sheriff Magee. Everyone. He'd won his last election in a landslide. And everyone liked Hazel. So how did these two not like one another?

Now wasn't the time to ask.

"Willa, come on back."

"Okay." I nodded and took a step toward the door but stopped when Logan touched my shoulder.

"I think you should wait until the lawyer gets here," he said quietly.

"That's still at least an hour away, and it's already three o'clock." I turned to Sheriff Magee, a man who I trusted to give me sound advice. "Should I wait for a lawyer?"

"That's your call and you have the right to wait. But I don't think you need one for this. I just have a couple easy questions."

"Then I'll come back now." If answering some simple questions meant that Jackson might not have to spend the night in a jail cell, I'd cooperate.

Logan frowned. "Willa—"

"It's okay. If I get uncomfortable, I can always stop talking and wait for the lawyer."

The door buzzed and the lock popped, so before Logan could stop me again, I opened it up and went inside.

I met Sheriff Magee in the short hallway behind the front desk. He led me around a corner and down a hallway toward a bull pen. We skirted past empty desks, going straight for a small room along the back wall.

As I stepped inside, I realized it was an interrogation room. The overhead fluorescent lights were bright, but without windows, the room was gloomy. The beige walls were dull and the wooden table in the middle of the room had seen better days.

There wasn't a two-way mirror, but there was a camera in the upper corner of the room. Its blinking red light made me even more nervous than I already was.

I took the chair on one side of the table, sitting on my shaking hands. Sheriff Magee sat across from me, slapping down the yellow legal pad and pen he'd been carrying. Then he pulled a small black recorder from the breast pocket of his brown shirt. He clicked it on and set it down, its red light intimidating me too.

"Sheriff Xavier Magee questioning Willa Doon on December eighth." He wrote down my name and the date on the paper, then looked up.

I held my breath, waiting for his first question as I sweated underneath my coat.

"Willa, could you state your relationship to Jackson Page?"

I swallowed hard, clearing the lump in my throat. "I'm his girlfriend."

"And how long have you been dating?"

"A little over three months."

He scratched something on the paper. I didn't try to read it upside down, focusing instead on trying to calm my racing heart. What if I said something wrong? What if I made this worse for Jackson?

Maybe I should have waited for the lawyer. I wasn't equipped to deal with this kind of pressure. I was a good girl. Good girls didn't know how to act when being questioned about a murder.

"Do you recall where you were on the night of November sixteenth of this year?"

"I'm not sure," I answered honestly. "I'd have to look at a calendar. But I was probably either at home or at Jackson's." That was three weeks ago. I would need a calendar to see the exact day of the week, but I had a feeling I already knew which night that was.

"Do you stay the night there often?"

I nodded.

Sheriff Magee smiled and looked at the recorder. "If you could say yes or no, Willa. Thanks."

"Sorry," I muttered, taking another breath. "Yes, I stay there often. Especially since he has Ryder now."

"And did you ever meet their mother?" he asked.

"Twice."

"When was that?"

"Um, the first day she came to Lark Cove. I was in the bar when she came in."

"And what happened that day?"

"Uh . . ." I searched my memory, trying to remember all that had happened that afternoon. "She came in and said she was looking for Jackson. Thea was there too. We didn't know who she was and when Jackson came out from the kitchen, she didn't recognize him. He told her to leave."

"He told her to leave? Or did he physically remove her from the bar?"

"He, um, escorted her out."

Sheriff Magee didn't need to write anything down. He already knew things had gotten heated that afternoon. But the only person who could have told him was Jackson since Thea had been with me in the lobby all day. Where was he going with this?

"And what happened next?" he asked.

"Nothing. I spent the evening at the bar with Jackson and then went home." There was no way in hell I was going to tell him anything about the fight we'd gotten into that night.

"You went home alone?"

"Yes."

"But you normally spend the nights together."

Why did I feel like this was a trap? "Yes."

"So you don't know what else happened that night after you left."

"Nothing else happened. I stayed until Jackson closed down the bar. Then I drove home and went to bed."

"And when did you see Jackson again?"

"The next morning."

He hummed and wrote down another note on the paper. He tilted it back, resting it at an angle to hide his notes.

"When was the second time you met Melissa Page?"

"The next day. I went with Jackson to visit her at her motel room."

"And what happened?"

I took a deep breath, though it didn't help soothe my

hammering heartbeat. "Melissa introduced Ryder and Jackson. Then she told Jackson he needed to take Ryder for a while."

That was the CliffsNotes version of our visit to the motel, but I was starting to feel like the less I shared, the better. If Sheriff Magee wanted details, he could drag them out of me one question at a time.

"Then what?"

"That's it. We loaded up Ryder and his stuff, then left. We went to the bar for pizza."

He set down the paper and pen, then steepled his hands by his chin. "And did you ever see or talk to Melissa again?"

"No."

"Did she ever call to talk to Jackson or Ryder?" he asked.

"Not that I know of."

"You're sure?"

"Yes." I locked my eyes with his. "I'm sure. If she called, Jackson didn't tell me. Ryder doesn't have a phone."

"Okay. Let's go back to the night of November sixteenth. You're sure you don't remember where you were that night?"

I shook my head. "Not really. Nothing specific stands out from that date. But can I check my phone? I might have something in my calendar."

"Go ahead." Sheriff Magee waved me on.

I dug my phone from my coat pocket and opened up the calendar, swiping to November. I kept everything in my calendar, mostly because I didn't ever want to forget a birthday, special occasion or dinner with the girls.

I noted everything, including my lunch dates.

And November sixteenth was the day I'd had a lunch date with my dad at the school.

That was the day that Jackson had been in to discuss Ryder's grades. It was the day he'd gotten that late-night phone call and disappeared for three hours and seven minutes, only to come home smelling like tequila and women's perfume.

"I spent the night at Jackson's house," I told Sheriff Magee.

"And was he there all night?"

I looked up, wanting to cry.

Sheriff Magee's eyes were waiting, his gaze gentle and understanding. He knew the answer already and he knew it was going to hurt to say it.

He knew that with one word, I'd be turning against the love of my life.

"No."

twenty-six

JACKSON

M Y FUCKING MOTHER. EVEN IN DEATH SHE WAS RUINING MY life.

I was sitting in an interrogation room at the sheriff's station. I wasn't sure how long I'd been here, but my ass was sore from sitting in this metal chair for so long. My head was pounding and my back ached.

"Fuck." I dropped my head into my hands and closed my eyes.

This was not how I'd planned on spending my day.

I'd stopped at the bar this morning to say hello to Thea, who'd been working on payroll. I needed some ideas on what to get Charlie for Christmas since I was going to do some shopping in Kalispell after I got Willa's car cleaned.

When Sheriff Magee came through the door, I assumed it was just to say hello. He came in every now and again to make sure we knew he and his team were always available if there was trouble.

I certainly didn't expect the sheriff to "invite" me down to the station for questioning—and request that I ride in the back of his cruiser.

At least he didn't put me in cuffs or throw me in a jail cell. He just brought me into this room and explained that my mother had been found murdered. Then he told me that, at the moment, I was their number one suspect.

I was a murder suspect.

That was not a concept I could grasp. What I did know for certain was that I never should have answered Mom's phone call three weeks ago.

My skull felt like it was going to split in two at any moment, so I rubbed the back of my neck, hoping to work out some of the kinks and get my headache to disappear. The pain was just beginning to let up when the door to the interrogation room opened and Sheriff Magee stepped inside.

He looked as tired as I felt.

We'd spent most of the day in here. He'd ask me questions and I'd answer into the recorder. Then I'd ask questions and he'd tell me what he could.

The only reason I'd agreed to talk to him without a lawyer present was because I trusted him. More importantly, Hazel trusted him. Those two butted heads all the damn time, but if she were in my shoes, she'd work with Sheriff Magee, not against him.

I just hoped my cooperation would be the key to my release, not my incarceration.

"Are you charging me?" I asked.

He shook his head and sank into the chair across from me. "Not today."

My shoulders fell. "I didn't do it."

"That's what everyone says."

"You don't believe me."

He thumbed through a pad of paper he'd brought in with him. "I'm not sure what to believe. The evidence I had this morning only pointed to you. But I'm still collecting puzzle pieces. Good news for you is that the more I get, the less the picture resembles your face."

That was the best news I'd had all day. "So what now?"

"You go home for the night. I keep working until I have all the pieces." He blew out a long breath and kept his seat. I was ready to bolt, but the sheriff had something more to say. "You've got a lot of people who love you. I hope you're grateful for them."

"I am."

"And you've got a smart woman who pays attention to details."

The hairs on my arms stood up. "You talked to Willa?"

"In that room." He pointed to the wall at my back.

I nearly shot out of my chair to go next door. The last place I wanted her was in an interrogation room, but I kept my seat. "What did she say?"

"She told me you left your house that night after a phone call. And that you came back three hours and seven minutes later."

She'd been awake? *Fuck.* I'd been so drunk and exhausted that I hadn't realized.

"So . . ." Sheriff Magee drummed his fingers on the table. "Like I said. This morning, the evidence pointed to you. But now I know you were at home for a good portion of the night."

"I told you that earlier."

"You did." He sighed. "And if I could take everyone at their word, my job would be a lot easier."

"I didn't kill her."

"And I'm inclined to believe you, Jackson. I really am. But I need proof. Until then, you're still my number one suspect. I'm going to keep digging until I can prove it wasn't you or I find someone else with the same means and motive."

"Understood." I nodded. "Did you call Dakota?"

"Just got off the phone. He's coming right down."

"Good." I rubbed my neck. Dakota would provide an alibi for two of the hours I was away from home. Then all I needed was for something to come up to show Mom was alive during the other hour.

"Goes without saying, but I'll say it anyway." Sheriff Magee pointed at me. "Don't leave town."

"No, sir."

"I expect to hear back from the medical examiner sometime this week. Expect a phone call asking you to come back down."

"Okay." I stood from the chair. My lower back pinched and my legs were stiff, but I ignored them and held out a hand to Sheriff Magee.

"We'll talk soon." He shook my hand, then walked out the door.

I followed him out of the room, hoping to get a glimpse of Willa next door, but it was shut.

"She's in the lobby." Sheriff Magee glanced over his shoulder. "You've had a whole crew in here today, drinking all my coffee."

I didn't respond as I followed him through the bull pen and down the hallway that led to the lobby. Sheriff Magee opened the door for me, then stepped to the side.

I strode right past him into the lobby, where Logan and Thea were standing against a wall, whispering to one another. Hazel was sitting in one of the lobby chairs with her knee bouncing. And Willa was in the seat next to her.

The second they spotted me, the room breathed a collective sigh.

Thea said something. Hazel stood. But I kept my eyes on Willa.

She sat perfectly still, not leaving her chair. The look on her face was part relief, part frustration.

Was she pissed? She should be. I'd lied to her and made a huge fucking mistake, so she had every right to be mad.

I opened my mouth to apologize, but the front door to the station opened and Dakota walked inside, kicking the snow from his boots.

"Dakota?" Thea asked, turning to look at our employee. "What are you doing here? Who's at the bar?"

"No one," he told her. "I locked up when the sheriff called."

"Thanks for coming down," I told him, sending Thea a look that meant we'd talk later.

Dakota crossed the room and walked right up to Sheriff Magee. "Uncle."

"Hi, bud. Come on back."

Dakota nodded, clapped me on the shoulder, then followed the sheriff back into the station.

When the door closed behind them, the room went silent again. My gaze went back to Willa, where she still sat frozen.

"Willa." I took a step forward, ready to get on my knees and beg for forgiveness. But before I could, she shot out of her chair and ran across the room.

She flung herself into my arms and the weight of a thousand worlds fell off my shoulders.

"I'm sorry," I whispered. I hugged her tight, burying my face in her hair and breathing it in deep.

"You didn't do it, so don't apologize."

"I *didn't* do it."

Her arms around my neck got tighter. "I know."

She knows. Without any kind of explanation, she knew. She had that kind of faith in me.

"I love you."

She leaned back, her blue eyes full of tears. "I love you too."

I pulled her back in, wishing we were alone. There was so much I had to explain and I wanted some time for the two of us to just talk things out. But that wasn't going to happen. First, I had to tell my little brother that our mother was never coming back for him because she was dead.

"Meet up at the bar," Hazel declared as she collected her coat and purse. "We'll talk there."

I let Willa go and took Hazel's hand. "I need to talk to Ryder."

"It can wait." She gave me the look I didn't argue with. "He's fine. He's with Betty at home, probably doing homework. And I want to know what's going on. Now."

"Okay." I sighed. "I need to get my things. I'll be right behind you."

As I went to the deputy at the desk to collect Willa's car keys and my coat, everyone else hurried to leave. When I turned back around, the lobby was empty except for Willa, who stood by the door, waiting.

I took her hand as we walked outside, leading her right to my truck. "I didn't get your car cleaned."

She gave me a small smile. "You can do it later."

"I will." That was, if I wasn't in prison. It all depended on what Sheriff Magee could dig up to prove my innocence.

Or whatever I could dig up to save myself.

"You drive." She handed me my keys, then stood on her tiptoes to give me a quick kiss before going to the passenger door.

We got in and went directly to the bar, parking next to her car before going inside.

When we walked through the door, Hazel was already pouring Thea a glass of water and Logan a shot of whiskey. She held up the bottle, silently asking if I wanted a drink, but I shook my head.

Until this was all over, I wanted a clear head.

"Willa?"

"Just water for me." She shrugged off her coat and took a chair at the table in the middle of the room where Thea and Logan were sitting.

"Jackson, lock the door," Hazel ordered. "We're closed for the rest of the day, and I don't want any distractions."

I nodded and turned back around, locking the door. Then I snagged an extra chair and slid it next to Willa's.

"Okay. Start at the top," Hazel said after she'd brought over drinks and we'd all sat down.

With a deep breath and an apologetic look at Willa, I dove in. "Mom called me about three weeks ago. That was the phone call I got the night I left the house."

"I kind of figured that one out today," she muttered.

"I'm sorry. I should have told you."

"You should have told all of us." Thea crossed her arms over her chest. "Was she calling you this entire time?"

I shook my head. "Just that once."

"Why didn't you tell us?"

"I don't know." I shrugged. "I guess I didn't want to talk about her." She'd been theoretically dead to me. Now, she actually was.

"What did she want?" Willa asked.

"Money." I took a drink of my water, then sat back in my chair to explain the entire night. "She asked me to meet her somewhere. She said if I didn't talk to her, she'd go to the authorities to take Ryder back. I didn't want to even take the chance that she'd put him through it, so I met with her."

I had just been trying to do right by Ryder. Even though I was working to get legal custody of him, my claim hadn't been approved yet. Mom was still his legal guardian. I'd figured the fastest way to get her the hell out of Lark Cove again was a quick meeting to hear her out.

"I told her to meet me here in the parking lot. It was snowing pretty hard and I offered to talk inside, but she didn't want to come in. She just told me that if I wanted to keep Ryder, I needed to give her three thousand dollars."

"Did you?" Logan asked.

"No. I told her to go to hell, then got in my truck and drove off."

Willa put her hand on my knee. "Then what?"

"Then nothing. I got back in my truck and drove around for a while. I was pissed and needed to think. After about an hour, I came back here and drank with Dakota for a couple hours."

"That's why Sheriff Magee called him down." Thea snapped her fingers. "He's your alibi for part of the night."

I nodded. "He poured me tequila shots for two hours and kept me company, then drove me home." Poor guy had walked from my house to his in the snow, but thankfully, Lark Cove was small and he didn't live more than five minutes away.

Logan leaned forward in his chair. "So we just have to prove that during the hour you were driving around, you didn't kill your mother."

"That's right," I told him.

"How did she die?" Thea asked.

I shuddered as the photographs Magee had shown me earlier flashed through my mind. I think he'd shown me pictures of Mom's lifeless body in order to gauge my reaction as well as to confirm she was in fact my mom.

I don't know if it was what he'd been going for, but I'd almost puked up breakfast in the interrogation room's trash can. The images of her gray skin and dead eyes were burned into my brain forever.

"She was strangled," I said quietly. "In her car, they think. That's where they found her. She'd turned off the highway onto Old Logger's Road. I have no idea why she'd take that turn. Maybe she was lost or something, but that's where they found her. Her car had been run off the road into some trees."

"She died three weeks ago. Why are they just now finding her body?" Logan asked.

"It snowed," Hazel explained. This was Logan's first year in Montana, so it wasn't a wonder he didn't understand. Once upon a time, she'd taught me about those old roads too. "That road gets closed every winter because it sits at the base of two mountains. It drifts in so badly during the winter they can't keep up with the plowing, so they just close it off until spring."

"Someone must have followed her up there and killed her, then driven her car off the road," Thea guessed.

I nodded. "And somehow we have to prove that someone wasn't me."

"But why?" Willa asked. "Why would they even think it was you? They just assumed that since you're her son, you'd kill her? That makes no sense."

I took another drink of my water, buying myself a minute. This was the part of my story I didn't want to confess.

"I threatened her. When we were at the motel and after she dumped Ryder, I threatened her never to come back. I guess she thought I might be true to my word because when I met her in the parking lot here, she recorded our conversation on her phone. And I threatened her again, right before I drove off. I told her if she ever came back, I'd use her body as fishing bait."

"Oh, Jackson," Hazel muttered, shaking her head. "You didn't."

"How the fuck was I supposed to know she'd end up dead?

I just wanted her to leave town." I'd been pissed and not thinking clearly. I said some nasty words in the heat of the moment and now they might cost me my life.

"Magee found the recorder in her car," I told them. "He found her phone and got the records so he knows I was the last person she called. So the evidence basically points to me following her out of the parking lot and killing her on an old deserted road."

"What about fingerprints? Or her time of death?" Willa asked. "If she died after you were home, then you don't have anything to worry about."

"They didn't find any prints in the car other than hers. Her body was frozen so Magee said the medical examiner might not be able to pinpoint exactly when she died. They're doing an autopsy, but it will take a while. But the bottom line is, if they come back and say she died anytime during the hour when I was driving around, I'm fucked."

I didn't know what the odds were that he'd find more evidence, but at least they were better now than when he'd arrested me. This morning, Magee didn't know that I'd gone home to Willa, and without her alibi, my window of opportunity was wide open.

Logan's phone rang and he excused himself from the table to answer. The rest of us sat quietly, each staring blankly at the table.

"You smelled like perfume," Willa whispered.

"Huh?"

She looked up at me. "You smelled like tequila and perfume when you came home."

"It was Mom." I sighed. "She was wearing strong perfume and she hugged me."

She'd done it right before she'd asked me how Ryder and

I were doing. The gesture had caught me off guard, so I'd just stood there. For a split second, I'd actually thought she'd regretted her decision to abandon him. But then she'd begged me for some money, giving me some bullshit sob story.

Looking back, I think the hug and the interest in Ryder were all part of her plan. She'd been recording me at the time. She'd put on a good show, pretending to be a mother who had fallen on hard times and needed some extra cash from her oldest son.

"How did they find her?" Thea asked. "The body and her car."

"Magee told me that a couple was out cross-country skiing and came across her car yesterday afternoon." I felt bad for those skiers. The image on the photograph I'd seen was bad enough; seeing it in person would have been awful.

Logan returned to the table and raked a hand through his hair. "We've got a lawyer coming down from Kalispell. She'll be here soon."

"Thanks." I appreciated that he'd called in some help. And I had a feeling he wasn't just doing it because Thea was his wife. Somewhere over the last couple of months, Logan and I had become . . . friends. I actually liked the guy. He was funny and smart. And he cared for the people in his life, me included.

"No problem." He nodded. "I'm sure she'll want to meet and discuss this with you as soon as she gets here."

"Okay." I blew out a long breath, glancing at the clock.

I needed to talk to Ryder, but I also needed to talk to this lawyer. I was going to need legal help if the autopsy came back with an incriminating time of death. This wasn't a road to walk alone, and for the first time in a long time, I wasn't even going to try.

I'd let the people at this table walk alongside me every step of the way.

"Do you think Magee believed you?" Willa asked. "That you didn't do it?"

"Yeah." I nodded. "I do. He told me more about Mom's death and the evidence stacked against me than he had to. If he really thought I was guilty, he wouldn't have shown me all his cards."

Instead, Magee had treated me like an ally. He wasn't trying to prove me guilty, he was trying to prove me innocent. So I'd told him every little detail I could think of, hoping it would help him put the puzzle together.

Magee had done a lot for me after I'd moved to Lark Cove. In part, I think he'd done it because of Hazel. But I'd learned over the years that he was one of the most honest men I'd ever met, so if he questioned my innocence, he would have told me so today.

"Okay. That's that." Hazel stood and clapped her hands. "We'd better get some dinner started. It's going to be a long night."

"I'll help." Thea stood too, holding out a hand for Logan. "Come on, gorgeous."

The three of them disappeared behind the bar and into the kitchen, leaving me and Willa alone.

"I'm sorry." I took her hand in mine. "I'm so sorry. I should have told you the truth."

"Yes, you should have." She gave me a sad smile. "But I understand why you didn't."

"Are you mad?"

"At your mom for putting you in this position? Yes. At you? No."

I squeezed her hand tighter. "Do you believe me?"

"I believe you." She slipped her hand free of mine to cup

my cheek. Then she leaned up, kissed me gently and wrapped her arms around my neck. "It'll be okay."

I pulled her into my lap and held on tight. I really fucking hoped she was right, because as tough as I tried to be, going to prison and leaving her would break me apart.

twenty-seven

WILLA

"WILLA," JACKSON SAID QUIETLY.

I turned around from my spot in front of the stove, spatula still in hand. I was in the middle of making pancakes for breakfast. I smiled at him, but it dropped as I took in his face. "What?"

He held up his phone. "Magee called. He wants me to come down to the station. First thing."

"Did he say anything?"

Jackson shook his head and crossed the room. He came right into my space and wrapped his arms around me.

I didn't hesitate to hug him back, even with the spatula still in my grip. I pressed my cheek against his heart and slipped my free hand around his waist. "It'll be okay."

He nodded, holding me so tight I couldn't move. "It'll be okay."

Over the last week, the two of us had said those words at least twenty times a day.

It had been the longest seven days of my life. Every day, we waited anxiously for a phone call from Sheriff Magee. Most days, they didn't come. Usually by midafternoon, Jackson would be so tense that he'd drag me down to the sheriff's station to check in with Magee personally—which meant I'd been to the sheriff's station seven days in a row.

The entire week, Jackson and I had been glued at the hip. We hadn't left the other's sight, not once. When he went to work, I went too. When I had to run errands or go to the camp, he came along. And both of us had spent as much time with Ryder as possible.

I'd expected Jackson to push me away some because of the stress. I was braced and ready for him to be distant like he had before Thanksgiving. But instead, he'd just pulled me in even closer. He confided in me. He leaned on me. When he was worried, we talked it out.

And though the last seven days had been pure agony, there was beauty in them too.

We'd finally gotten to an *us*. A real and lasting and true *us*.

"When do we need to be at the station?"

"Magee said as soon as possible."

I nodded, taking one last inhale of his shirt before letting him go. "Let me get breakfast done and I'll hop in the shower."

"Okay, babe. I'll wake up Ryder."

"I'm up."

I looked past Jackson as Ryder shuffled into the kitchen. He dropped his backpack by the kitchen table, then sat down. He'd already showered and gotten dressed for school, but he looked exhausted.

Ever since we'd told him about Melissa's death, Ryder hadn't been sleeping or eating much. One night I'd woken up with too much on my mind and had come to the kitchen for some tea. Ryder had been on the couch, watching TV on mute. He picked at his breakfast, and not even my wheat chili could entice him for seconds.

I'd never forget Ryder's pained cry when Jackson had told him about their mom's death. After we'd met with the attorney,

Jackson and I had come back here to talk with Ryder. We'd sat him down on the couch, one of us on each side, and Jackson had delivered the news.

Ryder had broken down and cried for almost an hour into Jackson's chest until he'd finally passed out and Jackson had carried him to bed.

Even though Melissa had disappointed him and left him behind, she was his mom. I think Ryder had always held on to a little slice of hope that eventually she'd come back for him.

"Hey, kid." Jackson walked over to the table and sat down next to Ryder. "You okay?"

Ryder shrugged. "Just tired."

"Couldn't sleep?"

"No."

I flipped my pancakes, then went to the cupboard for a coffee cup. I filled it for Jackson, then took it and my own over to the table.

"Thanks, babe." Jackson squeezed my thigh after I sat down. "Sheriff Magee called me this morning."

Ryder's eyes widened. "What did he say?"

"He didn't tell me anything. He just asked that I come down to the station this morning."

"I'm coming too," Ryder declared.

Jackson shook his head. "Not this time."

"But—"

Jackson cut him off. "It could take a while and I don't want you missing any school. You've got that social studies test today."

"Fuck school and fuck the test."

I flinched like I always did when Ryder cursed. He was so frustrated and angry and scared. He'd lost his mother and he was terrified he was going to lose his brother too.

"Listen." Jackson reached over and put a hand on Ryder's

shoulder. "As soon as we know what's happening, I'll come to the school. But you might as well try and ace your test like I know you can."

Ryder's frame slumped. "You didn't kill her."

"No, I didn't."

"This isn't fair." Ryder's voice cracked. So did my heart.

"You're right," I told him. "This isn't fair, but we'll get through it. You just stay strong."

Ryder looked up from his lap, his dark eyes glassy. "That's what your mom says."

"Yeah, but it sounds better when I say it," I teased.

The corner of his mouth twitched. It wasn't a smile—I hadn't seen one of those in a week—but it was a start.

Jackson winked at me and took a sip of his coffee.

"Pancake time." I stood from the table and went back to the stove.

"Willa?" Ryder called.

I looked over my shoulder. "Yeah?"

"Can I have the woogidy one?"

"Sure." I nodded and got his plate ready with three pretty pancakes and a woogidy one.

Just the way he liked it.

Jackson and I were at the sheriff's station an hour later.

After breakfast, we'd dropped Ryder off at school, then made a quick call to our attorney.

The lawyer Logan had found was incredible. The night she'd come to Lark Cove, she'd spent two hours with us. I'd left the bar with a deeper understanding of the criminal justice system than I'd ever cared to know. But she'd given Jackson some great pointers on what and what not to do or say.

We talked to her daily, keeping her fully briefed on whatever we learned at our sheriff's station visits, even if it wasn't much.

This morning, she'd given Jackson some advice on what to do if he was officially charged with murder. *Call me. Say nothing.* But otherwise, she told him to be smart and saw no reason not to meet with Sheriff Magee informally just to hear him out.

I had a feeling she was waiting by the phone, ready to hop in her car and drive down from Kalispell at a moment's notice.

So here we were, walking back into the sheriff's station.

Let this be the last time. I looked to the light-blue sky and made my wish on all the sleeping stars.

As we came inside, the deputy at the front desk didn't say anything other than good morning before immediately buzzing us into the back.

Jackson and I went right through the door, finding Sheriff Magee waiting for us. He was wearing his signature Stetson today, making him look more like the man I'd known since childhood.

"Thanks for coming down." He shook Jackson's hand. "Willa, would you like to wait in the lobby?"

"No sirree," I chimed, inching closer to Jackson as I held up my chin. I'd never spoken to an officer of the law like that before—with cheekiness—but he was going to have to physically remove me from this discussion because I wasn't leaving Jackson's side.

"I had a feeling you'd say that." Sheriff Magee grinned. "Come on back."

As the sheriff turned, Jackson bent down and whispered, "'No sirree'?"

"Shh. I'm nervous," I whispered back.

He chuckled quietly, then took my hand. We followed the

sheriff through the station to the same interrogation room he'd put me in before. Jackson and I each took one of the chairs on one side of the table while Sheriff Magee closed the door and sat on the opposite.

There was a file folder on the table already and it captivated me.

If only X-ray vision were a thing.

Jackson chuckled again. So did Magee.

So I'd said that out loud. "Whoopsie."

"Willa's nervous," Jackson explained. "So am I. Should I call my lawyer?"

"I don't think that will be necessary. I've got good news for you today."

Relief washed over Jackson's face and the air whooshed out of my lungs so fast I had to clutch my heart to keep it from blowing out too. His hand squeezed mine tight.

It'll be okay.

I nodded, not needing him to say the words because I was thinking them too.

Sheriff Magee opened the file folder and pulled out a small stack of papers. The writing was small, but with the stencil of a body on one quarter of the page and annotations in various spaces, I knew it was Melissa's autopsy.

"The medical examiner was extremely thorough with his report. He took into account everything he could, but with the body being found so long after death and in the cold conditions, all we have is a 24-hour estimate."

I held my breath as he picked up the report to read from the second page.

"Melissa Page died sometime on November seventeenth."

"The day after she saw me?" Jackson asked.

Sheriff Magee nodded. "She was killed during the time

when your whereabouts are accounted for, meaning I have sufficient evidence to rule you out as a suspect."

My eyes welled with tears, but I fought them back. As I blinked the moisture away, Jackson's face was one of utter disbelief.

He'd been preparing for bad news all week. He'd been mentally imagining the worst possible situation because he had always expected to be found guilty.

He didn't trust in justice.

But today it was on our side.

I wanted to leap across the table and hug Sheriff Magee. Instead, I just held Jackson's hand tighter, letting the immense joy in my heart chase away the last of my fears.

"So, that's it?" Jackson asked.

The sheriff shook his head. "Not exactly. I still need to find a killer, and to do that, I need some help."

"With what?" Jackson asked.

The sheriff slid out another paper from the folder. He spun it on the table and pushed it closer for Jackson and me to read.

It was a list of phone calls. I didn't recognize any of the numbers and they all had out-of-state area codes.

"What's this?" Jackson asked.

"Your mom's phone records. I've been digging into her finances this past week and came across her cell phone payment on a credit card. The number was awfully high for a single line, so I got ahold of the phone company. Turns out she was paying for two phones even though we only found one in her car. The second one is registered to Ryder Page with an incorrect birthdate."

"But Ryder doesn't have a phone," I told him.

"I remember you telling me that. Are you sure?" the sheriff asked.

"Positive."

"Okay." Sheriff Magee nodded. "Well, this phone number sent out a few texts the morning of November seventeenth. If you're sure it wasn't Ryder, then I'm inclined to believe it was your mother."

"But you didn't find that phone with her?" Jackson asked.

"Nope."

"Then where is it?"

"That's the life-in-prison-sentence question. Whoever has that phone is probably the person who killed her."

Jackson's jaw ticked, but he stayed quiet as Sheriff Magee leaned his elbows on the table.

"Look, here's my theory. Your mother came up here and asked you for money. You denied her, but she didn't leave town. I didn't find a charge for a hotel room on her credit card so my guess is she slept in her car. Maybe she stuck around to try and ask you for money again. Maybe she was going to try and contact your brother. I'm not sure. But during that time, she was in communication with the person who murdered her."

Jackson rubbed his jaw. "It actually surprised me that she didn't try harder to get some money. I didn't know her, but after she asked me for that three thousand bucks and I said no, she didn't put up as big of a fight as I'd expected. When I drove off, I would have bet my boat she'd be back."

"Do you know of anyone who might have wanted to kill your mother?" the sheriff asked.

Jackson blew out a breath, sinking back into his seat. "No. I hadn't seen her in years. Like I said, I didn't know her."

"But we know someone who did," I whispered, looking up at Jackson. "Ryder."

"With Melissa gone, you'll be appointed his legal guardian," Sheriff Magee said. "I know he's just a kid, but we need all the information we can get. With your permission, I'd like to talk to him."

"I get to be in the room."

"Of course."

Jackson nodded. "We'll bring him down later this afternoon."

"Good." The sheriff collected all of his papers, putting them back in the folder. "I'll walk you guys out."

I stood from my chair, still holding Jackson's hand. We hadn't bothered to take off our coats when we came inside, so we went right out the door, escaping the station as fast as we could.

"I don't want to bring Ryder here," I told him as I buckled my seat belt in his truck.

"Me neither." Jackson sighed. "But I don't think we have a choice. Let's go home and wait until his test is over. Then we'll go get him."

"Okay." I glanced at the clock on the dash. "Maybe we could go get him after lunch." That would give him time to finish his test, though I didn't have a lot of hope that he'd pass. He'd been distracted during each of our study sessions this week.

Jackson drove us back home, parking in the driveway. The boat got the garage in the winters so I braced for the cold as I opened the truck door. I followed behind Jackson as he led the way to the front door, staying close as we hurried inside. But the minute he put his key to the door, he stopped.

"What?" I peered around him. His eyes narrowed at the door, which was open a crack. The hairs on the back of my neck stood on end.

"Did you lock up when we left?"

I nodded. "Yes. I always do." Ever since the night Ronny had come after Thea, I'd made sure to lock all of our doors.

"You're sure?"

"Positive."

Jackson looked over his shoulder, inspecting the footprints on the sidewalk.

"What's wrong?" I asked, sticking close.

He held up a hand, silencing me as his eyes narrowed on a particular print in the snow. It was larger than the prints left by my shoes. It was larger than the prints left by Ryder's sneakers. But it was smaller than the prints left by Jackson's boots.

One thing was for certain: it hadn't come from any of us.

My heart was racing as Jackson followed the prints along the sidewalk as they led back to the front door. We both knew something wasn't right. This wasn't the mailman delivering a package or a solicitor visiting the house.

I knew without asking that someone had broken inside his house.

Maybe they were still in there.

Jackson turned to me, the same worries etched on his face as I was sure were on mine, and pointed over my shoulder. "Get in the truck and call Magee. Tell him to get here. Now. I think someone tried to break into the house. I'm going to go check it out."

"Jackson, no y—"

"Go, Willa."

Reluctantly, I did as I was told, running back to the truck, careful not to slip on the snowy sidewalk. I closed myself inside and took out my phone, ready to call the sheriff just as Jackson disappeared into the house.

twenty-eight

JACKSON

SOMEONE HAD BEEN IN MY HOUSE.

The couch cushions in the living room were turned up at odd angles. The drawer of one of the end tables was hanging open. Even the movies in the entertainment stand had been pulled out, like someone had searched behind them.

The disarray continued into the kitchen, where all of the cupboard doors were open and the drawers ajar. I walked as quietly as possible down the hallway toward my bedroom, hoping that if the intruder was still inside, I'd catch him or her in the act.

But my bedroom and adjoining bathroom were empty except for the items tossed and turned out of their normal place.

I turned from the bedroom, retreating quietly down the hall toward the other end of the house. My heart was racing, but I did my best to keep my breaths shallow and even as I approached Ryder's room.

As I peered around the door, I saw no one. Though his room was in much worse shape than the rest of the house. Whoever had come in here had obviously spent most of their time in this room. The mattress had been upended completely, tipped on its side against the wall with a huge gash cut into the back. The nightstand was smashed to pieces and the drawers to his dresser were scattered across the floor, each of them broken.

I finished my search of the house, hitting the laundry room and other bathroom, but I was alone. Whoever had come in here had either found what they were looking for and left or run before they could get caught.

"Fuck," I cursed in the living room, taking it all in.

Who had done this? What were they looking for?

The screech of tires outside sent me hustling out the front door. Willa was still inside the truck, watching with panic from the passenger window as Sheriff Magee and two of his deputies hopped out of their cruisers.

With hands on their holsters, they rushed toward the house.

"Is anyone inside?" Magee asked.

I shook my head. "No. I checked all of the rooms. They're all trashed but there's no sign whoever did it is still in there."

"Mind if we check, just to be sure?"

"Be my guest." I stepped out of the way as he and his deputies rushed inside to sweep the house.

Meanwhile, I went over to the truck, opening the door for Willa.

"What happened?" she asked, clinging to my hand as I helped her out.

"I don't know, babe. Someone broke in and made a mess of the place looking for something."

"What?" she gasped. "Who? Why?"

I pulled her into my chest, hoping some of my body heat would stop her shivering. Though I doubted it was from the cold.

"I don't know. Let's go inside and talk to Magee."

She nodded, leaving her arms wrapped around my waist as we walked. The minute we stepped inside, she gasped again and slapped a hand over her mouth. "No."

"Better stay there," a deputy warned from the kitchen. "We're going to dust this whole place for fingerprints."

Fuck. Even with the carnage all around us, it was hard to believe this was happening. When were we going to catch a break?

"All clear, Sheriff," one of the deputies called from the direction of my bedroom.

"Same here." Sheriff Magee's shout preceded him as he emerged from the hallway going to Ryder's room. As he stood in the living room, he surveyed the mess and shook his head. "Your brother's room is the worst. Whoever did this spent more time in there than anywhere else."

I nodded. While things in the rest of the house had been upended, his room had been fucking destroyed. "I noticed the same thing."

"I think you'd better go get him from school and bring him to the station," Magee said.

I sighed, tucking Willa closer to my side. "I think you're right."

My brother had some explaining to do.

Willa and I left the house immediately, driving straight to the school. We went inside, stopping at the office to request Ryder's early release. One of the aides went to get Ryder from his classroom and it only took a couple of minutes for him to come rushing around a wall of lockers. The moment he saw us in the hall, he jogged toward us.

"So?" he asked, hiking his backpack over his shoulder. "What happened?"

"They know I didn't do it," I told him.

Ryder dropped his backpack and flung himself at my chest.

I wrapped my brother up in a hug, realizing then just how much of his worries this past week had been for me.

"I was worried they'd take you away." Ryder's voice was muffled in my chest. "Then they'd take me away too."

"I'm not going anywhere." I dropped a cheek to the top of Ryder's head. "Neither are you. Love you, kid."

"Love you too."

I looked up at Willa just in time to see her turn to a bulletin board and swipe a tear from the corner of her eye. Did she know that it was because of her I could even say those words to someone?

Besides her, I'd never said them to another living soul, not even Hazel or Thea or Charlie. But since I'd begun saying them to Willa often, they'd become easier to speak. And if there was another person on earth who deserved to hear them, it was the kid in my arms.

After a few moments, Ryder pulled himself together and stepped back, looking up at me with pleading eyes. "I don't want to go back to class. Do I have to?"

"No." I clapped him on the shoulder. "But we need to talk."

"About what?"

I took a deep breath. "Someone broke into the house today and tossed the place."

"No way." His dark eyes widened.

"They went to town on your room."

This time there wasn't just shock on his face, but guilt as he dropped his chin to study the floor.

"The sheriff needs to talk to you."

Ryder nodded. "Uh, okay."

"We'll be with you the whole time, but you have to be honest with him. About everything."

"What if I get in trouble?" he whispered.

Willa stepped up to his side and took his hand, just like she did for me whenever I needed some reassurance. "Then we'll help get you out of it."

Ryder and I might have gone through a lot of our lives alone up to this point, but from here on out, we'd tackle problems together. Like a team.

"Go get your coat, kid." I motioned for Ryder to go down the hall to the lockers. "Then we'll get out of here."

It didn't take us long to be right back in the place where I'd vowed earlier never to set foot again.

The interrogation room.

Ryder, Willa and I sat on one side of the table with Magee on the other, his recorder in its place.

"Okay, Ryder." Magee steepled his hands under his chin. "I'm going to ask you some questions and it's imperative that you tell me the truth. The whole truth. Can you do that?"

Ryder, who'd had his gaze locked on the table since we'd arrived, nodded along with a murmured, "Yes."

"I'm trying to find the person who—"

"Killed my mom?" Ryder interrupted.

"That's right. And to do that, I need to know more about her."

The kid nodded, keeping his eyes focused on the table.

"But before we talk about her, I'd like to know more about you."

Magee looked to me, asking silently for permission to launch into his questions. I gave him a slight nod, then looked over Ryder's head at Willa sitting on his right side.

I wasn't sure if it was a mistake or not to be in this room again without our attorney, but I was going with my gut. And my gut said Magee would do everything in his power to make this the last time we met here.

For the next hour, Willa and I sat quietly as we listened to Magee's questions and Ryder's answers. It took the kid a while to open up, but once he did, Magee only had to guide the conversation.

We learned a lot more about Ryder's childhood and the lifestyle he'd had with Mom. It made me realize that maybe bouncing from foster home to foster home wasn't all that bad. At least I'd always had a home, whereas Ryder had slept a lot of his nights in the backseat of Mom's old car.

Ever since he was a baby, she'd driven him from state to state, following whatever boyfriend she'd been with at the time. Occasionally, they would move in with one and stay for a year or two. But Mom's relationships never lasted. Just as Ryder would get settled, she'd yank him out of his home and they would be off to somewhere else.

From what Ryder could remember, the longest Mom had stayed in one spot was right after Ryder was born. They'd lived in West Virginia, next door to one of Mom's cousins, until he turned six.

Then she'd gotten restless. Instead of leaving him behind like she had with me, he became her traveling companion.

It was no wonder he'd gotten so far behind in school.

"So eventually you ended up in Las Vegas, is that right?" Magee asked.

"Yeah." Ryder nodded. "We lived there with Mom's ex-boyfriend Christopher."

"And what was he like?"

Ryder scoffed. "He was a dick."

"Really?" Magee perked up. So far, Ryder hadn't had anything negative to say about anyone in his past, even our mother. "Why do you say that?"

"He used to push her around a lot." Ryder frowned at the recorder. "One time, I came home from school and I saw him yanking her around the living room by her arm. She was crying and had a red mark on her cheek. She made some bull excuses for him, but the guy was a loser. It wasn't the first time he'd put his hands on her."

"Do you know what caused that argument?"

Ryder shrugged. "Probably money. That's what they normally fought about. Christopher always had stacks of cash lying around."

Warning bells rang in the back of my mind and Willa had the same alarm on her face.

Magee, on the other hand, kept his expression neutral. "What did Christopher do for a living?"

"Some kind of banker, I think," Ryder answered.

Warning bells turned to blaring sirens.

"Interesting." Magee jotted something down on his notepad. "Do you happen to know Christopher's last name?"

"Unger."

"Good." Magee kept taking notes. "I don't suppose you know why they broke up?"

"Not really. They got in a big fight and the next day, Mom told me she was sick of his shit. While he was at work, she loaded up all our stuff and we left."

"And where did you go?"

"Denver. Mom bought a new car and we camped out in hotels for a while."

"No school?" Magee asked.

Ryder just shook his head. "No. Mom said we weren't staying long so I could just hang out and watch TV."

My hands fisted on my thighs, not for the first time today, in anger at Mom. Instead of doing something for her son, like enrolling him in school or getting a fucking job, she'd let him sit on a hotel bed and watch television for the month of September.

Beside Ryder, Willa's fists matched my own.

"Then what happened?" Magee asked.

"We came up here to look for Jackson. Mom was running out of money and thought he'd have some."

I scoffed, earning a *shut the fuck up* glare from Magee.

"Any idea how much money we're talking about here?" the sheriff asked.

"Um . . ." Ryder hesitated, looking between the adults in the room before muttering, "About fifty thousand dollars."

"What the fuck?" I exploded, earning another glare from Magee. But I was too pissed to keep quiet. "Mom spent fifty thousand dollars in a couple of months?"

Her car was nice, but not fifty-thousand-dollars nice. And months in a cheap hotel wouldn't have used up the rest of her cash. So where the hell had she spent it? Why had she been so broke that she'd had to beg me for money?

Ryder's shoulders curled in on themselves at my outburst. He looked over at me with guilty eyes.

Magee sat poised. He gave me a single nod to keep pushing.

"Ryder?" I warned.

He shook his head, clamping his mouth shut.

"What happened?"

He still didn't speak.

"You need to tell me. Now," I demanded. It was the sharpest tone I'd ever used with him. It was the same one Hazel had used on me countless times when I'd needed to get my act together. "I won't ask you again. What happened to the money?"

His chin began to quiver and he dropped his eyes. "I . . . I took it."

"*You* took it?" Willa asked. "Why?"

His teary eyes found his backpack at his feet.

The backpack he never went anywhere without.

"It was just a little bit at a time," he confessed. "I'd sneak it from her purse when she wasn't looking and hide it in my backpack. I wanted us to be out of money by the time we found Jackson. Because every time she ran out of money before, we'd stay somewhere for a while, with her friends or whatever. I thought maybe it would make her want to stay here."

My anger deflated and I put my hand on his shoulder. "It's okay. Do you still have the money?"

He nodded frantically. "It's in my backpack. I didn't spend any of it." Ryder's panicked eyes shot to the sheriff. "I swear. None of it. Not even a dollar. And I have some of her recorders too."

"Recorders?" Magee leaned forward. "What recorders?"

"The ones she gave me to carry for her."

The room went silent.

Mom had given Ryder recorders? Could they contain the link to her killer?

"Would you mind if I took a listen?" Magee asked me, not Ryder.

"No. Go for it."

Ryder immediately began digging in his backpack.

From over his shoulder, I watched as he lifted a flap in the bottom, one I wouldn't have noticed, and started laying stacks of cash on the table.

Willa's eyes stared unblinking at the money as it just kept coming. How the hell had he been carrying all of that around and we hadn't noticed?

Soon the cash stopped and out came three recorders. They weren't as fancy as the one the sheriff had used in all of our interrogations. These were single use only, so once they were full, you either recorded over what you had or bought a new device.

"Mom didn't notice you took all of this money?" I asked Ryder.

He shrugged. "She wasn't so good with numbers."

"Why didn't you tell us about this?" Willa asked him.

Good fucking question. This information could have saved me from a week of being the number one suspect in a murder.

Ryder hung his head. "I thought I'd get in trouble for stealing and they'd send me away."

And since he had nowhere else to go, he would have gone right into the system.

The same system I'd been telling him horror stories about since he'd arrived in Lark Cove.

I sighed, then looked at Magee. "Is he in trouble?"

The sheriff shook his head, then nodded to the cash and recorders. "As long as I can have that as evidence, I don't see any reason to punish Ryder." He stood from his chair. "I think we're done for the day. We'll need you to stay out of your house until my team is done dusting for prints. But I expect that to be done soon."

"Take your time." I stood and held out a hand for a shake. Then I nudged Ryder's arm so he'd do the same.

With my hand on the back of his neck, I steered my brother out of the interrogation room with Willa trailing close behind.

"Thank you, Sheriff Magee," she told him as he escorted us out.

"You're welcome. I'll be in touch."

He left us alone in the lobby and we all shrugged on our coats. With mine on, I tossed the truck keys to Ryder. "Why don't you head on out and turn the heat on for us."

"Okay." He nodded and hurried out the door.

When he was gone, I turned to Willa and let out a deep breath. "That was . . ."

"Intense? I can't believe all of this."

I pulled her into my arms. "Me neither, babe."

"I have a feeling this Christopher guy is about to meet Sheriff Magee. Do you think that he's the one who killed your mom? Could he be the one who broke into your house looking for those recordings?"

"That's my hunch, but we'll know more once Magee tracks him down." There was a flurry of activity behind the lobby desk as two deputies whispered to one another. I was guessing the sheriff had already started his search for Christopher Unger.

"One thing I know for sure," I said. "We're not going home until the sheriff rounds him up. I'm not taking any chances."

Willa nodded. "We can just stay at my place and Ryder can crash in my parents' guest room."

The deputies behind the desk both disappeared deeper into the station. "For Ryder's sake, I hope they find out who killed her. He deserves to know."

"So do you," Willa said.

"I said good-bye to her a long time ago, babe. Years before she ever came to Lark Cove. I just want to put it all in the past."

She held me tighter. "It'll be okay."

With her in my arms? "It already is."

twenty-nine

JACKSON

"YOU GUYS WANT SOMETHING TO DRINK?"

Willa, Ryder and Nate didn't look up as I stood from the dining room table. All I got were three slight headshakes as they stared at the cards in their hands.

They'd been playing three-handed pinochle for an hour. I'd helped Ryder out at first, but he'd gotten the hang of it quickly, so I'd just been watching them.

I pushed in my chair, then bent to kiss the top of Willa's head. "I'm going to see if your mom needs some help."

She gave me another absent nod before I left them for the kitchen. It was Saturday, over a week since my name had been cleared, and Betty and Nate had invited us all over for the day. We were going to play games, watch college football and then have Betty's famous pot roast for dinner.

"How goes the battle?" Betty asked as I walked into her kitchen.

I chuckled. "If Willa wins this game, it's tied at one win apiece. But I'm thinking Ryder might beat them both."

"Good." She smiled. "How's he doing?"

"Better." I went to the fridge for one of Nate's cans of Sprite. "Yesterday was rough, but I think he's just glad to know what happened to her."

"I'm sorry it was difficult, but I hope you both can find some closure now."

"Me too, Betty."

Magee had personally come over yesterday to break the news.

Because of Ryder's information, they'd found Mom's killer.

"What else did Sheriff Magee tell you yesterday?" Betty asked, taking a seat by their kitchen island.

I slid into the chair next to her, then glanced over my shoulder. Willa and I had decided not to give Ryder the dirty details about Mom's murder. We'd explained to him that Christopher, her ex-boyfriend, had killed Mom just as he'd suspected. But we hadn't told him even half of what the sheriff had explained.

We were protecting him, at least I hoped, because it wasn't a pretty story.

But it was one I felt comfortable sharing with Betty.

"Christopher was basically supporting Mom and Ryder for the year they lived with him in Las Vegas. Mom met him through a mutual friend. They hooked up. Two weeks later, he moved Mom and Ryder from Iowa to Vegas and right into his house."

I don't know if he really loved Mom or not. My guess was yes and the reason she was dead now was because she'd betrayed him.

"Christopher was a bookie," I told Betty. "And he kept a lot of cash around the house. Mom decided to relieve him of some of that cash when she and Ryder left Vegas for Denver."

"And that's when she started to look for you, right?" Betty asked. "Just because she needed a place to drop Ryder?"

I shrugged. "I don't know. Probably. I think she was also running out of money while they were in Denver. She'd been spending it like crazy, buying a car and living out of a hotel. Plus Ryder was sneaking it away from her. Either way, I'm glad she came looking. Who knows where Ryder would be if she had decided to keep him along."

I hated to think that he could have faced Christopher's wrath too.

"So after she dropped off Ryder with me, I guess she went back to Vegas. I assume it was to blackmail Christopher for more money."

That was what Magee assumed too. He'd been working nonstop to find evidence, though the most condemning pieces were the recordings she'd stashed with Ryder. Once Ryder handed those over, Magee found enough puzzle pieces to make sense of the picture.

Christopher had been skimming from his clients. Mom had found out. Just like she'd probably done with countless other people, she'd made recordings of Christopher admitting to taking extra "fees."

"It backfired on her," Betty muttered.

"Yes, it did."

Instead of getting more money from Christopher, he'd threatened to kill her. She'd fled Vegas again. That could have been the end of it, except Christopher had followed her.

Magee had gotten transcripts of the text messages sent from the phone Mom had falsely registered under Ryder's name. They showed an exchange between Christopher and Mom, further proving she was alive after I'd left her at the bar.

Thanks to the exchange, Magee knew Christopher had followed her to Montana. He'd likely promised to pay her off for her silence. Mom had sent him instructions of where to meet, down Old Logger's Road. But instead of giving her a payday, he'd strangled her with his bare hands, then driven her car into a ditch.

We didn't have proof that Christopher was the one who'd

broken into my house. But based on his credit card activity, it looked like he'd been hanging around Montana ever since he'd killed Mom. He'd probably been watching, waiting to see if they'd find her body. And when they did, he must have panicked. He waited for the right time and broke into my house, likely in search of the recordings he'd known Mom had taken.

Or the last of his cash.

I actually thought the break-in was a good thing. Without that incident, we might never have pushed Ryder as hard in the interrogation room.

"So what happens now?" Betty asked.

"Magee arrested Christopher at the hotel he'd been staying at in Kalispell. They've already pressed charges."

"And the phone registered under Ryder's name? Did they find it?"

"No. I'm sure Christopher destroyed it. But they got the text history from the phone company, so at least there's that."

Betty sighed. "What are the chances he'll get away with this?"

"According to Magee, slim to none. I hope to hell he's right."

Christopher hadn't confessed to the murder, and I doubted he would. His conviction would all come down to the evidence. But Magee was a good cop and would find enough to put that asshole away for the rest of his life.

"So that's it?" Betty asked.

I nodded. "That's it. Now we move on."

"Yes, we do." She stood from her seat and looked around the kitchen. "All right. What do I need to do before dinner? The meat's ready to go in. I need to peel some potatoes. Run the dishwasher. Take out the garbage."

I smiled as she continued with her verbal reminders. Willa did the same thing when she was planning. Her to-do lists came out in a whisper as she thought them through.

I stood from my seat and went to the garbage, opening the lid and tying up the bag. "I'll take this out."

"Oh, thank you. Once upon a time, Nate and I made an agreement. I'd do all his ironing if I never had to take out the garbage. Let's just say I haven't ironed one of his shirts in twenty-five years."

I chuckled. "I'll make you a deal. If I'm here, I've got the garbage. Just ask."

"Willa's a lucky woman."

"Nah." I grinned. "I'm the lucky one. I don't know if I deserve someone as good as your daughter. She's had to put up with a lot of my bull—er, crap lately."

"Yes, but dealing with the *bullshit* is how you know it's real." Betty smiled. "It's easy to love someone when times are good. Real love is about holding on to one another when times aren't."

I nodded, letting her words sink in.

Somehow, the timid woman who'd occasionally come into the bar—the girl whose name I'd fucked up for years—was the only person who'd made it past my barriers. She'd broken them down, one by one, and given me a love I'd cherish always.

"I do love her." For some reason, it was important to me that Betty knew I was truly committed to her daughter.

Her eyes softened and her mouth opened, but before she could respond, Ryder came bounding into the kitchen.

"I won!" He clapped and went right for the fridge, taking out the SunnyD that Betty kept stocked for him.

Nate and Willa came into the kitchen too, smiling at one another.

"Oh, I'll take that garbage, Jackson." Nate went for the bag, but I waved him off.

"No worries. I've got it."

"Thanks." He clapped my shoulder. "I hate garbage duty. I guess it's good that Betty and I made a deal years ago. I do my own ironing and she takes care of the garbage."

"What?" Betty's mouth fell open.

Willa giggled. "Uh, Dad? I think you might have that backward."

"No, I don't."

"Yes, you do!" Betty shouted.

I laughed, escaping the kitchen with the garbage bag in hand as the two began arguing over when and where they'd made the deal. When I got back inside, I hovered in the hallway outside the kitchen, just watching.

Willa and Ryder were doubled over, laughing hysterically. Betty and Nate were still arguing, though both had smiles on their faces. I bet they hadn't had a knockdown, drag-out fight in a decade.

They made marriage seem like the best damn idea in the world.

It was hard to believe that just a few months ago my life had been so lonely. Worse, I'd been okay with it.

I hadn't even known what I'd been missing.

Willa's laugh seeped into my heart, filling the last remaining cracks until it was whole.

From the corner of his eye, Nate caught me watching his daughter. He grinned, then went right back to arguing with his wife.

He knew why I was watching, and he knew why I was smiling.

Tomorrow, Willa would too.

"What about that one?"

I followed Willa's finger to the fir tree she was pointing at, then shook my head. "Too small."

"Too small. Too big. Too many pine cones. Too thin." She huffed. "You're the pickiest Christmas tree hunter in the universe."

I chuckled and stopped hiking. "Don't you want the perfect tree for our first Christmas together?"

"Yes." She stopped by my side. "That's why we should have bought one from the church's fundraiser. Those are grown to be perfect."

"What's the fun in that?" I put my gloved hands on each side of her face, then bent to kiss her forehead. "How are you doing?"

"Good." She smiled. Her nose and cheeks were pink from the cold and her chest was heaving as she breathed. "I didn't realize I was so out of shape."

"You're doing awesome. It's just because the snow is so deep."

"Should we look around here?" Her gaze ran over all the trees around us. "Or keep going?"

"Let's keep going. Just a little farther."

She didn't know it, but we were following the trail I'd left here this morning.

"It looks like we aren't the only ones who have been up here," she said. "There are tracks everywhere."

I grinned. "Yeah. Popular spot."

Ryder and I had hiked up here at first light to find the perfect tree. We'd told Willa that we were going ice fishing when we'd really come up to the mountains. So while she'd spent a quiet Sunday morning at my place, Ryder and I had trekked all over this area of forest in search of the perfect tree.

When we'd finally found it, we'd spent two hours setting everything up before hiking back down the mountain. Along the way, I'd made sure to make note of landmarks and leave a few of my own markings behind to guide us back to the spot.

I turned on the trail and took a couple more steps.

Behind me, Willa followed. "Can I ask you something?"

"Sure, babe."

"What's up with Hazel and Sheriff Magee?"

"Caught that, did you?"

"They either hate each other." She giggled. "Or don't hate each other at all."

"Hazel would never admit it, but she's got a thing for him. When I first moved here, he used to come into the bar all the time when she was working."

"Really? Did they ever date?"

"No. She turned him down every time he asked." I shot a look over my shoulder. "Kind of like someone else I know."

The red in Willa's cheeks got brighter. "I eventually gave in."

"It was the sticky notes, wasn't it?"

"And the Snickers." She wagged her eyebrows. "So what happened with Sheriff Magee?"

"I don't know." I shrugged. "He just stopped coming in to see her one day."

"Nooo," she groaned. "They'd be so cute together."

"He's like ten years younger than she is. I think the age difference freaked her out at first."

"That's too bad. I like him."

"So do I. Did you know I bought my house from him?"

"You did?"

I nodded. "When I moved here, I rented it from him. Hazel set it up. I didn't have shit at that point and I was broke all the time. There were a couple of months where I wasn't going to make rent by the first and he worked with me. I did improvements for him. He cut me a break. After I got on my feet, I told him I wanted to buy my own place. He said he'd sell me that one so I didn't have to move."

He'd given me a fair price and had been patient while I'd gotten a loan. It wasn't much of a payback, but when Dakota had moved to Lark Cove and needed a job, Thea and I had hired Magee's nephew immediately.

It was a win for the bar too. Dakota was good at his job, and as a bonus, he entertained the single ladies who used to drool over me.

"I'm glad you bought that house," Willa said.

I paused and looked back. "You are?"

"Yeah. It's got such great potential."

"Potential, huh?" I asked. "Does that mean you want to help me do some remodeling?"

"I might have a few ideas brewing." She smiled, excitement dancing in her blue eyes.

If she wanted to redesign the entire house, I'd let her. I couldn't afford to build her some fancy house on the lake or a lodge in the mountains. What I could give her was a nice home in town, someplace we could call ours.

"Come on, babe." I reached back for her hand.

She took mine immediately and I held it tight, my gloves to her mittens, as we walked around the last bunch of trees on the trail toward the clearing where I was taking her. When we rounded the evergreens and hit a flat spot, I stopped and turned around.

Willa's eyes were on the ground, watching her steps. But when she looked up, the happiness on her face nearly blew me over. "Need a break?"

"Yeah." I smiled at her, then jerked my chin so she'd look past my shoulder.

When she did, her smile fell. Her eyes got big and she looked between me and the tree. "What's going on?"

I kept her hand and pulled her toward the tree in the middle of the clearing—the tree that Ryder and I had decorated with silver and gold Christmas ornaments this morning.

In the sunny afternoon, the bulbs shone brightly. Along with the snow, they made the entire tree sparkle. And they made the single red bow tied right in the center of the tree nearly impossible to miss.

I led Willa right to the bow and waited for her to notice.

"Jackson, what is . . ." Her hand came to her mouth as she saw the ring I'd tied to the red velvet.

I shucked off my gloves, tossing them into the snow, then untied the bow, careful not to drop the ring I'd bought in Kalispell the day after Magee had cleared me of Mom's murder. Two days after that, I'd gone to the school and asked Nate for permission to marry his daughter.

"Willa Doon." I held the ring between my thumb and index finger, then dropped to a knee. "I love you. You're the reason I smile every day. You're the best friend I've ever had. You're my everything. And I want to be yours. I want to make every dream you've ever had come true. Will you marry me?"

Tears filled her eyes. "I thought you didn't want to get married to anyone."

"I don't. I want to get married to you."

"Are you sure? Because I don't want you to feel pressured to do—"

"Willa." I stood up swiftly, capturing her face with my free hand. "It's cold and I'm worried I'm going to drop this ring and then we'll have to spend the rest of our day digging for it in the snow instead of celebrating in the backseat of my truck. So I'm going to try this again."

She sniffled, a smile stretching across her face as I went back down on my knee.

"Marry me?"

"Yes."

"Now that wasn't so hard, was it?"

She laughed as a tear dripped down her cheek.

I stood again and wiped it away before taking off the mitten on her left hand. With steady fingers, I slid the delicate band to the base of her knuckle. "Do you like it?"

"I love it," she whispered, not taking her eyes off the ring. The center diamond sparkled in the sunlight. So did the halo of smaller white diamonds surrounding it.

The jewelry store would be receiving a monthly payment from me for a few years and I'd be delaying the purchase of a new truck, but it was worth it. Whatever I could give her, I would. Even kids.

Willa looked up from the ring. "I love you."

"Love you too, babe."

She smiled wide and a squeak escaped her lips. She giggled again, then launched herself into my arms.

I scooped her up, slamming my mouth down on hers. Then I kissed my fiancée long and deep. I explored her mouth with my tongue and nipped at her top lip. I sucked at the bottom. By the time we broke apart, we were panting, our breaths forming a frozen cloud around us.

"Do we need to take these ornaments down?" Willa asked, her eyes dark with heat. "Or can we celebrate?"

I grinned. "Fuck the tree. I'll come back up tomorrow."

"Okay, good. Let's go." She jumped out of my arms and started jogging down the trail.

I laughed, following close behind to catch her if she slipped.

The second we spotted the truck parked at the trailhead, Willa stripped off her coat. Her hat came next. She was bent over, untying her boots as I dug the keys out of my pocket and unlocked the doors.

She hopped into the backseat first and I followed, slamming the door to keep out the cold. Then we spent an hour fogging up the windows before we got dressed to drive back home.

As I pulled my truck onto the highway, Willa laughed out her passenger window.

"What?"

"I was just thinking." She smiled at her ring, then looked over. "When I was seventeen, I wrote in my diary that I was going to marry you one day."

My heart skipped. "You did?"

She nodded. "Seventeen-year-old Willa is doing a victory dance right now."

"Do you still have your diary?"

"Yeah. They're in a box at my parents' place. Why?"

"Research." I took her hand and kissed her knuckle, right above her ring. "Need to see what other dreams seventeen-year-old Willa had for her life."

I'd start with those, ticking them off one at a time, until all her dreams had come true.

epilogue

WILLA

Two and a half years later . . .

"WHAT IS THIS?" I ASKED JACKSON, STANDING IN front of a painting on the mantel above our fireplace.

"A present from Thea. I asked her to make it for me and she dropped it off this morning."

"But it's my birthday." I planted my hands on my hips. "Why are you getting presents?"

Jackson chuckled and wrapped his arms around me, pulling my back into his chest. "Don't worry. You get presents too."

"That better be plural," I mumbled.

He kissed my neck. "When have you ever gotten the shaft on your birthday?"

I smiled and reached behind me, palming the growing bulge behind his zipper. "I get the shaft every year on my birthday."

He laughed again, his voice booming in the living room. "This is true."

"Speaking of . . ." I turned around and went right for his belt. But before I could get it undone, he grabbed my wrists.

"We don't have time."

"Come on," I begged. "Real quick."

He shook his head, grinning before he kissed me. "We've done 'real quick' three times already. If we go again, we're going to be late."

"Ugh," I groaned. My hormones were out of control, but we had to get going. "Fine."

I was five months pregnant and wanted sex all the time. And if I wasn't having sex with Jackson, I was in search of food. My appetite was twice what it normally was. I could eat as much as Ryder, which was saying something.

At twelve, he'd had an appetite. At almost fifteen, it was nearly impossible to keep the fridge stocked. Jackson and I joked that the money I made from working as Logan's assistant in the winters all went directly to groceries.

"Ryder is staying with Hazel tonight," Jackson reminded me. "So as soon as we get home, I'm all yours. But we can't be late to your own birthday party."

"Okay." I huffed. "Let's go."

"I need to grab your presents, plural, then we can go."

I waved him off, then turned back to the painting.

It was beautiful, of course, because Thea was a gifted artist.

She'd painted me from behind, standing in front of the lake. My hair was down and a few pieces were blowing in the wind. You couldn't see my face, which I was glad for.

It was weird enough seeing it from the back.

"Ready." Jackson came from down the hall, carrying one gift bag and a wrapped box.

"Can I peek?"

"No way." He shook his head as he walked through the living room.

I took one last look at the painting before following. "So why did you ask Thea to do that painting?"

"I wanted one. She was bitching about needing a new art

project one night at the bar so I told her to paint me a picture of you."

"Why?"

He looked over his shoulder and shot me a *why do you think* look.

"Does it have to be on the mantel?" It was a beautiful piece, but on the mantel, it was the focal point of the living room. I didn't like to be so front and center.

"Yes."

"How about the hallway? Or our bedroom?"

"No."

"Jackson, be reasonable. It looks like you've built a shrine up there for me."

He ignored me, walking to the front door and setting down the presents on the little table I'd dragged him through five antique stores to find.

We'd spent the last year remodeling our house. I moved out of my tiny apartment above my parents' garage right after Jackson proposed. We saved up for a year and then hired a contractor to come in and remodel. There was a month where the place wasn't livable, so Jackson and I had stayed over the garage, for old times' sake, while Ryder camped out with Hazel.

But when the contractor finally finished the bedrooms and kitchen so we could all move back in, it was perfect.

Everything was updated and bright. We'd gotten new windows and floors. I'd even gotten a brand-new kitchen to make the guys breakfast every morning.

For the most part, Jackson and Ryder didn't care at all about the things I'd done to decorate. Ryder had done his own room, but the rest of the house had been mine.

But slowly, I was losing control over the mantel.

The first thing Jackson insisted on putting up there was our wedding picture. Since it was an amazing picture from an amazing day, I didn't argue.

The summer after Jackson proposed, we got married in the same church in Kalispell where my parents had gotten married. Then we drove back to Lark Cove and had a small reception at Hazel's lakeside cottage.

The picture on the mantel was of me and Jackson dancing under the twinkle lights in the tent we'd rented. My dress had a simple silhouette, fitted from the bodice through my hips. It was white with a lace overlay that went up to my neck and ended in delicate cap sleeves. My hair was curled and hanging loose down my back.

I loved that picture, especially seeing Jackson all dressed up in a tux. I would have put it on the mantel had he asked for it or not.

But over the last year, I kept coming home to find new additions up there. One by one, he'd built this Willa shrine. One framed picture was of me on the boat last summer, fishing. One was of me at camp, standing under the tall trees. The latest was one he'd taken of me barefoot in the kitchen, making french toast.

And now this painting.

It was too much.

"Please can we move it to the hallway?"

"No," he declared and pulled on his boots.

"Why?" I asked, getting frustrated.

He sighed and stood tall, stepping close to rest his hands on my shoulders. "Did I ever tell you why I came to your apartment above the garage that first night? That night you were all pissed off at me and I didn't know why?"

I thought back over the years, remembering that night. "No, I guess you didn't."

"I was at the bar that night, hanging with Thea. It was right before she went on that trip to New York, remember? Well, she was drawing in one of her sketchbooks that night. Guess who she was drawing?"

"Logan?"

He shook his head.

"Charlie?"

"You. She was drawing you."

"Me? Why me?"

"She used to do that a lot. She still does actually. When she gets bored, she draws the people who come into the bar. I guess you'd been there that night."

"Okay. So?"

"So . . . I saw that sketch and it opened my eyes. You'd been there, right in front of me all that time, and I'd been a blind fool. I left the bar and called Hazel, begging for your address. Then I showed up at your door and you yelled at me."

"Yes, I did." I smiled. "You deserved it."

He grinned, tucking a strand of my hair behind my ear. "Yeah, I did."

"So how does that lead to a painting above my fireplace?"

Jackson reached into his back pocket and pulled out his wallet. He thumbed through it and carefully pulled out a folded piece of paper. Slowly, he opened it up and handed it over for me to see.

It was the drawing he'd just described.

He'd kept it in his pocket all this time.

"Jackson," I whispered.

"I like to keep that with me, but I can't look at it every day, or it'll get ruined. So instead, I have those." He pointed over my head to the mantel. "Now tell me, what does this picture and all of those have in common?"

I turned and followed his pointed finger. Just like the sketch in my hand, all of those pictures and the painting were of me with my hair down.

"My hair."

He twisted a couple of strands around his finger. "Your hair. Your hair looks the same in all of them. So if I can't pull out this drawing every day, then I get those instead."

"We could just get this sketch framed," I offered.

He took the paper from my hands and carefully refolded it before returning it back to his wallet. "It stays with me."

I stayed with him. That's what he was really saying.

I stroked my baby bump. "If we have a little boy, I hope he's as sweet as his daddy."

Jackson pulled me into his arms. "If we have a little girl, I know she'll be as beautiful as her mommy."

I relaxed into his chest, enjoying this quiet minute together before we went to the chaos of my birthday party. It would be fun, but there wouldn't be time for a peaceful hug with so many people around.

My parents would be there, along with some of my aunts, uncles and cousins from Kalispell. We'd invited Leighton and Brendon to come and introduce us to their new baby girl. June and Hannah were driving down too.

I didn't see my high school girlfriends as much as I used to, but we'd settled into a different kind of friendship. One where we made it a point to attend birthday parties and baby showers.

Hazel was hosting my party. Ryder was already there to help her set up. Thea, Logan and their two kids would be there too. Thea was pregnant again—a couple months ahead of me—so at least I wouldn't be the only one pigging out on birthday cake.

I had fully embraced the excuse of eating for two.

To my surprise, Jackson had been the one to bring up the

topic of children. I'd been perfectly fine just enjoying our time as husband and wife, but on his birthday last fall, he'd asked me to go off my birth control.

When I'd asked him why, he'd told me it was because of his time spent coaching. He was co-coaching Charlie's soccer team with Logan, and he was an assistant for Ryder's football team. He didn't want to be too old to coach his kids in sports.

That day, he'd given me another dream. It was one I hadn't written about in my diaries, but it was one I'd always held in my heart.

"Do you love me?" I whispered.

He kissed my hair. "I love you so much, Willow."

"Hey!" I pinched his side, making him chuckle.

"Still too soon, huh?"

I leaned back, trying not to smile at the smirk on my husband's face. "Just for that, you owe me two orgasms tonight and you have to bring me ice cream in bed if I wake up hungry."

"Orgasms and ice cream. I can do that." He took my hand, scooped up the presents in his other and led me out the door.

Later that night, he gave me the two promised orgasms before I passed out, exhausted. And when I woke up hungry at three in the morning, he brought me a huge bowl of ice cream to eat in bed.

He catered to my every whim for the next four months, right up until our little boy, Roman Page, was born.

And he did the same when I was pregnant with our daughter, Zoe, two years later.

BONUS
Story

XAVIER

"Thanks for coming to my party." Willa hugged me as Jackson loaded up a stack of her birthday gifts into his truck.

"Thanks for the invite." I smiled, taking in her growing baby bump. "Take care of yourself and this little one."

"I will." Willa's eyes softened as she stroked her belly. "Can I ask you something?"

I nodded. "Of course."

"I overheard you tell Jackson you were going to announce your retirement next week. Are you doing okay with that decision? I know you've been talking about it for a while, but I wasn't sure if you were serious. I don't know if I can imagine someone other than you as the sheriff."

"You and me both." I sighed. "But . . . yeah, I'm serious. It's time to hand over my star. It's been a good job, but it's taken its toll. Lately I'm just feeling . . . tired."

I'd lived in Lark Cove for over thirty years now, and a good portion of that had been spent as the sheriff. I'd worked my ass off for decades, not wanting anything bad to happen in town on my watch.

And because a piece of me wanted to prove that a Native

American sheriff could be successful in a predominately white town.

I'd caught a lot of flak from my family on the reservation when I'd made the decision to move away. They couldn't understand why I didn't want to work for the tribal authorities like my father had before he was killed.

They couldn't understand why I wanted to find my own path.

No one in my family had ever lived anywhere but the reservation, and it had been like that generation after generation. I'd broken the chain and gone away to the police academy. Then my mother and grandparents had disowned me when I hadn't returned.

Those first few years working as a deputy for the former sheriff had been hard. I'd fought stereotypes and had been tempted to return home more than once. But I'd stuck it out and eventually earned the trust of the community.

I'd bought a nice house in town, then when I could afford it, I'd upgraded to another. Both were nicer than anything I'd lived in before. I'd made Lark Cove my home and heritage.

Then one day, my nephew Dakota had called, asking me to help him break away from the reservation too. Maybe it was because I'd paved the road for him, maybe not, but I was pleased to see that he'd been welcomed to town with open arms.

"We'll miss you at the station." Willa wrapped her arm around my side for another hug. "But I guess that just means you'll be free for more family functions."

I chuckled. "This is true."

"Bye." Willa waved, then walked over to her husband.

Jackson nodded good-bye to me, then helped her into the truck, practically lifting her inside. His younger brother hopped in too, then waved as they pulled away from the curb.

Over the last couple of years, I'd spent a lot of special occasions with Jackson and Willa Page. Ever since that ordeal with Jackson's mother, Willa had pulled me into their circle.

She invited me to birthday parties and holiday events. They had me over for dinner a few times a year. And whenever I came into the bar to catch a ballgame, she'd sit in the stool by my side.

Willa had this way of issuing an invitation that was impossible to turn down. And for it, I was grateful. Work had come first for so many years it hadn't left much room for a personal life.

But now, as retirement was looming, I realized the life I'd created was lonely. The next ten or twenty years didn't seem all that appealing.

Especially without the one person I'd always imagined by my side.

That one person who had been avoiding me for too damn long.

Hazel Rhodes.

The first time I saw her in the Lark Cove Bar, the wind had gotten knocked clean out of me. I remembered it like it was yesterday, not years ago. I'd come in to introduce myself to the bar's new owner, and there she'd been, laughing with a customer and smoking a cigarette.

Her eyes shone so bright, I fought the urge to shield my eyes. Her smile, white and unwavering, held a hint of mischief as she looked me up and down. She waved me over to a stool, poured me a beer and I stayed until closing.

I spent a lot of long nights at the bar during those days.

Then I spent a lot of long nights in the very cottage I was standing outside of now.

I let things fall apart between us. I let what once was love—at least for me—turn into frustration as she pushed me away. Now we could barely stand being in the room with one another.

Hazel was angry at me for things outside of my control.

I was angry at her for being so damn stubborn.

Maybe it was time to retire the anger too.

Was this why Willa always invited me to family functions? Because she knew Hazel would be here too? My feelings for Hazel hadn't been as hidden as I'd thought.

I chuckled to myself. Willa Page was one sharp cookie. She may be shy, but she didn't miss much.

A noise came from the back porch of the cottage—Hazel busy tearing down the party remains.

It was just me and her left tonight. While Willa and I had been chatting and Jackson had loaded her birthday gifts, the rest of the party had cleared out.

I shook my head, laughing to myself again.

She'd set me up.

And I guess it was time for me to make a move a decade overdue.

HAZEL

"Here's two more."

I turned from the hall closet at the deep voice behind me. I frowned as Xavier Magee strode inside carrying two folding chairs from the porch. It was bad enough that Willa kept inviting him to our family functions. He could at least have the decency to leave when everyone else did.

"I thought you'd left."

"Nope."

"I can do it." I tried to take the chairs from him, but Xavier shot me a glare, then came right into my space, essentially pushing me out of the way so he could fit the chairs next to the others.

"See?" He shut the closet door. "I can do it too."

I frowned again and went to the kitchen, doing my best to ignore his presence in my home.

It was like this every time he came to an event. I'd get assaulted with a rush of memories from the affair we'd had all those years ago. How long had it been? Ten years? No, more like eleven or twelve.

Yet, I could still picture him at my kitchen table, drinking his morning coffee. I could see him lazing on my couch, both of his arms across the back as he watched reruns of *Bonanza* on the television. Every now and then, I'd swear I could still smell his spicy cologne on my bedsheets even though I'd washed them a thousand times.

After hosting a large birthday party, I didn't have the energy to deal with those memories tonight.

I went to the back door and opened the screen for him. "Good of you to come to Willa's party. I'm sure she was happy to have you."

Xavier stood on the opposite side of the kitchen, casually leaning against the wall. "It was nice of her to invite me."

I looked to the door, then back to him. "It's getting late."

"Yeah. It is." He didn't move. He just held me with those dark eyes.

My heartbeat kicked up a notch. The only person in the world who could unnerve me with a stare was Xavier Magee. No one had power over me anymore, I was too old, but Xavier had always been the exception.

"See you around." Again, I looked at the door, then back at him.

He pushed off the wall and I breathed a sigh of relief. But instead of crossing the kitchen to leave, he slid off his black Stetson and set it upside down on the dining room table. Then he went back to the wall, leaning as he crossed his arms. His eyes stayed locked on me the entire time.

I looked at his hat and frowned. Once upon a time, Xavier had taught me the proper way to set down a cowboy hat. They had to be upside down; otherwise the brim would bend. It was one of a million things we'd talked about on the nights he used to come to the bar and keep me company.

Those nights were ancient history now. I'd asked him to stop coming down to the bar. I'd asked him to stop coming to the cottage at night.

I'd ended our relationship before it had really ever gotten off the ground.

Xavier had been pissed. He'd pushed back for a couple of weeks, but finally he'd given up.

That might have hurt worse than anything. So how had I handled it? I'd gotten pissed too.

For a year or so, we'd barely been able to stomach being in the same room together. Needless to say, his visits to the bar had stopped. And I avoided the diner during the lunch hour because he ate there more often than not.

It was for the best. He had the county to worry about. I had Jackson and Thea, who each needed some attention. After a few years, we learned to be civil—barely—to one another.

So what was he doing here tonight? Hadn't we settled into a good routine where we avoided eye contact and one-on-one time?

As I stood there doing my best to figure him out, Xavier untied the elastic band from his long hair, setting the strands free. He combed his hair out with his fingers, shaking it loose.

More memories came back to me as his hair settled down his back.

I'd always hated that part of the night when he'd come over and let his hair down before relaxing. His hair was always such a stark reminder of our age difference. Maybe it was due to his Blackfoot heritage or maybe just the luck of the draw; regardless, the man had always looked younger than his years. His black, shiny hair made me resent the gray, colorless strands of my own.

Except now, Xavier's hair was dominated by gray. His face, one that was just as handsome as ever, was beginning to show some wrinkles. The differences between us didn't stand out as much.

Still, numbers didn't lie.

"Did you need something, Xavier?"

He stood stoically in his place. "No."

"It's getting late. Time to get on."

"I'm staying."

"What?" I gaped at him, then let go of the door to cross my arms over my chest. "What exactly gives you the impression you've been invited to stay?"

"I got an invitation a long time ago."

"Which has since been rescinded."

He chuckled and pushed off the wall. He went to the cupboard where I kept the glasses and got out one, then strode to the sink and filled it with water.

I stood there, dumbfounded, as he drank. When he finished, he opened the dishwasher and set it inside. He was still courteous. *Damn it.* I sent him my best glare, hoping it would chase him away.

The bastard had the balls to laugh. "Save that scowl for Jackson or Thea. You should know by now it doesn't work on me. Well, except to turn me on."

My mouth fell open. Weren't we too old for turn-ons? Maybe not. Xavier's presence made my body . . . react.

He noticed. "Come on, baby. Lock the door and hit the lights. Let's go to bed."

Damn, I liked it when he called me baby. I always had. But *why* was he calling me baby? "Are you drunk?"

"Nope."

"Then what makes you think you'll be staying in my bed tonight?"

"Not just tonight. Every night."

"You're drunk." He had to be.

Xavier came closer, taking one of my hands in his. "I'm not drunk. But I am staying. We had a good thing a while back and I gave up too easily when you told me to stop coming to the bar. That was a mistake. One I'm rectifying tonight."

"By trespassing?"

He grinned. "You need me to call the sheriff?"

"Xavier, this is ridiculous."

"No, it's the best damn idea I've had in twenty years."

"What exactly do you think is going to happen?"

"I've got a couple of ideas." He stepped closer, his large fingers skimming my cheek. A shiver rolled down my back. It was familiar, a sensation he used to give me daily. Funny how you don't realize how much you've been missing something until you get it back.

I stared into his dark eyes, wishing things were different. But if I was too old for him a decade ago, I was certainly too old for him now.

"I'm too old."

"For what? Sex? Who says?"

"Me."

He laughed, his barrel of a chest shaking as the rumble

spread through the kitchen, making my knees weak. When he stopped, he grabbed one of my hands and pulled me away from the door. Then he locked it himself.

With my hand tight in his, he pulled me across the kitchen.

"Xavier, enough. Go home." I tugged, trying to get my hand free but he didn't let go.

"Don't fight me, woman. You know I'm not going to hurt you. Just . . . let me show you something, okay?"

I frowned, glaring at him again. It really didn't affect him, did it? Damn.

"Why are you dragging me into the powder room?"

"Quiet." He squished our bodies together, positioning me in front of the oval mirror. Our faces stared right back.

"What do you see?" he asked.

I sighed, taking in my crow's feet and the lines around my face. "An old woman."

He shook his head. "I see a beautiful woman with the brightest eyes I've ever seen. I see a woman with white hair who I've been in love with for years, but she thinks she's too old for me."

"I'm ten years older than you."

"Nine years and four months," he corrected. "And I don't give a fuck about your age."

My heart twisted and I sucked in a sharp breath. "It's too late."

"It's never too late."

"Xavier—"

He cut me off. "You know what else I see? A man who isn't all that young anymore. I see a man who would very much like to live out the rest of his days with someone he loves. So that's what we're going to do. We can either live out those years here or at my place."

"I'm not giving up my house."

He grinned. "Fine. Then I'll let Dakota take my place."

"This is crazy."

"This is real, baby," he whispered. "This is two adults deciding that they've wasted enough time being pissed at one another for a whole slew of reasons I'm not getting into tonight and saying to hell with them all. They're in the past and we're done with them. We've got some good years left, so let's enjoy them together. What do you say?"

I looked at his reflection in the mirror, holding his eyes. Could it really be this simple? Could it really just be me and him living out our final days in my house, watching all the kids grow?

Wasn't I too old for this? We'd probably kill each other. I'd made peace with my lot in life. I'd never believed I'd get this. Love. Really, I'd never given myself a chance to find it. I'd been too busy raising two broken kids who'd needed a mother more than I'd needed a man.

But now we were past it all. And the future looked . . . lonely.

Except it didn't have to be. It didn't have to be empty.

There was no use denying that I was in love with Xavier Magee. I'd loved him from the moment he'd walked into my bar and handed me his phone number to tape by the phone in case there was ever a problem.

"Hazel?" He nudged my side and I turned from the mirror, blinking away a sheen of tears.

When I searched his eyes, I found my answer.

Simple. It really was this simple.

So I grabbed his face and kissed him.

His soft lips melted against mine, his tongue sliding inside to sweep across mine. The desire he'd stirred in the kitchen surged to new levels as my arms roamed that broad chest and moved up to tangle in the silken strands of his hair.

He wrapped his arms around my back, sighing as we fell

into one another. The feel of his arousal pressed into my hip.

We were definitely *not* too old for sex.

Xavier's kiss was powerful and claiming, like the ones I watched in my favorite black-and-white movies. It rivaled the time Humphrey Bogart kissed Ingrid Bergman, or Clark Gable laid one on Vivien Leigh.

Though a bit dirtier, just how I liked it.

When we broke apart, the smile on his face made my heart skip. *God, don't give out on me.* I needed that heart for a few more years.

"I don't want to make a big deal out of this," I told him. "You can just move in. This doesn't need to be some hoorah where the whole damn town shows up to watch you move your clothes into my closet."

"Fine by me. But we're getting married."

I narrowed my eyes. "You could ask, you know."

"Ordering you around seems to be working for me tonight, so we're going to keep on with it. Maybe tomorrow I'll be more chivalrous." He winked. "Maybe not."

I fought a smile but lost. "Fine."

"Fine, what? Fine, you'll marry me?" he asked.

"Yep. I'll marry you. But don't expect me to wear white. It's not my color."

"Baby, you can wear whatever the hell color you want as long as you say yes."

Yes.

Finally, yes.

Enjoy this preview from *Tragic*,
book three in the Lark Cove series.

tragic

prologue

KAINE

ONE OR TWO.

"Kaine?" Mom's voice echoed off the cement walls as she stepped outside. The glass door swished as it closed behind her.

I didn't look at her as she stepped up to my side. My eyes were aimed blankly ahead as I wrestled with my decision.

One or two.

"What are you doing out here?" she asked. "We've been looking all over the hospital for you."

I wasn't sure how long I'd been standing out here. I'd told Mom that I was going to the bathroom and that I'd be back soon to talk with the doctors. But when I'd passed this exit door, hidden on the bottom floor in the back wing of the hospital, it had beckoned me through.

I'd needed a few moments away from the red-rimmed eyes and sniffling noses. I'd needed just a few seconds to pass without a single person asking me if I was okay.

I needed some quiet to decide.

One or two.

The parking lot ahead of me was shrouded in darkness. The night itself was pitch-black. There were no stars shining. There was no moon glowing. A thick fog had settled in, dulling the light of the streetlamps so their beams barely illuminated the few cars parked on the asphalt. The air should have been cold on my bare arms, but I couldn't feel it.

I was numb.

I'd felt this way for hours, ever since they took her from my arms.

One or two.

It was an impossible choice, one I shouldn't have to make. But because of *him*, it was inevitable.

"Kaine, I'm so sorry. What can I do?"

"I can't decide." My voice was rough as I spoke, the burn of rage and sorrow and pain making it nearly impossible to speak.

"Decide what?" she whispered. I didn't need to look to know that Mom's eyes were full of tears. Her dark hair had gotten a dozen new grays tonight. Her normally cheery and bright hazel eyes held their own fog of grief.

"One or two."

"One or two what?"

I swallowed the fire in my throat. "Graves."

One or two.

"Oh, Kaine." Mom began to weep and her hand reached for my arm, but I shied away. "Please come inside, sweetheart. Please. We need to talk about this. *He* needs to talk to you. Give him a chance to explain."

"I have nothing to say to him." He'd done this. He was the reason I had to decide.

"Kaine, it was an accident. A tragic accident." She hiccupped. "He—"

I walked away before she could finish. I walked right into the dark, wishing this blackness would swallow me whole.

Mom's voice rang across the parking lot as she called out, but I simply walked, my boots carrying me into the black.

One or two.

An impossible choice.

As if the heavens sensed my despair, the clouds opened. Rain poured down, soaking my dark hair. It dripped over my eyes and coated my cheeks. The water soaked my jeans, making them cling to my legs.

But I couldn't feel the water droplets as they streamed down the bridge of my nose. I couldn't feel the locks of hair that were stuck to my forehead. I couldn't feel the wet denim on my thighs as it rubbed my skin raw.

I was numb. There was nothing.

Nothing except the weight of four pounds, two ounces wrapped in a pink blanket resting in my arms as I said good-bye.

One or two.

What would Shannon want?

One. She'd choose one.

So I'd bury them together.

Then surrender to the black.

one

PIPER

"YOU'RE HERE!" THEA RUSHED ACROSS THE RUNWAY.

"I'm here!" I stepped off the last stair of my boss's private jet just as she threw her arms around me. The Kendrick family, Thea in particular, was arguably more excited about this adventure of mine than I was.

Montana, meet your newest resident: Piper Campbell.

I loved it here already.

The sky above me was blue with only a few wisps of feathered clouds. The sunshine was warm on my shoulders and the April air fresh in my nose. Any doubts I'd had about moving floated away in the mountain breeze.

Thea gave me one last squeeze for good measure, then stood back so her husband could take her place.

"Hey, boss." I gave Logan a mock salute as I infused the word *boss* with as much sarcasm as possible.

Logan chuckled, shaking his head as he came in for an embrace. His hug wasn't quite as enthusiastic as his wife's, but it was a close second. "It's good to see you."

"You too," I told him as he let me go. Then I gave him a diabolical smile. "It will be much easier to give you orders in person than over the phone."

"Maybe this was a bad idea." He frowned and looked over

my shoulder at his family's pilot standing on top of the plane's staircase. "Mitch, Ms. Campbell isn't staying after all. You'd better turn this thing around and take her back to the city."

"Ignore him!" I called over my shoulder to Mitch, who laughed and went back inside the plane.

I was Logan's assistant but gave him a hard time about who was really in charge. His ego could use a little razzing now and then. It was all in good fun because we both knew that I'd be lost without him. He was the best boss I could have ever asked for.

Logan took the backpack from my shoulder and slung it over his. "I'm glad you're here."

"So am I." I stepped around him, going right for the cutest little girl on the planet. "Charlie!"

She smiled and left Thea's side, rushing forward for a hug. "Hey, Piper."

"I've missed you, kiddo. I want to hear all about school and your soccer team."

"Okay." She smiled and took my hand, showing no signs of letting it go anytime soon.

Spending time with Charlie Kendrick was pure joy—except for the tiny pinch of longing that poked me in the side.

With her quiet voice and sweet nature, Charlie didn't act like a princess or a diva. She was a tomboy, much like I had been at her age. Instead of a tiara, she wore an old, faded baseball cap over her long, brown hair the same color as her dad's. There wasn't a stitch of pink or purple anywhere in sight.

If I could have had a little girl, I would have wanted one as precious and unique as Charlie.

I ignored the pinch and held out my free hand to fist-bump her little brother, Collin. "Hey, bud."

He gave me a shy smile but held fast to his dad's leg. Collin was destined to be beautiful, like his siblings. While Charlie took after Logan, Collin was the spitting image of his mother, with nearly black hair and rich, dark eyes.

I winked at him, then went over to the baby carrier where eight-month-old Camila was fast asleep. "I can't believe how much she's grown in four months," I told Thea as I looked adoringly at Camila's chubby cheeks.

"They always say time flies after you have children. It's the truth."

Another pinch, but I ignored it too.

I'd have to get over those now that I was living here. Whenever Logan and Thea had come to New York, I'd always volunteered to babysit the kids so their parents could have a night out, and I planned to do a lot more of that now that I was living in Montana.

I was determined to become Aunt Piper, blood relation be damned.

"How much stuff did you bring along?" Logan asked.

"Not much." I turned back to the plane as one of the attendants hauled a large suitcase down the stairs. "That case plus two more. The rest is in storage until I find a place here. Then I'll have it shipped out."

"All right." Logan smiled at Thea. "You guys get loaded up and I'll take care of the bags."

Twenty minutes later, my suitcases were in the back of Logan's beast of a silver SUV and we were headed down the highway toward my new hometown.

Lark Cove.

"It's so beautiful." My nose was practically pressed against the window as I soaked everything in. "It takes my breath away every time."

Tall evergreens lined the highway, towering above us into the bright sky. Past their thick trunks, the water of Flathead Lake rippled and glittered under the sun's rays.

Paradise.

"And now you get to live here." Logan smiled at me in his rearview mirror.

I smiled back, then returned to the scenery. "And now I get to live here."

My parents thought I was crazy for giving up my apartment in Manhattan to move to a small town in Montana I'd only visited once—maybe they were right. But I needed this change of pace.

I'd spent months grieving the death of my marriage. I'd come to terms with what I would and wouldn't have in my life. And when the dust had settled, I'd realized New York wasn't home anymore.

The only thing that had kept me in the city after Adam and I divorced had been my job. Working for Logan at the Kendrick Foundation, his family's charitable organization, was the best part of each day. But after a while, even work couldn't fill the lonely void.

This past Christmas, I'd confided in Thea that I was looking for a change and that it might involve me quitting. She'd passed it along to Logan, who had adamantly refused to accept my resignation. Instead, he'd offered to move me anywhere in the world to work remotely.

When he'd tossed out the idea of Montana, it had stuck. I could *see* myself living here.

I wanted empty highways instead of crowded city streets. I craved more space than the six-inch personal bubble people allowed me on the subway. I was sick and tired of seeing my ex-husband's face on every corner, plastered to buses and billboards.

So I'd waited out the winter, enduring the longest four months of my life while I hid behind the walls of my apartment.

Then I packed up my stuff, bid farewell to my family and friends and said good-bye to the city of my past.

Adam got to keep New York in our divorce.

I was taking Lark Cove, a town he hadn't ruined.

The thirty-minute drive from the airport to Lark Cove went by fast. While the kids laughed, Thea and I talked about her latest art project and how things were going at the bar she ran with her best friend. Logan had tried to sneak in a few work topics, but his wife had shut him down immediately, reminding him it could wait until the weekend was over.

And then, before I knew it, we were here. Home.

"Don't blink or you'll miss it," Logan teased as we passed a small green sign that read *Entering Lark Cove*.

My smile got wider, my dimples no doubt deepening. "It's better than I remember."

He drove slowly through the quaint town, letting me take in all of the businesses clustered along the highway. I saw things differently than when I'd come out here a few years ago for Logan and Thea's wedding. Then, I'd only been a tourist, excited to witness my boss get married.

Now I was a resident.

I was giddy at the prospect of grocery shopping at the small mercantile. Bob's Diner looked like my new favorite cheeseburger joint. When I went into Thea's bar, it would be as a regular patron.

And maybe one day, I'd meet a handsome man in town who'd be up for a casual, uncomplicated relationship.

The majority of the homes in Lark Cove were set behind the businesses along the highway. They were normal-sized homes situated in friendly blocks where everyone knew their neighbors.

On the other side of the highway, the lakeside, the homes were larger. They reminded me of the houses in the Hamptons, though not quite as big and more rustic lake house than beach chateau.

Logan turned off the highway toward the lakeside of town, following a quiet road that wrapped around the shoreline until he pulled up to a house that screamed Logan Kendrick.

It was all class, like the man himself: handsome with its cedar shakes and gleaming windows and well-manicured lawn. The boathouse on the water was larger than most of the homes we'd passed in town. The loft above it was going to be my abode for the next couple of weeks or months, however long it took to buy my own place.

As Logan parked in the detached garage and shut off the SUV, Charlie hurried to unbuckle her seat belt. "Piper, do you want to see my fort?"

"You know it!" I told her, helping Collin free from his car seat. The two-year-old squirmed out and crawled to the front before I could stop him.

"Daddy! Daddy!" he yelled, then giggled as Logan swung him out of the car and tossed him into the air.

"Come on, little one," Thea said, opening the back door to get out Camila's carrier. "I bet you need a diaper change and a bottle."

Camila cooed at her mother, her tiny mouth forming a hint of a smile. The jury was out on which parent she took after, but I'd get a front-row seat to watch as she grew up.

I climbed out behind them all, deciding to leave my suitcases for the time being. I wanted to play with the kids some before dinner.

"When is the meeting with your realtor?" Thea asked as we walked toward the house.

"Tomorrow," I said as Charlie slipped her hand in mine. "He's got three places lined up for me to see."

"Want some company? Logan can watch the kids and I can tag along to give you the inside scoop on potential neighbors."

"You wouldn't mind? I'd love to have your input."

I'd thought of inviting Thea along on my house-hunting trip, but I didn't want to smother her. The last four months had been incredibly lonely, and since she was my only girlfriend in Lark Cove, the chances were real that she'd get sick of me soon.

"Of course, I wouldn't mind," Thea said. "Though I should warn you, I'm probably going to become that friend who calls and texts too often. Have I mentioned that I'm really excited you're living here?"

She couldn't have known, but I'd really needed those words and the enthusiasm in her voice. Thea Kendrick was good people.

"Ready to see my fort?" Charlie asked.

I looked to Thea, just to make sure it was okay. She nodded and smiled. "I'll get Camila changed and fed, then we'll come find you. White wine or red?"

I amended my earlier thought. Thea Kendrick was *great* people. "White, please."

"You got it." She smiled and disappeared into the house with the baby.

"I'll take care of your suitcases," Logan told me as he set Collin down to go play in the yard. "You just relax."

"Thank you, Logan. For everything."

He patted my shoulder. "You're welcome. Glad you're home."

Home. I was home.

As he followed Collin to a stack of toys on the deck, I turned down to Charlie. "Fort time?"

She nodded. "Want to race?"

I slipped out of my four-inch stilettos. "Loser is a rotten egg!"

The next day, Thea and I were hiking through the trees behind the home my realtor had just shown us. This particular property was located in the mountains and had some acreage in the forest. So while the two of us were exploring, my realtor was back at the car, giving us a moment to debrief without him hovering.

"What do you think?" Thea asked.

"I don't know." I sighed. "That house is . . . there are no words."

She giggled. "I've never seen a house so dedicated to a decade."

"Ugh. Have you ever seen such hideous carpet? It was like the designer looked at an orange creamsicle and said, 'How can I turn this into a paisley shag?'"

"Exactly." She laughed again. "I can't get over those yellow cabinets in the kitchen. And that wallpaper? Lime green stripes should never be paired with beige."

I looked over my shoulder to the house and grimaced. It was an old-style rancher with three bedrooms, each needing a complete overhaul to bring them into this decade. Did I have it in me to take on such a large project?

This was our last showing of the afternoon. The first two homes we'd seen were in town. Both were nice, far better than this sixties monstrosity, but they were within twenty feet of a neighbor on each side.

I'd spent over a decade in apartment buildings and townhomes, sharing walls and public spaces with neighbors. I was ready to have some space.

"You're sure you don't want to look for something down along the lake?" Thea asked. "Something newer?"

"I just can't afford any of those listings right now." Only a few lakeside properties were on the market, and everything available was way outside of my budget.

Thanks for that, Adam. In a dick move, he'd contested our divorce, forcing me to spend a chunk of my savings on an expensive attorney.

So to stay within my price range, I'd have to purchase a house in the middle of Lark Cove or buy this one and do a complete renovation. The first choice was by far the easiest. But the latter option had its perks too.

This fifteen-acre property on the mountainside was gorgeous, and there was only one neighbor, a cabin about fifty yards away. It was close enough to run over in an emergency but far enough that I wouldn't have to see them unless it was intentional.

"I do like it up here in the mountains." Though Thea's lakeside home was peaceful, there was something enchanting about being surrounded by hundred-year-old trees. The forest smelled rich and mossy with a hint of pine spice in the air.

"It's a beautiful spot with your own hiking trail. You wouldn't have to worry about setting up a home gym. Just climb this every day and you'd be in killer shape."

"No kidding." I was breathing harder than I ever had in a spin class.

We continued our hike, going up the steady incline behind the house that led to a ridge at the back of the property. My realtor had pointed us in this direction, encouraging us to hike to the top.

He was a good salesman, that one. The farther away from the house we walked, the more I was willing to buy it just so I'd have this as my backyard.

By the time we reached the final stretch of the trail, my

thighs were burning. Sweat was beaded at my hairline and a drop rolled down my cleavage. I was comfortable in my cuffed boyfriend jeans and a casual T-shirt, but what I really should have worn was my gym attire.

"Almost there," I told Thea as the trees opened up and the ridge came into view.

We pushed through the last twenty feet and smiled at one another as the trail leveled off, turning to run along the ridge. We followed it, stepping into an open meadow filled with spring wildflowers.

"Wow," Thea whispered. "I'm starting to think a remodel is the way to go. Who cares what the house is like when you have this?" She held out her hands to the view.

"This is . . . unbelievable."

From here, the towering mountains were visible in the distance. The one we'd just climbed was no more than an anthill in comparison. The valleys below were green and lush. The horizon went on and on for miles, and nearly the entire lake spread out behind our backs.

"Let's keep going." I took one step farther down the trail, but Thea grabbed my arm, holding me back.

"Wait," she whispered, her eyes aimed ahead of us.

A momentary flash of panic hit. *Is it a bear?* I didn't want to get eaten by a bear on my first real day in Montana. Slowly, I turned and followed her gaze, my feet ready to bolt at the sight of a grizzly.

But it wasn't an animal that had caused her to freeze.

It was a man.

He was kneeling on the ground, about thirty feet in front of us. His head was bent and his eyes closed. His hands were pressed against his cheeks, his fingers straight as they steepled at the bridge of his nose.

Was he praying? Or meditating? Whatever he was doing, he was so consumed with it that he hadn't noticed us down the trail.

His shaggy brown hair curled around his ears and at the back of his neck. His jaw was covered in a dark beard that tried its best to hide the fact that its owner was likely quite handsome. His green shirt was strung tight across his biceps and broad shoulders. It showcased the corded muscles of his back.

Even from a distance it was clear that he was the quintessential mountain man, big and brawny.

My first instinct was to get closer. I wanted to see what his face looked like if his hands dropped. I wanted to see the breeze play at the curled ends of his hair. But besides his rugged appeal, there was something else drawing me in. Something that made me want to wrap my arms around his narrow waist and promise him it would be okay.

He had a tragic allure, one that screamed sorrow and loss. I knew that pain all too well. Recognition hit me like a flash and I spun around, hurrying back in the direction we'd come.

That man was up here to grieve, and we'd just intruded on his private moment.

Thea was right by my side as I hustled to the trees, doing my best to keep my footsteps quiet. I held my breath until we disappeared into the safety of the forest. Neither of us spoke as we hiked down the trail, retreating to the house.

"I hope he didn't hear us," Thea said.

"Me too. Do you know who that is?"

She shook her head. "No, I've never seen him before, which is strange. I know almost everyone in Lark Cove. I bet he's just visiting. We get a lot of tourists who come up and hike in the mountains."

I nodded as my realtor spotted us. "What did you think?

Nice spot, isn't it?"

"It's beautiful." Except when I took in the house's exterior, my face soured.

The house was a tribute to midcentury modern design with a plethora of windows and odd roof angles. It was as far from my traditional taste as you could get, and to renovate this into my forever home, I'd have to change everything.

My head ached just thinking about the construction bill.

"I can tell you the sellers are motivated on this one," my realtor said. "It belongs to a brother and sister who each live out of state. It was a vacation home for their parents, who have since both passed. It's been empty for about a year now."

Which explained the musty smell and the recent price drop.

"Can I think about it?" I asked him.

"Of course. Take all the time you need."

Thea gave me a reassuring smile, then got into the back of the car. I took one last look at the house, frowned again, then turned toward the trail we'd come down.

Find some peace. I sent my silent wish to the man on top of the mountain.

Pushing the stranger from my mind, I went to the other side of the car and got in the passenger seat. We drove down the long gravel driveway, then took yet another gravel road, this one wider and more traveled, that led back to the highway. With a wave good-bye from Thea's front yard, I promised my realtor to be in touch soon.

"How'd it go?" Logan asked the minute we came inside. Camila was crying as he rocked her in his arms and Collin was bawling into his leg.

"Uh, it was good," Thea said, eyeing her children. "What's going on here?"

Logan blew out a long breath and handed the baby over.

"These two have gone on a nap strike. While I was trying to get Camila down, Collin climbed out of his crib. He started crying and woke her up. It's been chaos ever since. Charlie escaped to her fort when the wailing started."

Thea laughed, then nuzzled Camila's cheek. "Come on, baby. Let's go cuddle."

Now that both arms were free, Logan picked up Collin and settled him on a hip. Collin rested his head on his dad's shoulder and his eyelids sagged.

"So did you find a place?" Logan asked, swaying his sleepy boy side to side.

I sighed. "There are options. Nothing is perfect, but I guess it never is. I was actually thinking about driving by them all again. Would you mind if I borrowed the Suburban?"

"Not at all." He led me to the kitchen and swiped keys off the counter, tossing them over. Then, as he headed toward Collin's room, I went outside and to the garage.

It took me the entire trip through town to get used to driving a vehicle two times the size of my Mini Cooper, but by the time I headed up the gravel road toward the mountain home, I'd gotten the hang of it.

The moment I parked under the tall canopy of trees, my gut began screaming, "This one! This one!" When I'd driven past the two homes in town, the only reaction I'd had was one burp.

I got out and surveyed the area again. This house might be hideous, but the location was serenity incarnate. I would have peace here. I would have quiet. I would—

A pained roar from across the trees startled me, and I looked toward the neighboring property. The moment my eyes landed on the log cabin nestled between tree trunks, a loud shout filled the air. "Fuck!"

I flinched again, then froze, listening for another sound. It didn't come. Was someone hurt? Should I go check?

There was a path between this house and theirs, so I took it, hurrying in case someone's life was at stake. I rushed right past ferns and forest bushes to the steps leading to the cabin's front door. Without delay, I pounded on the wooden face since there wasn't a doorbell. "Hello?"

Angry footsteps thudded on the floor. The entire porch shook and I backed up a step. My fist was still lifted when the door whipped open and none other than the man from the ridge appeared in its frame.

"What?" he snapped, planting his hands on his hips.

"I, uh . . ." Any other words I'd planned to speak fell away.

This man was even more handsome than I'd expected. He was tall, standing at least six inches above my five seven. His nose was maybe the most perfect nose I'd ever seen, straight with a strong bridge set perfectly in the center of his high cheekbones. But it was his eyes that swayed me sideways.

They weren't green or brown or gold, but this incredible swirl of all three. The ring around the edge was like melted chocolate.

I hadn't been with anyone since my ex-husband and I had separated over two years ago. A rush of desire, one I hadn't felt in a long time, rolled down my body. It pooled between my legs, curling in my belly as I raked my eyes over this man's thick chest and flat stomach.

The man's eyes flared as he looked me up and down. He tried to cover it up with annoyance, but there was lust in his darkening eyes.

"What?" he barked, louder this time.

I came unstuck, breathing again as I forced my eyes away from his soft lips. He had an old rag wrapped around one of his hands and blood was soaking through.

"I heard a crash so I thought I'd come over to see if everything was okay. Are you hurt?" I reached for him, but he jerked back.

"Fine," he grumbled. And with that, he spun around on his brown boots, stomped inside and shut the door.

"Seriously?" I whispered.

I gave him a moment to come back and be neighborly. I got nothing in return.

"Nice to meet you!" I waved at the closed door. "My name is Piper Campbell, in case you were wondering."

Nothing.

"I'm thinking about buying the place next door."

Still nothing.

"Great talk, uh . . ." I searched the porch, landing on a red and white cooler by the railing. *KAINE* was written on the handle in block letters. "See you around, Kaine."

My crazy was starting to show, so I turned around and walked back to the Suburban. The minute I hopped up into the driver's seat, I pulled out my phone from my handbag and dialed my realtor.

"Hi, it's Piper. I've given it some thought and made my decision." My eyes stayed glued to the cabin across the way. "I want the mountain house. It's just what I need."

Some peace. The quiet forest. A project to throw myself into headfirst.

And maybe a hot, sweaty fling with my grouchy, soon-to-be-next-door neighbor.

He had no-strings-attached sex written all over his handsome face.

acknowledgments

Thank you for reading *Timid*! I am beyond grateful for each and every one of my readers. Because of you, I get to keep doing my dream job.

To my husband, kids, family and friends, thanks for loving and supporting me through another story.

A huge thank you to Elizabeth, Ellie, Julie, Kaitlyn, Sarah and Stacey. I have an incredible team of people who help me put together these books and I couldn't do it without them. And a special shout out to Danielle Sanchez, my publicist, for being all-around awesome and for dealing with my plethora of voice messages every day.

Bloggers are my superheroes! Thanks to each and every one of you who have helped promote this book and this series. Thank you to my ARC and street teams for how much energy and support you give with every release. And to Ana, Karen and Jennifer, thank you for being you.

also available from
DEVNEY PERRY

The Birthday List

Jamison Valley Series
The Coppersmith Farmhouse
The Clover Chapel
The Lucky Heart
The Outpost
The Bitterroot Inn

Lark Cove Series
Tattered
Timid

about the author

Devney is the *USA Today* bestselling author of the Jamison Valley series. Born and raised in Montana, she loves writing books set in her treasured home state. After working in the technology industry for nearly a decade, she abandoned conference calls and project schedules to enjoy a slower pace at home with her husband and two sons. Writing one book, let alone many, was not something she ever expected to do. But now that she's discovered her true passion for writing romance, she has no plans to ever stop.

Don't miss out on Devney's latest book news. Subscribe to her newsletter!
www.devneyperry.com

Devney loves hearing from her readers.
Connect with her on social media!

www.devneyperry.com
Facebook: www.facebook.com/devneyperrybooks
Instagram: www.instagram.com/devneyperry
Twitter: twitter.com/devneyperry
BookBub: www.bookbub.com/authors/devney-perry

Made in the USA
Middletown, DE
05 January 2024

47271326R00236